FALLING AGAIN FOR HER ISLAND FLING

ELLIE DARKINS

WHAT MAKES A FATHER

TERESA SOUTHWICK

MIX
Paper from
responsible sources
FSC FSC C007454

This book is produced from independently certified FSC™
paper to ensure responsible forest management.

For more information visit www.harpercollins.co.uk/green

Printed and bound in Spain
by CPI, Barcelona

MILLS & BOON

First Published in Great Britain 2019
by Mills & Boon, an imprint of HarperCollinsPublishers,
1 London Bridge Street, London, SE1 9GF

Falling Again for Her Island Fling © 2019 Ellie Darkins
What Makes a Father © 2019 Teresa Southwick

ISBN: 978-0-263-27266-6

1019

Ellie Darkins spent her formative years devouring romance novels and, after completing her English degree, decided to make a living from her love of books. As a writer and editor, she finds her work now entails dreaming up romantic proposals, hot dates with alpha males and trips to the past with dashing heroes. When she's not working she can usually be found running around after her toddler, volunteering at her local library or escaping all of the above with a good book and a vanilla latte.

Teresa Southwick lives with her husband in Las Vegas, the city that reinvents itself every day. An avid fan of romance novels, she is delighted to be living out her dream of writing for Mills & Boon.

Discover more at millsandboon.co.uk

FALLING AGAIN FOR HER ISLAND FLING

ELLIE DARKINS

For my girls

CHAPTER ONE

MEENA LAY ON her back, the sand hot beneath her, the sun reaching her face through the leaves of the coconut trees, and breathed deeply, grateful for the shade even this early in the morning. By lunchtime the heat would be fierce, and she would be forced indoors, so she really should be making the most of her time here on the island of Le Bijou before she had to get back to the St Antoine mainland. But lying on the beach, alone in the sunlight, was still something of a dream. Especially here. Something that she had imagined for so long. Had started to fear would never happen again. It was something she could never take for granted.

She took another breath, long and slow, relaxing her body from the tips of her fingers down to her toes. It was still a marvel that she could make it follow her commands so easily, after the years that she had spent relearning how to use it. It had taken more strength than she'd known she had to get her body working again after the accident, and still more for her to be able to face the world and reintegrate herself into real life.

From the outside now one would never guess what

had happened to her. Her thick dark hair, worn in its natural curls, did a perfect job of hiding the scars on her head. Her standard-issue Environmental Agency polo shirt or a wetsuit over a one-piece swimsuit took care of the rest.

But the scars were still there. She could feel them on her scalp and her body. Feel them in her mind, every time that she tried to recall the months before the accident and found them blank. And then there were the looks and the whispers that she knew followed her around the island. She was the girl who had been hit by a car and lost her mind.

The dappled light grew darker behind her eyelids and she blinked them open, uneasy. She sat up quickly as she realised she was right to be concerned. A man was standing over her, casting a shadow where she had been lying in the sand. With the sun behind him, she couldn't make out his features, and she scrambled to her feet, heart tripping a little faster, glancing around her to see if there was anyone about who might hear her if she had to call out for help.

'Meena?' the man asked, sounding as if he was choking on her name.

'Do I know you?' she replied in English, picking up on his Australian accent even in that one word. Like most residents of St Antoine, an island nation in the Indian Ocean, she was fluent in the French the islanders used every day as well as English, the official language of government business, and of course the colourful creole that the islanders used amongst themselves. But she'd lived in Australia for a year while she'd been at university and the accent never failed to tug at her heart.

She narrowed her eyes, looking at him closely. Was there something familiar about him? She felt as if his name and the memory of who he was were right on the verge of making it into a functional part of her brain. But her brain didn't make the leap, so she launched into her well-rehearsed spiel, the words that she'd carefully formulated over the years to smooth this very social awkwardness.

'I'm sorry if we've met before,' she said, scrambling to her feet while she went through the speech. 'I suffered a head injury and lost some memories.'

She didn't even feel embarrassed any more, she realised, about giving her usual excuse when she didn't recognise someone but got the sense that she probably should. It happened rarely these days. Most of the people whom she'd met and forgotten that summer either knew about her accident already or had just been holidaying on the island and she need never worry about seeing them again. She had spent almost her whole life on St Antoine, the beautiful magnet for tourists and the developers who followed them. But most of the people who stayed here were on once-in-a-lifetime trips and would never know that she had completely forgotten meeting them. It had been a few months, at least, since she had had to make her slightly unorthodox introduction.

The man held out his hand to shake hers, still watching her with trepidation. Probably worried that she was going to fall into a fit or something, she told herself. She'd waited out the five-year danger period after her accident, desperate to get back to diving, her career and her life on hold until she could get back into the water; wondering every day whether this would be the one when a seizure struck. But it had never happened, and she had got herself recertified to dive and back to her conservation work on the island.

'Guy Williams,' he introduced himself. 'I'm—'

'The owner of the development company.' She'd received an email telling her that she should expect him tomorrow, yet here he was, interrupting her relaxation practice a day early.

'You've lost your memories?' he said, still looking at her strangely. Meena rolled her eyes; she used to get this a lot.

'Yes, just like in a movie. Should I remember something about you?'

He shook his head. He was taking this even worse than most people she told. Generally, people just looked puzzled but, even though Guy Williams was a stranger, she could tell from his expression that he was struggling to accept what she'd just revealed. Maybe he didn't believe her.

'Then this is a fresh start,' Meena said, eager to move the conversation along. 'I expect you want to know about the environmental impact assessment. I wasn't expecting you until tomorrow but I was just about to get started.' She glanced around, looking for her clipboard, sure that she had brought it out with her. Oh, way to make a good impression, she thought. Introduce herself with a side note about a brain injury and then look around the beach as if you have no idea what you're doing there.

She was not usually so distracted by a pretty face— even one as pretty as this. High forehead, golden tan, long, straight nose, full lips, a hint of a cleft in his chin. The body wasn't half bad either—she supposed, if she were absolutely pressed to give her opinion on the subject—from what she could see of it, anyway.

He was dressed for business in a conservative shirt and navy suit. But his collar was open, showing just a hint of his throat and making her want to lean closer, to let her fingers drift into that notch, feel the heat of his skin, the throb of his pulse beneath her fingers.

She shook her head. Where had that thought come from? She took a step away from him. She should *not* be thinking that way. She did *not* want a man in her life. She crossed her arms over her chest, suddenly feeling cold despite the growing heat of the day. She'd proved to herself a long time ago that she wasn't capable of making good decisions about men. About sex. It was safer to deny herself either rather than risk repeating her mistakes.

'Are you okay?' Guy asked.

'I'm fine, thank you. I was just about to begin.'

Ah, there. She spotted the clipboard from the corner of her eye and scooped it up in a single, easy movement that belied the many months of physio she'd endured after her accident to enable her to take even a single step.

She caught him looking at her from the corner of her eye and momentarily stopped. 'Are you sure we didn't meet…before?' she asked, hating the black hole in her memory that made the question necessary. She shouldn't have to look at every man she met and ask herself, *Was it you? Was it your baby I was carrying?*

He gave her a look so bland that she knew it couldn't possibly have been him. It was as if he barely saw her at all. As if she were barely *there* at all. Well, she supposed that answered her question well enough.

'I'm sure,' he said with firm politeness. Another one to strike off the list, she thought, trying not to cringe at this internal game of 'who's the daddy?' that she had been forced to play for the last seven years.

She could let it rest, of course. There was no baby. Not now. When she had eventually woken from the coma, the doctors in the clinic had broken it to her gently that it hadn't just been her memories that she'd lost. She didn't even know if she'd known before the accident that she'd been pregnant. Given the conservative attitude to premarital sex across almost every culture on St Antoine, she was sure that an unplanned pregnancy would have been more cause for anxiety than celebrations.

She still remembered the whispers that had followed a school friend who had fallen pregnant in her late teens, and who had hastily been married before the baby arrived six months later. Was that why Meena's lover had disappeared? Had he feared he would be forced into a shotgun wedding? Tied to a woman he didn't love?

Her parents were hardly traditional, though. They had raised eyebrows with their own marriage—

Meena's French-Mauritian mother and Hindu father had married at a time when such relationships had been even more unusual than they were now—but that didn't mean that people wouldn't talk. They always talked.

She had been unusual too in living away from her parents: it had taken every ounce of determination she'd had to move out when she'd been sufficiently recovered from her accident.

But if her family knew about any boyfriend she'd had they had never said anything. So she had no choice but to assume that the relationship had been a secret. How could she have been serious enough about someone to have slept with him but not serious enough to introduce him to her parents?

Her mind had spent many hours tying itself in knots trying to work it out. She hadn't been far along and what worried her the most was that she had no idea who the father could have been. She was only missing a few months of memory, and there had been no sign of a boyfriend in her life, so where had this baby come from—and what had happened to the father? Where had he been when she'd been trapped under that car, her memories and their baby leaving her body?

Leaving her broken.

Guy turned to look back up the beach to the scrubland where the hotel complex would be built. Where it *could* be built, Meena corrected herself, as long as the environmental studies were clear and planning permission was granted by the relevant government department. If she couldn't find something to hold up the development... She took a deep breath. She would find something—she had to—because there was something about this tiny jewel of an island on which she wasn't going to give up.

For seven years it had felt like her secret. In all the trauma and recovery of that time, she had spent more time here, at this secluded beach, than just about anywhere else. It was the only place where she felt still. At peace. Where her mind rested and her heart didn't hurt. So when she had heard about the upcoming development she had made sure that she was on the environmental impact team. If there was any way of stopping the resort from being built, then she was going to be the one to find it.

Meena Bappoo. Flat-backed on the beach, just as he'd left her. Eyes closed to the sun, as if it had been minutes since he had last seen her here rather than years. He'd nearly turned and walked away when he'd seen the Environmental Agency logo on her shirt and realised she was the agency marine biologist he was meant to be meeting. The notes that he'd received from his project manager's schedule hadn't mentioned her by name, only her job title and the time and location of the meeting, though it turned out that he had mixed up the date.

And then her lids had snapped open, he'd seen those warm golden-brown eyes again and he'd known he was too entranced to walk away.

Did he believe her story? Her memory loss seemed far-fetched. But she hadn't really given him a choice:

he had to believe her. The way she'd looked at him was so completely blank. Surely she couldn't have been so unmoved if she'd remembered even a moment of those few months that they'd spent together?

Because he remembered. He remembered *everything*. The way that she spoke, her island creole accent that he knew could slip so quickly into perfect French or her slightly American-sounding English. The way that she smelled—of salt, sand and the coconut oil that she rubbed into her skin. The way that she had looked at him after they had made love for the first time, as if they had just created the stars in the sky.

The way that he had waited for her as they'd agreed, after he had returned to Australia, and she had never shown up.

Had it been the accident? he wondered now. That would make sense, answer the questions he had been carrying around in the years since they had been together. It hit him like a blow to the chest, the thought that perhaps he had been wrong. That she had wanted to come as desperately as he had wanted it. But it didn't hurt any less when she looked at him and didn't *see* him.

He'd thought of her over the years. Thought of *them*. Thought of the days and the nights that they had spent on this beach. Thought of the night, years later, that he'd made the decision to buy the tiny uninhabited island of Le Bijou and build his resort. Thought of the pain that he had felt when he had been left alone, wanting her, wondering what had gone wrong. Thought of all the ways that he had tried to numb that pain, and the consequences that had spiralled out of control.

And then he couldn't think about it any more, because the loss and grief from that time of his life was still too painful, too raw even to glance at, never mind examine more closely.

He'd come here to get over her. To face their past, bury it, landscape over the evidence and then move on. But then he'd seen her lying there, looking exactly as she had the day that he'd left her, and known immediately that it was a mistake.

But maybe the fact she didn't remember him was a saving grace. She had no idea what they'd once shared and he had every intention of keeping things that way. He could never let her know what they had been to one another. What he had felt for her. He'd spent years trying to get over her. To shake the pain that her rejection had caused him. And he couldn't bear to reopen those old wounds. Not now.

They were over. They had been over for a long time. She didn't even remember that they had ever been together and, as far as he could see, that was a good thing. He wouldn't take that away from her and replace it with the anger and bile that had built up and then been fought down over the years. If she knew what he had done—who he had become—after the last time he had left this island she could only be relieved that she had escaped him.

It was kinder to lie, he told himself, convincing himself of its truth. He had to live with what they had lost and he wouldn't wish that on her too. Not now, when he knew that he could never again be that person he had been when they'd been together. Even though they were here on Le Bijou, they could never go back and be who they had been before.

He couldn't risk being in a relationship again. The only time he had tried it since Meena had ended in the worst possible way, and it was something for which he would never forgive himself. There was no way that he could ever let Meena get involved with him again. She was better off without him. Better off not knowing him.

Meena turned and looked at him, and he knew he'd been caught staring. He couldn't let that happen, he chastised himself. Couldn't let her see what he felt for her—what he *had* felt for her, he corrected—those long years ago. Before she'd failed to turn up as she'd promised and confirmed what he'd always known about himself—what his parents had made clear for as long as he could remember—that he just wasn't worth it.

She'd never let him become part of her life here on the island. Or vice versa. He'd agreed to it at the time because, more than anything, he'd just wanted her in his life and the sneaking around had felt fun at first. But he had realised, later, that she had done it on purpose, had kept their relationship separate from the rest of her life, so that when it was over she could move on.

He wouldn't let it happen again because they were done. She had no idea they'd ever started anything in the first place and that was a blessing.

'So I'm going to make a start on the detailed environmental impact study tomorrow,' Meena said eventually. 'You should have already received the initial report; this one will go into greater detail on the areas that were raised as a concern. I'll keep you updated with the results as I progress.'

'Do that,' Guy replied shortly, wanting this meeting at an end. 'I need those permissions in place as soon as possible if I'm going to keep to my schedule.' And he *would* be keeping to his schedule and leaving as quickly as possible. If his usual project manager hadn't broken his thigh bone in a nasty jet-ski accident, Guy wouldn't have had to take this meeting. He would have been on the island and off again within a couple of days, leaving everything in the capable hands of his team. It was the only way that he had been able to contemplate being back here at all, to minimise the risk of accidentally bumping into Meena. Now he was faced with the prospect of managing this himself, for the foreseeable future at least, and that meant managing Meena. Or trying to. He couldn't think that he had ever been successful at it before.

'Well, don't think I will rush it,' Meena said right on cue, confirming his fears of how this working relationship was going to proceed. 'There are reefs on this side of the island and the coral is very vulnerable. It's my responsibility to make sure that the environment isn't harmed by your building developments here, and I'm not going to cut corners. If you want to build here, you have to take care of the island first.'

He gritted his teeth, knowing that his tension was probably showing on his face. But why hide it? She didn't care what he was thinking. He was nothing to her. A stranger.

'I understand that—I think my plans have made reasonable provisions for the environment, so there should be no hold-ups. I will be following your work closely.'

She bristled at that, crossing her arms and fixing him with a glare. Good. He could handle her like this. He could handle angry. Angry was nothing like what he remembered between them. Angry didn't bring back memories that still—somehow—had the power to hurt him. Well, not for much longer. Once his plans were under way, this island would no longer be recognisable. Would no longer call to him. Would no longer be the yardstick by which he unconsciously measured his experiences and his relationships. Of course, no *real* woman could live up to an island fantasy, a summer romance with a beautiful girl while he'd been on holiday, barely into his twenties.

'Where are you going to start with your report?' he asked, trying to read her notes upside down. But her notes were in French. A language he had started to learn once—with scribbled love notes—here, with her—but had fallen out of using. Another very good reason he had hired a capable project manager to oversee this development. As soon as he got off this tiny island and back to the capital, he would be instructing his assistant, Dev, to find a temporary replacement for his injured project manager.

'I need to inspect the reef,' Meena said, checking her list. 'Many of the ones nearby have suffered from coral bleaching or damage from boats, and my initial look showed that these reefs appeared to be suffering similarly. At the very least we would need to do any remedial work before building is approved and make a plan for how it can be protected from further human damage. My other main concern is the turtle population. I saw tracks on the beach that indicate there may be a nesting site. We need to wait out the incubation period to see what, if anything, hatches, and to ensure that increased use of the beach won't impact on breeding or migratory patterns.'

He nodded, wondering how much time this was all going to take. But these were details, and he was no longer the details guy. He was the money and he was the vision. One of the joys of being the boss of your own multi-billion-dollar resort business was letting someone else worry about the bloody turtles.

'I'm sure your report will be fine, Miss Bappoo. Just submit your findings to my office and someone will be in touch.'

He turned away from her but then stopped, his feet halting in the sand. Was this it? Was it all finally going to end with a glib remark about turtles? With Meena having no idea that they had met before today? He turned back and looked at her. Really looked. He saw pink rise in her cheeks at his unmasked appraisal of her.

Seven years. That was how long it had been since he had seen her. And yet he couldn't see any sign of it on her face. Her cheeks, rosy beneath the warm bronze-brown of her skin, were still the smooth apples that he remembered. Her eyes were as golden and as full of challenge as they had been then.

What would she think of him, he wondered, if she remembered the man—boy—he had been? Would she find him much changed? His body was no softer—he had worked hard to ensure that. His heart, however, was harder—she was responsible for that. He shook his head. That wasn't fair. He couldn't entirely blame her for the way he had behaved after they had broken up. He had to carry that alone.

He held her gaze for a moment longer. He needed to know that she had seen him—really seen him. To give her one last chance to recognise him. To remember.

The blush faded from her cheeks as he refused to look away and her expression changed. He didn't know her well enough any more to guess what she was thinking. But in that moment it wasn't indifference. Curiosity, maybe. Desire. Did he want that? Would this feel better if she wanted him? If he was the one to walk away this time? Probably not, he conceded.

Anyway, those wounds had healed a long time ago, he told himself. He didn't need them to be reopened. 'So, goodbye, then,' he said, and turned from her, walking back towards his speedboat, knowing this would be the last time that he saw her. It had to be.

CHAPTER TWO

'COME IN.'

Guy glanced at the schedule on the computer monitor; he wasn't expecting a meeting and the knock on the door had taken him by surprise. In fact, he hadn't been expecting still to be on the island at all, but the search for a replacement project manager was proving to be more difficult than he had hoped. He'd already delayed his departure from the island by a fortnight, and the replacement that he'd hired couldn't fly out for another week at the earliest. Guy was going to have to get the environmental permissions he needed before he could get back to Sydney. Whoever was at the door had better be quick. He had three days' worth of work to do that evening. The last thing he needed was an unscheduled five o'clock meeting.

In the promotional brochures he'd had mocked up, he'd billed his island as paradise. But most of what he'd seen of the country in the last two weeks was the inside of its government buildings and his air-conditioned office. He could have been in the offices of any of his corporate buildings for all he'd seen of the local environment.

The door opened and he glanced up; his body registered her presence before his brain did. Before her name formed on his lips, his heart was beating wildly in his chest and there was a tightness, low in his belly, that seemed a response unique to being close to her.

'Meena, what are you doing here?'

Way to play it cool, he chastised himself, angry that she still had that hold over him, the ability to make him say what he was thinking without any regard for whether it was a good idea. When they'd been younger, it had felt like a blessing: their mutual honesty helping them past the barrier of dive instructor and pupil. Past the social conventions of a conservative culture and into the realms of something much more personal.

'Your environmental reports,' she replied, her brow furrowed into a curious expression. 'I emailed them over to Dev and he told me you'd want me to come and talk through my findings in person.'

'And why is that?' he asked, wondering why his assistant had thought that another meeting would be the way to cap off today. 'Never mind. Just give me the highlights.' He leaned back in his chair and folded his arms. The last thing this project needed was more delays.

'Well, the headline is, I'm not giving the approval for your permits.'

Guy sighed, leaned forward again, rested his elbows on his desk and gestured towards the chair opposite, inviting her to take a seat.

'Why not? What's the problem?'

She crossed to his desk and laid out the paperwork in front of him. 'The main problem right now is that the reef won't withstand an increase in boat traffic or sedimentation from the building work. There's been extensive bleaching and it needs to be stabilised and then an ongoing regeneration plan put in place.'

He gritted his teeth. *Ongoing.* 'Ongoing' wasn't a word he wanted to hear in the context of this development, and not from Meena of all people.

'Anything else?'

'There's still no sign of hatchlings from the possible turtle nesting site. We need to wait out the incubation period and see what we're dealing with before I could give the go-ahead.'

'How much time are we looking at?'

'A couple more wee—'

'Unacceptable,' he interrupted. 'This needs to be wrapped up within a week maximum, Miss Bappoo. I can't leave the island until they're done, and I need to get back to Sydney.'

'With all due respect, that isn't for you to say,' she replied, crossing her arms. 'This will take as long as it takes. It's not something you hurry. It's not something you *can* hurry. This is my call.'

He looked at her, assessing. Was she doing this on purpose? he wondered. Because of their past? And then he had to remind himself that she didn't even remember their past. She wasn't angry with him. She didn't feel *anything* for him. He envied her ignorance. He wished that he could see this as she undoubtedly did: a simple business matter with no personal feelings involved.

'That's not good enough,' he stated, leaning back in his chair.

She mirrored him, implacable. He remembered that look and he knew that it meant that there was no changing her mind. 'Unfortunately for you, your feelings on the matter aren't a criterion in my report.'

He shook his head. A standoff wasn't going to get them anywhere fast. Cooperation was the only way that he was going to get this project moving again. 'Tell me what I can do to make this happen faster.'

He saw his more relaxed demeanour soften her. 'You can stop asking questions like that for a start,' Meena said. 'Faster isn't the aim here; environmental conservation is. I'm not letting this island come to harm because you want to throw your hotel up *faster*.'

'I'm not *throwing* anything,' he retorted. 'And you say that like you think I want to cause harm. I don't; that's why you're here.'

'Good to know. I'll note it in the report.'

He paused. 'Meena, I…'

She was doing all this to protect the island. *Their* island. The tiny speck of sand and rock in the Indian Ocean. Could it be that she remembered it? That that was why she was being so fiercely protective of it? The thought warmed him somewhere deep but he shook off the feeling. That wasn't what this was about. She didn't remember him. She didn't remember anything about who they had been to each other.

'Look,' Guy said. 'I want this application to go

through and I have no interest in doing any harm to Le Bijou,' he lied. 'Tell me what I need to do to make that happen.'

She narrowed her eyes as she looked at him. 'You really want to do this right?'

He nodded. 'I really do.'

'Then you need a marine biologist on your team once building starts. Someone to ensure you are considering environmental impacts at every stage. You need short-term and long-term sustainability plans, and someone to hold you to account.'

He gave an ironic smile. 'You seem to be doing a pretty good job of that.'

'For now.' She smiled back. 'But my job's done when the reports are completed. This island needs a permanent guardian.'

'You're right. And you're perfect for the job.'

As he said the words he knew that it was true. Much as he hated to admit it, she would be the perfect person to make sure that the island was protected through the building of the resort, and after. And once his new project manager started he would be gone and he wouldn't have to see her again. If this was what it took to get the permits approved, he would do it. He could see from her face that she was surprised by the offer nonetheless.

'I have a job,' she said abruptly.

'True.' He shrugged. 'But here's the offer of another. Because you're right. An in-house marine biologist should always have been a part of the plan. I think this offer shows how serious I am about getting these permits. Your report proves you know what you're doing. And you love the island.' He knew what love looked like on her. He had seen it before. He remembered lying on that beach, seeing her look at him and knowing—*knowing*—that she loved him. He didn't know what he'd done to deserve it then. He knew that he didn't deserve it now.

Which was why it was such a spectacularly bad idea to offer her the job. He should be putting as much distance between them as he could right now. Not creating yet another bond.

It was fine, he reminded himself. As soon as he had a replacement project manager in place, he would be leaving this island and not coming back. In his headquarters in Sydney, he would have no more contact with Meena than with thousands of his other employees and contractors. She wouldn't be his problem any more. Wouldn't be in his life any more.

'I'll have to think about it,' she replied slowly, as if looking for the catch in his offer.

She could do a lot for Le Bijou as the resident marine biologist, Meena acknowledged, turning Guy's job offer over in her mind. She had done a lot of good when she had worked at another resort before her accident, she reminded herself, educating holidaymakers and divers about the local area and how to dive without impacting the coral reefs. She had even started a programme of coral regeneration with newlyweds, planting out coral, something that would carry on growing long after the honeymoon was over.

She could do the same at Le Bijou, she thought, if she took up Guy's job offer. She could stay on the island. Do her best for it. Protect it as best she could once the works were completed and the worst of the damage had been done.

Perhaps damage limitation was all she *could* do. Guy owned Le Bijou, and it was going to change. Her sanctuary. It just wouldn't exist any more. Not in the way that she wanted—needed—it to.

But something made her hesitate before telling Guy that she wanted the job. Working with Guy, specifically, made her hesitate.

She'd thought a lot about men the last few years. A lot about specifically what sort of man would make her fall for him. She knew she wouldn't have slept with someone she didn't love. Last she remembered, she had been a virgin planning to wait until she was married, as was expected of her. And then she was waking from a coma, finding out that she had been pregnant, and the only clues she had to her mystery boyfriend were notes she'd found months after she had finally left the clinic, scribbled in French on the back of a dive planner.

I love you. I can't wait to see you again. Meet me at our beach.

She had wondered ever since then who he could have been. Who her type was. What sort of man she had fallen in love with.

And now here was Guy and the strange sense of

déjà vu she felt around him. It was probably just his accent, she thought. The twang of his Australian vowels that was so familiar from her scholarship year studying there. That was what was giving her this strange feeling, she decided. There was no way that Guy was her mystery boyfriend. The way that he looked at her was so cold, so impersonal, it couldn't possibly be him.

Which made the dreams she had been having about him all the stranger. They felt so vivid, so real. She had touched him. Smelled him. Tasted him. In her sleep last night she had run her fingertips over every part of his body and then followed them with her tongue. He had spanned her waist with his hands, cupped the curve of her hip and her buttock, teased her with his lips.

All of which was making this meeting extremely awkward.

She risked another glance up at him, but his eyes were still fixed on his computer screen.

'I want to know what working with you will mean.'

'I'm glad you're considering it.' He didn't look as if he thought it was great. Considering he'd made the offer in the first place, he looked as if he didn't want her there at all. Well, it was too late. She'd been thinking about Le Bijou. What it would mean to stand guard over it. However awkward things got with Guy.

'Are you sure we haven't met before?'

She wasn't really aware of thinking the question before it popped out of her mouth. He was just so… unsettling. He unnerved her. And she couldn't help thinking that there must be a reason he had this effect on her. Must be a reason why her body reacted to him every time that he was close. A reason her heart was racing and her palms were sweating.

Was it you? Her mind jumped to the familiar question. *Did you love me? Did I carry your baby? Lose your baby?*

He sighed, looked up and made eye contact with her for the first time since she had walked into the room.

'What period of time are you missing memories from?' he asked. 'I've only visited St Antoine once before.'

She told him the date of her accident, and that she didn't remember the three months before, wondering at the change in his demeanour.

'I was here then,' he said. 'My parents own the Williams resort on the mainland. I was staying there for the summer.'

'But I worked there!' Meena exclaimed. 'I was working at the dive school before my accident. It was the summer after I got back from Australia,' she added, realising she'd never mentioned to him that connection. Was this the reason for his strangeness? For the strange familiarity she felt around him? Would she have mentioned that if she'd bumped into an Australian guest? Would she have struck up a conversation about that common link?

'So maybe I have seen you before, or maybe we spoke back then? I'm sorry,' she added, realising she was speaking out loud. 'It's just, it's hard, having this gap in my memories. It makes me question myself. Question what I know, you know?'

Of course he didn't know. How could he? How could anyone know what it felt like to live in a body and a mind that didn't fully belong to them?

'Maybe we did meet.' Guy shuffled some papers on his desk, not looking at her. 'I went to the dive school when I was here before. Maybe we crossed paths.'

'But you don't remember? You don't remember me?' It was clear from the way that he had turned back to his work that he was ready for this meeting to be over. But it had been so long since she had had any new information about that time that she couldn't let this drop, no matter how annoying Guy seemed to be finding her.

Just once in her life, she wanted a straightforward answer. No, scratch that. Once in her life she wanted to know the answer to questions about her life herself, without relying on near strangers to fill in the gaps. But as that didn't seem to be an option, no matter what she or her medical team had tried, she would have to settle for getting answers from someone else. For trusting other people to paint this picture of who she had been.

'I don't remember you,' Guy said, looking back at his screen. 'I'm sorry.'

'No need to be sorry.' Meena shrugged, tried to cover her disappointment. No answers, again. No reason for why she felt this strange familiarity around Guy. For him and for Le Bijou.

'Get in touch with Dev about the details of the new job, if you want to consider it. And keep him updated with your progress on the environmental reports. If there's nothing else…'

It was clear she was being dismissed.

'Okay, great.' She forced professionalism back into her voice. 'Well, I'm going to go have another look at the reef tomorrow. To see if there is any way that its decline can be reversed, or at least halted. If you want to come and see for yourself, you would be welcome.'

Guy glanced up at her, meeting her gaze again. Maybe this was why he avoided it, Meena thought, as she felt her cheeks warm under his scrutiny. Maybe he could see the effect he had on her when he turned his full attention on her like that. No wonder he didn't want to encourage it.

'I'll see what I can do. But I have a very full week.'

Did he remember her? Only every night in his dreams, in waking moments when his mind wandered, and for a moment he was back there, the sun and her lips on his body once again. He remembered everything.

And it broke him, almost daily now.

Because whatever, wherever they were now, they were never going to get that back. What they had had back then had been beautiful. It had been pure. It had been innocent. And then the darkness in his heart when he'd thought that she had abandoned him had sullied it. And that simply couldn't be undone.

He must have been broken before he had even met her, for that rot to have set in and cause the damage that it had.

If he told her what they had shared, what would she think of that? What could she take from it? Worst-case scenario, she would want to try to turn back time. To see what had brought them together then. To see if it still existed.

She had lost all the time that they had been together. He had spent three months on this island, ostensibly getting to know his family's resort on the St Antoine mainland as preparation for a formal role in the company. But in truth he had spent most of it getting to know Meena. His parents hadn't even been disappointed when they'd realised how little work he'd done that summer. As if they'd been expecting his failure all along. It was so easy to disappoint them, he realised, when they had such low expectations of him.

Meena thought that she wanted to know him, but she was wrong. The only possible outcome was her getting hurt, and he could spare her that at least.

Of course, his heart had hurt when he'd seen how lost she was without those memories. And he could fix that, he knew. He could tell her everything, and she wouldn't have to worry and guess at what had happened in those months.

But would that help her, really? To know that she had been in love with a man who didn't exist any more? No, it was kinder to say nothing, he told himself. Kinder— and safer—that she never knew what they had once had, and what they had both lost.

CHAPTER THREE

WHY HAD SHE invited him? Meena asked herself for the millionth time that day. It had been a stupid idea at the time, and felt even stupider now that she was sitting in her boat, in a rash-guard swimsuit and shorts, wondering if he was going to show up.

Of course he wasn't. He had been awkward and uncomfortable for the entirety of their short acquaintance, so he was hardly going to be signing up for extracurriculars. And no wonder, considering the way that she had quizzed him the last time that they had met, making a near stranger uncomfortable by trying to use his memories to patch together her defective one. And it had all been for nothing anyway. He hadn't known her then and didn't care now.

She checked over her equipment one more time, including the battery and memory card on her underwater camera. Ideally she needed some close-up shots of the unstable areas of the reef so that she could make a more thorough assessment of whether the damage could be reversed. She was hoping that transplanting in new corals would stabilise it. But if the damage had already gone too far and the reef was starting to crumble she would have to rethink her options. The best way to decide was to get down there for another look. But if Guy didn't show she would have to make do with photographing from the glass-bottomed boat. Even seven years after her accident, when the chance of having a seizure was minimal, she wouldn't risk being out in the water alone.

She needed to choose the best sites for transplanting in the coral pieces she'd retrieved after a storm a few months before, and had been growing out in the lab ever since. If Guy turned up and she had a buddy, then she could get her fins wet and take a closer look.

She looked along the beach, wondering how long she should wait for him, then shook her head; it was time to get to work. She steered her boat over to the reef, anchored carefully in the white sand, taking care not to damage the reef, and pulled out her clipboard and her camera, ready to make her observations.

As she took her first shot, she heard the steady buzz of motor. She looked up, shielding her eyes from the fierce morning sun, and spotted the company-branded speedboat rounding the far side of the island. Guy. She took a moment to calm her nerves and gather herself before he stopped on the beach. He didn't know that she was still dreaming about him, and he definitely didn't know about the X-rated images her brain was now happy to summon at will. The light, golden tan of his skin beaded with sweat. His eyes creased with intensity as he moved above her. His body a collection of hard planes that her hands had explored and come to know so well.

In her sleep.

It wasn't real life. And he would never, *ever* find out about those dreams.

The speedboat pulled up to the jetty and she watched Guy climb down the couple of steps to the sand and then look around. He spotted her and gave a brisk wave as she pulled up the anchor and steered back to the shore. Guy came over and helped her to tie the boat to the small wooden jetty. He was dressed more casually than she had seen him before, in cargo shorts and a polo shirt, and she tried to keep her eyes on his face, well away from the extra skin that he was showing.

The last thing her brain needed was new material. It had done quite a good job of conjuring up a naked Guy from just the skin of his hands and his face, and that triangle of his throat where he left his shirt open at the collar. But it turned out her peripheral vision was doing a more than okay job of measuring him up: the golden-blond hair on his forearms that caught the morning sunlight. The strong lines of his calves above his beach shoes. Even his feet seemed familiar. Her brain had been remarkably thorough. And accurate. She had to give herself credit for that.

She must be retrofitting, that was all, she told herself. Her brain was seeing the real thing now and simply slotting the new images into her memories of her fantasies.

Of all the people to be unsurprised by what the human brain could remember and forget, it should be her. Her brain had forgotten everything: who she was, how to walk, how to feed herself. And then it had relearned or remembered almost all of it again. Even with the whole 'missing summer' issues, she couldn't deny being impressed by what she and her brain had achieved between them. Summoning a perfect, naked Guy from just the glimpses she had seen so far proved that various important parts of her were functioning just fine.

She shook her head, trying to dislodge those thoughts before Guy could guess what she was thinking.

'You made it,' she said, offering him her hand to shake, trying to remember to be professional. She simply refused to be affected by the touch of his skin on hers. Nor to remember anything about her dreams inspired by the spark of electricity she felt. She was going to be working with him in her role at the Environmental Agency even if she didn't take up his job offer.

Although, with Guy due to be far away at his Sydney office in a couple of weeks, she barely needed to know that he existed at all in order to do her job. That was for the best, she told herself. Being distracted by a man was in no way a part of her plan for her life. She was here to work, to protect as much of the islands that made up St Antoine as possible, and nothing else.

'Do you have snorkel gear?' she asked Guy, setting a professional tone. 'I have some spares in the lockbox,' she went on, trying to avoid meeting his eye, instead busying herself with equipment and checklists. 'You can stay on the boat if you prefer; see the reef through the glass floor. It's not a bad view from there, and then I can do the underwater stuff.'

'I have my equipment in the boat,' he said shortly.

'Great.' She kept her voice neutral, refusing to react to his brusque tone. There was no reason he should be anything but cold and short with her. They were business colleagues and nothing more, she reminded herself. 'I always prefer to have a buddy in the water, even if I'm only snorkelling.'

'I only have an hour.'

She tried not to bristle again at his tone. She had no reason to court his approval. She didn't want to be his friend. In fact, the more brusque he was with her, the better. The last thing she needed was to think about getting close to this man. Any man, in fact.

She had already proved that she couldn't trust herself to manage her own desires sensibly. In the space of a summer she had met, slept with and then lost her only sexual partner. A man who, it seemed, had been happy to take her to bed but less keen on sticking around after her accident, for her miscarriage or her rehab. If that was the kind of man that she chose for herself, she was better off single. Or even giving in and allowing her aunties to arrange an introduction to someone that fit the older generation's idea of a 'nice young man'.

But that didn't exactly appeal either.

And what nice young man would want her, if they knew? A woman with a brain injury, with the scars of the accident still clear on her body and in her mind.

Who had carried and lost a baby without even knowing who the father was.

She didn't need to worry about that with Guy, at least. He looked at her with disdain, spoke with impatience and was in a hurry to leave the country. He hardly needed warning off. He clearly didn't share the fantasies playing through her mind.

She checked over the equipment that he fetched from the boat. Guy might be experienced, but if he was accompanying her then she would be responsible for his safety, even if it was just a shallow snorkel for the most part. The equipment was top of the range, of course. Far superior to her own snorkel, mask and fins.

She glanced over at him as they both sat on the edge of the boat, steering the way over to where she had anchored by the reef before, and felt a stab of déjà vu. It wasn't an unusual feeling for her; with an injury like hers she was constantly unsure of whether a memory was real or imagined. Before the accident, she would have just shrugged it off. But Guy had piqued her curiosity, telling her that he had attended the dive school when she had been teaching. Could they be sure that they hadn't dived together before? There had to be some reason why she was feeling this way around him.

'What?' Guy asked when he turned and caught her staring at him.

'It's nothing,' she said, creasing her brow, still getting that feeling of déjà vu. Trying to unpack whether there was any truth to the feeling that they had sat like this, on the side of a boat, before.

'Just that…this feels familiar. Us, on a boat like this. It feels like a memory. I'm sorry. It's hard to explain.'

Guy frowned, his forehead lining in what she knew must be a mirror image of her own.

'You remember something?'

'No.' She shook her head. 'I'm sorry. It's not a memory, just a weird feeling. I'm sure it's nothing.' She shrugged, trying to rid herself of the weird sensation. She almost gasped in shock when his hand landed on hers.

'I'm sorry,' he said. 'It must be difficult.' She hadn't been expecting to see empathy in his expression, but there it was. With most people who knew about her amnesia she saw pity. Or gratitude that it had happened to her and not them. But she could see her own pain reflected in Guy's eyes—real understanding—and she didn't know what to make of it.

'It's fine, mostly,' she lied. He didn't need to know the nights she lay awake, trying to force those memories back. Trying to remember who she had been with that summer. And then, maybe, to try to understand who *she* had been that summer. The person who had taken risks. Who had snuck around with a secret lover none of her friends or family knew about. Who'd been stupid enough to fall pregnant with a man who hadn't cared enough to stick around when she'd been hurt.

Guy squeezed her hand and let go, rubbing at the stubble just starting to shadow his jawline. Looking away, she reached over the side of the boat to dip her mask in the water, then slid the strap behind her head and tightened it. It was impossible to be serious with a person wearing a snorkel, and she was counting on that to break the atmosphere that seemed to have grown and thickened between them in the last few moments.

She glanced over and smiled at the sight of Guy in his mask. She was right; not even Guy—as sexy as he was, as vividly sensual as her dreams had been— could carry off that look. He grinned at her in return, and she breathed a sigh of relief.

'Ready?' she asked, and then slipped off the side of the boat and entered the water with a splash. She looked around to make sure Guy had followed her in. He was right behind her, and her body bumped his as she turned. She moved away, dipping under the water, exhaling through her snorkel, leaving a trail of bubbles behind her. His skin on hers was too distracting; she needed to put a sensible amount of space between them. She swam over to the reef, her camera on a tether clipped to her top, and waited for Guy to catch her up. She pointed out the areas where the coral bleaching was at its worst, and then over to the other side of the reef where there was a large unstable section and some damage that looked as if it had been caused by a boat anchor.

This was where she could do the most good. If the bleaching had gone on for so long that the coral had died, that couldn't be reversed, and even if she transplanted new coral into those areas it might suffer the same fate. But over on this side of the reef she had a chance to repair the damage. If she could secure the unstable sections of coral by transplanting in new colonies from other parts of the islands, then it stood a chance of growing back as healthy and vibrant an ecosystem as it had been in the past.

But there were no guarantees. She'd been part of several transplantation efforts over the two years that she'd been back at the Environmental Agency. Some of them had flourished; some of them she'd watched as they'd faded and died, despite every intervention that she could think of to try.

She signed to Guy to let him know what she was doing and dived a little deeper, holding her breath as the end of her snorkel dipped below the water. She took some more photographs, going as deep as she could within the reef without touching the coral and adding to the problems it was facing. She tried to decide if underneath the unstable sections it could support a transplanted colony, and the evidence that she would have to present to the Environmental Agency and to Guy if her plan was going to be approved.

She looked up towards Guy and kicked her legs to come up to the surface. He had stayed near the top of the reef, watching her rather than looking at the coral. There wasn't much of interest on this part of the reef to look at, she acknowledged. With most of the coral dead or dying, the rest of the marine life had followed suit.

When she'd first dived at this reef, back before her accident, before she'd even gone to Australia, it had been a vibrant landscape of marine life. Brightly coloured fish had swum in and out of the coral, and anemones had waved gently in the light current. She had known where to watch out for well-camouflaged stone fish, and where to give a wide berth to avoid getting too close to a lion fish. But global warming and other human interventions had worked fast, turning it into an underwater wasteland.

She tried not to despair. She was here; Guy was here. They were going to try to fix this. If she thought too much about what the reef had lost, she'd never be able to concentrate on what she needed to do to bring it back to life.

When she had all the pictures she needed she signed to Guy that they should head back to the boat, and then she bobbed up above the surface, checking that Guy was alongside her. She climbed back onto the deck of the boat, pulling off her mask and fins and squeezing salt water from her hair.

She was aware of Guy sitting next to her, taking off his equipment, but it wasn't until he spoke that she turned to look at him and saw the expression on his face.

'My God, what happened to it?' he asked, his face pale.

She narrowed her eyes.

'What do you mean?'

'I mean, the last time I saw it, it was teeming with life. We could barely move for fish.'

We? She didn't ask. Didn't want to know with whom he'd been here before.

'You've swum here before?' she asked, surprised that he'd not mentioned it yet.

He nodded. 'Last time I visited St Antoine.'

The shock was evident on his features, and she softened towards him a little. It was clear that he did care about the environment of the island, despite his impatience to move on the building project.

'What happened to it?' he asked again.

She explained about coral bleaching, the effects of rising sea temperatures and the impact of tourism and watched his face as the information sank in. She would have to wait and see whether that carried through to the decisions that he made as the project progressed. It was easy to be shocked by environmental issues when you were sitting on the water with the evidence right in front of you. In her experience, developers started caring a lot less about the coral when they were back in their offices, staring at a spreadsheet and a schedule.

Well, that was why she was here, she reminded herself—so that Guy wouldn't forget. She smirked to herself at the irony of the amnesiac being the one responsible for reminding someone of anything. She softened towards him, though. He clearly was very shocked by what he had seen.

'I know it's hard to see,' she said. She knew that all too well. It broke her heart, seeing what had become of what had once been a lively, vibrant reef. 'But this is why we're here. You're doing the right thing, putting this right before the building work starts. Not everyone would.'

Guy shook his head. 'Looks like we were too late.'

'Maybe not. I've seen other reefs recover.' Not many. Not often. But she had fresh young coral growing in the lab, waiting to be transplanted out. 'The situation's bad, but not hopeless,' she said as she steered them around the coral, back towards the little dock on Le Bijou. 'We have to try.'

* * *

Seven years hadn't seemed so long until he went down under the surface of the water and saw for himself the evidence of how much time had passed. How different the world was now compared to the last time that he had been here. How something that had once been beautiful had been so completely destroyed. Meena had said that maybe the reef could be saved, that they at least had to try. But he could see for himself that it was a lost cause.

When Meena had denied his applications for the permits he needed, he'd not been able to see it as anything but an inconvenience—and an expensive, time-consuming one at that. But now he could see why she was so concerned.

He looked around the island after he had waved her off in her boat and tried to imagine how it would look when the resort was finished. He had artists' renderings and a three-dimensional model, but they couldn't tell him how it would feel to lie on the beach with the resort behind him and the sea creeping towards his toes.

Could he lie on the sand, imagining what was happening to the crumbling coral below the sparkling water? That was why he was going to hire Meena, he reasoned. It would be her job to worry about that. Not his. And, now that he had seen her out here, he was satisfied that she knew what she was doing and he shouldn't have to worry about it any more.

Except, he owned this island now. He was always going to worry about it. He wondered, not for the first time, if he had made a mistake when he had bought it. He looked back at his thought-process; he'd been so sure that he was making a rational decision, but the more he pondered it the more he realised that he just couldn't bear the thought of anyone else having it.

He remembered the first time they had come to the island. Meena had mentioned it when they'd been sitting in the back of a different boat, on their way out to a group dive at the resort he'd visited before—back when he'd just finished university, had been an apprentice in the family's global, multi-million-dollar business, trying to impress his parents. Before he'd started his own company, trying to earn their respect if he couldn't have their love, instead being accused of trying to undercut them and steal corporate secrets. Long before he'd realised that it wouldn't matter how hard he tried: he would always be a disappointment to them.

That summer he'd noticed the beautiful dive instructor—of course he had. But, in a large group, he hadn't had a chance to speak to her. So, when he had spotted a space beside her on the boat, he'd jumped at the opportunity. They'd chatted as they'd motored through the waves out to the dive site. He'd not been able to take his eyes off her: the way her eyes had lit up with excitement as she'd explained the dive to him. The way she'd gestured with her hands to emphasise what she was saying. The passion in her voice as she'd spoken about the reef ecosystem.

They'd been diving at one of the larger reefs with the group, a regular stop on the tourist train. He'd wanted to see what was on offer at the other resorts on

St Antoine, still trying to find his place in the business for which he'd just found himself responsible decades before he'd expected it.

'If you want a quieter dive site,' she'd said, 'there's an island I love—Le Bijou.' 'The jewel'. 'I could take you out there some time, if you wanted.'

If he'd wanted? He was fairly sure that what he'd wanted had been written all over his face. He'd been too young, too green in business and too in love to have mastered hiding his feelings.

Anyway, back then, he'd had no reason to. He'd been free to fall for Meena. And he had—hard. And then he'd gone back to Australia and had waited for her to call. To email. To turn up on his doorstep as they had arranged. But she hadn't. He'd never heard a word from her.

Because she'd been lying in the clinic, with no idea who she was, never mind her feelings for anyone else.

And no one had called him about it, because no one had known about him. They had been so careful to keep their relationship a secret. She'd said that it was because he was a guest at the resort, the owner's son, and she just an employee. Because the conservative society of the island would judge their relationship. Would judge *her* for having a relationship with a white guy from a wealthy family.

She'd been worried that she would lose her job for breaking the rules. That the gossip that would follow her around the island would be unrelenting. He hadn't pushed her then because it hadn't occurred to him that he needed to. He'd gone back to Australia full of plans for their future, and when she hadn't turned up he'd assumed that she'd changed her mind about him. Her mobile number had stopped working. He couldn't ask about her at the resort without risking getting her into trouble. So he'd had to let it go.

Except he hadn't, had he? He'd buried his feelings in drink, had partied harder than he ever had before. Convinced himself that he was over Meena. He had started a relationship with a woman he'd met in a nightclub, who'd agreed that all he needed to cheer himself up was her and a bottle of something potent.

And it had worked, for a while. They'd distracted each other from the pain that had driven them to numb rather than face their feelings. Until the morning that he'd woken in a too-quiet flat to dozens of missed calls, and realised that something was horribly, horribly wrong.

And now it turned out that Meena hadn't abandoned him at all. The opposite. He was the one who had left her fighting life-threatening injuries. Alone. There could be no doubt that she was better off without him in her life. The sooner he could get off this island, get himself well away from her, the better.

She looked at him now and had no idea of what they had once shared. He'd come here because he'd wanted to wipe his memories of that time. To overwrite them. To overwrite the whole island. And instead he found himself as sole guardian of these memories—if he wanted the job. If he chose to forget, it would be as if they had never happened. But it didn't feel right, doing that. She had lost enough. He couldn't tell her what they had shared—not when being so close to him could bring her nothing but harm. Not when he himself knew that he couldn't offer what he had once promised.

Keeping it a secret was for the best. Telling her would only hurt her. It would have hurt him, if that was even possible any more. No. He had to plough on with the plans he had made before he had arrived here. Get work on the resort under way and then start forgetting he and Meena had ever been here. Even if it seemed that she was remotely interested in him. Which she most definitely didn't seem to be. He couldn't risk hurting her all over again. Even though he knew now that Meena hadn't meant to hurt him, that didn't change who it had made him.

The fact was that he hadn't been able to trust in any relationship that he'd had since then. His inability to trust and commit had hurt people. No—she was better off without him. Better off not knowing. If he told her how they had once felt about one another, she'd be curious. She'd have questions. She'd want to pick at wounds that had long ago scarred over.

He walked back towards his boat, feeling the sand beneath his feet, the sun pounding his shoulders. Was this it? The last time he would stand on their beach? The last chance to remember what they had shared here before he went back to Sydney, the bulldozers moved in and he moved on with his life?

CHAPTER FOUR

THIS WAS PROBABLY a huge mistake, Meena told herself for the hundredth time as she scrolled to Guy's office number on her phone and her thumb hovered over the call button. It was fine. She could just leave a message with Dev, letting him know that she was going to be visiting the site of one of her coral transplants. Let him know that Guy was welcome to join her if he was interested in how the restoration of the reef might go and then hang up. She wouldn't have to talk to Guy. And there was no way that he'd even turn up.

So why bother inviting him?

Because she wanted him to care, she told herself. When they had been on the boat before, she had seen the shock on his face at the state of the reef of Le Bijou. And at that moment she'd thought that maybe she'd misunderstood him. Yes, he wanted to build a big hotel complex on this beautiful, untouched island. But that didn't make him evil. He had offered to hire her to ensure that no harm—or, realistically, as little harm as possible—came to Le Bijou. That counted for something.

The look on his face when he'd seen the destruction of the reef haunted her. It was as if he had lost something important to him. She didn't want him to leave here thinking that the reef was a lost cause. That nothing they could do could restore it. She wasn't sure why it was so important to her, didn't want to look too closely at her motivations, but the fact remained that she was compelled to do something.

And it was time that she went to check on her other transplants anyway. They had been in the water for two years now and were growing better than anyone had hoped. Other sea life had returned to the area and a young, vibrant ecosystem was growing up again around the reef. She wanted Guy to see that. To understand that they didn't have to resign themselves to losing the reef by Le Bijou.

Was that the only reason? she asked herself. Or was the reality of the situation that she just wanted to see him again? That she had enjoyed spending time with him? Had enjoyed the sight of his bare chest, studying the shape of his calves, the blond hair on his arms.

She shook her head. She shouldn't be thinking that way about him. About anyone. Thinking that way about men had never led her anywhere good in the past.

So what if her body wanted him? She had been there before, she assumed, and listening to her body then had left her miscarrying alone, afraid of what would happen if her family or their friends ever found out what had happened. She had to be smarter than that.

She had to second-guess what she thought she wanted before her desires led her into any more trouble.

She didn't want to spend her life alone. And she assumed that at some point down the line maybe she'd meet a nice, sensible boy and have a nice, sensible marriage, just as she knew was expected of her. Her body had betrayed her in the past, her passions had left her hurt and alone, and she couldn't risk that happening again.

She chewed at her thumbnail as she listened to the phone ring. Maybe she'd get voicemail, she thought—hoped—and wouldn't even have to talk to Dev.

'Hello?'

The greeting in English threw her momentarily.

There was only one person who would answer the phone in English.

'Guy?' The last thing that she had expected was for him to answer his own phone. 'Where's Dev?'

'Meena?' She resisted a thrill at the thought that he had recognised her voice and forced down the sensation it had triggered in her belly.

'Guy, sorry, I wasn't expecting you.'

'You just called my office.'

'Yes, but…' But she'd been hoping she wouldn't have to speak to him? She knew how stupid that would sound and caught the words before they left her mouth.

She shook off her embarrassment and surprise and remembered that she was a professional. 'I'm diving at a reef today where we transplanted in some coral a couple of years ago. I wondered if you would like to see it. It'll give you an idea of what we might be able to achieve at Le Bijou with some careful conservation.'

She could imagine him in his office, looking at a packed schedule, amused that she thought that he could simply drop everything and head out to look at some coral. The silence at the other end of the line spoke volumes and she was about to die of embarrassment and hang up when he said, 'I can clear my day from four. Would that work?'

Clear his day? She'd been expecting another snatched hour at most. Hopefully by four the fierce lunchtime heat would have started to abate and being out on the water in her boat would be a little more bearable.

'That works for me,' she said, hoping that she was adequately hiding her surprise. 'Should I meet you there?'

'I'll pick you up,' he said. 'I prefer to dive from my own boat. Where shall I collect you?'

She hesitated, but then gave him the details of the marina, bristling at his overbearing tone. 'I'll see you in a few hours, then,' he said, sounding distracted, and then hung up.

The hours passed slowly, but as the clock ticked towards four she headed out to her boat to check and gather her diving equipment. Cursing herself for looking out over the water, she tried to catch sight of Guy's boat. She wasn't sure what to expect. The marinas around the island were peppered with super-yachts and speedboats more luxurious and expensive than she could possibly dream of owning. Judging by his taste in speedboats and snorkel equipment, she shouldn't expect Guy to have skimped.

She looked at the worn wooden boards and tired paintwork of her own vessel. She was proud of how she had kept it afloat all these years, having rescued and restored it when she'd been at university before she had gone to Australia. She wouldn't have made the strides she had in her education without it. It had allowed her to carry out the research that had won her a scholarship for her postgraduate study at the world-leading university in marine biology.

It had kick-started a career that had fallen by the wayside since her accident. After that had happened, she had needed to keep things simple. And sanding and oiling the board of this boat had brought her hours of pleasure. It had always been the plan to go back to Australia to work, to continue her research, which would have a far wider effect than saving a coral reef or two here on the islands. But after her accident she'd lost the drive to return. Had stayed home, and safe, instead.

A luxury yacht cruised into the marina and, though she could only see crew on board, she had no doubt that it was Guy's boat. It didn't have the company branding—it was clearly for pleasure, rather than business—but it had an unmistakable air of Guy Williams class.

She looked down at her humble, though no longer leaky, little boat. She couldn't summon any jealousy for the larger craft. Sure, luxury must be nice. She had heard, anyway. But she liked her own hands on the tiller, setting her own course. Liked being able to navigate around the coral and into the smallest lagoons.

She wouldn't swap the freedom of taking out her own boat alone, on her own whim, for the convenience of a couple of luxury cabins and a well-stocked bar. Well, not for more than an afternoon or so, anyway.

She watched the yacht slow to a standstill, and then launch a speedboat from the aft deck. Of course. She smiled. Of course.

As Guy drew closer she waved from her own mooring and saw the change in his posture when he spotted her. Creasing her eyes against the glare of the sun, she wished she could read him better. She sensed there was more to him than just the brusque businessman he presented to the world. Certainly, in her dreams there was a lot more to him.

It was just fantasy, she reminded herself. However real those dreams felt. However often she was having them—and she was having them a lot—they weren't real. She didn't know him better because she had dreamed of his hands on her body and his whispers in her hair. And she would do very well to remember that.

He tied his boat to the dock, jumped up onto the worn wooden planks of the walkway and headed over to her.

She straightened her shoulders, resisting the urge to lift a hand to her hair, which was being caught and played by the ocean breeze, the only respite against the heat of the summer day.

'Guy.' She pasted on a neutral smile. 'Hi. I'm glad you could make it.'

He nodded. 'Yes,' he said. That one syllable was

maddeningly vague. Yes, he was glad he was here too? Yes, he knew she was glad he was here? She was starting to see that Guy Williams was pretty opaque, impossible to read, even without her amnesia in the mix making her second-guess every man that she met, looking for clues to a shared past.

'Good,' Meena said, attempting to be equally enigmatic. 'Let me just grab my gear and we can head off.' She started lugging air tanks and the bags containing her dive gear from the small cabin, but froze at the feel of Guy's hand on her shoulder.

It shouldn't do that to her, she reasoned. It shouldn't make her stop like that, as if the rest of the world had ceased to matter and there was just him, her and touch. She should be able to breathe normally, even when he was standing so close. Her skin should feel like just skin, rather than a tissue-thin, failing barrier between her and pure sensation, fireworks, lightning strikes and every cliché she could think of, all from the innocent touch of a hand on a shoulder. She was starting to see, being around Guy, how she must have got it so wrong last time. How easily her body could be led astray by a man she desired, whoever that man in her past had been. How he had made her forget what was important to her.

Well, this time, she was prepared. She knew the consequences of oohing and aahing over those fireworks. Of looking to find where those sensations led. She wasn't going to make the mistake with Guy that she had made in the past. He was leaving the island in two weeks anyway. As if she needed another reason why she couldn't act on her feelings.

At least she didn't have to try to convince herself that following these feelings she had for Guy would be an equally colossal mistake. She was well aware of the fact. Every rational, sensible part of her brain—at least, all of those that she could readily access—was signalling to her on high alert that he was dangerous. Dangerous to the status quo. To her way of moving through the world, which was largely based on avoiding entanglements with the opposite sex.

'You can leave it, if you want,' Guy said. 'I have some on the yacht you can borrow.'

If she hadn't already seen his snorkelling equipment, she might have hesitated. But she knew that his scuba gear would be top of the range too. If you were stocking a luxury yacht for a dive, you were hardly going to cut corners. And if it would save her having to lift and carry her air tanks, she would say yes to anything. She threw her dive watch, underwater camera and dive plan into her backpack, though—those were non-negotiable—and accepted Guy's offer.

'Okay, sure, thanks,' she said, locking the strong box and stepping up on to the walkway.

'So what's the plan?' Guy asked as they jumped down onto his speedboat and left the sleepy Saturday afternoon capital behind them.

'Deeper water,' Meena said with a smile. 'There's a few reefs on the ocean side of the island that have coped better than most over the last few years. We collected coral fragments from them after a storm and grew them out in the lab. Then we transplanted them on to the reefs that were suffering the worst from bleaching. We're checking them both out today.'

'Does it harm the healthy reef, taking the fragments?' Guy asked.

Meena pulled a face. 'It's not a perfect solution, because those fragments would normally fall and grow on the reefs nearby. But I don't want to go breaking handfuls of coral off a healthy reef. So…it's the best we have. It's a risk. And if it doesn't take on the other reef—it's heartbreaking,' she admitted.

A huge part of her job was weighing up benefits and risks like this, and it felt as though the stakes couldn't be higher. And so much of the time it didn't work. The damage that had been done was irreversible.

'But sometimes, like the reef we're going to see today, the transplant takes, the coral grows, the fish and all the other marine life come back and it's…' She smiled and gestured with her hands as she searched for the right word. 'It's…*glorieux*,' she said at last. *It's glorious.*

She was glorious, Guy thought as the gentle breeze off the water teased her hair into soft tangles and her passion for the reef brought a glow to her face that he recognised from a younger Meena. She invested so much in these reefs. It was obvious from the look on her face when she spoke about them how personally she took each success and failure.

Had that been there before? he asked himself, trying to remember. Back then, he was pretty sure that he'd been only interested in her passion for *him*. That wasn't fair, he corrected himself. It hadn't just been about lust, or the thrill of the chase. It hadn't been a physical thing. Or *just* a physical thing. Though, while they were talking about glorious…

The connection between them had gone deeper than that. They'd cared for one another. Cared for one another's passions as well. It seemed important to him now that he was the only keeper of those memories that he got them right.

He'd come here wanting to forget, to pour concrete over his memories. To stop them seeping into his consciousness, making it impossible to move on. But once he'd found out about her amnesia that hadn't seemed fair any more. He couldn't tell her about what had happened between them that summer. Not without hurting her. But if he wiped those memories from his own mind too then they were truly gone. He was the backup copy. And Meena had lost so much already that he didn't want to take that from her as well.

After they had swum together alone the other day, he had known that spending more time together— just the two of them—was a bad idea, but here they were. It would be too easy to slip back into old ways of thinking. Old ways of feeling. He had to remember that things were different now. That *he* was different now. That the things that he'd had to offer her back then were no longer his to give. He had wanted to love her. To protect her. To be her partner. But he'd failed her back then, and failed the woman he had replaced her with, and he knew that it would happen again. And he wouldn't hurt her like that again. She had spent seven years moving on from what they had shared, and lost, and he wouldn't drag her back.

'What do you hope to see?' he asked, keeping their focus on the dive.

'I want to check the transplant sites first; make sure that the new coral is still growing well. We used a couple of different attachment methods, so it'll be interesting to see whether there's any difference in how they are faring. I'll need to survey the marine life, as well, to see if there are any new arrivals since I checked it last month.'

He nodded; that all seemed reasonable. 'I'll show you to where you can get changed,' Guy said as they both looked up to the full height of the yacht. The little speedboat had brought them to the lower deck and the white of the cabin towered, blindingly bright, above them.

He could let a steward show her to the guest cabin that he'd put aside for her use. That would be the sensible thing to do. But it was inhospitable, he justified to himself. She was his guest on the yacht, so it was his responsibility as host to make sure she was comfortable.

That was a lie. He wanted to spend time with her. He was excited by her presence in his life and he wanted to make the most of it. There was no point denying the way that he was drawn to her. But that didn't mean that he was going to be stupid about it. He knew that he was bad news for her. Knew that he was walking on glass, trying to keep their shared history from her even if he genuinely believed that knowing the truth could only hurt her.

As they climbed the steps to the upper deck of the yacht, he wondered what she would make of it. The Meena that he had known so many years ago wouldn't have been impressed by it. She loved the boat that she had rescued from a junk yard before university and had lovingly restored. He had felt a pang in his gut when he had seen it earlier, remembering all the times they had taken that boat out to Le Bijou. It had been their escape, somewhere they could relax without the fear of being spotted by someone from the resort, without risking Meena's job.

He watched her as they moved along the yacht. Her eyes had widened as they had entered the main cabin, but he could see the slight rise of her eyebrows that showed that she was amused rather than impressed by the luxury.

He had bought this yacht, as he had done almost everything else in the last few years, because it was the furthest thing that he could imagine from how they'd travelled around the islands when he had been on St Antoine before. He hadn't wanted to remember her boat. Hadn't been able to think about going out on it with her. That was why he had taken the speed-boat to meet her on Le Bijou. It was only when he'd seen that she had that unfamiliar glass-bottomed boat that he had finally decided that he would go out on the water with her.

They arrived at the cabin and he hesitated at the door. Crossing the threshold of her private cabin was a line both literal and metaphorical that he wasn't prepared to cross.

'You can change in here,' he told her. 'The stewards will get you anything you need.'

He turned to go, but the sound of Meena's voice pulled him back.

'This yacht is very impressive, Guy.'

Of course it was. It was all part of the image. He owned a string of luxury resorts. His billionaire customers expected to see the owner playing the part. More important, they expected to be wined and dined by him occasionally, and the yacht was a part of the deal. It was all for show. So why did it bother him that she saw that? That she saw through the image that he had constructed?

Why did that ironic crook of her eyebrow unsettle him?

'I'll meet you on the lower deck. The equipment is all down there, but there are wetsuits in the wardrobe here. Choose whichever you prefer.' He turned away so that she couldn't read his face. He hadn't expected her still to be able to read him. He'd assumed that that had been lost along with her memories. But he had the uncomfortable feeling that there was still something there, some understanding of who he was.

He headed to his own cabin and changed into his swim shorts before he headed down to the deck where the dive gear was kept to change into his wetsuit and wait for Meena to arrive. As he pulled the neoprene over his legs, working the tight fabric up his body, he steeled himself for the sight of Meena in hers. He had seen her in a rash suit just a few days ago and, though he had averted his eyes as much as possible, the sight of her body in that skintight material had brought back more memories than he could comfortably handle.

He heard bare feet padding up behind him and turned to see Meena walking along the side deck towards him. It was good that he had prepared himself because, even with trying to keep his eyes locked somewhere over her shoulder, his peripheral vision couldn't miss the fact that the wetsuit emphasised the sumptuous curves of breasts, waist and hips.

Once, his hands had known those curves as well as they had known his own body. Over the course of that summer, they had explored her body together until he hadn't known where he had ended and she'd begun. He would lie with her in his arms, her limbs entwined with his, feeling the rise and fall of her breath as if it had been his own.

As one of the stewards showed Meena where the various masks, fins, air tanks and other equipment were stored, Guy kept his gaze fixed firmly out on the water, aware that he was being rude. But that was infinitely better than the alternative, which was turning to look and talk to her, knowing that he wouldn't be able to keep his feelings under control. He couldn't allow that to happen.

He pulled on fins and his gas tanks, feeling their protection like a charm. It was impossible to find someone anything other than funny in full scuba equipment, and he was counting on that to see them through today. He concentrated on the dive plan as she talked him through it, impressed by her attention to detail. Though he had no reason to be surprised. She had taught him to dive, after all. He knew how good she was. He checked his watch and with a final nod at Meena tipped himself backwards from the side of the boat.

As the water engulfed him, he took a second to orient himself in the whiteout of bubbles and then surfaced to look and see that Meena had followed him into the water.

He gave her the okay sign as the water settled around her as the ocean adjusted to their presence.

The reef started just a few metres away, and he put his face under the water, marvelling as he always did at that line between the above and the below—the reflective mirror of the surface that hid the wealth of life underneath the surface. As he watched, schools of neon fish darted past in flashes of yellow and blue, and as he relaxed below the surface, his breaths slowing into the familiar huff of the regulator, he began to take in more—anemones swishing in the current, the slow crawl of a hermit crab down on the sand.

He looked over at Meena, who signed that they should dive deeper, and he gave her another okay sign. It was a long time since he'd dived, and he'd forgotten the otherworldly feeling of being beneath the water, his soundscape reduced to the slow, steady rhythms of his own breath and heartbeat, light restricted to those rays that struggled through the body of the ocean, growing fewer and dimmer the deeper that they dived.

He followed Meena's fins through the water, looking when she turned and pointed out something on the reef that he hadn't noticed. A tiny crab, a sea snake, a lion fish guarding its territory, spines erect and fearsome. They skirted away from that last one, giving it plenty of room, not wanting the underwater emergency of a nasty sting even through the neoprene of their wetsuits.

The yacht was a dark shadow on the surface of the water, growing more distant as they rounded another side of the reef. Meena stopped again and pointed her index and middle fingers in a V at her mask, divers' sign language for 'look', and then pointed into a dark nook of the reef. He didn't want to risk damaging the coral with his fins by getting too close, so he stayed as still as he could, calling to mind everything he had learned about buoyancy in order to be completely immobile above the reef. Mask below fins, breathing slowly and steadily, he didn't even need to adjust his buoyancy control to keep him in position.

He followed where Meena was pointing to what seemed like a stony piece of coral. But as he watched longer, buffeted only slightly by a gentle current, he realised that he was looking at a stone fish. Something he never would have noticed if he hadn't been with Meena. Something he would have swum straight past if he hadn't been with someone who knew these reefs like they were a part of her. He looked up, the regulator in his mouth making it impossible to smile, but from the expression on Meena's face his excitement must have been showing in his eyes.

He slowly swam up from the reef until he could

gently kick his fins without risking touching the coral. As they continued on around the reef, Meena taking photos and pointing out where new pieces of coral had been cemented or tied into place, he lost count of the number of species that he saw. The contrast with the reef at Le Bijou, where they had snorkelled together, was astonishing. And he knew that he would do anything that he could to restore the reefs there. Seeing that it could be done, that it had been done here, was more moving than he could have expected.

Through perseverance, stubbornness and her meticulous research, Meena had found a way to turn the clock back here. To undo the damage wreaked by careless tourists and the inexorable warming of the seas; to bring life back to this barren reef. He could have watched it all day. Watched the fish darting and the anemones swaying, and Meena click, click, clicking away with her camera. Always looking for more information, more ideas, more ways to help return this ecosystem to its former glory.

When she was finished with her camera she glanced at her watch and then with a thumbs-up sign suggested that they return to the surface. He signalled okay and kicked his fins as they swam straight up. They hadn't dived deep enough to need more than a quick safety stop, so they kicked up through the water, his fins an extension of his body propelling him gently, as if he were a creature of the ocean rather than the interloper that his gas tanks and wetsuit proved him to be.

As they broke the surface, Guy looked over to make sure Meena was still with him. They had surfaced away from the yacht but he knew that his crew would be watching for him. Would bring the speedboat over to collect them if he gave them the signal. But the sea life beneath them was so tranquil, so delicately balanced with the new coral transplants and the recently returned marine life, that he didn't want to disrupt it by bringing the boat closer and scaring away the fish.

Or maybe it was that he didn't want to disrupt this, he thought as Meena pulled off her mask and smiled at him. Under the water, there had been no place for complications. No thoughts about their past, or what they had been to each other before. Diving together, they were responsible for keeping one another safe. It was important to be in the moment. To communicate. There were enough barriers between them, with not being able to speak to each other beyond simple hand signals, to prevent anything to distract them.

But now that they were back above the surface, back in the real world, those doubts came flooding back. He never should have mentioned that they had known each other before. He had seen how she had reacted to that. How she had started to wonder whether she had the full story. Had tried slotting that new piece of information into her memories and seeing if it stirred up anything else.

He was suddenly struck with doubt that he was doing the right thing by keeping their past from her. But he couldn't see a way of telling her without hurting her. He had loved her then, and she him, but he didn't—couldn't—love her any more.

What if she had questions? How could he tell her

what he had done, who he had become? No. He had
been right the first time round. Telling Meena could
only lead to more pain for them both. Knowing what
they had shared, what they had lost, felt like a knife
in his chest every time that he saw her. Every time he
remembered what they had hoped for in their relationship, and how pitiful the reality had turned out to be.
He couldn't spare himself that pain but he could spare
her. And he would. He owed her that.

They swam over to the boat with barely a word spoken, just a smile passing between them. With his buoyancy adjusted, it felt more like floating, a lazy kick
of his fins moving him through the water with barely
any effort. They climbed aboard the yacht, water drip-
ping from their wetsuits puddling around their feet on
the smooth, oiled deck, as his staff appeared to collect their dive gear and hand out warm, fluffy towels
and dressing gowns.

With the activity around them, he could barely see
Meena. He glanced over her way to say something,
but when he saw her hand on the zip at the back of
her suit he immediately looked away. He didn't want
to see that. Never mind that it wasn't appropriate to
watch her as she was undressing. He couldn't. To be
reminded of the wonder of her body would be too
much. The reminder of making love to her. Of how
she had trusted him. And he her. How together they
had explored one another, fulfilled one another. Loved
one another.

He pulled on a towelling robe over his tight, wet

swim shorts and waited until Meena cleared her throat before looking round again.

'That was wonderful,' she said, her expression matching the smile and passion in her words. 'The coral is doing even better than the last time that I was here.'

Guy couldn't help but return her smile. 'Shall we dry off,' he suggested, 'and have a drink while we talk about it?'

'Perfect. I have so many ideas for Le Bijou. I'd like to know what you think of them.'

She'd been so inspired by what she had seen on the reef, she couldn't wait to adjust her plans for how to put that into action. Her mind raced with ideas as she headed back to the cabin to change.

When she emerged, clean and dry in a cotton sundress, the sun was lower in the sky, its burning intensity now merely a hot glow on her skin. Still, she pulled her shades over her eyes, as glad for the subtle barrier they would provide between her and Guy as she was for their UV protection. But when she reached the deck Guy was nowhere to be seen. A steward had left a selection of drinks in an ice bucket, and a basket overflowing with fruit on a table between two sun loungers stretched under a sun shade, so she poured herself a glass of water and perched on the edge of one of the loungers, waiting for Guy to appear.

He strode out onto the deck with the confidence only a man on his own yacht possessed and came to sit beside her. Grabbing a beer from the ice bucket, he flipped off the lid and sat back.

'So what was your verdict on the coral?' he asked, looking across at her as he eased back onto the lounger. 'Were you happy with how it was doing?'

She could feel herself glow with pleasure as she answered him. 'I really was. There's such a difference from the last time that I was here.' So many of the bare, dead areas of coral were now teeming with life, and she'd recorded at least a dozen species that had moved in since her last survey. She couldn't have hoped for a better result. 'What did you think of it?' she asked.

He smiled, and she was tempted to melt at the way the lines softened his face. It made him more human. 'It was a relief, to be honest, after seeing the reef by Le Bijou. That was how I remember the diving here. Was it as bad as Le Bijou?' Guy asked. 'Before the transplant, I mean.'

She noticed that mention of diving here before, and again it tugged at something in her mind. A memory lurking just out of reach. She shook the feeling off, trying to stay in the present. Resisting the pull to that black hole in her memories.

'It was different,' she said. 'Not exactly as bad, but it definitely wasn't good. We've made a real difference. We have every reason to hope that we can replicate the results.'

Guy's smile took her aback.

'Well, anyone would think you actually care,' Meena said, smiling back at him.

He frowned. 'Of course I care, Meena. Why do you think I came?'

Of course he had come because he wanted to see the coral, she chided herself. Did he think that she was sitting here imagining that he had some sort of ulterior motive for seeing her? She could laugh at that. *Should* laugh at that. The only answer that made sense was that he had a real interest in how the reef was recovering. How that could be applied to Le Bijou.

So that he could get his building permits.

As her brain raced through the permutations of the different reasons that Guy could have had to come out to the dive today, of course it all came back to that. He wanted his permits so that he could get his building project moving again and get off the island.

'I'm sorry. I shouldn't have said that. I know that you care,' Meena said quickly.

'You should know,' Guy said, and then stiffened, as if he had said something wrong. Meena watched, confused, as his body language became more and more uncomfortable. Eventually, he sat up on the edge of the lounger, facing her, his expression deadly serious.

'What do you mean by that?' she asked, the tension in his body contagious, putting her on edge too. They were sitting so close their knees were almost touching, their pose laughably tense on two pieces of furniture designed specifically for relaxation.

'Nothing,' he said, refusing to meet her eye.

'It's not nothing,' she countered, trusting her gut. Trusting that feeling that there was a memory lurking just a little way out of reach. Trusting that Guy was hiding something, something that she would want to know.

'Why should I know that you care?' Meena asked. 'I've only known you a week. You've not wowed me with your passion for environmental conservation. There's something you're not telling me. What is it?'

She stared him down. She needed him to be truthful with her. She had spent so long questioning her body. Questioning her mind. Now she just knew that she was right about this. She had picked up on something that Guy had said and now she needed him to follow through and fill in the blanks.

'It's nothing,' Guy said.

'You're lying.' She held his gaze a little longer. 'Why?'

He shifted uncomfortably on the lounger, then stood and walked over to the railing, turning his back on her and looking out over the ocean.

'I'm right, aren't I?' Meena asked, watching his back. 'You're hiding something from me.'

'I'm trying to do the right thing here,' he said, turning around and leaning back against the rail, his arms crossed over his body.

'Let me make that easy for you,' she said, walking over to him, feeling perspiration prickle her skin in the late afternoon sun as she mirrored his crossed arms, holding his gaze and refusing to back down. 'Tell me the truth.'

'I don't want to hurt you, Meena.'

There was something in the familiar tone of his voice, the way that his eyes softened as he looked at her, that told her most of what she needed to know. They weren't strangers. Hadn't been strangers even when she'd met him on the beach a week ago. He had known her before. Remembered her from when he had stayed at his parents' resort on St Antoine seven years ago, before her accident.

That hole in her memory loomed before her, menacing with its secrets and the hidden parts of her soul. He knew what lurked in there; she was sure of it. And, if she wanted to know, she was sure that she could make him tell her.

Was it him? Was he the mystery man she had been looking for all this time? And, if he was, did she want to know for sure?

She knew she could find out now if she pushed. He would tell her.

But she didn't know if she was ready.

'I don't want you to hurt me either,' she told him.

Guy shook his head, arms dropping from where they had been crossed to grip the railing behind him. 'Then don't make me talk about that time.'

She thought for a few long seconds about letting this lie. About protecting herself from whatever it was that he thought would hurt her. She could leave this yacht and they could never mention this conversation again. When Guy was gone from the island, she would never have to think about him again.

But the unease in her chest as she considered it told her what she needed to know—she had to find out what had happened to her that summer. Who she had become. She had spent the last seven years of her life wondering about that time. She couldn't turn away from this opportunity, even if it did mean more pain. What could be worse than not knowing who she had been? Who she was now?

'I need to know, Guy. I need you to tell me everything.'

He let out a long sigh, lifted a hand and rubbed at his hair, and a chill went down Meena's spine at the expression on his face. If they had been romantically involved before, if he was the man that she'd lost her virginity to, then she would expect embarrassment. Not fear. Not this pain that etched lines into his forehead.

'I've already guessed that we knew each other that summer,' she said. 'But my memories are missing,' she added, hoping that would prompt him to continue. 'How did we meet?'

The look on his face had already confirmed what she had been starting to suspect. That he was her mystery boyfriend from that summer. But his expression was scaring her, rather than reassuring her. What had happened between them to cause the pain that was so clearly emanating from him?

'We were friends, weren't we? More than friends.' She made it a statement, rather than a question.

She couldn't tell him how she knew, though. Couldn't tell him she'd known all along that she'd had a lover that summer because she'd been pregnant. Unless he already knew that. She'd been six weeks along when the accident had happened. Had she told him? Had she even known herself? This was why she needed to know.

Guy shook his head, and for a moment she thought that he was going to deny everything. If he did that, she wouldn't know what to do next. She would know that he was lying. His face had already told her that they had a past. What she needed now were the details.

'Yes, we knew each other,' Guy said without meeting her eyes.

'More than knew each other. We were…involved.'

He looked up then, meeting her gaze briefly before looking away again. 'Yes. We were involved.'

CHAPTER FIVE

INVOLVED. THAT ONE word didn't come anywhere near to what they had been to each other. He had never even wanted to reveal this much. But she'd looked at his face and read exactly what she needed to know. He'd expected her to have lost that knack. They barely knew each other any more. She shouldn't be able to see into his thoughts like that. But, as usual, he had underestimated her.

So what if she knew that they had been involved, though? Could that be enough for her? Could he extricate himself from this conversation without having to open a vein and bleed every single moment of their history onto the deck in front of her?

'We had sex?' she asked, doing away with euphemisms.

His head snapped up at the question and he held her gaze. Her expression was fierce, and he knew that he couldn't lie to her.

'Yes, we had sex.'

It seemed both so simple and so cold to say those four words. They didn't come anywhere close to describing what they had shared. But revealing even that much was going much further than he had ever wanted.

What was he meant to say? *Yes, we had sex. I loved you, but you never came to me. You broke my heart, and me. And now I'm dangerous and no good for you and I'm not going to risk hurting you by telling you all this.*

But of course he couldn't.

Knowing now that it wasn't her fault that she had never come to Australia didn't matter. He didn't hold that against her, wasn't angry. How could he possibly be, in the circumstances? But, even though it hadn't been intentional, the damage had still been done. He had made the decisions that he had made, and someone had died. He couldn't undo that. Would never be free of the responsibility or the guilt. The wound to his heart had turned him into someone who hurt the people he tried to love.

If only he had been there. If he had managed to curb his drinking enough to actually make it out of his apartment and to the nightclub, he could have stopped his girlfriend, Charlotte, taking those pills. He would have noticed that she needed help. He would have called an ambulance before she collapsed and everything would have been different. She would have been alive and he wouldn't have been a monster. But that hadn't happened. Instead he had downed beer after beer and then a bottle of whisky, trying to drown his memories and numb himself enough to get out of the house and face the people he called his friends.

He wasn't making that mistake again.

After Charlotte had died he'd stopped the partying. Stopped the drinking. Had concentrated on growing his business. But he could never forget what had happened. And he had no doubt in his mind that if he and Meena started a relationship again one of them, or both of them, would get very badly hurt, and he had no interest in either outcome.

Guy tried to read the expression on Meena's face as she took in what he had said. The shock at his straight answer came first; that one was clear. But it mellowed into something subtler. Something he was less sure of.

'Just once?' she asked eventually.

He huffed in a deep breath. He could lie. But he'd had enough of lying. He would answer her questions truthfully. But that didn't mean he had to volunteer anything more than she asked for.

'No. More than once.'

'But then you left.' She narrowed her eyes at him, taking a step closer. He could feel her scrutiny on his face. In his heart.

'Yes.'

'Why?' Her arms remained crossed, her expression unreadable now. Not quite hurt. Not quite curious. Somewhere between the two, perhaps.

'Because the summer was over.'

He caught the huff and the eye roll that let him know she didn't believe him. It wasn't the whole truth. But it wasn't a lie. 'And you never knew about my accident?'

'No,' he said softly. 'I swear I never did. Not until

you told me yourself.' It was important that she believed him on that. Whatever else had happened between them, he didn't want her to think he was the sort of man who would have left her to cope with that alone, not if he had known what she'd been going through.

'And why did you decide not to tell me about all this?' This question was forced out through gritted teeth, and he understood for the first time what a risk he had taken by keeping the truth from her until now. He had to make Meena see that he had only ever acted in what he'd thought were her best interests, even if it didn't seem that way now. He had only ever wanted to save her from the hurt that he felt every time he remembered what they had once been to each other. But, again, that was more than Meena needed to know. He wasn't lying to her any longer.

'It didn't seem relevant…any more.'

'It didn't seem relevant to our current working relationship that we used to have sex with each other?'

He shook his head, firm in his resolve to protect himself. To protect Meena. He would give her the facts that she needed to fill in the blanks in her memories. But she had no claim on knowing his emotions. Those were his and his alone.

'No,' he said bluntly.

Unforgivably bluntly.

'Why not?' she asked, clearly determined not to let him off the hook so easily.

'Because it's in the past.' He uncrossed his arms and rubbed his hands through his hair, wondering how long this Q&A was going to last. The longer it went on, the harder it was to conceal what his feelings for her had once been. And if that came out then, yes, this would get complicated. 'I thought if you couldn't remember it, it was less complicated not to tell you,' he said with complete honesty.

'So you lied to me.' Her brow creased together in a way that made him uncomfortably aware that she was not going to take his answers at face value. Of course she wasn't. When had she ever? She was too smart not to have figured this out. Not to keep probing at his feelings until he had revealed everything. But he was on his guard, and he wasn't going to let her do that. 'Even though I told you how hard it was, living with these holes in my memory.'

'I tried not to lie,' Guy said.

Though in truth he hadn't really tried that hard. He should have told her sooner. He saw that now. But he had been trying to protect her. He winced a bit at that thought. That wasn't entirely honest, he acknowledged. She wasn't the only one he was trying to protect.

'You failed,' she stated.

He nodded. 'And I'm sorry for that. There won't be any more lies.'

She held his gaze but didn't answer for a long time.

'I still don't remember.'

His face softened with sympathy. How could it not, in the face of what she had suffered, and the disappointment in her voice? 'Did you think…?'

'That my memories would be back in a flood? No, not really,' she admitted, looking downcast. 'But I'd hoped that maybe there'd be…something.'

His arms ached to pull her in at seeing the despondency in her expression. He fought it, hard, and spoke instead. 'You said you knew that we were together before. How did you know that?'

She shrugged, blushing a little. 'You were behaving strangely. I just guessed the reason.' She looked away, though, which made him think that this time she was the one keeping secrets.

Fine, she could keep them if she wanted. The less they said about the past, the better, as far as he was concerned. He had meant what he'd said. What had happened in the past made no difference to who they were now. They had a business relationship and nothing more. All he needed was to get these permits signed off and get off this island. Then Meena could continue working with the project manager and he would never have to speak to her again.

A pang of regret hit him in the chest with that thought.

It was just an echo, he told himself. An echo of the feelings that he used to have for her. That wasn't what he felt now. It would be a relief, he told himself, to be off St Antoine and away from Meena. Except that thought didn't seem to ease his pain.

It was him, Meena told herself with certainty. She'd known deep down as soon as she'd seen that expression on his face that he was the one. By the time she'd asked the question, she already had the answer.

And yet, she didn't have the answer. She had a thousand more anxieties and a thousand more unresolved questions.

But this she knew: she had had sex with Guy Williams. More than once. And from the blank, expressionless look on Guy's face, it had meant less than nothing to him. So why had she done it? How could he sit with her, talk with her and dive with her now as if nothing had ever happened?

Why hadn't he known about the accident? Why had he never got in touch?

Now it was answered, what had seemed like the most important question in her life seemed suddenly irrelevant. She'd had sex—that wasn't new information. She'd known it since she'd been in the clinic.

But all along she'd thought that knowing the 'who' would answer all the other questions that she had. Principal amongst them: why? Why had she changed her mind about waiting? She knew that Guy was attractive. Knew that her body reacted whenever she saw him. That she wanted him. She'd thought that as soon as she knew who her partner had been, who had fathered the baby that she had been carrying, everything else would make sense. Her life, her decisions.

She'd been wrong.

Because nothing that she knew about Guy Williams made her decisions any more understandable. He was cold. He was evasive. He was bulldozing her island, or as good as.

How could this man have been the one? How could she ever possibly know? It wasn't as if she could ask him outright. It was clear in every line of his body and his face that he didn't want to talk about their past. He had said he wouldn't tell her any more lies, but how was she meant to get the important questions out: did you love me? Did I love you? Did you know that we were going to have a baby? Would you have been happy? Why did I love you? *Who was I when we were together?*

She couldn't even think about posing a single one of those questions to the hard, stern man standing in front of her, answering her questions with monosyllables while the breeze whipped at his hair.

There had been a moment when they were diving, communicating using only their eyes and their hands, when she had thought that she had felt a connection between them. An understanding and a shorthand that spoke of some deeper understanding than the one that they had formed over the last week. That was what had given her the confidence to ask the question that needed to be asked.

But it turned out that she had been wrong. Sex didn't equal intimacy. Or, if it ever had, it didn't apply indefinitely. The knowledge that Guy had once been inside her body didn't mean that she knew him any better now. And it didn't mean that she understood herself better, either.

What had she expected? She wasn't sure, but she did know what she'd wanted. She'd wanted to meet the man that she had fallen for, and she'd wanted every decision she'd made in the past, whether she could remember it or not, suddenly to make sense. She wanted to lose this shame and doubt that had dogged her since she had woken from her accident in a broken body with a broken mind and a broken heart.

But she'd been foolish, childish, thinking that that was going to be the outcome. All she knew now was what she'd known before. She'd had sex with a man who no longer wanted to be a part of her life.

Now that she knew that for certain, it was time to move on. To put to rest the questions that had been burning through her. To concentrate on the future, rather than focussing her energies on something that couldn't be changed. And that meant moving on from Guy. The more distance she could put between them, the better.

CHAPTER SIX

GUY GLANCED AT the inbox that he shared with his assistant, hoping for a message from Meena. Because he needed these permits sorted so he could get home to Sydney, he told himself. Not because he was feeling awkward over their last conversation, when he had confessed that they had been lovers and that he had returned to Australia and never been in touch again.

But three days had passed since she had made her excuses and they had awkwardly parted at the marina and there had been no word from her since. He wasn't surprised that she didn't want to rehash that last conversation, but he had been expecting to hear something about the report from their last dive. Without a plan for the reef at Le Bijou, she wouldn't sign off the permits. He wanted off this island, and he needed Meena's co-operation if that was going to happen.

He drew in a pained breath and reached for his phone, scrolling through his contacts until he found her number. As he listened to the ringing tone, he dropped his head into his hand, sure that this was a bad idea. If he was thinking as a developer, this call was essential. As her ex, it was a disaster waiting to happen; he was certain of it. But if she was avoiding him because of their last conversation, and that was holding up the development, then he needed to address the situation.

Just as he was about to hang up and send an email instead, the ringing stopped.

'Hello,' Meena said, a little out of breath. 'Sorry, I was in the lab,' she added by way of explanation for the delay.

Guy gulped, suddenly lost for words. 'We need to talk,' he said eventually.

'Guy, I…' He could hear the hesitation in Meena's voice and it actually reassured him. Hopefully she was as disinclined as he was to rehash their past.

'We need to talk about Le Bijou,' he added resolutely, leaving no room for her to interpret his last comment as being about their personal rather than professional life. 'I want to know what progress you have made since the dive.'

Meena took a deep breath to reply, but on an impulse he cut off whatever she was about to say.

'It would be best if you came here,' Guy said. 'I want this sorted as soon as possible. The best way to do that is in person. That way we can be sure there are no more delays.' He glanced at the clock in the corner of his computer screen. 'This afternoon?'

Meena paused, and he was already preparing to counter her arguments when she said, 'Fine. I'll be there in an hour. But I'll need to finish before sunset.'

'Sunset?' he asked, momentarily confused.

'I'm watching for turtles hatching on the beach tonight,' she explained. 'I'm not signing off the permits until I know what's going on with the nesting site. It's the last possible day of the incubation period, and I want to be there in person to see what's happening.'

'Fine,' he said. 'I'll see you in an hour.'

He watched the minutes crawl by slowly for the next sixty-four, and was about to pick up his phone and find out where Meena was when a knock sounded at the door. He looked up to see her standing in the doorway, laptop case slung over her shoulder, a hard look on her face.

'Where are we going to do this?' she asked without preamble.

He wasn't sure what he had been expecting from her today. But he was sure that it wasn't this…hardness in her eyes and her body. If she cared at all that they had once been lovers, she wasn't letting it show now.

He gestured her over to the table, then pulled out a couple of chairs for them both. 'Have you written your report on the dive?' he asked while she was booting up her computer.

She nodded, not looking over at him. 'It's nearly done,' she said, still looking at her blank screen.

How were they meant to work together if she couldn't even look at him? He understood that this was awkward. God, of course it was. But this was about more than their personal relationship. His whole development was dependent on getting these permits approved. If she couldn't even talk to him, they weren't going to get anywhere.

He hadn't exactly helped matters, he acknowledged.

Now that she was in his office, it suddenly seemed like an insane idea. They could have done this over email. Over the phone. There were a million ways to finish this project without ever being in the same room, never mind holed up in his office together. And he hadn't thought that any of them were good enough. He had insisted that she come here, and had made them both uncomfortable.

'Meena?' he asked, trying to keep the frustration out of his voice.

'What?' she asked, not looking up.

'Will you look at me?' he asked.

She shrugged, finally looking over and meeting his eye. 'I am.'

'You know what I mean.'

She shook her head. 'I really don't, Guy. What's the problem?'

She was putting on a front. He could see that. He had thought that he remembered everything there was to know about her when he had seen her lying on the beach on Le Bijou nearly two weeks ago. But the more time that they had spent together, more was coming back to him. The easier it was to know what she was thinking from the set of her mouth or the angle of one dark, angled eyebrow.

'You're stalling,' he said, calling her bluff. 'That's the problem. This report should have been done days ago.'

She crossed her arms, leaning back in her chair, aiming a death stare in his direction. 'Are you questioning my professionalism?'

'Yes. No. No, of course not. I'm sorry,' he blustered, wondering how she had grabbed the upper hand in this conversation. He had called her here because he thought that by looking over her shoulder he could push this report through faster. But now he realised his mistake. She was a consummate professional. Summoning her here was going to do nothing but slow her down.

He was the one being unprofessional. There was no way that he would have accused someone of that if they didn't have a shared past. It was unforgivable for him to say that to Meena. 'I didn't mean it and I'm sorry,' he added. 'That was indefensible. I know you're a professional.'

'Good,' she said, uncrossing her arms and returning her gaze to the laptop, typing in a password and clicking through login screens. 'And thank you. Because annoying me isn't going to get this finished any faster, you know. I've told you that before.'

'I know. I should have listened. It's just, the last time we spoke…'

She took a deep breath and he saw her brace herself.

'Last time we spoke was very awkward,' she confirmed. 'We spoke about stuff from the past that probably should have stayed there. I'd prefer it if we didn't speak about it again.'

'Fine by me.'

Perfect by him, in fact, he thought, letting out a long, relieved breath. He had never wanted to talk about it in the first place. He never would have if she hadn't pushed him so hard. Now that it was out there, the best thing that they could both do was ignore it and push it back into the sealed box where it belonged.

But he was surprised, nonetheless. Because Meena was the one who had pushed and pushed him to reveal their past—and, now that she knew, she had decided she wasn't interested any more? The last thing that he wanted was to rake over it all again, but he couldn't deny that he was surprised that she had dropped the subject entirely.

Maybe it was him, he mused. He had been giving off signals that he wasn't good for her from the moment that he had met her. He couldn't blame her for taking notice of them and deciding to wipe their relationship from her memory—voluntarily this time.

Meena talked him through the report from their last dive and her updated plans for the reef off Le Bijou. He couldn't fault her work. Her research was precise, and her plans for the project detailed and thorough. As far as he could see, the only remaining question mark over the permits were these bloody turtles.

'Will you definitely see the turtles hatch tonight?' he asked her when they reached the end of the report.

'I've learned not to get too hung up on "definitely",' she replied, annoyingly obtuse.

'Okay, do you think that you *will* see them tonight, then?'

She shrugged. 'I hope so. But I hoped that last night too.'

'You were on Le Bijou last night?'

'I camped on the beach,' she said. Her words sparked a host of memories, of the night that they had camped out, their two blankets on the sand doing less to keep them warm than the heat of one another's bodies. They'd made a small fire, eaten sticky mangoes and then watched the stars appear one by one in the sky.

'What?' Meena asked, and he knew that some of what he had been remembering must have shown on his face.

'It's nothing,' he said quickly, trying to cover his tracks. Cover his feelings.

'A memory?' she asked.

He hesitated. She was the one who had said they should leave the past where it was. But he had promised not to lie to her.

'Yes.' Monosyllables were safest.

'Ours?'

He nodded. 'Yes.'

'Le Bijou?'

'Yes, Le Bijou.' He cracked; holding these memories himself was too much of a responsibility. She had shared in the making of them, and she was as entitled to them as he was. He could talk about Le Bijou without talking about how he had felt for her. He could give her something without giving her *everything*. 'We spent the night there,' he said simply, leaving out the details.

Meena looked thoughtful.

'We went there a lot?' she asked.

He could have ignored the question. He had promised not to lie; he hadn't promised always to answer every question. But the look on her face, the eagerness for new information, meant that he couldn't deny her.

'Yes,' he said eventually. 'We went there a lot.'

It was where she had always felt safe since the accident. Where she had always been comfortable. Where she had eventually learned to be happy again. And now she knew that she had shared that place with him.

Was that why he had bought it? Because it had been special to them?

It would have been sweet, she thought, if he hadn't been bent on trying to destroy it. Despite her best efforts to limit the impact of the development, despite the relatively sensitive plans that Guy had submitted, her tranquil island retreat would never be the same once building began.

Was he trying to erase what had gone on there? What they had shared?

'Was that why you bought the island?' she asked, unsure of whether she would get an answer, never mind one that she would like.

'Yes.' Another monosyllable. Marvellous. Piecing together her history one syllable at a time wasn't remotely frustrating…

'Fine,' she said, her patience finally snapping. 'You don't have to tell me, Guy. You hoard those memories to yourself, and I'll pick up the crumbs and try and piece those few months together from the scraps that you throw me. It's not like I mean anything to you. I wouldn't expect you to try and understand.'

'It's not like that,' Guy protested.

'Four syllables this time. Lucky me.'

'I'm serious. You're better off not knowing. Trust me.'

'Trust you?' She raised her eyebrows in disbelief. 'And what possible reason have you given me to do that? What I know about you can be summed up in a handful of paragraphs, and the fact is that we had sex and you no longer care. That's fine. But this isn't just about that for me. Can't you see? I can't pretend that I don't care. I can't *not* care. Because to me that summer isn't about what happened between *us*. It's about *me*. It's about who I was. And the only clues that I have are the ones that you throw me, and I'm fed up of turning up here hoping for scraps and having to deal with your attitude to get them. Either start sharing our history with me or stop calling, Guy. It's not fair to trap me between the two.'

Guy let out a long breath, then came over and sat opposite her.

'We spent a lot of time on Le Bijou,' he confirmed, letting out another long breath. 'It was special to both of us.'

'And that's why you bought the island?' she asked. He nodded. 'And that's why you are intent on destroying it?'

His head snapped round to look at her. 'I'm not destroying it.'

'You're building a hotel on it. It'll never be the same again. It's hardly preserving it.'

'Fine, yes. I wanted to destroy it.'

She sat and looked at him for a long moment, the impact of that statement hitting.

'You hate it that much?'

Guy sighed, shaking his head. 'I don't hate it,' he said.

'Then why?'

'Because while it's sitting there, just as I—we—left it, I couldn't stop thinking about it.'

Meena felt the silence settle uncomfortably between them before she spoke again.

'It was that bad?' she asked, her voice soft.

'Bad. Good. I don't know.'

Meena was seriously starting to regret pulling on this thread. Answers were meant to be reassuring, but she wasn't liking the sound of where this was going. She thought again about what Guy had said—how he had kept the truth from her in order to protect her— and wondered if she had made a mistake in pushing for it.

'Did you really leave because your holiday was over?' she asked, not sure that she wanted the answer. But, now they had started, she wanted everything out in the open. She wanted to know how bad it could get. And then once it was done, flushed out of her system, she could move on. She *would* move on.

He nodded, but she could see there was more, so she waited. 'It wasn't really a holiday. It was an apprenticeship. I was here to see how the resort worked, before I went back to head office in Sydney to work with my parents. We didn't have much of a choice about me leaving.'

'Did I want you to go?' she pressed. He fixed her with a stare, as if he was challenging her. He didn't want to tell her this, but she wasn't going to let him off the hook. This was her history too. She was entitled to know it.

'Yes,' he answered. She thought about that. Thought about where he'd been going back to. Thought about her scholarship to Australia, and her plans to continue her research there.

'Was I meant to come with you?' she asked.

It felt as if they were fixed in this space between her question and his answer for days. Until eventually he nodded, his eyes dropping from hers, staring out at the water. 'Yes.'

This time, she could forgive him the monosyllable. 'I never came,' she said, her voice full of sadness. Sad for him. Sad for herself. Sad for the fact she was having to ask Guy these intensely personal questions; that she couldn't know the answers for herself.

He shook his head and shrugged. 'And now I know why. It wasn't anyone's fault.'

She traced the line of a scar under her hair, almost without realising what she was doing.

'You never knew,' she said, her voice low. 'You never knew why I didn't follow you?'

No wonder he had seemed so angry with her, she thought. She had assumed all this time that she was the one who had been abandoned. When she'd been working through her recovery and rehabilitation, she had wondered where her lover was. How he could be moving on with his life while she was left with a devastated body and a broken heart, even though she didn't know the cause. To find out that she had hurt Guy just as badly winded her.

'I'm sorry,' she said. 'That must have been hard for you.'

'It was a long time ago,' he replied, which didn't really answer her question. 'Are we going to discuss the dive?' Guy continued, dragging their conversation back to the professional.

'I'm not sure that this conversation is finished,' Meena said, sensing his barriers flying back up but hoping that she might get some more information out of him if she trod carefully.

'It is for me,' Guy replied, his eyes hard.

Part of Meena bristled, wanting to push back, demand her answers. But she could see that Guy would not be receptive.

She thought again about how it must have been for him—waiting to hear from her, assuming that she had made up her mind not to come to him. And then he had turned up here and found that she had no memory of him. She decided not to push. Not just now. If she did, he was just going to clam up. And if that happened, and he decided to put more distance between them, she might never find out everything that she wanted.

'Fine, let's get to work, then,' she said, pulling up the relevant files on her laptop and talking him through her findings from their dive. He nodded along as she pointed out what she had recorded and the adjustments that would be needed at Le Bijou as a result.

'And once we have an answer about the turtles on the beach, I can finish my reports,' she said at last.

He let out a long sigh, and she could practically feel his relief.

'And you're going tonight?' he asked. 'To see the turtles?'

She nodded. 'Yes. I'd hoped to see them last night— we're so close to the end of the possible incubation period—but nothing happened. It's been sixty days since I found the nest, so I'm hoping something happens tonight. If it doesn't…' She didn't even want to think about what it would mean if she didn't see any hatchlings.

'You were out there *alone* last night?' Guy asked sharply, and Meena didn't know quite what to make of his tone.

'Of course,' she replied, trying to keep any hint of annoyance out of her voice, but bristling all the same from his questioning how she did her job or how she took care of herself. Either way, it was none of his business.

Guy narrowed his eyes. 'Why "of course"?'

'Who did you think I would take with me?'

'I don't care who you take,' Guy said with a nonchalance that stung. 'I just don't think you should be out there all night on your own.'

She crossed her arms and stared him down in a way that was starting to feel familiar. 'It's not a big deal, Guy,' she told him, hoping that he would pick up from her tone that she didn't care for his input on this matter.

'I don't care. I don't like it.'

The message obviously had not been received. 'Well, then,' Meena said, wanting this conversation to be at an end. 'It's a good job it's not your decision, then, isn't it?'

'You work for me,' Guy said, his words eerily cool.

Meena leaned forward and rested her elbows on the desk, fixing him with an equally cold stare and hoping that he couldn't see how her heart was racing in her chest.

'When the permits are approved,' she said, making her words deliberately slow, 'I will be considering whether to come and work for your company. Right now, I work for the government of St Antoine. I don't report to you, no matter how much you like to call and demand my presence.'

Guy huffed. 'I do not do that.'

'Then what am I doing here?' she asked, a false note of sweetness in her voice.

'You're working.'

'Right, because I couldn't possibly update you over email. Or the phone.'

'It's easier this way,' Guy stated, as if the strength of his opinion could make it fact.

Meena snapped the lid of her laptop shut and started to gather up her papers. 'For you, maybe,' she said, knowing that Guy would get the subtext.

He stayed silent long enough for her to break her resolve and turn and look at him, wondering what he was plotting. 'Look, Meena, I'm sorry for annoying you. I was just concerned about you being on the island on your own overnight.'

'You don't need to be.'

'Well, I am.' He was back to monosyllables, but they were softer than they had been before—less combative—and Meena felt her shoulders relax down from her ears a fraction in response to his change in tone.

'I'm sorry you feel that way, Guy. But there's not a lot you can do about it. Like I said, I need to get this job done, and this is how I work. You're not my boss, and you're not my boyfriend. You can't stop me.'

His forehead creased in the way that Meena knew meant he was plotting something. 'I can come with you,' he said.

She laughed—couldn't help herself. 'Oh, right, the great Guy Williams camping out on a beach waiting to see turtle babies. I can really see that happening.'

'It's happening. I already told you, I've done it before.'

She stopped and stared at him for a moment. 'You're not serious. That was a million years ago.'

'It was seven years ago and I'm deadly serious. I'm not letting you stay out there alone.'

'Letting me? You wouldn't have got away with talking to me like that when we were together, Guy. Never mind now. No one "lets" me do anything.'

'How do you know how I spoke to you when we were together?'

It was a low blow and it hurt—a lot. He was right. She didn't know. Perhaps when she'd met him she'd turned into the sort of woman who had done as she was told, gone along with what he had wanted. Perhaps that was how she had ended up pregnant. But, even as she had the thought, she dismissed it. That wasn't who she was. It wasn't who she had ever been, and meeting Guy wouldn't—couldn't—have changed that.

'I just know, okay? I might not remember you, or us. But I know myself, Guy, and I would never stand for that.'

A small smile betrayed Guy.

'You're right,' he said, the smile creasing his eyes. 'You never did.'

'So stop trying it on now.' She tried to be cross, but his smile was contagious and she could feel it softening her features even as she tried schooling them into something stern.

'I'm not trying to force anything, Meena. I would love to keep you company on Le Bijou tonight, with the added bonus of knowing that you are safe. Am I welcome to come and watch for the turtles with you?'

She sat in silence while she considered the proposition. Truth be told, she hadn't been all that happy about sleeping out on Le Bijou alone and she would have been grateful for some company. More important, if Guy came along tonight, spent more time on Le Bijou, maybe he would soften his plans for the development. If he remembered how special the island was, he might rein in his development plans, so they made less of an impact on the environment of Le Bijou. Perhaps he would even abandon the plans altogether.

'Fine. You can come along,' she said eventually. 'But bring your own tent.'

CHAPTER SEVEN

SHE HAD DECLINED Guy's offer to bring his yacht to the island. She didn't want it anchored off shore, not knowing what impact it might have on the marine life. Her little boat had been puttering around Le Bijou for so long that it felt like part of the ecosystem, and it was perfectly capable of getting them to and from the island, even if it lacked a bit in the luxury stakes. She had half-expected Guy to pull a face when she had insisted that they both use it, but if he had been annoyed he hadn't shown it.

Instead he had turned up at the marina wearing a casual pair of cargo shorts and a polo shirt with a stuffed rucksack on his back. She could see a tent and a sleeping bag, and was glad that he had taken her instructions seriously. She'd meant what she'd said about not sharing.

Even with separate tents, though, this was probably not one of her best ideas, she thought as she steered them up to the little jetty and tied up her boat. Guy scrambled out first and held out a hand to help her up, and she hesitated before she took it. But it was just a polite gesture, she told herself as she made herself reach out for it, trying to ignore the zing that she felt when his fingers touched hers. They walked over to where she had set up camp the night before and pitched the tents quickly. The sun was setting fast, shadows growing long around them as she knocked tent pegs into the earth and tightened the lines. She was unrolling her sleeping bag when she felt Guy's eyes on her back and turned to find him watching her.

With the setting sun behind him, she couldn't make out his expression. He was just a dark silhouette against the bleeding orange of the sun dipping into the water.

'What is it?' she asked as the last rays of sunlight streaked around them.

'It's…' Guy hesitated, as if he was making up his mind whether to speak. 'It's just strange, being back here again,' he said eventually, coming round to the front of the tents and spreading a blanket on the ground. 'We spent so much time here before. And I've had this place in my mind for so long.'

'It's so strange not being able to remember it,' Meena said, sitting on the blanket and wondering whether this conversation would have been different if she'd had her memories. If Guy would even have talked about the past at all if she hadn't been reliant on him to fill in the missing parts for her.

'It's strange for me too,' Guy said, lit now only by the full moon as he dropped down beside her. Darkness had fallen fast, and Meena didn't want to risk interfering with the natural instincts of the turtles by turning on a torch or lighting a fire. 'It's hard to know what to tell you.'

'I want to know it all,' she said, glad of the darkness that hid her expression, letting her ask questions she'd never have dared to if she'd properly had to look him in the eye.

'I know…' Guy said. 'I know you think that you do, but…'

'But what? But you know what I want better than I do?'

'But me telling you isn't the same as you remembering.' He explained his thinking. 'Would it really change anything?'

'It might,' she countered. He could never know what it was like for her to live with this hole in her memories. To feel as if she didn't know herself. 'I want to know everything I can about that time when my memories are missing.'

He sighed, shaking his head. 'Why does it mean so much to you? It all happened such a long time ago. Why can't we just leave it all in the past?'

How could he ask that? Had their relationship meant so little to him that he could just pretend that it had never happened in the first place? Had she meant so little to him?

She could see why it wouldn't matter to him. He was clearly a womaniser who picked up women and dropped them with barely a thought for what came next. But she wasn't like that. Had he known, then, that she'd been a virgin? She couldn't think of anything more mortifying to ask. If he hadn't known, it would be mortifying telling him now. That he had been so special to her when she had clearly meant nothing to him.

'Because I deserve to know my own past,' she told him. 'You're hoarding these memories like it's your decision only. But I helped make those memories, and I think I'm entitled to have them back. Perhaps not everyone with amnesia feels this way. But what I've pieced together of that summer doesn't make sense. The Meena that I see through those memories doesn't make sense to me. I want to understand her. Want to understand who I was.'

'I don't remember you changing,' he said, as if that was the end of the matter. How could it be? How could she have been pregnant with his baby if she hadn't become someone else over those months?

'That's not possible,' she said eventually. 'I know that I changed. I want to know why.'

'Is this because—?' Guy stopped himself, and that was all she needed to hear to know that he was about to tell her something important.

'Just say it,' she told him.

He hesitated, but she knew that her tone hadn't given him any choice but to answer. He must remember something of her, to know that. 'Is it because of me? Because of our relationship. Is that what you're confused about?'

'Partly,' she confirmed, though she couldn't tell him about the baby. Assuming that he didn't already know, of course. It was impossible trying to pick through these conversations when both of them were hiding so much. Surely if he had known then that she was pregnant he would have asked about it by now?

But even if it hadn't been for the baby she would still have been confused about what had happened. The Meena that she remembered wouldn't have slept with Guy. So she must have been someone different those months.

'I just don't understand…*us*,' she said at last, not sure that it was a good idea mentioning their relationship, but unsure of how else to get the answers that she needed. 'The me that I remember wouldn't have…' She was grateful for the dark hiding her expression. If she'd done it, she should be able to talk about it. But as she didn't even remember having sex with him—having sex with anyone—she figured that it didn't count.

'Wouldn't have slept with me?' Guy asked outright.

The blood rushed furiously to her face and she could feel her skin burning even as the evening was starting to turn cooler.

'Yes,' she said, forcing out the word to break the awkward silence.

'I know that you hadn't before,' he said after a long pause. 'That I was your first.'

She kept thinking that it wasn't possible to be any more embarrassed than she already was, and then Guy would go and open his mouth and suddenly she was dying all over again.

'It wasn't a casual thing,' he went on when her silence continued. 'If that's what you were thinking. It was important to you. To both of us.'

She blew out a breath, hoping that it would take the

heat in her face with it. 'I… I'm glad. That helps,' she told him. And she meant it. It was a relief, if she was honest, to know that it had been important enough to her for Guy to know that. They must have talked about it, for him just to come out and say it like that. And he still knew her, to know that that was what she was wondering.

It was so strange, she acknowledged, the asymmetry of their relationship. He knew so much about their past. But they had both made so many assumptions, got so much wrong, that their last few years hadn't been so different really. They must both have been wondering what had happened to the person who they had loved that summer. She must have been as much a mystery to Guy as he had been to her.

And she was keeping a secret too, a huge one. Because Guy hadn't mentioned anything about the pregnancy. She was demanding honesty from him but couldn't offer it in return and she couldn't pretend that that didn't make her uncomfortable. But if he didn't know… She thought of the pain that she had felt, finding out that she'd lost a baby. And she'd not even had any context for that knowledge. She hadn't known whose baby it was. Hadn't known whether she had been happy or anxious to know that she was pregnant. Hadn't known how she had felt about the father.

Guy had all that.

That baby would have a meaning to Guy that she might never be able to understand. And she had a choice about whether or not he should know. An option that had never been open to her—to keep something from him that could only hurt him. She had been angry when she'd realised that Guy had been doing the same thing to her, hiding things that he thought would hurt her, but, faced with telling him about the baby that they had lost, she knew why he had made that decision. Who would choose to deliberately hurt the person that they cared about? Especially if it was all in the past. If there was nothing that they could do about it.

She could spare him that.

She didn't want to think too hard about why it seemed so important to her to protect Guy from pain. What that meant about how she felt about him. It could be purely human compassion, she considered, but knew that she was lying to herself. Regardless of the reason, she knew that she would do it. She would carry the memory of their baby by herself as the only person in the world who knew and cared that that life had existed, even for such a short time. She would treasure it, keep it safe, and she would spare Guy the agony of imagining what might have been, as she had so many times over the years.

Or at least she wished that it could be as simple as that. But it could never be, not between them. She sat on the ground beside Guy and looked out over the water.

'Do you want to hear more?' Guy asked, both their eyes fixed on the reflection of the moon on the gentle waves of the sea, the hush and swoosh of the water over the sand the only other noise in the night.

'Yes,' she breathed, wondering how much of her history she was going to rediscover tonight.

'We sat here,' Guy said, something wistful and distant in his voice. 'Right here. We camped, just like tonight.'

Meena held her breath, wondering how far this was going to go.

'We'd been struggling to find somewhere to meet,' Guy continued. 'You were living at home with your parents. We didn't want to meet anywhere in the resort, because we were worried about your boss finding out. It wasn't worth risking your job over. So we came out here, in your boat.' He fell silent, staring out over the water, and she wondered if that was it. If that was all he was going to tell her.

'That was the first time,' he went on, and she knew exactly which *first time* he was talking about.

She felt a shiver completely at odds with the still sweltering temperature.

'We'd been…close…before. But that night…was something else.'

He didn't say it, and he didn't have to. She knew exactly what he meant. She could almost feel it. Flashes of memories, or dreams, came back to her. His hands were on her beneath her sweatshirt. Her heart was beating faster, her breath coming shorter, and heat was rising in every part of her body.

Was that real? she wondered for the millionth time. Were those real memories, pulled up from a deep, damaged part of her brain that she couldn't reach when she was awake? Or were they pure fantasy, drawing only on an overactive imagination and out-of-control libido? That was one answer she'd never get, she supposed. Guy couldn't tell her what it had been like to be her in that moment. What she might have felt for him. How she might have felt when he had been inside her.

She looked out over the water, wondering if he was remembering it as she was. Or as she was trying to. Could he remember the touch of her fingers on his skin? The feel of the sand beneath them, the rush of the waves their soundtrack?

And then she remembered that he wanted to destroy everything that he remembered about this island. He was going to build a generic luxury resort here, in the place that he told her had once been so special to them, and it was like ice down her spine.

That was how much it meant to him, she reminded herself. The night that he was recalling here. He wanted to pour concrete over it, bury it. Destroy it, so that he no longer had to be troubled by it.

She must remember that, she told herself. They hadn't come out here tonight to reminisce. They were here to complete her environmental survey so that Guy could continue with his work of building over everything that they had shared here.

'It was a long time ago,' she said, hearing the frost in her voice and wondering if Guy would recognise it. Had he had cause to hear it back then, she wondered, or had everything always been happy between them? A simple summer romance that never would have weathered the slightest storm. 'I suppose it doesn't matter any more. I don't want to hear anything else,' she said.

Despite what she'd said about having to fill in the gaps, the reminder that Guy wanted to destroy those memories took the shine off any new information. The past was important, but so was the present. And she shouldn't get confused between the two. She was in danger of doing that, she realised. That was why Guy had wanted to keep this from her, after all. Because he assumed that if she knew what had been between them in the past she wouldn't be able to keep herself from bringing that relationship into the present. From expecting him to act like someone who had loved her, rather than someone she simply had to work with. He had been right. She had to remember the boundaries between them.

'It *was* a long time ago,' Guy said, still sounding thoughtful. 'But, sitting out here like this, I guess it doesn't feel that way.'

Her gaze shot across to his, trying to catch the expression on his face in the moonlight. What was that supposed to mean?

'Well, that's the point of bulldozing this place, I guess,' she reminded him. 'So you don't have to remember any more.'

He sighed and shook his head.

'I thought that was what I wanted.'

Meena held her breath, waiting for him to say something more, to explain, but he didn't. She couldn't leave it at that, though.

'Does that mean it's not what you want now?' she asked hesitantly, not sure whether she wanted the answer.

'I'd forgotten how it felt to sit here like this,' he said on a sigh. 'To be the only people on this island. To be

so alone, in a good way. All I could think about was…
what had come after.'

'When you were alone in a bad way?'

'Yeah.' He nodded. 'I thought that I didn't want
this place to exist any more. But I'm not sure that
that's true now. I think… I didn't want it to exist if I
couldn't have it.'

'Guy, we're not—'

'It feels petty now,' he interrupted her. 'And I don't
want to be petty. What we had was special. Even though
it's over, it doesn't mean I have to tear through here to
try and assuage my ego.'

'I don't think you're being petty,' she said gently.

'You don't think I'm doing the right thing,' he countered. There was an edge to his voice that hinted at
self-reproach.

'I don't,' she agreed, surprised at the self-awareness
Guy was offering. She hadn't expected this tonight.
Hadn't expected him to be honest with her about how
painful he found their past. She had assumed that she
had meant little to him. But if that were true he wouldn't
be hurting like this now. 'I don't think you're doing the
right thing. But that doesn't mean I think you're being
petty. I think you were hurt, and you had every reason
to feel that way. You thought that this would make you
feel better. But I don't think it will.'

'I don't know any more,' he said. 'But it's too late
now anyway.'

Meena shook her head. 'Please don't say that. It
doesn't have to be, not for Le Bijou.'

He looked at her, surprised. 'You don't understand my business, Meena. It's not as simple as you think.'

'No,' she said simply. 'I don't understand. But I know that no harm has been done yet—you could stop this, if you wanted to.'

'I never said that I wanted to.'

Meena sat up a little straighter at the bite in his tone. She had thought that they were getting on better, and here was the payoff, she guessed. He opened up and then snapped back shut when he realised what he had done.

'Guy, if all this has been to punish me, then consider it done, okay? Even the thought of what you're planning to do here breaks my heart. Is that enough? Will you stop now?'

'It isn't about punishing you, Meena. It was never about that.'

'Then what? Because whatever you think, this is punishing me. It's hurting me. And I don't believe you think that it's the right thing to do.' She held his gaze, refusing to let him look away, challenging him to tell her that she was wrong.

'You tell me what the right thing to do is, then,' he replied at last. 'Because I've already sunk millions of dollars into this development. I have a whole team waiting to get started on it. You tell me what I'm supposed to tell them. That I've changed my mind because I've been reminiscing with an old girlfriend?'

'If you think I'd care about what you're going to tell them, or about the money, Guy, you don't know me as well as you think you do.'

He huffed out a small laugh, breaking the tension between them. 'I didn't think you'd care about that at all, actually.'

She managed a small smile, pleased that the atmosphere was gradually easing. 'Do you mean it?' she asked. 'Would you really stop it, if you could?'

'It's not that simple.'

'We don't have to decide anything tonight,' Meena reminded him, not wanting the conversation to turn hostile again. 'We're meant to be watching for the hatchlings.'

'I'd almost forgotten,' Guy acknowledged.

Meena fixed her eyes on the sand, looking and listening intently for any sign of activity on the beach.

Guy moved closer, so they were sharing the same line of sight down to the beach, and she was hyper aware of the heat of his body beside her. Her own skin was still stickily warm, and the knowledge that Guy was so close was doing nothing to cool it.

'Does it help?' Guy asked, settling beside her, his gaze following hers out over the sand towards the water. 'Knowing more about what happened?' His voice was soft, almost sensuous, and Meena repressed a shiver.

'It helps,' she agreed, intensely aware of the heat of his body beside her, the bulk of him. It seemed so familiar from her dreams, as if she could strip his shirt off and know every line of his body from memory. He turned and caught her looking. She held his gaze, caught in the stream of energy that seemed to flow between them. It must have been because they were talking about their past, she thought. That was what had charged the atmosphere like this. There was definitely something between them, something pulling her towards him, that hadn't been there before.

Or maybe it had just been easier to ignore it before, when they hadn't been talking about the fact that she had lost her virginity to him, perhaps in this very spot.

'What are you thinking?' Guy asked.

'Nothing,' she replied, though she didn't look away. Didn't break the connection between them.

That look she was giving him was dangerous.

It was knowing.

It shouldn't be—she'd told him that she couldn't remember being with him, but that was not what her face was telling him. He knew that look; he remembered it well. It was the look she got when she was thinking about sex. About him. He should know. He'd seen it often enough. Looked for it, in fact, knowing that they could share a heated look and then she would seek him out later and find a way for them to sneak off together and meet somewhere. That look had led them to this island once. And here they were again, Meena with that look on her face, though he knew that she couldn't remember what they'd shared here.

'I don't believe you,' he said with a smile that he couldn't help forming, regardless of the danger they were heading towards. 'Tell me.'

She didn't have to. He knew that she was perfectly capable of ignoring his command. It was a question of whether she wanted to share with him. He wasn't sure that he wanted her to. Whether that was a good idea.

'I don't know,' Meena said. 'I have these…images… in my head, and I don't know if they're real or if I'm making them up.'

'Why don't you tell me what they are? I'll tell you if they're real.'

'I—I can't,' she said, and he knew that he had been right. She was thinking about sex. Which was interesting on so many fronts. Had she remembered something? If she had, that was huge. From what she'd told him, they would be the first memories that she'd recovered of that time before her accident. And if they weren't really memories, if it was her imagination, that meant that she was fantasising about him. About them together. And that meant that their past was still very much in the present. He could feel it between them. How could he not when she was positively humming with sexual energy?

'They can't be memories,' she said, shaking her head, her voice uncertain.

'Why not?' Surely there was the possibility that her memories could return. She'd acknowledged that to him before.

'Because I don't have any memories!' she stated. 'These are just…flashes. Feelings.' Her voice trailed off, but he couldn't leave this unfinished. It didn't matter that he knew that he was leading them towards danger.

'About me?' he asked.

She narrowed her eyes, clearly fighting with herself about whether to answer honestly. Or at all.

'Yes, about you.' She paused. 'Always about you,'

she added with a sigh. Her body softened beside him and he ached to draw her into his arms. He could see the toll that it was taking on her, not knowing their past. Searching for memories that her brain couldn't access. He knew how much strength it was taking her to ask him to fill those missing memories for her.

'What about me?' Guy asked. She needed this. She wanted this. Wanted to know the answers to these questions.

He knew that he was strolling into danger. But he couldn't help it. Couldn't stop himself. Out here, on this beach, on *their* beach, knowing that Meena was running X-rated fantasies of them through her mind, looking for clues that might tell her if they were real, the real world felt too far away. It could have been that night. It could have been the night that they had come out here and lain on a blanket just like this one, and she had loved and trusted him, and he had been deserving of that love.

While they were here, he could make himself believe that he was that man again, *could* be that man again. That he could be deserving of her trust.

He turned to her at the same moment as she turned to him, and suddenly she was closer to him than she had been for the past seven years.

His eyes never left hers as his arm curved around her back, watching for any sign that she wanted him to stop. Hoping that she would be the one to be sensible and put a stop to this, because he wasn't sure that he could. His other hand still rested on the soft, worn cotton of the blanket they had spread on the sand beneath them. Meena's eyes drifted closed and he watched those long, thick lashes as they brushed against her skin before she opened them again. When she met his gaze this time, there was something new in her expression. A determination and a fearlessness that he had seen before.

He sighed, smiled. Knowing that he was lost. Helpless, as he always had been with Meena.

She leaned in, those eyelashes sweeping shut again as she closed the distance between them. His hand came up to cup her cheek, holding her just before that moment when their lips would meet. Wanting to stretch this moment, to soak in it. In the promise of everything that was to come. To stretch that moment before their lives became so much more complicated.

Their first kiss hadn't been so considered. It had been furiously hot, between two young, inexperienced kids who had no idea what they were getting themselves into.

He couldn't launch himself in blind this time. He knew too much for that. Knew where this could lead. Knew how good this was going to be.

And with that memory he groaned, slipped his hand through the thick curls of her hair and brought her mouth to his.

At the first touch of her lips, he wanted to explode. To push her back on the soft cotton of the blanket and show her exactly what they had been missing out on for the last seven years. Instead, he shut off his imagination and channelled every firing neuron into the present moment. To fully experiencing the subtle friction of her lips. To hearing every nuance of the moan that escaped her as his tongue touched hers for the first time. His hand reached for the soft curve of her waist and he schooled it to stay gentle. To ignore the impulse begging him to squeeze her hard. To wrap both arms tight around her waist and never let her go. He dragged himself back to the present, drowning in the smell of her hair, the soft give of her flesh beneath his hands, and wasn't sure he would ever be able to stop.

They had to stop, Meena thought as she reached for Guy's shirt to pull him in tighter. She'd thought that this could be a simple test, to see whether her fantasies were based on reality or entirely constructed in her mind. But as soon as he had touched her, pushing her hair behind her ear and cupping her jaw, she'd known that this was so much more than that. This was her giving in to every temptation of the past week. Every time she had fantasised about this man had led them to this moment.

But they had to stop. She hesitated, and it was enough to break the spell. Guy lifted his head and looked at her, his expression as shocked as she felt by what had just happened.

'I…' he started, and she was touched to see that he was as affected by the kiss as she was.

'It's fine,' she interrupted, speaking quickly. 'I'm sure it was just nostalgia getting the better of us,' she added, trying to explain away what had just happened between them, though she was still feeling drunk from it. The last thing that she needed was Guy thinking that she thought that a relationship between them would be a good idea. How could it be, when she didn't even know who she was? When being around Guy made her act in a way that meant she didn't even recognise herself?

Guy stared at her for a beat longer than was comfortable, as if he didn't believe what she was saying.

'Nostalgia,' he repeated.

'Or curiosity. Maybe both,' she added quickly, aware that she was rambling. 'We should just forget about it,' she added, hoping that they could finish this conversation before she died of embarrassment.

That kiss had been hot. Seriously hot. But also seriously confusing. Because her and Guy were in the past. Were meant to be in the past. He had made that completely clear from the minute she had forced him to confess that they even had a history. He had made it abundantly clear that he had no interest in rekindling what they had once had. Well, until he had kissed her.

She had seen his expression when they had talked about how she had never come to him in Australia. It didn't matter that she had been in a coma at the time. He had been hurt, and it was perfectly evident from the expression on his face that he hadn't forgiven her. Couldn't forget. Probably never would, if he hadn't by now.

And she didn't want to be with him either. Couldn't be with him. She was still trying to find out who she was. Who she had been. She had thought that being around Guy would help with that. That he could fill in those parts of her past that she couldn't remember herself. But she had been wrong. Because, when she was around him, she barely recognised herself. In the past fifteen minutes, she had done things that she had never done before—or probably had, but she didn't remember. And that was the point. The way she reacted to Guy was so unlike her that she couldn't deal with it. She didn't need that reminder that there were vast parts of herself that she just didn't understand.

'So,' Guy said, edging away from her subtly, just enough that her breathing could slow to a normal rate, and pulling his arm back from around her waist, crossing it over his body. 'These turtles…'

They sat on the beach for hours, the silence between them becoming more and more strained as the time passed. By the time the sun began to rise and she realised that the hatchlings weren't going to appear, the atmosphere was so charged that she was surprised neither of them had spontaneously combusted.

It would be better tomorrow, she told herself. The sunlight would wash away the memories of that kiss, they would climb into her little boat and they would leave what had happened on the island safely on the island.

CHAPTER EIGHT

HOW COULD HE have been so stupid? Guy thought to himself as Meena navigated them around the coral reefs and away from Le Bijou. Since the first moment he had laid eyes on her again he'd known one thing above all else—he could not get involved with her. He would not be in a relationship again. Not with her, not with anyone. He had already proved that a relationship with him brought nothing but pain and danger, and he wasn't going to put anyone else at risk.

In the time that they had been apart, he had turned into someone who no longer deserved Meena. He had to protect her more than anyone because their shared past and her amnesia made her vulnerable. It had been unforgivable of him to forget that last night. He should never have let himself kiss her, however tempted he had been. It only went to prove his point. He knew that getting involved with her would only ever lead to her getting hurt, and yet he'd done it anyway. He'd kissed her, knowing that he could never be with her. If she hadn't stopped him, God only knew how far it would have gone before he'd come to his senses. If he'd been able to. He'd never been one for self-control around Meena before.

And now she wouldn't even meet his eye. She was the one who had written the whole thing off as curiosity or nostalgia, but she didn't entirely mean it. That much was clear from the way that she was avoiding his gaze. The way that she had jumped a mile when his hand had brushed hers when he'd helped her pack away the tent. In the strained silence between them now, as he looked out over the water, or up at the clear blue sky, or anywhere but into her curious brown eyes.

Well, this was the final part of the environmental survey, so as long as she approved the permits he could be off the island and back in Sydney in just a matter of days.

He was blindsided by the wrench that he felt as he had that thought. A pain that reminded him of the heartbreak he had felt those years ago when he had said goodbye to Meena before. Back then, he had at least been able to tell himself that he would see her soon, when she flew out to Australia to continue her research. But she'd never come, and his heart had cracked and then broken for good. And, when he'd turned to drink and partying to numb the pain, someone had died.

Now he was back here, feeling more of that pain, and wondering whether it was possible for him to be any more broken.

Meena looked over her reports, desperately trying to keep her head in the present and stop her thoughts drifting back to last night on the beach. She was a professional. She had a responsibility to her position to give this environmental survey the consideration that it deserved. She couldn't let her personal feelings for the applicant, or her memories of the area in question, colour her judgement.

Despite all her hopes, no turtles had hatched last night. She'd been keeping an eye on the spot every day since she'd seen the tracks which looked like they were leading to a nest. Legally she had to wait a week to excavate the nest and find out what had happened. Maybe she'd missed the hatchlings somehow? But she knew that she hadn't. The nest hadn't produced any live young.

It had been the last certain thing that she could think of to delay this development. If there were turtles nesting on the beach, producing live hatchlings, she could have used that to put a stop to it, or at least stall for more time. Without it, what did they have? The bleaching to the coral might be enough, perhaps. But, perversely, her successes with reviving reefs elsewhere made that argument weaker. And she wasn't sure that her bosses would consider that enough of a reason to reject the applications.

She would try, though.

She drummed her pencil on the draft of the report as she thought it over, but her mind wouldn't leave alone the memories of last night. When she closed her eyes, she could see Guy's face, bent towards her, the second before his lips met hers. She could smell the salt of the sea and the unique scent of Guy as their bodies had pressed together. She could feel the soft, cool cotton of the blanket beneath her bare legs, and hear the gasp of their breath as they'd broken off the kiss.

Memories. All real. And the sensations were so close to those that she had dreamed that she could no longer write them off as mere fantasy.

They shouldn't have done it. It was clear to her that Guy did not want a relationship. And she couldn't see how she could let someone into her life when she was still so unsure of who she was. When she had so many unanswered questions about her past. There was no chance of her being able to commit to another person—or of wanting to—when she did not even know herself.

No, last night was a mistake, and they would be foolish to repeat it. But they had both known that it was foolish last night and that hadn't stopped them.

She added a couple of lines to the report and then considered the options on the screen in front of her. Accept or reject. There was no grey area where this computer program was concerned. If she rejected the application, Guy would not get his permits. He could appeal the decision with revised plans, or he could forget the idea of building on Le Bijou altogether.

He had hinted last night that that was what he had wanted.

She shook her head. She couldn't let that influence her. This had to be based on the facts. The evidence. The science.

Meena looked up at the sound of the heavy knock on her office door and started when she saw Guy standing there. His face was drawn into hard lines, and she swallowed, nervous for a moment before she squared her shoulders and stood, refusing to let him intimidate her.

'Guy, what a—'

'What the hell is this, Meena?' he asked, brandishing a piece of paper.

She couldn't actually read it, with him waving it around, but she didn't have to be a genius to work out that he had received the email formally informing him that his planning applications had been rejected on environmental grounds.

'You tell me, Guy.'

'You rejected the application? Why?'

'The information is all there in the report. The potential harm to the environment of Le Bijou is too great. I couldn't approve the development.'

'But we've been working together on this, Meena, and you never suggested...'

'I never suggested what, Guy? That the application might not be successful? If that were the case then we wouldn't bother with a report at all. We would just rubber-stamp the application of every billionaire developer who happened to take an interest in our country.'

'Take an interest? What's that supposed to mean?'

'I didn't mean anything. What do you think it means?'

'I think it means that you're angry that I'm back. That I've chosen to develop an island that used to mean something to us. That you're letting our personal relationship cloud your judgement.'

Meena placed her hands on her hips. 'I wasn't aware that we have a personal relationship,' she stated, angry that he could accuse her.

'You know what I mean,' Guy said, grinding the words out. It was clear that he was as angry as she was. But she would not let that make her change her decision. 'Our history,' Guy continued. 'Our history on Le Bijou—that's why you rejected the application.'

Meena crossed her arms, not bothering to try to assuage her anger.

'You are accusing me of being unprofessional. It is not acceptable to come to my office and make those sorts of accusations. If you have a complaint, you can make it in writing,' she told him. Adding, 'To my boss,' to make her point. Guy was the one bringing their relationship into this. It had never been a part of her decision-making process. She'd only ever been thinking of Le Bijou, she told herself, and what was best for the ecosystem there. Never about him.

'Fine. I'll do that,' he said, turning for the door.

Meena was about to watch him walk out—storm out—without either of them mentioning that kiss on the island. Fine. It clearly meant nothing to him. But that wasn't the only thing that had happened that night. They had talked. Specifically, they had talked about the fact that Guy wasn't even sure that he wanted this development to go ahead.

'Guy…' she said, and he paused at the doorway. His shoulders dropped slightly, some of the tension leaving his body, and she guessed that his initial anger was fading along with the adrenaline that had no doubt fuelled his outburst.

'What?' His voice was still hard, though, the word pushed through a tense jaw and gritted teeth.

'If you wanted to stop the development…this would be a way.'

She knew that she was taking a risk, saying the words out loud. But she wanted him to know that he didn't have to fight this if he didn't want to. He could back out of the development gracefully, without losing face, if he accepted her report and didn't push back.

He stared at her, a muscle ticking in his jaw. 'You'll be hearing from me.'

Guy stalked out of her office and she collapsed back into her seat, trying to control the shake in her hands.

As the sound of Guy's footsteps faded down the hallway, she pulled up her emails and started drafting a note to her boss, reiterating why she had made the decision to deny the application and backing it all up with evidence. If Guy wanted to fight this, fine. She would treat it just as she would any other application. And that meant defending herself to her boss if her judgement was called into question.

She hadn't been expecting him to be so angry. Perhaps she should have… After that kiss, maybe he thought that she'd go easy on him. That he would get special treatment. Maybe that was why he had done it in the first place. But if that were the case, he was going to be sorely disappointed. Her only interest here was Le Bijou.

* * *

Guy sat on the deck of his yacht, willing away the shame that he felt at his outburst in Meena's office. He never should have accused her of being unprofessional. But he had been so shocked when he had received the email telling him that his application had been denied that he hadn't stopped to think. He had marched straight round to her office to have it out with her.

Would he have reacted that way if they hadn't kissed the last time that he had seen her? He couldn't deny that the kiss had affected him. He'd barely been able to think about anything else since it had happened.

So when Meena's name had popped up in his inbox he had thought, for a second, that maybe she wanted to talk about what had happened that night. He had thought that maybe *he* wanted to talk about what had happened that night, rather than give in to his instinct to ignore anything that came remotely close to emotional introspection. But then he'd read the message and understood that it had meant nothing to her. That she'd sent him this boilerplate message crushing all his plans for the island without even a single personal word to him.

Well, that told him everything that he needed to know about what she thought about that kiss. Good. He hadn't meant to kiss her anyway. And if she'd just been satisfying her curiosity then it had meant nothing to him either. There was no reason for either of them to mention the kiss, or their past together.

But he had to fight this ruling on the permits. So he had emailed her boss, knowing that it was a petty thing to do to Meena, calling her decision into question and asking that they reconsider.

When his phone rang, he was only half-surprised to see Meena's name on the screen. It was inevitable, really, that they would have to speak again in order to sort this out.

'Yes?' Guy asked, his voice tart and impersonal.

'Hello, Guy,' Meena said, and he winced at the formality in her voice. 'I've been asked to give you a call to see if we can reach a compromise on your application. My boss agrees that we cannot approve your plans as they are and has asked me to see if we can find a compromise. It may mean significantly altering your plans, if you are amenable to that.'

Amenable? He couldn't believe that just a few days ago he had sat on the beach with her in the moonlight, remembering the first time that they had made love, and had then shared a kiss so intensely emotional that it had been haunting him ever since. And now they were going to haggle over bureaucracy and blueprints. He wondered, not for the first time, if any of this was worth it. If he should just forget his plans completely and go back to Australia, where he would never have to see her again. Never be reminded of what they had had, and lost, on Le Bijou.

He shook his head, because he knew that was impossible. He'd tried it before. Tried burying those feelings. And it hadn't worked. That was why he'd come back in the first place. To try to do something different. To do something proactive to sully the memories he had of Le Bijou. And what had he done instead?

He'd made new memories. Made it harder than ever to forget.

'Fine,' he said eventually into his phone, because he was as determined as he had ever been to get this development built. 'Tomorrow. My office. Nine o'clock.'

'I can't make that, I'm afraid. I'll be excavating the possible nest on Le Bijou. But I can come afterwards.'

'No need. I'll meet you on Le Bijou.'

'Guy, I'm not sure that that's a good—'

'Nine o'clock. I'll see you there.'

CHAPTER NINE

MEENA WASN'T SURE what to expect when Guy's speed-boat skittered to a stop the next morning. Would it be the fiery anger he'd shown her the last time they'd spoken in person, or the ice that she'd heard on the phone?

Well, either way, she was prepared for him. She had all her red lines drawn clearly in her mind for what would and would not be acceptable to the Environmental Agency. And if she could just find some evidence of live hatchlings this morning, even if they hadn't made it to the sea, that would be everything that she needed.

That was probably why Guy had invited himself along, she told herself. Nothing to do with what had happened the last time that they'd been on Le Bijou together. He probably just wanted to be sure she wasn't going to plant evidence or do something else nefarious with the nest.

She shuddered at the thought of having to compromise her ecological principles just because of Guy's money. She recognised that her superiors in the St Antoine government had their own priorities. But if she didn't speak to him about this, then someone else would. Quite probably someone who cared a lot less about damage being done to Le Bijou than she did. She couldn't trust anyone else to value the environment of that island as much as she herself did. So, as much as the idea of compromises pained her, she would be the one to make them.

Unless, of course, Guy had had a huge change of heart overnight and was prepared to scale back the resort to the point where it would no longer have a significant impact on the environment. Not likely, she acknowledged, preparing herself for a fight.

'Good morning, Guy,' she said as politely and formally as she could when he walked up the beach to where she was waiting for him, avoiding meeting his eye.

'Meena,' Guy said, nodding. 'Let's get on with it. I need to know what I finally have to do to get this report going my way.'

'What you need is plans that don't harm the environment of Le Bijou.' Meena didn't even look at him as she spoke. What was the point? It was the same thing that she had been saying for weeks. It wasn't her fault that Guy wasn't getting the message.

'Because this island is important to you,' Guy countered, trying to make this personal. She wasn't going to rise to it. She was here to do her job and that was the end of it. She dropped onto her knees on the sand and started digging carefully at the nest site, scooping sand with her hands, reaching further and further into it up to her wrist, then her elbow, until she was almost lying on the beach, her whole arm reaching into the sand.

'Because Le Bijou is protected by the government of St Antoine,' she pointed out, still looking down into the hole because she didn't trust herself to look at him.

'And that's the only reason you rejected the application?' Guy asked, still determined to make this about them rather than about her job. He had no right. 'Because I thought we had been working towards a solution.'

She couldn't answer. All she could think about now was the nest and why, after she had dug down so far that practically her whole arm was disappearing into the sand, she didn't have even a small piece of egg shell to show for it. She concentrated on widening the hole, wondering whether she had got the location wrong. Whether the marker she had used had moved somehow.

'I just find it strange that, just a couple of days after we kiss, you decide that you're not granting the permits after all,' Guy said.

Well, she wasn't rising to the bait. She had made that decision based on evidence. He was the one bringing their relationship into this, when there was really no need. 'You should never have assumed that they would be approved. That was your mistake, not mine.'

'You gave me every indication—'

'I did nothing of the sort,' Meena retorted, sand slipping through her fingers as she searched for any evidence of egg shell. When she had come out here in her boat this morning, she'd had visions of finding hatchlings still in the nest, perhaps unable to find their way out through compacted sand. Now a hollow feeling was growing inside her at the thought that she might have made a mistake. Even a nest full of un-hatched eggs would be something. Something that she could use to prevent the development. But if her fears were correct, and the nest was empty, she would be left with nothing.

'I have maintained throughout this process that the permits would only be granted if you were able to show that the environment around Le Bijou would not be sig-nificantly harmed. You failed to do so. This was the only possible conclusion.' She tried to hide her fears from Guy, tried to hide the worst-case scenario that was playing out under the sand. Until Guy caught her expression.

'What's wrong?' he asked. And then, 'Shouldn't we have found something by now?'

'Yes,' she said shortly, not offering more than that monosyllable as she kept on digging,

But when she finally looked up he fixed her with a stare and she couldn't look away. Because as much as she might be a professional, they both knew that there was more to their relationship than that. She was man-aging to keep that under control, for now. But the lon-ger that she was forced to look at his face, the harder it was to keep memories from her mind. Those early, hazy memories in the private clinic, as a kind nurse had taken her hand and explained about the baby that had slipped away while she had been sleeping.

'What's wrong?' Guy asked, and she knew from

the tenor of the voice that her despair was showing on her face.

She fought to keep the words from her lips, but it was going to be impossible to conceal for ever. The best she could do was get it over and done with. 'There's…there's nothing here. Nothing at all.'

An emptiness opened up inside her as she spoke the words, as she started to accept them.

'What? What does that mean?' Guy asked.

'It must have been a false crawl,' Meena said, finally sitting back on her heels and rubbing the aching muscles in her arm. She stripped off her blue latex gloves and threw them on the sand. 'Sometimes, turtles will crawl up the beach, dig a nest but not lay any eggs. That's what must have happened here.'

'And that means no baby turtles.'

'No hatchlings,' she confirmed. And no hope for a reprieve for Le Bijou. Guy would get her report overturned with her superiors; she knew it. There just wasn't enough to stop the development. Not without the hatchlings.

She nodded, then moved to the blanket that she'd spread out under the shade of a coconut tree, picking up her water bottle and her clipboard. The longer that she stared into that empty nest, the larger the empty feeling inside her grew. She had to get away from it.

Guy came to sit beside her.

'Meena,' he said, the ice melting from his voice. 'Are you okay? We never talked about what happened the last time we were here. I'm sorry that I accused you of letting that interfere with our work. But…'

She couldn't do this now. Couldn't have this conversation. Not with the emotions that seeing that empty nest had brought rushing to the surface. It was more than the loss of the hatchlings she was feeling. It was another loss, another time, when she had felt all the potential of a life to be lived snatched away before it had started. And she couldn't let Guy see those feelings, because it would mean telling him about the miscarriage, and she had already decided that she couldn't do that to him.

'I should have called you,' Guy said. 'To talk about what happened. We shouldn't have left it like that.'

'Or I should have called,' Meena conceded. 'I should have dealt with our personal relationship before I sent you my decision about the permits.'

'Dealt with it?'

She shrugged, choosing her words carefully, not sure in what direction she wanted this conversation to go. 'I should have spoken to you about what happened between us.'

She had barely even let herself think about what she felt about that kiss. The kiss itself she hadn't been able to hide from. It had played in her mind, over and over, since the minute that it had happened. But as for where that left her and Guy? It was safer not to think about it. Not to wonder whether he was thinking of her at all. Whether he was replaying that kiss in agonisingly intense detail, as she had been.

'And what would you have said?' Guy asked, his voice dropping.

Meena held her breath. She didn't know what she

would have said. She still didn't know what she wanted to say. She wanted to say that the kiss had shaken her and grounded her at the same time. That she was terrified and also desperate to do it again. She wanted to ask if that was how it had been before. If there was something between them that had survived her accident—a part of who she had been that summer who was still living in her skin.

But she couldn't say any of that. Because the hard, cold look on his face told her he didn't want to hear a word of it. 'I would have said, I hope we can be adult enough to keep what happened separate from our professional life, and that my decision had nothing to do with what happened that night.'

For the first time since he had walked onto the beach, she saw a crack of warmth in his expression, and she breathed a sigh of relief. 'How am I doing with adulting so far?' he asked with a wry smile.

She grinned in return. 'Not great. Me?'

'Mixed reviews.'

She felt the tension leaching from the atmosphere as they both laughed out loud.

'Maybe we should talk about it, though,' Guy said, his voice taking on a serious tone that made Meena inexplicably nervous.

'What is there to say?' Meena asked, avoiding meeting his eye.

Guy shrugged. 'I think I should apologise. I shouldn't have done it.'

Meena drew her eyebrows together. 'I don't remember it being done to me,' she objected. 'I'm fairly sure I remember joining in.'

Guy shook his head, and she knew that he was shaking off her words too. 'But I knew that I shouldn't be doing it even as it was happening. And so I should apologise.'

Meena swallowed. Just because she had been equally sure that the kiss had been a mistake, that didn't mean that it was any less bruising to her ego to hear it out loud.

'Let's not mention it again, then,' she said, making her voice extra bright to cover her feelings. But still, she was…curious. She knew her own reasons for resisting the urge that had tried to convince her to take that kiss further. The urge that was trying to convince her it was the right thing to lean in and kiss Guy again. But what were his?

He had wanted her. She might be inexperienced, but she had known that much from the second before Guy's lips had touched hers. And he had had feelings for her once. So what had happened in the meantime to make the thought of a relationship with her so abhorrent?

She had broken his heart, she reminded herself, when she hadn't come to Australia to meet him as they had planned. That would be reason enough for him to not want to go over old ground, she was sure. But it seemed like more than that. As if he was hiding something. As if there was something about himself that he didn't want her to see.

'It's probably best,' Guy said. 'What happened between us all those years ago, it's ancient history. There's no need to drag it all back up again. The other night, that was just a…a slip.'

Of the tongue? Meena thought, remembering the English idiom. Interesting choice of words…

Guy's eyes were fixed on her face, and Meena felt suddenly uncomfortable under his gaze, the way that he was studying her and the crease that had just appeared in his forehead.

'What?' she asked, against her better judgement.

'I just don't…' He hesitated but then seemed to come to a decision. 'I don't understand how you knew,' he said. 'How you knew that we had been together before. I did nothing that would give it away.'

Meena fought to keep her expression under control, not to give away anything about how she had known that she'd had a lover that summer. That she'd been looking for him for all the years since. But, with thoughts of the miscarriage so fresh in her mind, it was harder than ever to pretend that it had never happened. 'Well, you might have thought that you hadn't. But you must have done, because I guessed. What other explanation could there be?'

She hoped that she sounded more confident than she felt…

Guy shook his head slowly and she guessed that she hadn't quite pulled it off as well as she had been hoping. 'I don't know,' he said, creasing his forehead once more as he looked at her. 'But I can't shake the feeling that I'm missing something.'

She shook her head in what she hoped was a casual

manner. 'You think I'm keeping secrets?' She felt the blood rush to her face as she asked the question, because of course she was keeping a secret.

She wondered for a moment if she could just tell him about the pregnancy. In the years since it had happened, she had never told anybody. Had never spoken to anyone about it since the nurse who'd first told her that it had happened. She didn't even know if her parents knew about it. They had never said a word if they did. With so much to focus on with her recovery, she'd buried thoughts about the baby as best she could. But, with Guy back in her life, it was suddenly impossible to do that any more, and she couldn't help but think that everything she was thinking must be written on her face.

Guy was watching her through narrowed eyes, and she knew that he suspected that something was wrong. If he had had a sneaking suspicion before that she was keeping secrets from him, then he must be certain of it now.

But she was entitled to secrets, she reminded herself. She didn't owe him her honesty, or anything else, for that matter. He was an associate and nothing more. That kiss on the beach of Le Bijou was a throwback to a different time. It didn't change anything about who they were to each other in the present.

But she felt different from how she had before it had happened, she acknowledged. She couldn't help it. She had wanted that kiss and, now that she knew how good it was to kiss him, to really kiss him, rather than just fantasise about it, she wanted more. And, from the heated look he gave her as he held her eye, she guessed that everything she was thinking was showing on her face.

Guy moistened his bottom lip, and with that tiny movement she was so very nearly lost. Because she knew that he was thinking the same as her. That he could taste her, as she still had the taste of him in her mouth. If she closed her eyes she could feel his hands skimming the curve of her waist, dropping lower, pulling her closer. She could feel the thud of his heart under her hand and hear the rush of blood in her ears as she had abandoned rational thought and let instinct take over.

She closed her eyes for a long moment, took a deep breath, and when she opened her eyes she was in control again. Memories of that night had been banished.

'What happens next?' Guy asked, and for a moment she thought that he was talking about them, and she was almost at the point of telling him that nothing happened next when she realised that he was trying to bring the conversation back to work. That he was talking about the permits. She felt another flush of blood to her face and hoped that Guy hadn't noticed.

'You submit revised plans,' she told him simply, trying to get her mind back into the game. 'Address all of the points in the environmental report and we will reconsider your application. If you meet all the requirements, the permits will be approved.'

His plans *would* probably be approved eventually, she knew. Guy wouldn't stop until they were. And then he expected her to come and work here, to oversee the destruction of the island in the guise of trying to protect it. She had thought that accepting his job offer would be for the best. That Le Bijou needed someone to stand up for it, and she would be the right person. But, with everything that had happened here in the last week, she knew that she couldn't be the person to do it. The memory of their kiss, the fresh raw grief of that empty nest: it was too much.

'Even if they're approved, though, I can't accept your job offer,' Meena added suddenly.

'Excuse me?' Guy said, his head snapping across to look at Meena. Of course he sounded surprised— she was surprised too. She hadn't meant to say it like that. Or say it at all to his face yet. She had planned to send an impersonal email to Dev and then never have to see the look on Guy's face when he heard the news.

She wasn't sure what she was so scared of seeing there. Or maybe it was more a case of what she *wanted* to see there. Did she want him to be disappointed? To be sorry that after she completed her report there was going to be no reason for them ever to talk again? She couldn't read him well enough to know which it was. His face was hard, stony, giving nothing away.

'I thought you were going to take it,' he said, his words calm and measured, giving her no clue to what he was thinking.

'I thought I would too,' she admitted, lifting her shoulders and letting them fall.

'What changed?' he asked, his voice hard.

'I can't,' she said. 'I can't watch that happen to Le Bijou.'

Guy's jaw tensed further, and she knew that he was angry. 'Fine.'

The careful control behind that monosyllable didn't make him seem any less irritated. He couldn't really make it any clearer that it was anything but fine. Well, that was okay with her. She wasn't going to stand here and pretend that she was happy about him destroying the place that she loved more than any other. It wasn't up to her to make him feel better about what he was doing.

'Has it got something to do with the secret that you're keeping?' Guy asked out of nowhere, taking Meena off guard.

'No! And there is no secret!' she said, a little too forcefully, making Guy narrow his eyes at her. Great— she'd made him more suspicious of her. It wasn't fair— her decision genuinely had nothing to do with having lost the baby. But now her over-the-top denial was making her look more suspicious than ever.

'I'm not sure that I believe you,' Guy said, taking a step towards her.

That was fine. She didn't need him to believe her. She just needed him to drop it.

'Never mind,' Guy said at last, when it became clear that she wasn't planning on answering him. 'It's none of my business anyway.'

Her face fell. She knew that her expression was giving her away but she couldn't stop it. Because of all the things that he could have said to her, that was by far the worst. Because of course it was his business. As much as she had tried to put the thought out of her head, it had been his baby that she had lost. If the accident had never happened, it would have been his baby she would have given birth to. Of course that was his business. She had kept the secret, trying to protect him from the hurt that she knew was inevitable. But she wasn't sure any more that that was her decision to make.

'What? What have I said?' Guy asked. 'Is your secret something to do with me, with us?'

She wanted to shake her head and deny it, but there was a difference between lying by omission and lying outright, and it turned out she wasn't actually great at either of them.

'I think you should probably just tell me what's going on,' Guy said, giving her a stern look.

'I don't know how,' Meena admitted, not wanting to look up and meet his gaze. Even after all this time, the pain she felt when she thought about what she had lost felt as fresh as the day she had first found out. How could she inflict that on Guy when she had the choice to spare him?

Was that what she would have wanted? she asked herself. She realised she had never considered the question before. But if she could have woken from her coma with no idea about the life that had once been growing inside her—would she want that?

No.

The answer came to her as quickly as it was decisive. That life had been important. Valuable. And she wouldn't want to diminish that by forgetting. And she owed Guy the same consideration she had been shown.

She sank into a chair, knowing what she had to do, that knowledge making it more impossible than ever to look him in the eye. Before she realised what was happening, Guy was sitting beside her, reaching for her hand, and she wondered what must be showing on her face for his sudden change of mood.

'Is it something I can help with, Meena?' he asked, and she nearly broke at the tenderness in his voice. She shook her head.

'There's nothing you can do. Nothing anyone can do. It's in the past but it still…'

'It still hurts,' Guy said simply, and she nodded. 'It's something to do with when we were together. Or your accident.'

'Yes. Both.'

With gentle fingers, he lifted her chin, forcing her to meet his gaze.

'What is it? You can trust me, Meena.' And she knew that she could. Despite everything, when she was with him she got that same feeling as she did when she was on Le Bijou. A feeling like nothing could touch her. That she was protected from the worst ravages of the real world. She took a deep breath, knowing that nothing was going to happen that would make this any easier. That she couldn't delay any longer.

'I was pregnant, Guy, when the accident happened. I lost your baby.' She watched as his face creased with confusion, then shock and pain, coming to rest firmly on the latter.

'Why didn't you tell me before?' he asked, leaning away from her, subtly putting space between them.

Meena shook her head. 'I thought it would be better for you not to know. I didn't want you to feel the pain that I did.'

His expression registered shock, and she waited for it to shift or change, but it was fixed there, much as she remembered her own world stopping when she had first been told the news. She squeezed his hand, knowing what a blow he had just received. Wanting him to understand that he wasn't alone in this.

'Why did you change your mind?' he asked eventually.

'You had a right to know,' she conceded. 'I finally understood that.'

'I was going to be a father?' he asked, a slight tremor in his voice.

Meena gave a sad smile. 'I think so.'

'You think so?'

She took a deep breath, facing some of the uncertainties that had haunted her the longest. That had made her life the hardest over the years. Exposing the depths to which she had lost her sense of herself when the accident had stolen her memories.

'I know that I was pregnant,' she explained, 'because the doctors in the clinic told me that I had had a miscarriage. But I don't remember it, Guy. I don't remember knowing that I was pregnant—*if* I knew that I was pregnant. I don't know what we would have wanted for the future. I don't know how we would have felt about a baby coming. We weren't married. I was going back to my research...'

He reached for her hand, looking closely at her face as he narrowed his eyes.

'You thought we wouldn't be happy about it?' he asked.

'I… I don't know.' It was just one of the many, many things that she didn't know about that summer. Who she'd been, what she'd wanted. How she'd changed.

'I do,' Guy said, squeezing her hand and moving closer again. 'You would have told me, if you'd known about the baby. I know it. And we would have been excited.' She was sure that his sad smile mirrored her own as they both thought about a life they hadn't lived. A future that had been wrecked out on that road.

'But…?' How could he be so sure? How could he be so sure about what she would have wanted when she didn't even know these things about herself?

'It wouldn't have mattered,' Guy said, and she clung to the certainty in his voice. 'Any of it. We would have been happy.'

She shook her head. 'I can't believe I have to rely on you to tell me how I would have felt. How do I know if you're telling the truth?'

He shrugged. 'I'm sorry. I can't begin to know how difficult that must be. I guess you have to decide whether you can trust me or not. I'm sorry I can't give you more than that.'

She breathed out and realised how much of a relief that was. How long she'd been carrying the fear that, as painful as it was to have lost the baby, perhaps before the accident she hadn't wanted it.

'We'd talked about it,' Guy said, and Meena's eyes widened in surprise.

'But how could we have? You said you didn't know I was pregnant.'

'No, not this baby.' He shook his head and she wondered what he was thinking. Wished that she knew him well enough to guess what he was feeling right now. 'But we had talked about the future,' he went on. 'About children and marriage.'

How had they become so serious in so short a time that a smashed skull could erase it? she wondered, disbelieving. And how could it have ended so abruptly? Both of them going on with their lives as if it had never happened. As if it had never mattered.

'Did you not wonder why I didn't come to Australia?' Meena asked, wanting answers to the questions that had haunted her for seven years.

'Of course I wondered,' Guy snapped, pulling his hand away. 'I called your phone, but no one answered. I emailed. Same. You weren't on social media. I could have called the resort, but you'd been so scared that if anyone found out about us that you would lose your job and I didn't want to risk it. What would you have done, if the situation had been reversed?'

What would she have done? How could she possibly know? She had no idea why she'd made any of the decisions that she had when it came to Guy. No idea about who the woman making those decisions had been.

Except that wasn't really true any more, was it? Not after that night on Le Bijou when she'd started kissing him and never wanted to stop. For the first time, she'd started to understand what had happened that summer. Had started to feel like the woman who had made those decisions.

'I would have tried to find you,' Meena said, but added on a sigh, 'But I'm not sure I could have done more than you did.'

'After a while, I just assumed that you had…moved on. And it made sense, really. Plenty of people have summer romances and they just…end.'

She shook her head. She thought that he'd known her better than that. At least, that was what she'd wanted to believe. 'I don't. I didn't.'

'I know.' He reached for her hand again and she didn't stop him. Didn't want to. She felt anchored, with her hand in his. As if she could start to put the pieces of herself back together again. As if she could finally start to understand herself.

'Can you tell me any more about the baby?' Guy asked, his voice quiet.

Meena took a deep breath. 'I'm so sorry, Guy, but there isn't much to tell. I was only a few weeks pregnant. Barely far enough along to take a test. That's all the doctors were able to tell me when I woke up.'

'So we won't know whether it would have been a boy or a girl.'

She shook her head. 'I'm sorry.'

He squeezed her hand again, and Meena felt it in her chest. 'You don't have to keep apologising,' Guy said. 'It wasn't your fault.'

'Well, it certainly wasn't anyone else's,' Meena

said, voicing a thought she'd always shied away from. 'Whose fault was it, if not mine?'

'How about the person that caused the accident?' Guy asked. 'You know, you've never told me what happened.'

Because there wasn't much to tell, and she'd had it all second-hand anyway. She didn't remember a moment of it. 'It's not much of a story. I was crossing a road and apparently a motorbike came too fast around a corner, lost control and knocked me over. Head injury. Internal injuries. I think you can imagine the rest.'

'How long were you in the clinic?'

'In total? A couple of years.'

She laughed at the surprise on his face; what else could she do? 'Did you think I just got up and walked out? Guy, I had to learn to walk. I had to learn to talk. I was lucky that I had health insurance. If it wasn't for all the support at the clinic, I don't know that I would have ever been able to live independently. I've only been diving again for a year or so. Did you know they make you wait *five years* after a serious head injury? I'm lucky that I haven't suffered from fits since it happened. If I had, I wouldn't have been allowed back in the water at all. I was worried, every day of those five years, that I would never be able to get properly back in the water again.'

'So by the time you got out of the clinic…' Guy started, finally piecing together the timeline of their relationship.

'Everything from that summer was gone. My phone

was destroyed. I couldn't access any of my online accounts for months because I barely knew who I was. By the time I was even thinking about it, the tech companies made it impossible and I didn't have the energy to fight them. I had to let it all go, start fresh, concentrate on my recovery and rehab.'

'You let me go,' he said sadly.

But it wasn't as simple as that. She hadn't let go, not really. She hadn't even known what she was clinging to, but she'd never stopped thinking about who the man she had given herself to might have been. 'I didn't know who you were. All I knew was that I had been pregnant. I found a couple of notes, scribbled on the back of a dive plan, that made me think that maybe I'd had a boyfriend. They were the only clues that I had. It wasn't enough to go on.'

'I wish I'd been here.'

She couldn't let herself think about that. About all the ways that her life might have been different if his flight had been a week later, or if she'd crossed the road in a different spot. They could have a family now—could *be* a family now. It was too strange even to consider.

It still didn't feel like her, the woman who had been hit by the motorcycle. In a way, Meena was glad that she couldn't remember that time. Because she didn't have to think about how much she had changed. What had motivated that change. She could try to get on with her life as she had been before her memories had gone.

Until Guy had turned up and reminded her that that wasn't possible. She couldn't pretend that she hadn't changed that summer. Even without her memories, she had known that something was different. And that was why she'd spent the last seven years trying to make sense out of the different pieces of her life. And why she had consistently failed. Because she needed to know it all to make sense of it.

She realised with a jolt that her hand was still resting in Guy's, and with another jolt that she had no intention of moving it. Because this was the missing piece. She couldn't figure out who she had been that summer unless she followed through on these feelings that she had for Guy. Unless she acted now, as she had acted then, to see if that made her understand who she had been. She pulled his hand a little closer to her and then looked up, meeting his eye.

He had sat down close to her on the sand. He had taken her hand. But she was the one who was going to move closer. To tip her face up to his and make absolutely clear what she wanted from him.

'Meena…' he started to say, but she laid a hand on his arm and he stopped, his gaze moving from her face down to her hand and then back to her eyes. 'This is not a good idea,' he said eventually.

'Does that mean that you don't want to do it?' she asked, without a hint of guile, because really she just wanted to know that they were on the same page, that she hadn't misread the situation and was about to make a complete fool of herself.

'Of course I want to,' he said, and she thought that it might be the simplest, most uncomplicated thing that he had said to her since he had shown up in St

Antoine. But the consequences of his confession were anything but simple. 'That doesn't mean that I think we should. I'm going to be leaving soon,' he reminded her, as if the thought didn't already haunt her. 'Again.'

'I know that,' she said. 'I'm not looking to the future. But…but my past is so complicated. And so much of it is missing, and I think that… I think that we could fill in some of those gaps, if you wanted…'

He shook his head, spoke softly, one hand coming up to play with the curls that fell forward towards him. 'We can't recreate the past, Meena,' he said. 'I think we've proved that already. It's not going to bring your memories back.'

'I know that,' she said quietly, turning her face towards his hand, where it played gently with her hair. 'I'm coming to terms with that. And I don't want to just re-enact the past either. But I want to understand who I was then. And this is a way to do that.'

'So I'm just an experiment to you. Is that your plan? It's hardly fair to ask that of me, Meena. What do I get out of it?'

She pulled back, taken aback by the bluntness of his question. He looked startled, too, at having asked that.

'I'm sorry,' he said, moving closer as suddenly as he had retreated, the shock falling from his face leaving something softer, yet more intense. 'Stupid question.' His hand lifted to her face, cupping her cheek as he moved closer. So close that she could feel the warmth of his breath on her lips. 'I get you.'

'And that's not enough?' she asked, wishing her voice didn't sound so small.

'God, Meena.' He sounded as if the words were being ripped from his throat. 'It was always enough.'

His hands threaded through her hair, pausing as they encountered the bumps of her scar tissue, smoothing them with his fingertips. He tilted her face back up to his and then his lips were on hers.

That's not enough? He wasn't sure that anything was ever going to be enough when it came to Meena. From before the moment that his lips had touched hers, he'd wanted the wet heat of her mouth. From the instant that he'd felt her tongue against his, he'd wanted more, deeper. When her body pressed against him, he wanted heated, naked skin, cool silk sheets and weeks to rediscover her body.

It had always been that way for him.

When they had first been together, she'd been the one to hold back. To grant first kisses, then touches. And she had held back in other ways, too. She had been the one who had insisted that they keep their relationship a secret. Which he'd understood. Of course he had—St Antoine was a conservative country; women could be judged harshly for sex outside of marriage. And she'd been worried for her job, what might happen if she was found having a relationship with him.

But it had still angered him. Because what did any of it matter, if she was moving to Australia? But she had been insistent that she didn't want to be the subject of gossip, even if she was leaving soon. And she didn't want to be fired—she wanted a letter of recommendation. Which had all been completely reasonable, he could acknowledge now.

But at the time, once he'd got back to Australia, it had only fuelled this idea that he'd imagined it all. Not the kisses. Not the sex. There was no way his imagination was that good. But the rest of it. Their plans for the future. Their intimacy. The whispered words of love that they had shared, first shyly and then urgently, as his time on the island had drawn to a close and they had realised that they had a decision to make.

Now he knew that she would have come with him if it hadn't been for the accident… And that all his feelings of abandonment and hurt that he had carried with him for years had come from nowhere—or, probably more accurately, from his own fears and insecurities; they had nothing to do with how Meena had felt about him and everything to do with how he had felt about himself. He'd turned that self-doubt against himself, and it had done so much damage to his heart that the pain had radiated out and started to hurt the people around him. But the damage had been done, whether it was based on a misunderstanding or not. And he couldn't risk hurting Meena again.

She'd been through too much. Deserved better than him. Better than the person who he was now.

But, when he was kissing her, he didn't feel like that person any more.

He felt again like the man he had been when he had first met her. When he'd been trying to find a way to impress his parents, getting to know their business and hoping that they would see that he wasn't as useless as they seemed to think. Like a man who had found the person who made him feel strong, capable and decisive.

Meena moaned into his mouth, and he didn't care whether he was the boy he had been before or the man he was now. All he knew was that he was a man, and the woman he desired more than any other was kissing him back, and he wasn't going to stop her.

How could he stop her, when this was everything that he wanted? With Meena in his arms, sliding onto his lap, he could believe that he was wrong. That he could be the person who fell in love with her again. That he could love her without hurting her.

Meena's hands tightened on his shoulders and he wrapped his arms round her waist in response, rolling over so he was lying above her, the sun hot on the back of his head, her body soft beneath him. Her shirt had rucked up as he'd rolled them over and he couldn't resist the heat of that golden-bronze skin. His hand explored, and his eyes and lips followed, her fingers threading through his hair as he pressed first one kiss and then another to the soft skin of her stomach.

But then with a wrench she pulled her shirt down, and he lifted himself up on his elbows, looking into Meena's eyes as she lay beneath him.

Which was enough time for doubt to flicker over her features.

'Guy… I can't,' she said. 'This isn't me.'

His brows creased. 'I don't want to do anything you don't want to, Meena,' he said, putting more space between them. 'But…if this is what you want… Meena, it *is* you. It can *be* you.'

'But I don't do this sort of thing,' she said, wrapping her arms around her body.

He gave her a small smile. 'It doesn't have to be a *sort of thing* you do,' Guy said, giving her space, but looking at you so intensely that she felt herself squirm. 'It can just be something that you want to do now. Here. With me.'

He moved away from her a fraction more, leaving her cold where he had been pressed against her. She relaxed a little, secure in the knowledge that if she didn't want this then he wouldn't want it either. This would be so much easier if she actually knew what she wanted, though.

Except that wasn't right, she acknowledged to herself. She knew exactly what she wanted. What she wanted was laid out in front of her, waiting for her to come to him. The question was whether she was going to take it. She wanted him, but she couldn't shake that voice in her head that told her that she shouldn't.

Guy leaned towards her and kissed her lips so softly, so gently, that she felt herself melting. And with that, she knew that this couldn't be wrong. It didn't matter what she'd thought she'd had planned for her life. All she had to think about was what she wanted for herself now. And she knew that there was no way that this could be anything other than beautiful.

She kissed him back, her lips curving into a smile.

'Is this okay?' Guy asked breathlessly between kisses.

'Very okay,' she whispered back. This time it was her hands that went exploring, skimming over his skin, tracing out the shape of his shoulder blades, the bumps of his spine down the centre of his muscled back.

She had never imagined that she could want this so much. That she could want more—but she did. She couldn't imagine anything any more that would make her want to stop touching Guy, that would stop her wanting him to touch her. Guy's hands had stilled when she had drawn away before, but she wanted his fingers back on her skin, showing her everything that he had once known about her body. Things that she herself couldn't remember.

She reached down for the hem of her shirt and pulled it over her head. She soaked in the desire in Guy's eyes for a moment as he drank in the sight of her, and she was amazed by how powerful that made her feel. How intoxicating that feeling was. And then his eyes dropped to the scars that criss-crossed her stomach and she tensed.

'From the accident,' he murmured. It was more a statement than a question as he traced one scar from the curve of her waist down towards her navel and the waistband of her shorts.

She bit her lip and nodded. 'Uh-huh,' she muttered, not capable of forming words.

'I'm so sorry,' Guy said, dipping his forehead to rest on hers, his fingers never stilling on that scar, tracing up and down, up and so slowly down. 'I wish I had been here,' he said, and Meena held her breath, because how different would her life have been if that had been the case? 'I would have kissed these better,' he whispered, and then the sun was dazzlingly bright in her eyes as his head dipped lower, kissing her neck, collarbone, then the soft curve of her belly, his lips replacing his fingers, tracing over the bumps of her scars, lower and lower and lower.

CHAPTER TEN

HER BODY HAD never felt so heavy. Her limbs were jelly; her eyelids were a rockfall across the entrance of a cave. Who cared? Meena thought. She didn't need to move. To see. She'd just exist here, with the sun heating her skin and Guy's breath still stuttering in her ear.

She groaned as he rolled away from her, but he grabbed her hand and squeezed, then pulled her closer, so she was tucked under his arm, her cheek pressed against the hot, damp skin of his chest.

So, finally, she understood.

This was who she had been that summer she had first met Guy. *This* was why she had made the decisions she had. And this was how she had got pregnant. Because the pull of this was irresistible and, now that she knew these sensations existed, she wasn't entirely sure how she was going to get anything done ever again.

And yet, the feelings weren't entirely new. There was something comfortingly familiar about the warm heaviness that weighed down her limbs. About the way that her body and Guy's fitted together. There was something so right about being tucked up beside him that made her think that perhaps her body remembered him, even if her brain didn't.

It made her wonder if her memories were still in there somewhere, just waiting for her to find the right route back to them. But perhaps they weren't, and for the first time that thought didn't frighten her. Frankly, how could she care if it meant that she got all these firsts again? First kiss. First love…

She smiled, listening to the gentle crash of the waves, soaking in the rays of the sun filtered by the coconut trees swaying above them. Grateful for the touch of a gentle breeze over her damp skin. She couldn't imagine anything more perfect.

Couldn't imagine a memory that she would choose over this one.

And that was when it hit her. Any day now, this perfect scene would be destroyed when the builders moved in and started to dig up this island. All because Guy wanted to destroy the place that had been so special to them. She shuddered as real life filtered through her fantasy. She couldn't lie on his chest any more with that knowledge burning through her. And she couldn't even look at him.

So now she *really* knew. Knew what it was like to be so blinded by her desire for Guy that all sense was forgotten. Knowing that she'd repeated the same stupid mistakes she'd made when she'd been much younger and more naïve burned in her chest. She pushed herself upright, looking around for her clothes, scrambling into her shirt and underwear.

Guy pushed himself up on his elbows, his expression the definition of confusion. 'Meena?' he said, watching her battle with her clothes in a belated attempt at dignity. 'What's wrong?' he asked, his eyes narrowing as he took in the change in atmosphere.

'Everything,' Meena replied. 'This is wrong. A mistake. We never should have…'

'I don't understand what just happened,' he said, pulling on his shorts while Meena gathered up the blanket, her papers and started throwing everything into her bag.

'What just happened is I realised I've made a huge mistake.'

Guy frowned. 'Is there any way to take that other than as an insult?'

'Probably not,' she conceded, keeping her focus on tidying their things rather than seeing the censure she knew must be waiting for her if she looked at Guy.

'Are you going to explain it, then?' he demanded.

'I don't believe I have to, Guy. You already know—you want to destroy this island. The only reason you were here in the first place was to try to make sure that I approve your environmental report and help make that happen. I can't believe that I forgot that, even for a second.'

He stood watching her in silence, and any hope that they could somehow rescue this situation fled. There was no way around it. She would do anything to protect this island. He would do anything to destroy it. That had been the situation when he had first walked onto this beach and found her flat on her back on the sand,

and nothing had changed since then. The fact that she had fallen for him somewhere along the way—again—meant nothing. It meant less than nothing.

'If that's the way you feel,' Guy said, every word a violent slash at her heart. It wasn't the way that she felt. It was the truth. It was his truth. 'I should go.'

'You probably should,' she agreed. 'Get your revised plans to me by the end of the week. I'm sure we can find a way to put the application through, now that we know the nest was empty.'

He stopped and looked at her.

'Is that what this is really about? The turtles?'

'It's all the same thing, Guy. This is about Le Bijou, and the fact that I would do anything to protect it.'

'Including sleeping with me?'

She whipped her head round to stare at him, open-mouthed. 'Are you really going to accuse me of that, Guy?' she asked. 'You think I would do this to try and change your mind? Well, thank you for proving me right. This *was* a mistake. I barely know you. And you've just proved you don't know me at all. I thought you understood that this was special to me.'

He had the grace to look ashamed, at least. But it didn't make his words go away. They couldn't be unsaid. 'I know that.' He took a step towards her, but seemed to think better of it. 'I'm sorry, Meena. I didn't really believe that you would do that.'

'But you said it.'

'And I take responsibility for that. But I want you to know that I truly don't believe it.'

'Fine. I understand. Now, I think we should get off this island.'

She looked over at where her boat was tied up on the rickety old dock, glad that they had arranged to arrive separately. The last thing that she wanted was to be trapped in close confines with him for a moment longer. But, when they got to the jetty, Guy jumped down into her boat rather than into the cockpit of his speedboat.

CHAPTER ELEVEN

WHY HAD HE said it? The only answer he could give himself was that he had wanted to hurt Meena. He hadn't believed what he had said, so what other answer could there be?

Which proved that she had the right idea, ignoring what had just happened between them and resuming their former hostilities. Meena was right. He wasn't going to change his mind about Le Bijou. How could he?

But he wanted to. The voice at the back of his mind was too loud to be ignored now. He had wanted to build this development to erase Meena from his memories, but he realised now how impossible that would be. Even if every grain of sand on this island were removed, Le Bijou was soaked in Meena and in memories of their time here. There wasn't enough concrete in the world that could make him forget her. Instead, he had made things worse. Made new memories, which were all the more unbearable for their freshness.

And he had hurt Meena. Over and over this afternoon, he had hurt her without even meaning to, try-

ing to. He had hurt her when he had made love to her
with no thoughts for the future, and no intention of
dropping his plans for his development. He had hurt
her when he had accused her of sleeping with him to
push her own agenda, rather than…

Rather than what? He realised he had been so quick
with his accusation, hurt at the way Meena had suddenly cooled towards him, that he hadn't considered
why she *had* slept with him. Or why he had slept with
her, for that matter.

It was because he had wanted her so much he could
barely breathe, he acknowledged to himself. He had
wanted her as fiercely now as he ever had when they'd
been younger. And he'd seen that same desire in her.
Seen it overcome her hesitation and reserve.

He had loved her once. But that love had twisted
and soured in him until he was the man he was now—
incapable of having a relationship with a woman without hurting her. They had gone from perfection to
disaster in the space of a breath, and he had no idea
how.

But he knew now, more than ever before, that his
decision to stay well away from relationships was the
right one. How could he choose anything else, knowing what happened to the women that he got involved
with? Thank goodness Meena had seen sense while
they'd been lying on the sand on Le Bijou, because
he wasn't sure that he would have had the strength to
end it if she hadn't.

Being with Meena again was everything that he had
dreamed about almost every night since he had last

known her. But he knew that it couldn't happen again. That he couldn't risk hurting her again.

'I don't want to leave things like this,' he said as Meena stashed her bags in the storage locker, the side of the boat bumping against the jetty as it rocked under their weight. Meena kept her eyes on what she was doing, though he had to wonder why it was taking her so long. She was avoiding speaking to him, of course. The answer was as obvious as it was unwelcome. Because now he had to say goodbye. Again.

He had no doubt that Meena would make sure that they didn't meet again. She had all the information she needed for the environmental report. The turtle nest had been the last hurdle in the way of his development, and when she had excavated it and found it empty all his concerns should have fallen away as that final hurdle was cleared. Instead, all he could see was the grief that had creased Meena's face as she had realised that there were no eggs.

He wasn't sure which was worse for her. The loss of her fight against the development, or the reminder of the baby she had lost. But the pain had been raw and tangible.

The miscarriage hadn't been just 'her' loss, though, he acknowledged. It was his too. With everything else that had happened in the last few hours, he had barely had a chance to process that information. She'd been carrying his child when he had left St Antoine. Even though he hadn't known about the baby until it was already too late, he felt a wave of sadness for what might have been. Because he and Meena would have loved that baby. If he hadn't left, if Meena hadn't been struck by that motorbike, then they would be a family now. He could picture it as clearly as if it was real, and the loss of that life struck him with a painful intensity. His knees buckled and he sat on the edge of the boat with a heavy thump, feeling it rock beneath him.

At the sudden motion, Meena turned her head. 'Guy? What is it?' she asked, her expression so concerned that he wondered what was showing on his face.

'Nothing…' he said, but then hesitated. Because, if he left now, he was sure that he would never see her again. And if he never saw her again then who could he possibly talk to about the child and the future that they had lost? She was the only other person on the planet who shared this loss. Who could understand the alternative reality he was grieving for.

'I was thinking about the baby,' he admitted, and her face softened. 'I can't believe I never knew about it.'

'I guess we have that in common,' Meena said, coming to sit beside him. And he could see her point. He had never realised before that he had lost so much when Meena had lost her memories. So much of what they shared, what was important to them, was stored in one or other of their brains, each a backup for the other, and when half their collective memory had been wiped clean they'd both been left incomplete.

Meena, her hands tucked between her knees, her shoulders sloped as she stared down at the deck, said, 'It's only natural to think about it.' And for a moment, she looked as if she didn't hate him. And that lit up something inside him. Something he wanted to nurture, to keep alight.

'I'm glad you told me,' he said, realising suddenly that she had had a choice about that. She could have kept him in the dark and he would have lived his whole life never knowing about the baby they had made together.

'I wasn't sure whether I should,' Meena said in a small voice. 'It hurts so much, to think about it, and I thought I was sparing you that. But then when I excavated that nest…'

'I know,' he said, reaching for her hand and squeezing. 'I know how hard that was for you.'

He told himself that he shouldn't be doing this. That he shouldn't be reaching out to touch her, and the sensible part of his brain agreed completely. But the woman that he had once loved was beside him, hurting, and every part of his body ached to make that better. Holding her hand wasn't much, but it was solidarity. It was telling her that she wasn't the only one who had to carry those memories any more. That they would share this sadness and bear it together.

'I'm glad that you know,' she said at last, her hand still soft in his. He was waiting, he realised, for her to stiffen and pull away, and God knew that was what he deserved after the things that he had said. After what he was trying to do to the island that she loved. But for some reason he couldn't fathom, she wasn't pulling away. Instead her body was leaning closer; and her head had landed soft and warm on his shoulder.

'You've never spoken to anyone about it before?'

She shook her head. 'I couldn't. Not without knowing the full story. Not without being able to tell my parents or my friends who the father was.'

'Well, you're not alone in it any more,' he murmured, risking pressing his cheek to the top of her head. Waiting for her to pull away from him, to realise that she was making a mistake. Putting herself at risk of being hurt. Instead he felt her soften more, her head growing heavier on his shoulder, the weight of her body pressing warmer at his side.

He should be the one to do it, he knew. He wanted to protect her, and the best way that he knew to do that was to stay as far away from her as possible. But he wasn't sure that he could do it any more. He couldn't willingly put more than a breath of space between them. He'd spent every minute since he had arrived here and seen her again for the first time trying to resist her. It had made absolutely zero difference to the way that he felt about her, and he feared he didn't have the strength to keep going.

But she had to know what she was getting into. He was laying everything on the table and had no doubt it would send her running.

'I'm not good for you, Meena,' he said. He waited a moment for the words to sink in, waiting for her to pull away, but she still didn't.

'I don't think I believe that,' she said at last. 'If what you've told me is true, then the Meena who knew you before thought that you were. And I'm learning to trust her judgement.'

He let out a sigh. 'She knew a different me. It was a long time ago.'

'I'm not sure people change that much,' Meena said with a small shrug against his body. 'I think we might be proof of that. Neither of us planned this, or expected it. And yet here we are. Again.'

'I mean it, Meena,' Guy said, sitting up a little straighter, trying to break the intimacy between them. 'I've done things in the last seven years that I'm ashamed of. I've hurt people. People have died. I don't deserve you.'

She looked up at that, meeting his gaze with narrowed eyes.

'Someone died? You hurt them on purpose?' she asked, wary.

He sighed. It was always the wrong question. 'No. Not on purpose, but that doesn't mean that it wasn't my fault. I should have been able to save her. I just… couldn't. I was so wrapped up in my own problems…'

Which made it sound less bad than it had really been. If he had taken better care of Charlotte, if he had at least been with her when she'd taken those pills instead of passed out drunk at home, he could have done *something*. The fact that the damage he'd caused hadn't been intentional didn't absolve him. He should have known better than to get involved with someone when he was still so broken after Meena.

'Guy, you're scaring me. I need you to tell me what happened. Who died?'

He shook his head, unable to believe that he was going to have to tell her this. 'My girlfriend,' he said, trying to keep his voice light. 'The girl I started see-ing after I got back to Australia.'

'How did she die?' Meena asked, her frank gaze giving him nowhere to hide.

He shook his head, covering his eyes. He wished he didn't have to do this, but Meena needed to know. 'She took some pills in a club. I was meant to be there with her, but I'd passed out at home and never made it. If I'd been there, I would have seen that something was wrong. I would have gotten her help sooner. I know it.'

Meena went silent for a moment after he spoke, and he wasn't sure he wanted to know what she was thinking.

'You didn't give her the pills?' she asked, a crease appearing between her eyebrows.

His eyes snapped to hers. 'Of course not.'

'And you didn't make her take them?'

He shook his head. 'No. I didn't want her to take pills. I'd told her before that I didn't like it.'

Meena shook her head. 'Then I don't see how you can think that this is your fault.'

'Because I should have been there with her!' Guy burst out, emotion making his words sharp. 'Charlotte shouldn't have been alone in some disgusting toilet of a dodgy club. If I'd been there with her, I would have got her help sooner. If I'd been able to control my own drinking, control my own feelings…'

'You drank a lot?' Meena asked. 'After you got back to Australia?'

He nodded. 'I thought it would help.'

'Did it?'

'Of course it didn't. And then Charlotte died and everything was so much worse.'

'It wasn't your fault, Guy.' Meena said the words gently, dropping her head and forcing him to meet her eyes. 'You're a good man. You deserve to be happy.'

'I'm not sure I have it in me, Meena. After I left here, and you didn't come, my heart broke—I broke. I tried to start again. But it didn't matter how much I tried. Because I could never feel it. It was never the same. Never real. And so I drank to try and convince myself that it didn't hurt. Charlotte died, and it was a tragedy. But it wasn't the same as losing you. Nothing was real, after you.'

She fell quiet, and it wasn't until he finally looked up and saw her face that she said, 'This feels pretty real.'

'This isn't love,' he said, shaking his head. It couldn't be. Because the implications of that were just too frightening to consider.

'Right.' She edged away from him slightly, caution making her wrap her arms around herself. He hated that he had sent her into self-protection mode. But it was for the best. She *should* be on her guard around him.

'See! I'm doing it already,' he pointed out.

'I'm annoyed, Guy. Not heartbroken.' She sat up a little straighter now, pinning him with a glare before she continued. 'So, let me be sure I have this right. Because someone sold your girlfriend dodgy drugs, and she died due to events beyond either of your control, you've decided you're incapable of having a relationship.' Guy nodded. 'That sounds pretty stupid to me.'

'Well, thanks for your understanding,' he said, crossing his arms and standing. 'But it doesn't feel stupid from where I'm standing. I don't like hurting people, Meena, but I've been hurting you since the moment I arrived here.'

'Do you want me to hate you?' Meena asked, standing up to face him.

Why couldn't she just take his word that this was a bad idea? *Because if she was the sort of person who didn't question what she was told you wouldn't have fallen in love with her in the first place*, his brain told him, providing the inconvenient answer.

'Of course I don't want you to hate me,' he said.

'Right, I'm the one who decides whether I do, and I don't, as it happens.' She crossed her arms and planted her feet firmly against the slight jostling of the boat and he knew that he was getting nowhere.

'Well, you should,' he repeated, though with diminishing expectations of her taking any notice of what he was trying to tell her.

'I think that says more about how you feel than how I do,' Meena suggested, her posture softening slightly, one hand reaching to touch his arm. 'Why should I hate you, Guy? Because we disagree about the future of Le Bijou? I never expected you to change your mind about that. Not really. Not even when we made love. It was just more convenient for me to…not think about it. I won't let you take sole responsibility for the mistakes we both made. I'm sorry if I made you think that I hate you, because I don't.'

He shook his head. Why wouldn't she just believe him when he said that he didn't deserve her? 'Please, Meena. Just take my word when I say you're better off without me in your life.'

'Honestly, I don't know, Guy. What happened between us was so… I'm not sure I have the words to describe it. And knowing what's going to happen to Le Bijou makes having those feelings difficult for me. But, after everything that you've just told me, I'm not sure that running from them is such a great idea either. You've spent seven years feeling broken from what we had before, from what happened to you after you left here. I feel like there's more to be said. More to talk about. If we both walk away now, then everything is just as broken as it was before. We have a chance to put that right.'

'And I've told you that those chances always end up in someone getting hurt.' His shoulders stiffened beneath her cheek.

'This is different.'

'How?' he asked.

Meena sighed. 'Because we are having this conversation. Have you ever told anyone else what you told me?'

'No.'

'Then I doubt anyone has told you what I'm about to. It wasn't your fault, Guy.' She squeezed his hand and he tried so hard to believe her. 'And what we have is different to what came before. I don't think I've ever

stopped loving you. And if you felt the same way…
maybe you weren't broken, Guy,' she said. 'You aren't.
Maybe things were just…unfinished. And now we can
finish them. One way or the other.'

He shook his head. 'I don't think what we did today
helped things feel more finished, if I'm honest.'

'I know.'

She looked so bloody confused about that that he felt
terrible for pushing this. For making this about him,
when she was the one who had just taken a life-changing
gamble on him. She had chosen him to be her first—
again—and he had let her down—again. And he was
kidding himself if he thought that what had happened
today hadn't been life-changing for him too. Because
there was no coming back from what had happened on
the beach. Already he was thinking differently. Wishing differently. Trying to find a way that they could
give their relationship a second chance. But he knew
that it would be selfish. That any sort of relationship
with Meena risked her getting hurt, and he couldn't be
responsible for that.

He was so sure, Meena thought, watching Guy. So sure
that he knew what was best for her. So sure that his
history was going to repeat itself and that there was
nothing he could do to stop it.

Well, he didn't know the future. And it was time
to prove that to him.

'I never got the chance to tell you, Guy, that I'm
leaving St Antoine.'

The pure shock on his face gave her a tiny buzz of

pleasure. He was so sure that he could predict what was going to happen between them that it pleased her that she could wrong-foot him like that. She wasn't even sure why it was that important to her. But she absolutely knew that she didn't want him writing off her options.

'You're leaving? Why?'

'I decided it was time to get back to my research. I had a position at my old university that I couldn't take up after my accident. There are still opportunities for me there.'

'You're moving back to Australia?'

'That's the plan. And it's one of the reasons why I couldn't accept your job offer.'

'I thought that was because you didn't approve of my plans,' Guy said.

'I didn't. I don't. But that wasn't the only factor. Meeting you again has shown me how much I've put my life on hold. I've been obsessed with getting my memories back. Trying to work out who I was that summer. And I'm starting to understand that it's really not that important. Or, at least, it's not the most important thing. What's important is who I am now. What I want to do next.'

'But you don't have to leave to do that. If this is because of me, because of what I'm doing at Le Bijou, I'll drop it, Meena. I'll find a way to stop it.'

She stared at him, open-mouthed. 'You'd do that? To stop me moving to Australia? You've said all along that there's nothing you can do to stop the development. But now I'm talking about moving to the same country as you and suddenly you can find a way? Were you lying before or are you lying now?'

'What? No, it's not because we'd be in the same country. And I haven't lied. But I don't want to be responsible for you having to leave. I know how much you love St Antoine and Le Bijou. I can't have that on my conscience too.'

'You knew before how much I loved it. You weren't too concerned about your conscience then.'

'I did know it, but… I don't know. The thought of you having to leave here because of what I've done… I've hurt so many people already, Meena. I'm not sure I can handle that too.'

She was still staring, and he started to shift uncomfortably. Of all the reactions he could have predicted, anger hadn't been high on the list.

'How many times do I have to say it, Guy?' she went on. 'I'm choosing this. Me. This isn't something that you're doing to me. It isn't about you at all. This is something that I want, for myself. Can't you credit me with that? Not everything that I do has to be about you. And, if you're worried I'm going to be too close just because we happen to be sharing the same continent, don't worry. I'm still going to be two thousand kilometres away. I don't think you have to worry about bumping into me at the supermarket.'

'That's not what I was worried about,' he said, shaking his head.

'Good. That's settled, then,' Meena said, crossing her arms and willing him off her boat.

'I don't feel like anything's settled,' Guy countered,

making no move to jump back on the jetty. 'I feel like things are getting more confusing by the minute, Meena. I just told you that I'd cancel my development. I thought that was what you wanted.'

'I heard you. And you know already that it's what I want. But honestly, I don't know what to think any more. You weren't prepared to change your plans even when we made love. What's changed now?'

What had changed? He wasn't even sure he understood it himself, never mind being capable of explaining it to someone else. But something had changed. And it wasn't just that he'd told her that he could cancel his plans for Le Bijou, though that was part of it. It was why he'd done it. He'd been so horrified at the thought that he'd be driving her from her home, when she'd already lost so much, that he'd have done anything to right that wrong.

It was the realisation that he was still in love with her. He had to be, because nothing short of that would have made him change his plans. He'd spent years telling himself that he couldn't be in a relationship. That he was too damaged from what had happened with Meena. But what if he wasn't damaged? What if Charlotte hadn't died because he wasn't a good enough boyfriend? What if it had been nothing more than a tragic accident? Could he really let go of the guilt he had been carrying around for so long?

That would mean that he wasn't broken. That it wasn't impossible for him to have another relationship. That maybe he and Meena *could* try again, and see if they could make it work this time.

Yes, they would still be two thousand kilometres apart if she went back to her old university. But that kind of distance wasn't insurmountable. Not when you were your own boss and had money to throw at the situation. They could make the distance work.

If they wanted to.

And there was the crux of the matter. Would Meena want to? They'd talked round and round and round the issue without either of them facing it head-on. And if he wanted that to change—wanted his future to change— he knew that he was going to have to step up and make it happen.

'I'm killing the development on Le Bijou,' he said, and breathed a sigh of relief after the words were finally out. 'Whatever happens, Meena, I want you to know that. I started the project for all the wrong reasons, and I want to stop it now for all the right ones. I don't want anything to happen to that place. I wanted to destroy it, and all the memories it held for me. And I don't want that any more.'

'I'm glad to hear it,' Meena said cautiously. 'Though it doesn't change my plans.'

'I know. I don't expect it to. But there's something else I need to tell you. I love you, Meena. I never stopped loving you. And I can't believe it's taken me so long to realise how I feel, because my heart has been aching for you since the day that I left St Antoine. I should have grabbed you up the moment that I came back and done everything in my power to try and get you to fall in love with me again. I didn't because I was an idiot, and because I was so sure that I was wrong for you. But now…'

'Now?'

'Now I think I got that wrong. That all I ever wanted was a chance to love you.'

'And, if I gave you that chance, how would this work?'

'It works however you want it to work, Meena. It works in Sydney, or it works here, or on your campus in Queensland. I don't care where we are. I just want a chance.'

CHAPTER TWELVE

A CHANCE. That was all that he wanted. And now it all came down to this—what did she want for her future? Meena had spent so long thinking about her past, agonising over the decisions she didn't even remember making, that she had put off thinking about her future. She'd made one big decision already—that she was ready to get back to her academic career. She'd been so overwhelmed by the knowledge of her past that she'd never even let herself think about her romantic future, but here it was looking her in the face, asking her to take a leap.

Could she trust him? Yes. The answer came to her without deliberation. Even without the change to his plans for Le Bijou she trusted him. She loved him. And if he truly meant what he'd said about changing his mind, then there was nothing standing in their way.

He said that he'd never stopped loving her, and from the heartfelt expression he was wearing, she had no choice but to believe him. He'd been torturing himself over the tragic death of his girlfriend, unable to see that he wasn't responsible, no matter how terrible he felt about it.

She knew that she loved him, too. She had known it the moment she had learned about their history, and the uncanny emotions that she'd felt at seeing him again had suddenly made sense. Of course she still loved him. Her body had never forgotten him, and she was sure that somewhere in the recesses of her brain those precious memories of their summer together were locked away safe.

'I love you, Guy.'

He'd tried to scare her off with his failed romantic history, but none of that mattered. They were both bringing baggage into this relationship, but it didn't matter. Because at last they were being honest with each other, and she was convinced that there was nothing that they couldn't face if they did it together.

'We're going to make this work,' she added as she saw his smile grow. 'If we both want this, we'll find a way for the geography to work. And I *do* want this. I've wanted it since the minute I opened my eyes on Le Bijou and saw you, if I'm honest. Long before I knew what you meant to me.'

'And I've wanted it since the day I left you there, looking just the same as I found you. Lying beneath the coconut and filao trees, eyes closed, just soaking in our favourite place.'

'I don't want you to resent me for making you change your mind about Le Bijou,' she said in a softer voice, concern clouding her expression.

'Meena, I promise you, I will never resent you. This

whole project was about forgetting you. Because I was an idiot. I don't want to forget a second that we spend together. I want us both to treasure those memories. And the ones that you've lost, I'll treasure them enough for the both of us.'

She smiled at that.

'And we'll look after Le Bijou together,' Guy went on. 'And make sure it is always protected. And maybe, one day, we'll bring our family here to enjoy it with us.'

'Our family?'

He nodded and pressed a gentle kiss to her lips. 'It's what I want, Meena. It's what I wanted that summer, and what I've been grieving for ever since. If it's what you want too, then we can make it real.'

'And the distance?' she asked. 'Even when we're both in Australia?'

'It's nothing,' Guy said confidently. 'You're the one who said it. I have a plane. And a helicopter. If you want our home to be in Queensland, I will fly back to you every night.'

'Hardly the environmentally friendly solution…' she replied, eyebrows raised.

'Then I will work remotely. Or I'll move the whole bloody office to Queensland if I have to. I don't care, Meena. I'll make it work, if you just tell me that you want me to.'

She said nothing. For seconds. For days. For long enough that he was convinced that she had changed her mind. Until her face broke out into the beaming smile he'd not seen for seven years, and he knew.

'I want you too.'

She squealed as he wrapped his arms around her waist and lifted her up, the boat rocking beneath them until he had to reach out a hand to steady them. As she slipped down his body, held tight against his chest, he knew that, whatever happened, he wouldn't let her go again.

'I love you, Meena,' he said, half under his breath as he leaned in to kiss her. When her arms wrapped around his neck he finally felt it fall away—the heartache and the grief that he had carried for the last seven years. With her in his arms, he was whole again.

'I love you too,' Meena said, returning his kiss with a freedom and a passion she never remembered feeling before. 'We haven't taken the easy way here,' she added eventually when Guy's arms had loosened to a comfortable weight around her waist and her cheek had found a spot to rest on his breastbone.

'I don't care how we got here,' Guy murmured into her hair, tightening his arms around her for a second. 'I just care that we did. I'm glad that I'm old enough and wise enough to know that I would give anything for this, for you.'

Meena looked up at Guy, at the heartfelt love in his expression, and smiled. 'All you have to give me is yourself.'

'Well, that,' Guy said between kisses, 'is easy. You have me. You've always had me.'

* * * * *

WHAT MAKES
A FATHER

TERESA SOUTHWICK

To my parents, Gladys and Frank Boyle.
You made raising six kids look easy.
I love you both and miss you always.

Chapter One

Annie Campbell didn't know exhaustion of this magnitude was even possible. Since suddenly becoming a mom to newborn twins three months ago, she'd been tired, but in the last week she'd counted sleep in seconds and minutes rather than hours. Either Charlie or Sarah was always awake, hungry, wet, crabby or crying uncontrollably for no apparent reason. Childhood had been challenging for Annie, but raising twins was the hardest thing she'd ever done.

And she wouldn't trade being their mom for anything. With one toothless grin they had her wrapped around their little fingers. Now they had all the symptoms of teething—drooling, gnawing on their fists, crying—and Annie honestly wasn't sure she'd survive it.

Her apartment was small, perfect for a single woman. Then she brought infants home from the hospital, forced by circumstances to care for two babies at once and too overwhelmed to look for a bigger place. And she was still overwhelmed. On a good day she could sneak in a shower. Today hadn't been a good day but there were hopeful signs.

Sarah was quiet in the crib. Charlie was in her arms but she could feel him relaxing, possibly into sleep. Oh, please God. She would walk until her legs fell off if that's what it took. With luck he'd go quietly in with his sister and Annie could close her eyes. To heck with a shower.

Slowly she did a circuit of the living room, past the bar that separated it from the kitchen, around the oak coffee table, gliding by the window that looked out on the center courtyard of the apartment complex. As the baby grew heavier in her arms, she could almost feel victory in her grasp, the euphoria of having two babies asleep at the same time.

Then some fool rang her doorbell. Charlie jerked awake and started to cry just on general principle. Sarah's wails came from the bedroom.

"Someone is going to pay." Annie cuddled the startled baby closer and kissed his head. "Not you, Charlie bear. You're perfect. But if someone is selling something they'll get more than they bargained for."

She peeked through the front window and saw a man wearing military camouflage. This was probably daddy candidate number three, the last one on her sister's list of men who might be the babies' father. This had to be Mason Blackburne, the army doctor who'd been deployed to Afghanistan. She'd contacted him by email and he'd claimed he'd get back to her right away when he returned to the States. She hadn't expected that he actually would.

In her experience, men were selfish, hurtful and unreliable. His written response was a brush-off any idiot would see. Except maybe not since he was standing outside. Not to be picky, but the least he could have done was call first. Come to think of it, how did he get her address? She'd only given him her phone number in the email. Apparently she was taking too long because he followed up the doorbell ring with an aggressive knock.

The chain locking the door was in place so she opened it just a crack. "Your timing sucks."

"Annie Campbell? I'm Mason Blackburne."

"I gave you my number. You were supposed to call me. How did you get my address?"

"From Jessica."

Pain sliced through Annie when she heard her sister's name. Jess had died shortly after giving birth to the twins. The joy of welcoming her niece and nephew into the world turned to unimaginable grief at losing the person Annie loved most in the world. Her sister had lived with her off and on, couch surfing when she needed somewhere to stay. She didn't trust men in general any more than Annie, so if she'd given the address to this guy, her gut must have said he was okay.

Annie unlocked the door and opened it. For the first time she got a good look at Mason Blackburne. Two things stood out: he was tall, and his eyes were startlingly blue. And he was boyishly handsome. Okay, that was three things, but she was too tired to care. And some part of her worn-out brain was regretting that her hair was in a messy ponytail because she hadn't washed it. Or showered today. Or put on makeup. And she was wearing baggy sweatpants and an oversize T-shirt.

"Come in," she said, stepping back. "I've got a DNA swab right here. Just rub it on the inside of each cheek for thirty seconds and put it back in the tube. I'll send it to the lab with the other one and the results will be back in five business days."

But it wasn't clear whether or not he'd heard her. The guy was staring at Charlie. The baby had stopped crying and was staring suspiciously back at the tall stranger. And he was sucking his thumb. The baby, not the stranger.

She sighed. "Well, baby boy, now all my extensive research into the best pacifier on the planet to prevent thumb-sucking is down the tubes. Somewhere an orthodontist is doing the dance of joy."

Mason had a look of awe on his face. "What's his name?"

"Charlie."

"Did Jessica choose that?"

"No, she didn't get a chance. But she'd narrowed down the choices to Christopher and Charles. Sarah was always the top girls' name."

He looked past her to the hallway where the baby girl was still crying. "Can I see her?"

Annie wanted to say no. She didn't know this guy from a rock, but again, Jess didn't normally share her address with men and she'd given it to him. So maybe it was okay.

After closing the front door, she headed for the hallway with daddy candidate number three following. The master bedroom and bath were on the right, and across from it was her office, now the twins' nursery.

"She's in here. And before you ask, they share the crib. The pediatrician advised not separating them just yet."

"Because they shared quarters for nine months," he said.

"Exactly." They walked into the room where the crib was on the wall opposite her desk. "She probably needs her diaper changed. I'll have to put Charlie down since I haven't yet figured out how to do it one-handed. Fair warning—he's going to cry."

"Could I hold him?"

Annie's gaze snapped to his face. "Why?"

"You need help. And he might be my son." There was

an edge to his voice and intensity in his eyes that made her think it really mattered to him.

Annie thought it over. This guy *might* be Charlie's father. Why not push him into the deep end of the pool, let him know what he was getting into. She held Charlie out to him and he took the baby, a little awkwardly.

Annie walked over to the crib and lowered the side rail. She picked up the little girl to comfort her first. "It's okay, Sarah. You're fine. I'm here, sweet girl. I have to put you down again, just for a minute to change that diaper. Trust me on this. You'll feel a lot better."

Three months ago the top of her lateral file cabinet had become the storage area for diaper supplies. She settled the baby back in the crib and quickly swapped the wet diaper for a dry one, then picked her up again for a snuggle.

"What happened to Jessica?" He looked away from the baby and met her gaze.

"I told you in the email. She had a pulmonary embolism, a blood clot in her—"

"Lung. I'm a doctor. I get it. But why didn't she let me know she was pregnant? And that I might be the father of the baby—" He stopped and his gaze settled on Sarah. *"Babies?"*

"I told her more than once that the biological father had a right to know. Even though I suggested she let the guy screw up first, she was convinced that he would desert her anyway. She planned to raise them by herself."

"Why would she think that?" There was a tinge of exasperation and outrage in his tone.

"She had her reasons."

His gaze narrowed and irritation pushed out the baby awe. "So you talked her into it? She didn't intend to share the information."

"Not with you or the other two men she slept with."

Annie winced as those words came out of her mouth. That made Jess sound like a slut. Maybe it was a little bit true, but that's not who she was. Her sister liked men and sex. She'd been looking for fun, nothing more. "Men sleep around all the time and no one thinks less of them. But if a woman does it, she's trash. Don't you dare judge her."

"I wasn't judging—"

"Oh, please." When a person was as tired as she was, that person had to dig deep for patience. Hers was dangerously depleted. She looked at him and, judging by the uncertain expression on his face, it was possible that there were flames shooting out of her eyes. "And why is this all on my sister? You were a willing participant. Who didn't wear a condom."

"I just wanted to talk," he protested.

"Right. That's what they all say." Her voice dripped with sarcasm. "You should know that I'm not normally this abrasive, but I'm tired. And I was much more compassionate the first two times a potential father showed up—"

"What happened with them?"

"First one wasn't a match. Number two finally came by a few days ago. I have his sample for the lab along with a legal document from his attorney relinquishing all rights to the babies in exchange for my signed agreement not to pursue him for child support should he be a match. I was only too happy to do that and send him responsibility-free on his way. Sarah and Charlie deserve to be wanted more than anything. They don't need a person like that in their lives."

"Prince of a guy." Mason was still holding Charlie and lightly rubbed a big hand over the baby's back.

Annie loved her sister but that didn't mean she approved of her choices in men. "A few weeks before she gave birth, Jess had second thoughts and narrowed down potential daddy candidates to three. Before she could contact them, she went into labor and showed symptoms of the embolism. Tests confirmed it and the risks were explained to her. She got scared for the babies if something should happen to her and put in writing that I would be the guardian. It was witnessed by two nurses and is a legally binding agreement. No one really thought she would die, but fate didn't cooperate. Now Charlie and Sarah are my babies and I will do anything and everything to keep them safe."

"I'm a doctor. I took an oath to do no harm."

"There are a lot of ways to damage children besides physically." Annie knew from experience that emotional wounds could be every bit as painful and were the ones you didn't have to hide with makeup or a story about being clumsy. "And I wasn't implying that you would hurt them."

"I would never do that," he said fervently.

For the first time she noticed that he looked every bit as tired as she felt. And he was wearing a military uniform— if camouflage was considered a uniform. What was his deal? "When did you get back from Afghanistan?"

"A couple of hours ago. My family lives in Huntington Hills, but I haven't seen them yet."

"You came here first? From the airport?"

"Yes."

It was hard not to be impressed by that but somehow Annie managed. The adrenaline surge during her outburst had drained her reserves and she wanted to be done with this, and him. "Look, if you'd please just do the DNA swab and leave your contact information for the lab, that would be great. Five business days and we'll know."

"Okay." Gently, he put Charlie down in the crib.

Annie did the same with Sarah and miraculously the two didn't immediately start to cry. "Follow me."

They went to her small kitchen, where the sink was full of baby bottles and dishes waiting to be washed.

"I have the kits here." She grabbed one from the counter and handed it to him. He seemed to know what to do.

Mason took the swab out of the tube and expertly rubbed it on the inside of his cheek for the required amount of time, then packaged it up and filled out the paperwork. "That should do it."

"I'll send it to the lab along with the other one."

"Okay."

"Thank you. Not to be rude, but would you please go?"

He started to say something, then stopped and simply let himself out the front door without a word.

Annie breathed a sigh of relief. The uncertainty would be over in five business days but somehow that didn't ease her mind as much as she'd thought it would. After meeting Mason Blackburne, she wasn't sure whether or not she wanted to share child custody with him. Not because he would be difficult, but because he wouldn't. And that could potentially be worse.

"She researched pacifiers, Mom." Mason stopped pacing the kitchen long enough to look at the woman who'd given birth to him. "I don't know whether or not she's a good mother, but both babies were clean, well-fed and happy. Well, one or the other was crying, but it was normal crying, if you know what I mean."

"I do," Florence Blackburne said wryly. "And it's not like she staged the scene. She had no idea you were going to stop by."

"That's true." He'd arrived home five days ago and told her everything. He'd started his job as an ER doctor and he was house hunting. None of it took his mind off the fact that he might be a father.

"That poor woman. Losing her sister and now raising two infants by herself." His mom was shaking her head and there was sympathy in her eyes. "I don't know what I would have done without your father when you and your siblings were born. And I only had one baby at a time."

"Yeah. She looked really exhausted." Pretty in spite of that, he thought. He remembered Jessica and Annie looked a lot like her. But their personalities were very different. Jess was a little wild, living on the edge. Annie seemed maternal, nurturing. Protective. Honest. The kind of woman he'd want to raise his children. If they *were* his children.

The lab hadn't notified him yet, but this was business day number five and he kept looking at his phone to make sure he hadn't missed the call.

"Checking your cell isn't going to make the news come any faster. I'm sure the twins are yours." His mother gave him her "mom" look, full of understanding and support.

She loved kids and had four of them, never for a moment letting on that she'd sacrificed anything on their behalf. Mason was wired like her and badly wanted kids of his own. The woman he'd married had shared that dream, and the heartbreak of not being able to realize it had broken them up. The third miscarriage had cost him his child and his wife—he'd lost his whole family. If the experience had taught him anything, it was not to have expectations or get his hopes up.

"If only DNA results happened as fast in real life as they do on TV," he said.

"Did the babies look like you?" Flo asked. "Eye color? Shape of the face? That strong, square jaw," she teased.

"They actually looked a lot like Annie. Their aunt. Hazel eyes. Blond hair. Pretty." Something he didn't share with his mother was that Annie Campbell had a very nice ass. Her baggy sweats had hid that asset, no pun intended, until she'd bent over to pick up a toy on the floor. There was no doubt in his mind that a shower and good night's sleep would transform her into a woman who would turn heads on the street. "DNA is the only way to be sure."

"That's just science. It's no match for maternal instinct. And mine is telling me that those babies are my grandchildren."

"Don't, Mom."

"What?" she asked innocently.

"If you have expectations, you're going to be let down." Mason could give a seminar on strategies to avoid disappointment. The only surefire approach was to turn off emotion. Not until the science said it was okay could you let yourself care.

Flo's face took on a familiar expression, the one that said she knew what he was thinking and wanted to take away his pain. The woman was a force of nature and if she couldn't do something, it couldn't be done. Wisely she stayed silent about his past and the situation that had left him bruised and battered. And bitter.

There was something to be said for Jessica's philosophy of fun without complications. But Annie was right, too. He hadn't used a condom and chose to believe the woman who'd said she had everything taken care of. Now he was on pins and needles waiting for the results of a test that could potentially change his life forever.

It was almost five o'clock and the lab's business hours were nearly over for the day. Maybe Annie hadn't sent the samples as soon as she'd planned to. She did have a lot on her plate with two infants. It was possible—

Mason's phone vibrated, startling him even though he'd been waiting and checking. He stared at the Caller ID for a moment, immobilized.

"For Pete's sake, answer it," his mother urged, nudging him out of his daze.

He did, assured the caller that he was Mason Blackburne, then listened while the information was explained to him. "You're sure?"

They were completely confident in the results. Mason thanked the caller and pressed the off button on his phone.

Flo stared at him anxious and expectant. "Well? Mason, I'm too old for this kind of suspense. Don't make me wait—"

"They're mine," he said simply.

His voice was so calm and controlled when he was anything but. He was a father!

It was a shock to hear the news he'd hoped for but shocks seemed to be just another day in the ER for him these days. Images flashed through his mind of meeting Jessica the day his divorce was final. She'd sat next to him at the bar. He really had only wanted to talk. A distraction from the fact that his carefully constructed life had fallen apart.

For a while talking was all she'd done, telling him about her sister, Annie, living with her between jobs, and that he would like her. Then she'd flirted and charmed her way into his bed. He'd had a rough time of it and she promised sex without complications.

Surprise! Let the complications begin. Oddly enough, complication number one was Annie Campbell.

At least this time Mason called to ask Annie if he could come by. He'd gotten the news from the lab just like she had, so of course she agreed to see him. The problem was now she had to see him.

He was the twins' father, which gave him every right to be a part of their lives. But he made her nervous. Not in a creepy way. More like the cute-guy-at-school-you-had-a-crush-on kind of thing. And she had to figure out how to co-parent with a complete stranger who made her insides quiver like Jell-O.

There was a knock on the door. She noticed he didn't ring the doorbell again, which meant he was capable of learning. And it was a good thing, too, since the babies were asleep at the same time. Although not for long since they needed to eat.

Annie opened the door and Mason stood there, this time in worn jeans and a cotton, button-up shirt with the long sleeves rolled to mid-forearm. The look did nothing to settle her nerves.

"Come in," she said without offering a hello.

But neither did Mason. He walked past her, mumbling something about needing to buy a minivan and save for college.

"I suppose that means you don't want to sign away your rights as a father."

"No." His expression was intense, serious. "In fact, since I last saw you, I consulted an attorney."

Words to put fear into a girl's heart. "I'm their legal guardian. If you try and take them away from me—"

"Whoa." He put his hands up in a slow-down motion. "It's just that even though I'm their father, I have no rights because my name isn't on the birth certificate. Now, with DNA proof, I will acknowledge paternity and petition the court to legally claim my paternal rights."

"How long will that take?"

"There's a sixty-day waiting period, then however long it takes to get a court date," he said.

"And then you're going to sue for sole custody?"

"Of course not. No one is talking custody fight here. You clearly love them."

"I do. But how can you know that?" Where men were concerned, suspicion was her default emotion.

"Because you did copious research on a pacifier. And I just get the feeling that if I look at either baby funny, you'd cut my heart out with a spoon."

"You're not wrong." But how did he know her so well? They'd barely met. "Is that a negative critique on my mothering instincts?"

"Absolutely not. You're protective. And I think that's a plus. I happen to strongly believe in traditional two-parent families. That kind of environment is a positive influence in shaping their lives. It's the way I grew up and I didn't turn out so bad. I'd like my children to have that, too."

"I see." That was good, right? It was something she'd never had and desperately wanted. Especially for the twins she loved so much.

He looked around. "It's awfully quiet. Are the babies here?"

She wanted to say, "Duh." Where else would they be? There was no family to help her out. She'd barely heard from her mother and stepfather after they'd moved to the other side of the country. Jess was all she'd had. But there was no reason to be snarky to Mason.

"They're both asleep at the same time. It's a very rare occurrence." His grin made her want to fan herself but she managed to hold back.

"Maybe we should have a parade in their honor," he teased.

"Good grief, no. The marching bands would wake them up and I want to enjoy every moment of this quiet for as long as it lasts."

"Good point. A better use of this time would be for you and I to get to know each other."

He probably wouldn't like what she had to say.

Chapter Two

Annie tried to think of a reason getting to know Mason was a bad idea. She wondered how Mr. I Had a Perfect Childhood would feel about co-parenting with someone whose story wasn't so pretty. But he had a right to know.

Common sense dictated that she find out everything possible about her babies' father and she couldn't do that without giving him information about herself. But he made her nervous. To reveal her nerves would require an explanation about why that was and she didn't think she could put it into words. At least not in a rational way. Last time he'd been here, he was less than pleased about not being informed that he might be a father. Annie couldn't really blame him and wondered if he was still resentful.

"Getting to know each other is probably a good idea," she agreed. "I was going to have a quick bite to eat while Charlie and Sarah are sleeping. It's just leftovers but you're welcome to join me."

"Thanks. What can I do to help?"

"Set the table, I guess." She wasn't used to having help; it was nice. "I'm going to throw together a salad and

I have cold fried chicken. I'll nuke some macaroni and cheese." She pointed out the cupboard with the plates and the drawer containing utensils. Napkins were a no-brainer, right in plain sight in a holder on her circular oak table.

"Yes, ma'am."

"One thing about me you should know right now," Annie said as she put prewashed, bagged lettuce into a bowl. "Never call me 'ma'am.' It makes me feel like I need help crossing the street."

"Understood." He set two plates on the table. "So what should I call you? Miss Campbell?"

"Annie works." She put dressing on the greens and handed him the bowl containing long-handled serving spoons. "Toss this, please."

"Yes, ma—" He looked sheepish. "Sorry. I'm a civilian now."

"I guess you can take the man out of the military but you can't take the military out of the man." She felt a little zing in her chest when she looked at him and struggled for something to say. "So, you were in the army."

"Yes. I enlisted."

She put a casserole dish in the microwave and pushed the reheat button. "Why?"

"I wanted to go to medical school and couldn't afford it. My parents wanted to help, but it's a steep price tag and I didn't want them taking out a second mortgage or going into debt. It was the best way to get where I wanted to go without putting a strain on them. When I got my MD, I owed the military four years. The upside is that I was able to serve my country while paying back the government."

Watching him toss the heck out of that lettuce, Annie realized a couple of things. He was way above average-looking and it wasn't as hard to talk to him as she'd thought. Although, he was the one doing the talking. With a little luck he wouldn't notice that she hadn't revealed anything about herself yet.

Keep the conversation on him. She could do this. She was a grown woman now, not the geeky loner she'd once been. "So now you're a doctor."

"That's the rumor. Also known as an emergency medical specialist." He stopped tossing the salad. "I've started my job at Huntington Hills Memorial Hospital. Just so you know I'm not a deadbeat dad."

"I didn't think you were."

"Just wanted to clarify." He shrugged his broad shoulders. "This kind of feels like a job interview. Maybe the most important one I'll ever have."

"I hadn't thought about it that way. And it doesn't matter what I think," she said. "You are their biological father. Time will tell if you can be a dad."

The expression on his face didn't exactly change but his eyes turned a darker navy blue, possibly with disapproval. "Spoken like a true skeptic."

"I am and there are reasons."

"You're not the only one. Your sister wasn't going to tell me I'm a father."

Annie got his meaning. He was wondering if keeping the truth from a man was a shared family trait. Part of her wanted to remind him she was the reason her sister made the daddy candidate list. Part of her respected his skepticism about her. More often than not people let you down and the only way to protect yourself was to expect the worst. So, yay him.

"That was wrong of Jessica. In her defense, I'd like to point out that she was taking steps to do the right thing. It's not her fault that she couldn't see it through."

"Look, Annie, I didn't mean—"

"Sure you did," she interrupted. "And you're not wrong.

So this isn't a job interview as much as it's about finding a way to work together for the sake of those babies."

He thought for a moment. "Can't argue with that."

"Okay." The microwave beeped so she pulled out the casserole dish and stirred the macaroni and cheese, then put it back in for another minute. "So you have family here in Huntington Hills?"

"Parents and siblings," he confirmed.

"How many siblings?"

"Two brothers and a sister."

Annie felt the loss of her sister every day and not just because of caring for the twins. No one knew her like Jess had. They'd shared the same crappy childhood and her big sis had run interference at home and at school. She'd always had Annie's back—no matter what.

"You're lucky to have a big family."

"I know you're right, but I'm looking forward to having a place of my own," he said.

"Don't tell me." She grinned. "You're a man in his thirties living with his mother. You know what they say about that."

"No. And I don't want to know. Besides, it's not as bad as you make it sound." He smiled and the corners of his eyes crinkled in an appealing way.

"There's no way to make it sound good."

"I guess technically I live with my parents here in town. I sold my house before going to Afghanistan. I'm just staying with the folks until I can find a place of my own." His smile disappeared and there was a shadow in his eyes, something he wasn't saying.

And she didn't ask. The microwave beeped again and she retrieved the dish and set it on the table. "Okay, then. That makes it a whole lot less weird."

"Good."

"Dinner is served."

They sat across from each other and filled their plates. Well, he did. A couple pieces of chicken with a healthy portion of macaroni and cheese. He dug in as if he hadn't eaten in a week.

He finished a piece of chicken and set the bone on his plate. "So, what about you?"

"Me?"

"Yeah. I've monopolized the conversation. Now it's your turn."

She really didn't like talking about herself. "What do you want to know?"

"Do you have a job?"

"Other than caring for the twins?" She realized he had no frame of reference yet for how that was a full-time job. "I'm a graphic designer."

"I see." There was a blank look in his eyes.

"You have no idea what I do, right?"

"Not a clue," he admitted. "I was going to wait until you were busy with something else and Google it on my phone."

He was honest, she thought. That was refreshing. "Let me save you the trouble. I create a visual concept, either with computer software or sketches by hand, to communicate an idea."

"So, advertising."

"Yes. But more. Clients are looking for an overall layout and production design for brochures, magazines and corporate reports, too."

"So, you're artistic."

"Beauty is in the eye of the beholder, I guess. But I can honestly say that I've always loved to draw." She didn't have to tell him she was dyslexic and that made anything to do with reading a challenge. Was it genetic? He might need to know at some point but that time wasn't now. "Fortunately, I can do a lot of work from home. Which means I haven't had to leave Charlie and Sarah much. Yet."

"Oh?" He had finished off his second piece of chicken and half a helping of the macaroni. Now he spooned salad onto his plate and started on that.

Annie pushed the food around hers. Talking about herself made her appetite disappear. "We're developing an advertising package and bid for a very large and well-known company. I won't jinx it by telling you who. But if we get it, my workload could increase significantly and that would mean meetings in the office." She speared a piece of lettuce with her fork, a little more forcefully than necessary. "And the twins don't really have much to add to the discussion yet."

"What are you going to do?"

"I'm planning to cross that bridge if and when it needs crossing."

She put a brave and confident note in her voice because she didn't feel especially brave or confident. Leaving her babies with a trusted friend who bailed her out in an emergency was one thing. Turning them over to a stranger, even a seasoned child-care professional who'd passed a thorough background check was something she dreaded.

"It's really something," he said. "Taking in two infants."

"How could I not?" Annie swallowed the lump of emotion in her throat. "Their mother was my sister."

"Still, I know people who wouldn't do it. You and Jessica must have been close."

"We were. She was always there for me. No matter what—" Unexpectedly, tears filled her eyes and Annie didn't want him to see.

She stood, picked up her plate and turned away before walking over to the sink. She felt more than heard Mason come up behind her. Warmth from his body and the subtle scent of his aftershave surrounded her in a really nice way.

"Annie, if I haven't said it already, I'm very sorry for your loss."

"That's exactly what her doctor said to me when he told me she was dead. Is there a class in med school on how to break bad news to loved ones?"

"No. Unfortunately, it's just experience. The kind no doctor wants to get."

It had been three months since Jess died. Annie had thought she was out of tears and didn't want to show weakness in front of this man. Maybe because he was the babies' biological father and had a stronger and more intimate connection to them than she did. The reason didn't matter because she couldn't hold back her shaky breaths any more than she could hide the silent sobs that shook her whole body.

The next thing she knew, his big, strong hands settled gently on her upper arms and he turned her toward him, pulled her against his chest in a comforting embrace. He didn't say anything, just held her. It felt nice. And safe.

That was a feeling Annie had very little experience with in her life. Odd that it came from a relative stranger. Maybe Jess had felt it, too.

Annie got her emotions under control and took a step back. She was embarrassed and couldn't quite meet his gaze. "I'm sorry you had to see that."

"Don't be."

She shrugged. "Can't help it. I don't know why I broke down now. It's not a fresh reality."

"Maybe you haven't had time to grieve. What with suddenly being responsible for two babies."

That actually made a lot of sense to her. "Anyway, thanks."

"You're welcome. I hope it helped." He looked like he sincerely meant that. Apparently the business of helping people was the right one for him.

"Speaking of those babies, I'm going to check on them. It's not their habit to be so quiet and cooperative when I'm having a meal." The first one with their father, she noted.

"You cooked, so I'll do the dishes."

"Cook is a very nebulous term for the way I warmed up leftovers. But I'm taking that deal," she agreed.

The best one she'd had in a long time. She went to the "nursery" and found Charlie and Sarah awake and playing. Standing where they couldn't see her, she watched them exploring fingers and feet and smiling at each other.

Her heart was so full of love for these two tiny humans that it hurt, and was something she experienced daily. But having a man in her kitchen doing dishes didn't happen on a regular basis.

She found herself actually liking Mason Blackburne. So far. But she hadn't known him very long. There was still time for him to screw up and she had every confidence that he would.

Men couldn't seem to help themselves.

Mason was feeding a bottle to Charlie when he heard footsteps coming up the outside stairs followed by the apartment door opening. Annie walked in and looked at him then glanced around.

"Wow, it's quiet in here. And really neat." Was there the tiniest bit of envy in her expression? "I'm feeling a little inadequate because I can't seem to manage two infants and an apartment without leaving a trail of debris and destruction in my wake."

"Oh, well, you know—"

After several weeks of him visiting the babies every chance he could, she'd reluctantly accepted his offer to watch them while she went to her office for a meeting. He wasn't completely sure she hadn't done a background check on him before agreeing. Fortunately he'd already passed the diaper-changing, bottle-feeding and burping tests. Still, Annie had been very obviously conflicted about walking out the door and leaving him in charge. He'd assured her there was nothing to worry about and shooed her off to work.

She'd barely been gone five minutes before all hell had broken loose. Two code browns and a simultaneous red alert on the hunger front. His situational readiness went to DEFCON 1 and he'd done what he'd had to do.

Glancing at the hallway then at her, he said, "I thought you'd be gone longer."

She walked over and kissed Charlie's forehead. The scent of her skin wrapped around Mason as if she'd touched him, too, and he found himself wishing she had. The night she'd cried and he held her in his arms was never far from his mind. She'd felt good there, soft and sweet.

"I stayed for the high points then ducked out of the meeting. I just missed my babies and didn't want to be away from them any longer," she said. "How did it go? Where's Sarah?"

At that moment his mother walked into the room holding the baby in question. Florence Blackburne was inching toward sixty but looked ten years younger. Her brown hair, straight and turned under just shy of her shoulders, was shot with highlights. He'd been about to tell Annie that he'd called her for help, but he was outed now.

"You must be Annie. I'm Florence, Mason's mother."

Annie's hazel eyes opened wide when she looked at him. "I thought you said you could handle everything."

"When I said that, the ratio of adults to babies was one to one. And I did handle it," he said defensively. "I called for reinforcements." He set the bottle on the coffee table and lifted Charlie to his shoulder to coax a burp out of him. It came almost instantly, loud and with spit-up. "That's my boy," he said proudly.

"Seriously?" she said.

"Eventually he'll learn to say excuse me." Mason shrugged then returned to the subject of calling his mom. "I admit that I underestimated my multitasking abilities."

"Oh, please," Flo said. "You just couldn't stand that one of your children was unhappy."

"Yeah, there's that," he acknowledged.

"Even though I told him that crying isn't a bad thing. They'd be fine." Flo was talking to Annie now. "You know this already. You've been doing it by yourself since these little sweethearts were born."

"I have." Annie gave him a look that could mean anything from "You're a child-care jackass" to "Finally someone gets it."

"How nice that you had backup on your first solo mission."

Flo's blue eyes brimmed with sympathy and understanding as only another mother's could. She handed the baby girl to Annie. "You're not alone now, honey. Being a mother is the hardest job you'll ever do times two. And sometimes you need a break. Recharge your batteries. Take a deep breath. Go get your hair trimmed or a pedicure. I just want you to know that I'm here. Don't hesitate to call."

"I would never impose," Annie said.

"These are my grandchildren. It wouldn't be an imposition. I have a part-time job as a receptionist in a derma-tology office and my hours are flexible, so we can work around that. Mason will give you my number."

"Thank you." Annie kissed Sarah's cheek. "I appre-ciate that."

"What are grandmothers for?" She shrugged. "Full disclosure, I might spoil them just a little because I've waited a long time to play the grandmother card. Char-lie and Sarah will learn that my house is different, but I will never compromise your rules. I might be prejudiced, but these are the most beautiful babies I've ever seen. Al-though I don't see much of Mason in them."

"Gee, thanks, Ma," he teased.

"I didn't mean it like that, son." She smiled at him. "It's just that they look a lot like you, Annie."

She pressed her cheek to baby Sarah's. "There was a strong resemblance between my sister and me."

"Then she was very beautiful," his mom said.

"She was," Annie agreed.

The subtext was that Annie was beautiful, too, and Mason couldn't agree more. Today she was professionally dressed in slacks, a silky white blouse and black sweater. Low-heeled pumps completed the outfit, but he missed her bare feet. Her straight, silky blond hair fell past her shoul-ders and she was wearing makeup for the first time since he'd met her. And he'd been right. She was a knockout.

"Well, you two, now that everything is under control, I'll be going." Florence grabbed her purse, kissed Mason on the cheek and smiled fondly at her grandbabies. "It was wonderful to meet you, Annie. You don't need my approval, but it has to be said that you've done a remark-able job with your children. And I sincerely meant what I said. Call me if you need anything."

"Thank you, Mrs. Blackburne—"

"It's Flo." She patted Annie's shoulder. "'Bye."

And then the two of them were alone, each holding a baby, and Mason wondered what Annie was thinking.

"So that was my mom."

"You have her eyes."

He'd heard that before. "It turns out that when one of my children is crying because he or she has needs that I can't instantly meet, it's not something I manage very well."

"As flaws go, it's not an exceptionally bad one to have," she conceded. "So you called your mom."

"Yeah."

"And if I got home later and your mom was gone, would you have let me believe you sailed through your first time alone with them trouble free?"

He would have wanted to. There was the whole male pride thing, after all. But... "No. I'd have told you she'd been here."

"Why?"

"Because that's the truth and it's the right thing to do." He shrugged and a dozing Charlie squirmed a little against his shoulder.

"I'm not sure I believe you."

He remembered her saying she was a skeptic and had her reasons. Skepticism was rearing its ugly head now. "In time you'll be convinced that I embrace the motto that cheaters never prosper."

"And in time, if I'm convinced, something tells me your mom is responsible for that honest streak."

"Oh?"

"Yeah. She's really something."

"She's just excited and happy to finally have even one grandchild. In her world twins is winning the lottery."

"I didn't mean that as a criticism." There was a baby

quilt on the sofa beside him. Annie took it and spread the material on the floor in front of the coffee table. She put Sarah on it then sat next to him. "I meant just the opposite. She's full of energy in the best possible way. The kind of supportive, protective mother I wish my mom had been. The kind I want to be."

That little kernel of information reminded Mason that he didn't know much about her. The night they'd been getting acquainted he'd given her some facts about himself. She'd only offered up what she did for a living and then he'd held her when she'd cried. He hadn't been able to focus on much besides the soft curves of her body and hadn't noticed how little he'd learned. Now he was becoming aware of how guarded she was. And it wasn't just about protecting Charlie and Sarah. She held parts of herself back and he wondered why.

He stood with Charlie in his arms, then moved to the blanket on the floor and gently settled the sleeping baby next to his sister. After stretching his cramped muscles, he met Annie's gaze. "So, what you just said implies that your mother wasn't supportive."

"She had issues."

He waited for more but that was it. "Had? Does that mean she passed away?"

"No. She lives in Florida with her husband." When Sarah let out a whimper, Annie jumped up as if she'd just been waiting for an excuse to end this conversation. "Did she have a bottle?"

"No."

"Okay." Annie scooped up the baby and went into the kitchen to get a bottle from the refrigerator.

Mason didn't claim to be a specialist in the area of feelings but it didn't take a genius to see that Annie wasn't comfortable talking about herself. Either she was hiding something or there was a lot of pain in the memories. So now he knew she was a graphic artist, had adored her sister and missed her terribly. And there was stuff in her past that she didn't want to talk about.

That was okay. She was the mother of his children and he wasn't going anywhere. In his experience as an ER doc, he'd learned that often people held things back but eventually the facts came out. And he wanted all the facts about his children's legal guardian.

Chapter Three

Several weeks after Mason walked into her life Annie
got her first really powerful blast of mom guilt. There
had been some minor brushes with the feeling, but this
one was a doozy.

Because of him, and by extension his mother, Florence,
everything had changed. For the better, she admitted. The
woman was fantastic with the twins so when she'd offered
to watch them while Annie went to a mandatory meeting
in the office, she'd gratefully accepted.

It had only been a few hours ago that Annie had walked
out of her apartment but it felt like days. She checked her
phone to make sure there were no messages. The empty
screen mocked her and she felt the tiniest bit disposable,
followed by easily replaceable. There was a healthy dose
of exhilaration for this unexpected independence mixed
with missing her babies terribly. The verdict was in. She
was officially conflicted and on the cusp of crazy.

If all that wasn't guilt-inducing enough, she was going
to have a grown-up girlfriend lunch. She should call it off
and go be with Charlie and Sarah. Even as that thought

popped into her head, she saw Carla Kellerman walking toward her with a food bag. Her friend had stopped to pick up something, as promised. So if Annie bugged out now, Carla would be inconvenienced. She would just have to eat fast.

"Hi." Carla came into her cubicle and smiled.

This woman was completely adorable. Perky and shiny. Straight, thick red hair fell past her shoulders and went perfectly with her warm brown eyes. She had the biggest, friendliest smile ever. And a soft, mushy heart. The occasional loss of her temper was almost always on someone else's behalf and made her completely human. As flaws went, it was adorable.

"I forgot how much I love this office," her friend said, looking around. "If I didn't already have a job, I would want to work here."

C&J Graphic Design occupied the top floor of an office building on the corner of C Street and Jones Boulevard in the center of Huntington Hills. The light wood floor stretched from the boss's office at one end of the long, narrow room to the employees' lounge at the other. Overhead track lighting illuminated cubicles separated by glass partitions. The environment had a collaborative vibe and Annie loved seeing her coworkers' creative ideas and them having easy access to hers.

"Hi, yourself." Her stomach growled. Loud.

"Apparently my arrival with provisions isn't a moment too soon." Carla grinned. "I guess I don't have to ask if you're ready to eat."

"Follow me. There are drinks in the break room fridge. Or we could sit outside." It was October but Southern California was still warm. There was a patio with wrought iron tables and chairs shaded by trees and surrounded with grass, shrubs and flowers.

"That. Door number two," her friend said. "I need fresh air."

They grabbed drinks, walked to the elevator and Annie hit the down button.

"Maybe we should go wild today and take the stairs," Carla suggested. "I could use the exercise."

"Since when? Don't get me wrong," Annie added. "I'm a supportive friend who will follow you bravely down eight flights of stairs. But this switch from 'I can't stand sweat' to 'We should take the stairs' is different."

"Not really. I always think about it."

Annie opened the stairway door and they started down. "But I can't read your mind. You never said anything before. What's changed? Got a crush on the boss?"

"Hardly. I work for Lillian Gordon."

"I know. But didn't her nephew come in to help the company over a rough financial patch?"

"Yes. Gabriel Blackburne. But he's kind of a hermit. Keeps to his office, hunched over a computer, presumably strategizing how to turn the company around."

They'd reached the ground floor and both of them were breathing a little harder as they headed for the rear door that led to the patio.

Carla gave her a look. "You have the strangest expression on your face. Why?"

"Because Mason's last name is Blackburne."

"Who's Mason?"

"The babies' father," Annie clarified.

"Small world," her friend said. "We needed this lunch even more than I thought so you can fill me in."

"I wonder if Mason is related to your Gabriel Blackburne. It's not that common a name," Annie said.

"I guess it's possible." Her friend moved decisively to the table with the most shade, put the bag down on it and sat in one of the sturdy metal chairs. "From what Lillian tells me, Gabriel is not a fan of her business plan but he does approve of the branding campaign C&J did for Make Me a Match."

"Well, he sounds a little intimidating, but definitely has good taste in graphic design companies." Annie sat at a right angle to her friend. "You'd expect Mason to be that way, but he's not."

Carla pulled two paper-wrapped sandwiches and napkins from the bag. She handed one over. "I need details. A text saying 'twins' father showed up and DNA confirms' isn't much information."

"I haven't had much time in the last few months."

"Two babies. I get it. And you're a saint, by the way. So tell me everything."

Annie explained about contacting the men Jessica thought could be the father and Mason showing up last. "He's an army doctor just back from Afghanistan. So, military and medical."

Carla took a bite of her turkey sub and chewed thoughtfully before swallowing. "He sounds honorable to me. I haven't known you long but I'm learning that you're good at finding flaws."

Not so far, Annie thought. "You know me pretty well. I'm not holding my breath he'll stay honorable. For now he's good with Charlie and Sarah. Not too proud to ask for help. The first time I left him alone with them, he called his mom for backup." Annie wasn't sure why, but she'd believed him when he'd said he wouldn't have let her think he handled the twins without a problem. "Florence, his mom, is fantastic. Loves kids and thrilled to be a grandmother. She has them now."

"Lillian's sister is Florence. Has to be the same family," her friend concluded. "Like I said, small world."

"No kidding. If Gabriel looks anything like Mason, I can see why you think you could use the exercise."

"He's pretty, but a little too dark and brooding for me. Besides, he keeps reminding everyone that he's only there temporarily." Carla shrugged. "So the twins' father is a hottie? It could be a reality show—*Real Hotties of Huntington Hills.*"

Annie laughed then thoughtfully chewed a bite of her sandwich. "'Hottie' would be an accurate description."

"You like him." Carla's voice had a "gotcha" tone.

"Why in the world would you come to that conclusion from what I just said?"

"Good question," Carla mused. "Maybe the way you were so deliberately aloof."

It was a little scary how well this woman knew her, Annie thought. They'd hit it off when working together on the branding campaign for Make Me a Match. Annie had spent some time in their office to get a feel for the dating service but the nephew had never poked his head out of his inner sanctum. Her friendship with Carla was relatively new but her assessment of Annie's feelings about Mason wasn't too far off the mark. Still, an attraction was no reason to be giddy. Just the opposite, in fact.

"It doesn't matter whether or not I like him. Men are notoriously unreliable."

"You know I agree with you about that." Carla ate the last of her sandwich then wiped her hands on a napkin. "I know we're fairly new friends and this is probably invading your privacy. Feel free to say it's none of my business, but what's your story? Why are you commitment averse?"

"Let's call it daddy issues. And before you ask, it's both biological and step. My mother has terrible taste in men. And you already know about Dwayne." Her ex-boyfriend. The jerk had sworn to always have her back but couldn't get away fast enough when she'd become the twins' legal guardian and brought them home. "I'm not going to be complacent and starry-eyed then get blind-sided when Mason decides he can't handle being a father to twins. I can only deal with one day at a time and for now he's doing all the right things."

"Like what?" Carla asked.

"Well…" Annie thought for a moment and fought a smile she knew would look tender and goofy. "Hardly a day has gone by that he hasn't come to see them. He said he's already lost too much time being their father and doesn't want to miss another single moment with his kids that he doesn't absolutely have to."

"How sweet is that? Certainly not the behavior of a man who's going to abandon them," Carla pointed out.

"Maybe." It was hard to argue with that assertion so Annie didn't. "He works in the emergency room at Huntington Hills hospital and he looks so tired sometimes it's a wonder he can stand up, let alone hold one of the babies."

"Wow." Carla stared at her in disbelief. "Do you have recent pictures of the twins?"

"What kind of mom would I be if I didn't?" Annie proudly pulled a cell phone out of her slacks' pocket, found the most recent photos and then handed it over so her friend could scroll through.

"The twins are beautiful. And I say again—wow." Carla's eyebrows went up. "He's such a cutie, and I'm not talking about Charlie. This one of Mason holding both babies is a seriously 'aww moment.'"

Annie glanced at the picture and smiled at the memory of Mason dozing off while they were on his chest. He held them securely in place with a big hand on each of their backs. The moment did have a serious cuteness quotient, which was why she'd taken the photo. "More than once he's fallen asleep on my sofa."

"Oh?"

"Down girl." She hadn't been able to resist snapping the picture, but it didn't mean anything. Certainly not that she was looking at the future. One day at a time worked just fine for her. "Naps on my couch are about a demanding career, work schedule and his children," Annie said. "It has nothing to do with me. Or us."

"Still, he's not a troll and he likes kids. That's a good start."

"There is no start," Annie argued. "How can there be when he doubts my character? He made it clear that he doesn't trust me."

"What does he have against you? The two of you just met."

"He was justifiably curious about why my sister didn't contact him when she found out she was pregnant, about the possibility that he was a father. I got the feeling that, with him, that lie of omission extended to me because I'm Jessica's sister."

"Is it possible that you're inventing reasons to push him away? Like I said, you're good at finding flaws," Carla said. "Does it bother you that Jessica slept with him first?"

"Of course not. And, as you pointed out, I just met him a few weeks ago." Annie analyzed the question a little deeper. "And by *first* you're suggesting that I will sleep with him, too. That's just not going to happen."

Carla shrugged. "If you say so."

"You're seeing a relationship where none exists. Is Lillian working you too hard at Make Me a Match?" Annie teased. "Maybe you can't leave work at the office?"

Her friend laughed ruefully. "We need satisfied customers. And they need to spread the word about the valuable service we provide if the business is going to survive."

"I'll talk it up and, if I can, send clients your way," Annie promised.

But she wouldn't be one of them. She had enough on her hands without falling in love. Lust was a different thing altogether and had a mind of its own. Proof of that was the vision of twisted sheets and strong arms that had been keeping her awake at night. And those arms didn't belong to just anyone. They were definitely Mason's.

Mason was at the apartment with the twins several days after his mom had watched them. Annie was putting in more hours at her office because the deadline for the high-profile campaign was approaching fast. He'd gotten Sarah to sleep and had spent the last fifteen minutes walking Charlie. Now he carefully lifted the baby from his shoulder and put him on his back in the crib, beside his sister. He held his breath, fingers crossed that the little boy was finally sound enough asleep that the movement wouldn't wake him. No sound, no movement. Mission objective achieved.

He looked down at them—his children—and thought for the billionth time how beautiful and perfect they were. And how lucky he was to have them. Sure, he hadn't known from the beginning about the pregnancy and could whine about that, but it wouldn't have changed anything. A lot of active-duty service members missed out on big family moments because of deployment. The truth was, he couldn't have been there for their birth even if he'd known.

So he hadn't been able to support Annie through the shock and sadness of losing her sister. A little extra help with the babies wouldn't have hurt, either. Somehow she'd had the strength to do it all by herself. On the other hand, he wouldn't be going through the legal maze of securing his paternal rights now if things had been different.

It had been a month since he'd stood at Annie's door for the first time and he could hardly remember a life without his kids—and her—in it. He'd seen the commercials on TV for companies that facilitated meets for people who wanted a relationship. The tagline: Never More Ready to Fall in Love. Mason was the opposite of that. Never less ready for love.

The collapse of his marriage had been a horrible warning. He found out that even if one made all the right moves and everything was perfect, it was still possible to fail spectacularly. And painfully. Because of things out of his control. He wouldn't make the same mistake.

That didn't mean he couldn't be in awe of Annie Campbell. He thought about her more than he liked, even when he was slammed with patients in the emergency room. She was quite a woman—sexy, beautiful, maternal, funny and smart. Everything a man could want. So why hadn't a guy snatched her up?

The doorbell rang and he swore under his breath, then checked the babies for any sign it woke them. Neither moved so he hurried to the front door, ready to chew out whoever had been stupid enough to ignore the baby sleeping sign.

He opened the door and saw a thirty-something guy standing there. He was well dressed and nice-looking. Mason wanted to strangle him. "Can you read?"

"What?"

"Did you see the sign?" He pointed. "The babies are sleeping."

"Right. Sorry, man. I forgot."

"How to read?" Now he really wanted to strangle this guy.

"No. That the babies are here." He held out his hand. "Dwayne Beller."

Mason hesitated then shook hands. "Mason Blackburne."

"The father?"

"Of the twins? Yeah." Now his curiosity was on high alert. "Who are you?"

"Annie's boyfriend." He shifted uncomfortably. "At least, I was."

"So you're not now?"

"No."

Mason felt an odd sort of relief that she was no longer with this guy. "What happened?"

"Is Annie here?"

"No." He stood feet apart, blocking the doorway.

"Do you mind telling me where she is?"

"Yes." They were sizing each other up. "Mind telling me what happened with you and Annie?"

Dwayne shifted his stance uncomfortably. "Look, man, would you just tell her I stopped by?"

"Why?"

"Because I'd like her to know that I was here."

Mason didn't miss the fact that Dwayne was looking pretty irritated. It didn't bother him at all. "I meant why don't you want to talk about what happened?"

"Because it's none of your business. It's between Annie and me—"

"Dwayne?" Annie was almost at the top of the stairs and her eyes widened at the scene unfolding in front of her door.

She had several bags of groceries in her hands and didn't look happy to see the guy. That didn't bother Mason at all, either.

"Hi, Annie. You look good." The ex-boyfriend had a sheepish expression on his face and glanced at Mason, who was still blocking the door. "Can I come in?"

"Why?" she asked warily.

"To talk," he said. "I really miss talking to you."

There was hurt and disillusionment in her eyes, proof the line wasn't working. "I don't think there's anything left for us to say to each other."

"Please just hear me out."

"These bags are getting heavy." She elbowed past him and Mason stepped aside to let her through. "And you said quite enough the last time I saw you. At Jessica's memorial service. Your timing left a lot to be desired."

Dwayne elbowed his way past Mason and followed her into the apartment, watching her set bags on the table. "Look, Annie, that wasn't my finest hour. I admit it, but—"

"There's no but," she snapped. "At the worst time in my life you walked out on me. That doesn't deserve a but."

"No one feels worse about that than me." The jerk held out his hand, a pleading gesture. "The thought of being a father freaked me out, okay? Two at once is a lot."

"Yeah, tell me about it." Her tone dripped sarcasm.

"You were distracted and I was starting to wonder if you were ever going to be there for me. For us. But I've had time to think. I miss you. I can't forget you."

Mason could understand that. Annie was unforgettable and this idiot had voluntarily walked out on her. The last thing he should get was a do-over.

Fortunately she appeared unmoved by his words. "Honestly, I haven't had time to think about you at all, what with two infants to take care of. The fact is, you never cross my mind. In case that's not clear enough, there is not a snowball's chance in hell I would ever consider taking you back. You abandoned me once. I won't give you a chance to do that to me again."

"I wish you'd reconsider. We were good together. At home and at work."

Dwayne must be desperate, Mason thought. After what she'd just said it was clear she'd made up her mind.

Annie's eyes narrowed. "Oh, now I get it. And the verdict is official. You're a conniving weasel dog and I don't ever want to see you again."

"Annie, please. I really need this—"

"Oh? I needed you," she said. "And you couldn't get out of here fast enough then. I'd like you to do that now. Just go."

"Annie—"

Mason had seen enough. He moved next to her. "The lady asked you to leave."

Dwayne's ingratiating performance disappeared. "What are you going to do? Throw me out?"

"If I have to." Mason stared at him and knew the exact moment the moron realized it was over.

"Your loss, Annie. Remember that."

"In my opinion, I dodged a bullet," she snapped back.

Without another word, the creep left and slammed the door. Hard.

Mason and Annie looked at each other and said at the same time, "The babies."

They hurried down the hall to check on them but Charlie and Sarah were still sleeping soundly. In unison, they heaved a sigh of parental relief then quietly backed out of the room and returned to the kitchen.

She met his gaze. "So, that happened."

"He's determined. I'll give him that."

"Yeah." She closed her eyes for a moment, as if erasing any vision of Dwayne from her mind. After letting out a long breath she said, "I could have called him much worse than a weasel dog."

"Me, too, but that was pretty descriptive."

"It was a compliment compared to what I was thinking. He's lucky I didn't throw something at him."

Mason studied her face and realized he had never seen her furious. The cleansing breath she'd taken hadn't cleansed anything. There was more. "What else did he do? Besides leave you at the worst possible time."

She met his gaze. "The last thing he said before bailing on me was that raising some other guy's brats wasn't what he'd signed up for."

"Son of a bitch—" Mason felt the words like a body blow. He didn't like the guy but Annie had at one time. He couldn't imagine the scope of betrayal she'd experienced. Now he was furious, too. "Good thing you threw him out. I'd have tossed him over the railing."

Surprisingly, she laughed. "That's a very satisfying image."

"What did he mean about working well together?"

"He's a graphic artist, too. It's how we met, collaborating on a job."

So they had something in common, spoke each other's language. "And when he said he needed this? Any idea what that was about?"

"He's employed by a rival firm. My guess is that they're in competition for this big contract I've been working on. If I took him back, he'd have access to my team's creative direction and could take steps to counter in their own presentation."

"So he wanted to steal from you," he said, seething with anger.

"That's my guess."

"Prince of a guy. Just oozing integrity. Damn right you dodged a bullet."

"Wow," she said. "Don't sugarcoat it. Tell me how you really feel."

"I don't mean to hurt your feelings." That was completely sincere. He would never hurt her. Not deliberately. But he couldn't hold this back. "I just have to ask. What the hell did you ever see in that guy?"

Her hazel eyes turned more green than gold. It was a clue that he'd crossed a line. Her next words confirmed that he'd said something wrong.

High color appeared on her cheeks. "It's really easy to be on the outside looking in and draw conclusions. I've known you, what? Fifteen minutes? Yes, we share the babies and you're their father. Calling them brats makes him lower than pond scum. But I get to say that. You don't get a say about my personal life, especially for something that happened before I met you."

"Annie, I—"

She held up a hand. "Now is not a good time to talk. I have another bag of stuff to bring inside. I'll get it," she said when he was about to offer. "I'm embarrassed by what just happened and taking it out on you. I need the exercise to shake off this unreasonable reaction."

Without another word, she walked out the door. Mason let her go even though every instinct was pushing him to go after her. But moments later he heard her cry out just before a scream of pain. He rushed outside and looked down. Annie was in a heap on the cement at the bottom of the stairs.

Chapter Four

One minute Annie was walking down the stairs, the next she was falling and desperately reaching out for something to stop the downward plunge. Something stopped her, all right. It was called cement. A jarring pain shot through her right leg. She cried out just before it took her breath away. Moments later Mason was there.

"Don't move," he ordered.

"Fat chance," she managed to choke out. "Knocked the…wind out…of me."

"Where does it hurt?" He ran his hands over her head and down her body. "Did you hit your head?"

"No. My leg."

After helping her to a sitting position, he gently touched her knee and shin. Searing pain made her cry out. "Ow!"

He slid her sandal off and put two fingers on her ankle, a serious expression on his face. Apparently he noticed her questioning look because he said, "I'm checking the pulse—blood circulation."

"Why?"

"Make sure nothing is restricting it," he said.

She was almost afraid to hear the answer but asked anyway. "What would be doing that?"

"The bone."

Yup, she was right. Didn't want to know that. Then he checked her foot and dragged his thumb lightly across the arch. It tickled and she involuntarily moved, sending a sharp pain up her leg.

"Ow—" She gritted her teeth because she wanted so badly to cry.

"Do you have scissors?"

"Kitchen drawer. What are you—?"

But he was gone and she heard his footsteps racing up the stairs. He was back in less than a minute with her heavy shears in his hand. He positioned them at the hem of her slacks.

"You're going to cut them?"

"Yes. I'm concerned about swelling. They'll do it at the hospital anyway. I think your leg is broken."

"No. I don't have time for that."

He met her gaze, and his was serious and doctorly. "You're going to have to make time. I'm taking you to the hospital."

"Can't you brace it with a couple of tree branches and wrap it in strips from a dirty T-shirt?"

One corner of his mouth curved up. "You've been watching too many action shows on TV."

That was probably true. "You could be wrong. Maybe it's just a really painful sprain and you're overreacting."

"I hope I am." His serious tone said he was pretty sure that wasn't the case. "You still need an X-ray to make sure. I'm taking you to my emergency room to get it checked out."

"Oh, bother—" She closed her eyes and tried not to move and make it hurt more. "I've been up and down those stairs more than a hundred times. How did this happen?"

"My guess is you tripped over that box of disposable diapers." He pulled his cell phone from his pocket.

"Oh." Vaguely she remembered bringing bags from the car and trying to take as much as possible in one trip. Between her parking spot and the flight of steps, the box started slipping so she'd set it on one of the steps near the bottom, intending to grab it when she got the last bag. What with the Dwayne drama, she'd forgotten all about it. It was a big box because she went through a lot of diapers— "Mason, the babies!"

"It's all right. I'm calling my mom. She'll take care of them."

"But they're my responsibility—"

"And mine," he quietly reminded her. "But everyone needs help sometime, Annie. And you really don't have a choice right now."

She hated that he was right.

While they waited for his mother, he fashioned a splint from a cardboard mailing box and duct tape to immobilize her leg. Then he filled a plastic bag with ice, wrapped it in a towel and put it on the injured limb to reduce swelling. Flo got there in record time and gave Annie a quick hug and reassuring smile before hurrying up the stairs to handle the twins.

"Okay," Mason said, "let's get you to the car." He helped her stand without putting any weight on the injured leg but the movement sent pain grinding through her. There was a grim look on his face when she cried out. "I was afraid of that. Either I carry you or we call paramedics."

"No ambulance."

"That's what I thought. This will be faster and less painful. Brace yourself. Deep breath."

He gently lifted her and she slid her arms around his neck then held on. In spite of the pain, she had that familiar feeling of safety when he held her and closed her eyes while he moved as quickly as he could without jostling her too much. His SUV was at the curb in front of the complex and he got her into the rear, where she propped the bad leg up across the leather seats.

When they arrived at the emergency room entrance, someone in scrubs was waiting at the curb with a wheelchair. Mason quietly but firmly directed that she be taken to Radiology and he would meet them there with paperwork. He was as good as his word and while waiting for the X-ray tech to take her back she filled out medical forms and insurance information.

It turned out that the scrubs guy was an ER nurse who worked closely with Mason—Dr. Blackburne. He told her that Mason was smart, skilled and one of the best diagnosticians he'd ever known. Everyone liked him. And his combat medical experience saved more than one life during a recent MVA trauma—motor vehicle accident involving multiple cars and victims with critical, life-threatening injuries.

"I think this is just a bad leg sprain," Annie told him. "But Mason believes it's broken."

"Hate to say it, but he's probably right."

It turned out that he was.

After the films were taken, Mason got them to the front of the line to be read by the radiologist.

Annie was sitting on a gurney in Emergency with the curtain pulled when he came to give her the results.

"I have good news and bad," he said.

"Don't ask which I want first. Just tell me the worst," she said.

"It's broken." There was sympathy in his eyes, not the satisfaction of being right. "You'll need to be in a cast."

"How long?"

"That's up to the orthopedic doc. In a few minutes he's going to set it—"

"And plaster it?" she asked.

"Probably fiberglass. It's lighter. The goal is to control your pain and swelling, then keep it immobilized while the bone heals."

She folded her arms over her chest and frowned at him. "I see no good news in that scenario."

"It won't require surgery to set the bone."

"Does that mean I can walk on it?" she asked hopefully.

"No. Non-weight-bearing for six to eight weeks depending on how fast you heal and whether or not you follow doctor's orders."

"I'm sorry. Did you say eight weeks?"

"Max. Less if you don't push yourself too soon," he confirmed. "And, in the good news column, a broken bone heals much faster than soft tissue damage, like muscles, tendons, ligaments."

"Oddly enough, that doesn't make me feel a whole lot better. I have two four-month-old infants." This nightmare was expanding exponentially. "How am I going to take care of them? Go to the store? Walk the floor if they're crying?" Then the worst hit her. "I live in a second-floor apartment. I have to go up and down stairs. There's no elevator."

"If you put weight on it before that bone heals, there will be complications," he warned.

"So what am I supposed to do?" She was very close to

tears but not from physical discomfort, although her leg was throbbing painfully. Dyslexia had been a challenge in school and the bullying that resulted was emotionally devastating, but she'd learned coping skills. None of that had prepared her to cope with this.

"Move in with me," Mason said.

That sudden declaration kept her from crying. "Just like that? It was the first thing that popped into your head?"

"I've had time to process the situation."

She was still bitter about him being right. "Because you knew all along it was broken."

"Yes. I'm just glad it's not more serious."

"It's more serious to me."

That was self-pity, raw and unattractive. She wasn't proud of it, but couldn't deny the feeling. He probably thought she was being a drama queen, what with seeing patients who had injuries much more serious and life-threatening. But she had her babies to think about. How was she going to take care of them?

Through her shock she was trying to work out the logistics of what was happening to her. "I can work from home and have groceries delivered. But I can't hold a baby and walk on crutches. I won't be able to pick up Charlie to feed him. Or carry Sarah into the bathroom to bathe her. And it's my right leg. That will make driving difficult, if not impossible." Her heart was breaking. "How will I get them to the pediatrician? Maybe Uber…but the complications—"

"Move in with me," he repeated.

"I don't know you," she blurted.

He sighed. "Look, I know this is upsetting. But it's been a month now. Have I let you down? Have I done anything suspicious or weird?"

"You mean aside from living with your parents?"

"I haven't had a lot of time to go house hunting." He moved closer to the bed and looked down at her. "If it would make you feel better, you could do a background check."

Annie's eyes filled with tears. "I know I'm being silly. You've been terrific and your mom is a goddess. But it's hard for me to deal with the fact that I can't do this on my own."

"My parents have a single-story house and lots of room. Believe me when I say they would love it if you and their grandchildren stayed with them."

"How do you know? Have you talked to them about it?"

"As a matter of fact, I have," he said. "I would tell you if they were hesitant, but they couldn't have been more enthusiastic."

"I don't know—"

"Look, Annie, we can keep this up however long you want, but we'll end up in the same place." He sat on the bed, being careful not to crowd her injured leg, and took her hand in his big warm one. "The thing is, you don't really have a lot of options."

He was right again and she wasn't any happier about it this time. She nodded and one tear trickled down her cheek. "Okay. But only for the babies."

Mason carried the last box from Annie's apartment into her new room. She was sitting in the glider chair with her casted leg elevated on the ottoman. Charlie was sacked out in one of the cribs his parents had bought and Annie was holding a sleeping Sarah in her arms.

He'd spent his day off making trips back and forth for all the baby paraphernalia, her clothes and toiletries. In between carrying the babies to her for feeding and cuddling, he put everything away in the pine armoire and matching dresser. Using the top of it for diaper supplies, the second crib beside it was being turned into the changing table. His parents wanted their grandkids to spend a lot of time there and had insisted on buying a bed for each baby.

That meant Annie would be there, too. He liked the prospect of spending time with her, especially being under the same roof. For the next six weeks at least, he wouldn't fall asleep on that uncomfortable couch of hers.

"Hi," she said.

"Hey."

"What's in the box?"

"Toys." He set the box in a corner, out of the way. With her on crutches, the last thing he wanted was for her to trip and fall.

Two days ago he'd brought her here from the hospital and his mom had helped her care for the twins. This was his brothers' old room. It had bunk beds but was still a little crowded with Annie and the babies. Between working a shift and moving things from the apartment, Mason hadn't had a chance to talk to her. He'd missed it. He didn't want to, but it was pretty hard to ignore how glad he was to see her.

"This is the last of the things on your list. Unless you think of something else."

"You look tired," she said softly.

"Don't feel guilty."

"Who said anything about—?"

"I can hear it in your voice." Funny how he knew her that well in a relatively short period of time. "It's not your fault."

"Yeah, it kind of is," she said. "I left the box of diapers on the stairs."

"That's why it's called an accident. On the plus side, my folks are over the moon about you and the twins being here." And, though he didn't want to be, so was he.

Mason moved closer to the chair and smiled at his beautiful daughter. "How are the kids handling this change of environment?"

"It's different and they know. Not much napping going on today. I could tell they were a little restless and out of sorts." She looked up and there were shadows under her eyes, proving someone besides him was not getting enough sleep. On top of that she was pale and there were traces of pain around her mouth from the recent trauma.

"How are you holding up? Are you staying off the leg per doctor's orders?"

"Have you met your mother? She's the keep-that-leg-elevated police. If I get up for anything other than the bathroom, her feelings are hurt because I didn't ask for help." Her full lips curved upward. "She's completely fantastic, Mason. So is your dad."

"You'll get no argument from me."

"Flo must be exhausted. Basically she's been doing the work of three people, between the babies and me."

"I think she's asleep." The TV in the family room was off and the house quiet when he'd come home with the last box.

"Good." Annie nodded. "She checked in with me when you went for the last load and wanted to put Sarah in the crib for me, but I just want to hold her. Your mom, bless her, completely understood. She was turning in and wanted to make sure I didn't need anything. She said to holler if I did."

"Well, I'm back and just on the other side of the bathroom." There were entrances to it from each bedroom. "If Charlie or Sarah wakes up, I'll hear them."

Annie shifted the baby in her arms. "Can you put her in the crib for me?"

"Sure." Mason leaned down and slid his hands under the little girl and carefully lifted her. After a soft kiss on her forehead, he set her on her back beside her brother. "She's out cold. So is Charlie."

"Excellent."

"Now you can get some rest," he advised.

"Yeah." But she reached for her crutches leaning against the wall beside her. "After I take a shower."

What? He'd started out of the room and froze then turned back. "You can't get the cast wet."

"Not breaking news, Dr. Do Right. The ortho doc was very clear on that."

He could see she was determined to stand and moved the ottoman out of her way. "So it's going to be a hop-in-and-out kind of thing. Quick."

"Believe me, no one gets that better than I do." She pulled herself up awkwardly, winced with discomfort, then arranged the crutches beneath her arms. "But I'm stuck with this obnoxious thing for a while and I have to bathe."

"Of course. But my sister is off tomorrow. She's a nurse and could help you—"

"I can handle this, Mason. Don't try to talk me out of it. Another sponge bath isn't going to cut it. And I'm going to wash my hair or die trying. So get out of my way. I don't want to hurt you."

She looked fierce and beautiful and so cute. Something in his chest squeezed tight for a moment, then he laughed at the idea of a little thing like her hurting him.

She glared at him. "It's not funny. After two days, I can't stand myself."

He could stand her. A lot. What he couldn't stand was

her getting hurt. Seeing her at the bottom of the stairs
had taken time off his life and he didn't want to specu-
late on how much. Showering on her own was a disaster
in the making. She was still getting used to the crutches
and learning to balance on one leg to keep her weight off
the other. It wouldn't take much for this to go sideways,
literally, real fast.

"Okay. At least let me help you with a strategy. Figure
out the steps, pardon the pun, of this operation."

There was a suspicious gleam in her eyes. "Like what?"

"Keeping your cast dry for starters. A few drops on
the outside isn't a big deal. But if you get the inside wet
it can lead to a skin infection."

"That sounds pretty gross," she agreed. "So what do
you have in mind?"

"I'll be back in a minute. Wait here."

"Seriously? You don't want me to hobble along and
keep you company?" Letting the crutches take her weight,
she stood there with a teasing look in her eyes.

"Right." He grinned then left the room.

The logistics of this maneuver ran through his mind
as he hurried to the kitchen and grabbed the things he
wanted. That kept him from thinking too much about
Annie naked in the shower except for the lime-green cast
on her leg.

Actually the vision popped into his mind anyway,
along with the steadily increasing urge to kiss her. If he
did, that could be a problem. Clearly she didn't trust easily and he wouldn't be another Dwayne in her life who
made promises he couldn't keep.

When he came back to the bathroom, it was empty.
"Annie?"

"Coming." Her soft voice came from the other side of
the door. Then she shuffled back into the light wearing

a short, pink terry-cloth robe, under which she probably wore nothing.

Sweat popped out on his forehead and he nearly swallowed his tongue. "I thought you were going to stay put."

"I changed out of my clothes."

"Yeah. Because that's what you do when you take a shower." He sounded like a moron. *It's what happened when blood flow from your brain rerouted to another part of your anatomy.*

"What's all that stuff for?"

Apparently she was more focused on what he'd brought than what he'd said. Good. "A plastic trash bag, duct tape and a pitcher. Sit down and I'll show you."

She moved over and sat on the closed toilet lid then rested the crutches against the sink. "Now what?"

Now he would do his level best to act professionally and not let on that he was crazy attracted to her. "I'm going to put the bag over your leg. Before I secure it with the tape, I'm going to tuck this hand towel into the top of the cast so that if the bag leaks it will still keep the inside dry."

"Great idea. I love it when a plan comes together."

Not yet, but if his hands didn't shake when he touched her, he'd call it a win.

Mason went down on one knee and put her foot on his thigh. Then he did his thing with the towel. There was no way he could avoid touching her skin and the contact just south of her thigh was sweet torture. He tried not to notice, but the material of her robe separated just a little. Not enough to get a glimpse of anything he shouldn't but enough to torment him with what he couldn't see.

He took a deep breath, as if he was going underwater, then opened the plastic bag and slid it up over her cast.

Twisting it closed just below her knee, he wrapped it securely with the tape then ripped it off the roll.

Annie nodded her approval. "That looks watertight."

"You still need to keep it away from the running water. Hang it outside the shower stall."

"What's that for?"

He glanced at the small, plastic sixteen-ounce measuring cup she was pointing to. "I'll help you wash your hair in the sink. The less time you spend in the shower, the better."

Her mouth pulled tight for a moment. "So I need to let go of a long, hot, relaxing wash."

"Like I said, it will be quick. Sorry."

"Not as sorry as I am." She met his gaze. "Let's do this."

"I'll get towels." He went to the linen closet in the hall and brought back two big fluffy ones. "This one is for your hair."

"Okay."

"Ready?"

When she nodded, Mason helped her stand, then put his hand at her waist and tried not to wish she didn't have that robe on. He instructed her to bend over the sink. Her shampoo and conditioner were right where he'd put them after unpacking her toiletries.

He turned on the water and filled the cup to wet all that beautiful blond, silky hair. He was a doctor and had been married, but this was the first time he'd ever washed a woman's hair. There was something incredibly sensual about the soapy strands running through his fingers.

No way could he stop himself from picturing her, him in the shower together with water running over their bodies. Surely he was going to hell for impure thoughts at the expense of an injured woman. He rinsed the soap as thoroughly as possible then used the conditioner and went through the same procedure, wondering if a man could go to hell twice.

"All finished." His voice was a little hoarse and with any luck she was too preoccupied to notice. He helped her straighten then handed her the towel to wrap around her hair while he steadied her. It didn't escape his notice that the pulse at the base of her neck was fluttering a little too fast. If there was any satisfaction from this ordeal at all, it was that she might be as affected by him as he was by her.

"Okay. Now for the hard part. I'll aim the showerhead away from the door so you can stick your leg out."

After he did that, she looked at him pointedly. "You can leave now."

Here was the classic definition of conflict. He wanted to get as far away from her as possible. At the same time, he didn't want to leave her and risk a fall. But the fact was he couldn't stay. He was trying to be a gentleman, not picturing her naked. The last thing he wanted was to be a sleazeball who reinforced all her reasons for being a skeptic. This might just be the hardest thing he'd ever done.

"Okay. But I'll be just on the other side of the door if you need anything."

"Thanks."

He turned his back and walked out, shutting the door behind him. That's as far as he got. He'd never forget her cry of pain when she'd fallen on the cement and hoped to God he didn't hear it now. So he waited right by that door just in case he needed to get to her in seconds.

He waited to hear the shower go on and it was a while because she had to hobble over, take off that sexy little robe, step in and set the crutches aside. The water went off fairly quickly so she'd gotten the message about not standing under it for too long.

And speaking of long, he stood in that same spot by the door for quite a while after he heard her leave the bathroom and go into the other bedroom. What the hell was wrong with him?

Stupid question. If this was a clinical situation, he would be focused on the medicine. Only that wasn't the case.

It was personal. No matter how hard he tried to stop, no matter how hard he tried not to be attracted to Annie, this was getting more personal every day.

Chapter Five

A week after breaking her leg, Annie and the kids were pretty much settled into a routine with Mason's family. He worked twelve-hour shifts for a couple of days, then was off a couple. When he was gone, his mother took over helping with the twins, bringing one or the other to Annie for feeding and cuddles. When Mason's dad, John, got home from work, he pitched in, too. His sister, Kelsey, had nursing shifts at the hospital, but happily lent a hand when she was home. It occurred to Annie to wonder why a grown man living with his parents was weird, but not a grown woman.

Mason swore that as soon as there was time he was going house hunting. And she wondered why he hadn't kept his house before he deployed to Afghanistan instead of selling it. One of these days she planned to ask him.

Right now she was too busy feeling guilty and sorry for herself. She was only good for elevating her bum leg and petting the dog while the rest of the adults took care of her babies. She could hear them in the other room getting baths. There was a lot of laughing and splashing going on and she was missing out on all the fun. Broken legs sucked.

Dogs did not. Lulu was a black shih tzu–poodle mix and completely adorable. Annie rubbed her hand over the animal's soft furry back and smiled when Lulu licked her hand, like kisses to say "Thank you for paying attention to me." When she stopped for a moment, sad brown eyes looked up at her. "Sorry, Lulu. I have to get up off this couch and go see the kids."

Florence Blackburne picked that moment to come in and check on her. "Not so fast, young lady. Your orders are to stay off that leg as much as possible."

"But I'm missing them grow up." Annie knew she was being overly dramatic and…dare she say it? Whining? But she couldn't help it. "You don't understand."

"Maternal guilt? Boredom? Missing your children?"

"Yeah, that." The words backed Annie up a bit.

Flo sat in the club chair at a right angle to her position on the sofa. "When I was pregnant with Kelsey, my youngest, I had a condition known as placenta previa, which could cause complications during labor and delivery. I was put on bed rest until she was developed enough to take her by C-section."

"Oh, my."

"I had three small and very active boys who didn't understand why Mommy couldn't do all the things she did before. I'll never forget Mason's little face when he asked me to throw the ball with him outside and I couldn't. It broke my heart."

"How did you get through it?"

"My in-laws were fantastic. It would have been almost impossible if not for them."

"You were fortunate."

"Don't I know it. The children adored them. We all still miss them." Her voice went soft for a moment. "They died a few years ago, a couple of months apart. She went first and my father-in-law seemed in good health, except for missing her. He didn't know how to go on without her."

"He died of a broken heart," Annie commented.

Flo smiled sadly. "That's what I always thought. My family helped, too. My sister, Lillian, adored the boys and was here as much as possible on top of her full-time job."

"So you had support from both sides of the family."

"I always suspected there was a spreadsheet and schedule," the other woman said teasingly. "Lillian was in charge of that, but business and records weren't her thing. She was always a romantic and said there's nothing sexy about numbers."

Annie grinned. "That depends on who's using the algorithm."

"So I've been told," Flo said. "My son Gabriel is helping her out with her business right now and I'm told he's not hard on the eyes."

"My friend Carla works at Make Me a Match." Annie explained how they'd met. "It's not a rumor that he's a hottie. She has firsthand knowledge."

Flo grinned. "Family can be both difficult and indispensable. So, my advice is, since there's no way your broken leg is going to heal as fast as you want it to, just sit back and enjoy the help. We're happy to be doing it."

"Thank you. It's appreciated more than I can possibly say." Annie smiled when Lulu rested a paw on her left leg and whined just a little to be petted. She happily obliged. "Please don't think I'm not grateful, because I am. And maybe I'm a control freak. But I haven't had very much experience with backup."

"Do you have family?"

"My mother and her husband. Stepfather," she added.

"You don't like him." Flo wasn't asking.

"How did you know? I thought I was hiding my feelings pretty well."

"You didn't call him *your* stepfather." The woman shrugged. "No offense, but you're not a very good actress."

Sometimes Annie wished she was better at it. Like the night Mason had washed her hair and waterproofed her cast. She'd been a bundle of feelings and jumped every time his fingers had grazed her skin. Every touch was like a zing of awareness, but he probably hadn't noticed. He'd never looked at her, just concentrated on positioning duct tape.

The thing was, Annie liked when he touched her. A lot. But since he'd shown up at her apartment, there'd been no signal from him that he had the slightest personal interest, other than being a father to the twins. They had to parent together. That was all. If she let the secret of her attraction show, it would be humiliating, and her life was already filled with enough humiliation.

Annie looked at the other woman. "I don't hide my feelings well. That could be why Jess and I didn't see much of him and my mother after they moved to Florida."

"Did they know she was pregnant?" Flo asked.

Bitterness welled up inside Annie. "They knew. And they know she died after the twins were born. But they haven't seen their grandchildren even once."

Speaking of being an actress, Mason's mother couldn't or wouldn't conceal the shock and disapproval that showed on her face. "Grandchildren are our reward for not strangling our kids as teenagers. But… Never mind."

Flo seemed so open and Annie couldn't figure out why she was reluctant to say more. Just then the dog jumped off the couch and trotted to the kitchen. Moments later the doggie door slapped open and shut.

"What were you going to say?" Annie couldn't stifle her curiosity.

"I shouldn't judge people I don't know."

"But…?" She prodded.

"No. Florida is on the other side of the country. I have zero knowledge about their financial situation."

"I can tell you have an opinion," Annie nudged.

"Of course. I have opinions on everything." Flo shifted in the chair. "How's the leg? Are you comfortable?"

"I'm as comfy as possible." Annie had her leg elevated on the coffee table with the cast resting on a throw pillow. "And you're changing the subject."

"Yes." Flo sighed. "I don't want you to think I'm awful."

"Seriously?" Now it was Annie's turn to be shocked. This woman had been nothing but kind, welcoming and a godsend. "I could never think that. I can't imagine what I'd have done without this whole family and I don't even want to imagine it. I've actually thought this, so I'll just say it straight out. You're a goddess."

"Right back at you. The thing is, maybe I have strong feelings because I've waited for grandkids for quite a long time. I'd hoped Mason would…" Flo checked her words and sadness slipped into her eyes. "That was another life. It's just that I can't picture not knowing my children's children. They're a blessing."

"The babies are for me, too," Annie said.

"Thank you for sharing them with us. I just want to be included. If I overstep, you are to let me know. I mean that, Annie."

"I promise."

"If I do, just know that it comes from a place of love. I don't want to miss out on anything."

"Okay. And you should know that if I don't think to

reach out, it's nothing more than me being tired and brain-dead, certainly not deliberate. And you have to tell me."

"Thank you." Flo smiled and reached over to squeeze her hand.

Lulu returned to stand in front of Annie. The little black dog whined softly and Annie had learned this meant she wanted a treat for successfully going potty outside. The jar was beside her and she plucked out a bone-shaped biscuit, holding it just within the animal's reach. Lulu stood on her back legs, opened her mouth and snatched it from Annie's fingers then took it to her favorite spot underneath the dining room table. Annie was happy to be of use, at least to one member of this household.

But back to her folks. Annie thought about them. "My mom and stepfather have missed everything and don't seem to mind. That's in character. When I was growing up, they seemed happiest when they didn't have to get in-volved in mine and Jess's life."

"It's hard finding balance between hovering con-stantly, being a helicopter parent, and backing off to let your child's independence evolve." Flo looked as if she was remembering. "Mason was our oldest and it never seemed fair that we had to practice on him because we had no idea what we were doing. Unfortunately some-one has to be first. John and I always joked that he was our prototype."

Annie laughed. "At least Charlie and Sarah have each other and eventually a therapy buddy when they grow up and complain that we did it all wrong. At least me. Mason is so good with them."

It was clearer every day how much he loved his chil-dren, as if he'd been waiting a very long time to be a father. Unlike Dwayne, the douche who'd called her pre-cious babies another man's brats. When she'd told Mason that, she'd been afraid he'd chase down the jerk and pop him like the douchebag he was. The thought of that was pretty hot.

"Mason told me about your boyfriend abandoning you," Flo said.

"Ex-boyfriend." Annie was going to add "mind reader" to this woman's list of superpowers. "I couldn't have been more wrong about him. I won't make a mistake like that again."

"Not everyone walks out."

"Couldn't prove that by me." Annie was afraid the other woman could look into her soul and see the feelings she was trying to hide. Then the meaning of her words sank in. "I wasn't talking about you. I must have sounded completely ungrateful. I'm not sure how I would have coped if not for Mason and you guys, his family."

"We're your family, too."

"I appreciate you saying that." But she wouldn't let herself count on it. The *stepfather* had always said she and Jessica wouldn't have been so much trouble if they'd been his blood. The message had been received loud and clear. Mason's family were helping, but only because of the blood connection to the babies. Why else would they bother?

"I mean it, Annie. Of course having trust is hard." Flo hesitated then added, "You don't have any reason to believe someone who just tells you he loves you. Believe someone who shows you he does."

She was right about trust. Annie's biological father physically left. The stepfather emotionally dumped her. Then she made the mistake of letting her guard down with Dwayne. Three strikes and you're out.

Annie didn't believe in love anymore. Disillusionment hurt and the longer she stayed here in this house with Mason, the more she could get sucked into believing. As soon as she could manage on her own, she was going back to her place.

Mason sat in the rocker that was older than he was and held Sarah in his arms. Annie was next to him in the glider chair, her bad leg elevated on the ottoman and Charlie nestled to her chest. It was late and everyone else in the house was asleep. To keep it that way, they were tandem rocking the twins.

He glanced sideways and thought how beautiful she looked with a baby in her arms. She and the twins had been here for two weeks and it was the best two weeks he'd had in a very long time. Charlie whimpered restlessly and she softly shushed, settling him down.

Annie met his gaze and frowned. "What?" she whispered.

"Nothing." He studied Sarah and knew now that she was sufficiently asleep to handle a quiet conversation.

Annie kept staring. "You have kind of a dweeby look on your face. Why?"

"It's the same look I always have. Guess I'm just a dweeb."

"No." She shook her head.

"So you don't think I'm a dweeb?"

"I didn't say that. Your expression is just dweebier than normal." She rubbed a hand over Charlie's back. "What are you thinking about? It's making you look weird."

He hesitated. "I feel silly telling you."

"Now I have to know." There was a teasing note in her voice.

"You'll mock me."

"Probably. Suck it up, Doc. You're a grown man. A soldier. I can't believe you haven't developed a thicker skin."

Maybe a diversionary tactic would distract her. "Have you?"

"I had to." She laughed but there was no humor in the sound. "For survival. So let me help you exercise those muscles. What were you thinking to put that dopey expression on your face?"

"Well, I should start by saying that I'm sorry you broke your leg." *But not for helping you shower.* It was on his highlight reel of awesome memories, but he didn't think she'd want to know that.

"Not as sorry as I am. But how is that silly?"

"Because I'm not sorry about being under the same roof with you. And my children," he added. "So I can get to know them better. Like now."

"You're rocking Sarah to sleep," she pointed out. "How is that getting to know her?"

"I'm doing it in the rocking chair that my father bought for my mother when she was pregnant with me." It had been out in the garage and brought in because sometimes both babies needed rocking.

"So it's an antique," she teased.

"I'm not going to let you spoil this for me." He smiled at her. "I'm learning about her sleep patterns. And Charlie's. Figuring out what it takes to soothe them when they're upset. Their personalities. I get to just be around. Before it was like visiting hours at the hospital and now— It's not."

"You'd probably rather have them on their own. Without me."

"No," he assured her. "You're their mom. The engine that drives everything. The center of their world."

"And you really don't mind that your world is turned upside down because I broke my leg and the three of us had to move in?"

"Just the opposite. I love what I do for a living. I love

being a doctor and helping people, but it doesn't compare to being a father and spending as much time as possible with my children. Like I said, I'm glad you're here. In fact, I'd have to say, for maybe the first time in my life, I'm content."

He wasn't pulling all-nighters for grades to get him into med school or stressing about the money to go. It wasn't about looking at the calendar to gauge his wife's ovulation date or trying to get pregnant. There was no agenda except to just be. And while he was just being, he could feel Annie's gaze on him.

"What?" he asked.

"You're right. What you were thinking about was dopey. And sweet," she added.

"Haven't you ever experienced contentment?"

"It's hard to feel something you don't believe in. If contentment exists, it's just the bubble of calm between crises."

His mother had mentioned to him that she'd talked with Annie about her absentee parents and Dwayne the Douche. It explained her tendency toward cynicism, but he had the feeling there was more. He saw a lot of people in the emergency room and often they withheld information, reluctant to admit some aspect of their lifestyle might be contributing to whatever condition needed medical intervention. He couldn't help without all the facts and had learned to spot the signs. Annie was holding out, but maybe he could change that.

"Do you want to talk about what happened to you, besides a self-centered boyfriend who left you in the lurch?"

"Life happened," she said. "Dwayne was just the cherry on top of a bad-luck sundae."

"Tell me about it." Sarah was deadweight in his arms,

sound asleep. But if he put her in the crib, this moment of quiet reflection would disappear and he didn't want it to.

"My mother got pregnant in her senior year of high school and was pressured to marry the boy she slept with. They were on their own and hardly more than kids themselves. Barely two years later, I was on the way. He couldn't handle the responsibility of two kids and took off."

That explained why Dwayne's desertion had hit a supersensitive nerve. "You mentioned a stepfather."

"Right." Bitterness was thick in her voice. "He's the man my mother married, but calling him a father is really stretching the definition of the word."

"What happened?" It surprised him a little when she answered because she was quiet for so long.

"You should probably know that I have dyslexia. There could be a hereditary component."

"Okay."

"If either of the twins has trouble reading, we need to look into getting them help as soon as possible."

"That's good to know." The tension and snap in her tone told him diagnosis and help had been a problem for her. "What happened to you, Annie?"

She wrapped Charlie a little more securely in her arms and softly kissed his forehead. "In elementary school, they didn't pick it up with me for a couple of years. Most of the kids were reading and comprehending in first and second grade. They were off and running."

"But not you."

"No. They tested us and arranged everyone accordingly, giving each group a color. It was supposed to be discreet, but everyone knew who was high, middle and low. I got help through the school district's resource program but needed more than they could give. My teacher suggested private reading and speech therapy, but my mother's husband said it was a waste of money. That I was just stupid."

"Oh, Annie—" A fierce, protective feeling welled up inside him followed closely by an even fiercer anger. And he didn't know how to vent it. It wasn't like he could fly to Florida and punch the guy's lights out for being an insensitive moron. But he was afraid to say anything, partly because he was so ticked off at the jerk. Partly because he sensed she wasn't finished yet.

"He used to put me down every chance he got. Called me dumb. Idiot. Retarded. Whatever insult popped into his tiny little mind."

"Where was your mom?"

"Right there when he did it. Too timid to say anything that would make him walk out and leave her alone with my sister and me."

"So *you* were all alone." It took a lot of effort to keep his voice neutral, to not let her see how outraged he was on her behalf.

"No. I had Jessica."

"She was just a kid herself," he said.

"Which makes her actions even more special." She looked at him over Charlie's head. "When he'd start in on me for no reason, she would run interference. And sometimes it would distract him and she'd take the brunt of whatever verbal abuse he was handing out."

"Good for her." He remembered a tough self-awareness about the woman he'd spent one night with. And this was where it had come from.

"He liked to ground us for any small thing, but never together because we had fun."

"Piece of work—" Mason said under his breath.

"And at school. There were bullies who used to make fun of me. But not when my sister was around and she made it a point to be around as much as she could. She was my hero." Annie sighed and it was an achingly sad and profoundly lonely sound. "I miss her so much. She would have been a good mom."

"Her protective instincts were extraordinarily strong even then," he agreed. "Oh, Annie, I wish you hadn't had to go through that. No child should."

"What doesn't kill you makes you stronger, right? And I was convinced reading would kill me. For sure it was a challenge and I hated it. But art—" The dislike in her voice turned to reverence. "There's no right or wrong way to do it. It's about the artist's interpretation. I had fantastic teachers who took me under their wings and gave me the best advice I ever got."

"Which was?"

"Study what you love. I did that and found a career."

"And you're good at it," he said.

"I'm not looking for pity. I just thought you should know because we'll be co-parenting. And—" She caught her bottom lip between her teeth.

"What? You can tell me anything." And he hoped she would.

"You might have noticed that sometimes I have a chip on my shoulder. It's my hard outer shell, my bulletproof vest against humiliation."

"In the army I saw men and women ripped apart even with body armor. It can't protect against everything. Children can be cruel, but most grow out of it to become better human beings. You might want to cut people slack sometimes. No one is perfect."

"Says the guy with the perfect childhood. Raised by the perfect parents, with a father who bought his wife a rocking chair when she was pregnant."

"It was good," he admitted. "And I wouldn't change a

thing. It's the way I want Charlie and Sarah to grow up. But there's no such thing as perfect. You have to learn to roll with the punches."

She lifted Charlie from her shoulder and settled him on his back in her lap. He was getting so big he barely fit. Then she rotated her arm to ease the stiffness. "I'm not looking for perfect. I just learned to take things one mess at a time and always have a plan B."

Mason had studied anatomy, physiology; he knew how to heal bodies. But wounded souls were not his specialty. He wanted to take away her pain, and all the bad stuff in her past, and had no clue how to do that. For a man whose whole life was about fixing people, that was a tough reality.

All he could do was show up so she would know he wasn't going anywhere. They shared the same goal: loving these children. That would never change and it was safe for him.

Romantic love was different—mercurial—even when you thought you had all the bases covered. It was humbling and painful and something he was determined to never do again.

He wanted Annie. No question about that, but that was just anatomy and physiology. He wouldn't let it become more. Because of the children. And speaking of the twins...

"Tomorrow you and I are going to go house hunting," he said.

Chapter Six

The next morning when Annie walked into the kitchen Mason was there, leaning against the counter by the sink with a cup of coffee in his hand. Every time she saw him it was like being starstruck all over again, making her breath catch and her heart pound. Today was no exception. Most women would be excited about the reaction, but Annie wasn't most women.

Last night she hadn't challenged him about the house hunting remark because they were trying to settle the twins. Now she had questions. "About a house…" she said.

"I'm going out with a Realtor today and I'd like you to come along. If you don't have anything pressing at work," he added.

"No, I'm caught up. My boss has all my ideas and sketches related to the account we're going after, but…" She leaned on her crutches and stared at him. She had another question. "What about the twins?"

"My mom is working half a day and will be home soon to watch them."

Annie's first reaction was no way. She hadn't been

alone with him since the drive to the emergency room when she broke her leg. Although, technically, they had been alone that first night in this house when he'd helped her shower. She'd felt the burn ever since and not from hot water. It was all about the hotness of this man. So pretty to look at, which distracted her from the fact that he could not possibly be as good as he seemed. No man was.

"Annie, please say something." He set his mug on the counter.

"You can't want me to go. With these crutches, I'll just slow you down."

"Not that much. You're getting around pretty well now. Are you having any pain?"

"You sound like a doctor."

"Because I am." He smiled. "So, are you? In any pain, I mean."

"No. But my leg is itching like crazy."

"I know it's uncomfortable. Believe it or not, that's a good sign," he said. "On the bright side, getting out and doing something will distract you."

"Why?"

"You'll be focused on something else and not thinking about how much you want to find something that will fit down that cast and scratch the itch."

She couldn't help smiling because he was right about wanting desperately to do just that. But that wasn't what she'd asked. "I meant why do you want me to go along?"

"Since the twins will be with me half the time, I'd really like your input. A mother's perspective on their potential environment. I've been working with a real-estate agent and he's lined up some houses based on the criteria I gave him." Mason folded his arms over his chest. "I could really use another point of view, especially about safety concerns, kid-friendly floor plans. Another pair of eyes to pick up something I might not see or think about."

"You had a house before you deployed. Why did you sell it?" She wouldn't have blurted that out except he'd backed her into a corner. But when the happy look on his face faded to dark and his eyes turned intense, she felt guilty enough to let it go. "If you really want me there, I'll go. But you need to let me know if I'm holding you back. You don't have a lot of time, what with work, and I don't want to slow you down."

"Promise." With his index finger he made an X over his heart. "I'd really like to get this done. Find a place of my own. You know what they say about a guy in his thirties who lives with his mother."

She laughed. "Yeah. People are starting to talk. 'There's something odd about Dr. Blackburne. He still lives at home.'"

"I know, right?" One corner of his mouth curved up and just like that the darkness was gone. "And I think the twins need their own space. Sometimes we just need to let them cry and it's hard to do that here because we don't want them disturbing anyone else."

"Good point. Okay. I need to change." She glanced down at her old sweatpants, legs cut off to accommodate the cast. "If potential neighbors see a bag lady trailing you, no one will sell you an outhouse."

"Yeah." But something shifted in his expression when his gaze skimmed her legs, and humor was replaced by what looked a lot like hunger. He turned away and reached into the sink. "While you do that, I'll wash bottles and get them ready so Mom won't have to deal with it when she comes home."

Annie hobbled out of the room and prayed she wasn't making a big mistake going with him. However, she'd given her word and wouldn't back out. Besides, she had bigger problems. Like what to wear. Fortunately the October weather was still warm, at least during the day. Bermuda shorts would work. She chose white ones and a T-shirt with lime-green horizontal stripes and three-quarter-length sleeves.

Before going in the bathroom, she peeked at the babies in the crib and was glad they were still sleeping soundly. She was getting pretty good at balancing on one leg and braced her midsection against the sink while pulling her hair back into a ponytail. After taking more care with her makeup than normal, she told herself that it had everything to do with making a good impression on a potential neighborhood and nothing to do with impressing Mason. And she almost believed the lie.

Flo came home just as Annie was ready, so it appeared the universe was aligning for her to go with him.

A short time later they'd met the agent, George Watters, and were now pulling up in front of a house. "Note the beautifully maintained landscape," he said. "Brick walkway. Covered front porch. Four bedrooms, two-and-a-half baths. I'm sorry, Annie, but this is a two-story home."

"That's not a problem," Mason said before she could comment. "We'll check out the first floor and see if it's even necessary to look upstairs."

After everyone exited the SUV and went up the walkway, George extracted a key from the lockbox and let them inside. Using the crutches, Annie swung herself over the threshold and looked around. It was an older home with low ceilings and needed a fresh coat of paint. There was an eat-in kitchen, but not a lot of counter space. Still, the family room was adjacent, so being able to keep an eye on the twins while fixing dinner was a plus.

Annie couldn't tell what Mason thought. She wasn't

blown away, but he was the one buying it. "What do you think?"

He was staring out the sliding-glass door into the back-yard. Turning, he said, "I was hoping for a little more space for the twins to play."

"No problem," George said. "This is just the first one. I've got more for you and your wife to look at."

"We're not married," Annie said.

"I should know better than to assume." George was silver-haired, in his mid to late fifties, and looked apologetic.

"No problem. It was an honest mistake." Mason didn't elaborate.

That was for the best, Annie thought. The phrase "it's complicated" was tossed around a lot, but with her and Mason and the twins, it really *was* complicated. The situation would be a challenge to clarify in twenty-five words or less.

"So let's go look at option number two," the agent suggested.

They piled back in the SUV and George drove them to another property that wasn't far from the hospital. The front yard was basic but well cared for and there was a front porch. For some reason Annie was drawn to cov-ered front porches, picturing it with a couple of chairs for sitting outside in the evening. Chatting with neighbors. Watching kids play until it was time to go inside to get ready for bed. The vivid fantasy made her wistful.

George unlocked the door and let them in. The walls were painted a neutral shade of beige with contrasting white doors and trim. Mason checked out the rear yard and nodded approvingly. The kitchen had granite coun-tertops, an island and lots of cupboards.

"Thoughts?" Mason said.

"It's nice. Let me take another look." She walked, or rather, hobbled, the complete bottom floor again and stopped by the stairs. "It has possibilities."

"Okay. Let's look upstairs."

"I can't get up there, but you go ahead," she urged Mason. "I'll wait here."

"I want your opinion on the entire house." He instructed her to rest the crutches against the railing, then scooped her up and carried her to the second floor.

Annie protested but slid her arms around his neck. "For a doctor you're not too bright. Your back will not thank you for this."

"I'm showing off." He grinned. "And you don't weigh much."

That made her heart happy and way too soon the top floor was visible. There was an open loft that looked down on the entryway. Mason walked her through three bedrooms and then the master. One very nice feature was a balcony overlooking the backyard, but they both thought the rooms were on the small side. Annie made him look in the closet and she felt it left a lot to be desired.

"But that might not matter to you," she said.

Unless a woman moved in with him. The thought was vaguely unappealing. It shouldn't be, and the fact that it was bothered her more than a little. Then it occurred to her that another woman would be around her children. And she had no right to say anything about who he became involved with. Well, shoot.

"I wouldn't have noticed that," Mason said. "That's why I wanted you to come with me. Still, there are a lot of positive things here. We'll make a list of pros and cons."

"Okay."

Annie found herself wishing the trip back down those stairs wouldn't end too soon. It gave her the opportunity to hold him, to feel her body close to his. She wasn't the one exerting herself but was a little breathless anyway. It didn't mean anything, she told herself. Just that while her leg might be broken, her female parts were working just fine.

At the bottom of the stairs Mason set her down and she missed the warmth of him. He handed her the crutches and looked up to where they'd just been.

"I was just thinking about the twins. When they start crawling. They'll go right for the stairs."

George joined them. "You can get gates for the bottom and the top. Until they're old enough to go up and down by themselves."

"I suppose." But Mason didn't look sure about that.

So they got back in the SUV and went to two more houses. Both were adequate but nothing to get excited about.

"I've got one more," George said. "It just came on the market. And it's one story."

When they stopped at the curb Annie zeroed in on the covered porch. Check, she thought. The yard was landscaped with neatly trimmed bushes and flowers. Inside was a traditional floor plan: living and dining rooms separated by a marble-tiled entryway. There was no furniture and George explained that because of a job transfer, the family had to leave quickly. That meant they'd probably be willing to make a deal and escrow could move fast. But first things first. They needed to look at the whole house.

The kitchen was gorgeous—beautiful granite, white cupboards—and she didn't even care about toddler handprints. There was a copper rack for pots and pans hanging over the island.

The rest of the house had spacious bedrooms and big closets. Mason heartily approved of the backyard and there was a casita. She looked inside and couldn't help thinking what a great home office it could be. But it wouldn't be her home or her office. Or her man. He was the twins' father. That was all.

"What do you think?" Mason asked.

Without hesitation she said, "I love everything about this house."

He smiled at her. "Me, too. I'm going to make an offer."

While he talked details with the Realtor, Annie browsed the rooms again. With every hobbling step she took, the longing for a traditional family grew. What she wouldn't give for the twins to have a father and mother. Correction, they had that. What she yearned for was all of them together in this house, a family unit, a happy home with kids. And marriage. Traditional all the way.

She hated being right about making a mistake coming with Mason to look at houses. Now there was a happy picture in her head, but reality never lived up to the image. If she'd never seen this place, she'd never have known what she was going to miss.

And she was going to miss being a family and living in this house.

Once a month the Blackburne family had dinner together. Attendance was mandatory unless you were bleeding, on fire, working or deployed to a foreign country. This ritual was one of the things Mason had missed most when he was gone. Today the family gathering had grown by two with the twins. Three counting Annie. She was the mother of his children and a part of them now.

Mason put a big blanket on the floor in the family room, set out toys in the center of it, then settled the twins on their backs.

Annie was sitting on the large sofa that separated the

kitchen and family rooms. She was sporting a brand-new, hot-pink walking cast since her recent follow-up ortho-pedic appointment. After a month the bone was healing nicely, but the doc didn't want her to put weight on it for another two weeks. A cautious approach of which Mason highly approved. For any patient, but especially for Annie.

She met his gaze and smiled. "They're not going to stay put on that blanket."

"I know." They'd grown so much in the last two months, rolling all over and getting up on all fours to rock back and forth, the prelude to crawling. That mile-stone wasn't very far off.

"As you well know, those toys are far less interesting than electrical cords and everything breakable."

"And I couldn't be prouder," he said. "They're curious. Exploring their environment is exactly what they're sup-posed to do at this age."

His dad took the roast outside to barbecue and his mom walked over to stand behind the couch, wiping her hands on a dish towel. "Gabriel and Dominic aren't used to ba-bies on the floor. Charlie and Sarah aren't like Lulu, who can get out of the way. Will they be okay?"

"My brothers or the twins?"

Flo laughed. "I was talking about the babies. We have to make sure everyone watches their step."

"Don't worry," Annie said. "I'm on it. I may not be able to move very fast, but I can direct traffic and, if all else fails, I've got my crutches. To make a point."

"Funny," Mason said and she smiled. He really liked her smile.

"It's too bad Kelsey had to work." His mom leaned a hip on the back of the sofa. "You're a doctor. You couldn't pull some strings to get her off?"

"Two things, Ma. I haven't been there very long, so

zero influence. And I'm not in charge of the nurses' scheduling." He grabbed up Charlie, who'd already rolled off the blanket onto his stomach and had his eye on something across the room. "Hey, bud, where do you think you're going?"

When the doorbell rang, Lulu started barking and rushed to greet whoever was there, waiting patiently for someone taller and with opposable thumbs to open the door.

Mason put a squirming Charlie back on the blanket and looked at Annie. "It's about to get wild. Brace yourself."

"It occurs to me that for the last five months I've lived in a constant state of being braced."

And it looked good on her. Normally her hair was pulled up in a ponytail, out of her way when she was busy with babies. Today it was down and fell past her shoulders, shiny and blond. For some reason the silky strands framing her face made her hazel eyes look more green. Or it might be the pink lip gloss. She was a woman who would turn men's heads and his brothers were both single. The thought had him bracing—for what he wasn't sure.

The two men walked into the room and bro-hugged Mason. They all had blue eyes and brown hair—clones, his mother always said about the family resemblance. Gabe and Dom knew about Annie and the twins but this was the first time they'd met.

Flo smiled at her sons. "I have to finish getting the rest of dinner ready. Mason, you handle introductions."

"Okay." He looked at his brothers. "This is Annie, the twins' mother."

The taller of the two moved closer and shook her hand. "I'm Gabriel. Sorry about your leg. Nice to meet you."

"Same here." She looked ruefully at the cast. "My fault for not watching where I was going."

"I'm Dominic." He was the youngest of the boys and had a thin scar on his chin. The details were never clear but it had something to do with a girl.

"Nice to meet you." She looked past Mason. "And those two little troublemakers are your niece and nephew, color coded. Sarah's in pink and—"

"Charlie's the one in blue who is checking out the movie collection." Mason moved quickly to grab him up before the stack of plastic DVD containers toppled on him. "He's moving faster all the time."

"And Sarah is right behind." Annie indicated the little girl who was scooting in the same direction as her brother. "She's ready to follow into whatever trouble he leads her."

"Cute kids," Dom said. "They look like Annie."

"Subtle, bro." Mason held his son and the curious little boy checked out the neckline of his T-shirt then explored his nose and ear.

"So you're a graphic artist," Gabe said to Annie.

"Yes."

Mason hadn't mentioned anything about her job. "How did you know that?"

"Her firm did a branding campaign for Make Me a Match. It was well-done. Smart. Clever. Visual."

"Thanks." The dog trotted over to Annie and she patted the seat beside her. Lulu didn't have to be asked twice and jumped up for a belly rub. "My friend Carla works for you. We met while I was involved in the project."

"Actually she's my aunt's personal assistant. And I'm only working there temporarily."

"So she said. I understand the business is still not where you'd like, financially speaking," Annie commented.

"True." His mouth pulled tight. "Aunt Lil is more focused on idealistic notions of relationships than numbers."

Their mother walked over to join the conversation and

clearly she'd been listening in. "My sister is a romantic and always has been. Did you know she fixed up your father and me?"

The three brothers stared at each other with equally blank expressions. Mason said, "That's news to me."

"Did she charge you for her services?" Gabe asked wryly.

"Of course she didn't."

Lulu barked once and jumped off the couch then trotted over to Sarah, who was reaching for the DVDs her brother had just looked over. Mason put Charlie back on the blanket and picked up his daughter.

"Her romanticism is the problem," Gabe continued. "Aunt Lil is in love with love and wants to give it away for free. It's a business and by definition the purpose of its existence is to provide a service for which customers are prepared to pay. In other words, make money."

Flo looked at Annie. "Lillian is a widow. She and Phil were deeply in love until the day he died. They never had children but she always says they were rich in so many ways because they had each other. She wants everyone to have what she did with her husband."

"They were lucky." Mason wasn't interested in what his aunt was selling. "Not everyone is."

"Is that the voice of experience?" Annie asked.

"Yes. I was married and the magic didn't last."

Annie had asked him why he'd sold his house before he deployed. He could have kept it, shut things down until he returned. But it held nothing but bad memories—loss, pain and a marriage imploding with no way to fix it.

Lulu sat on the baby blanket and Charlie touched her back. The dog was extraordinarily patient with the babies and was loving, even protective. While Mason cuddled

Sarah close, he caught Annie considering him, surprise in her eyes.

Then she turned to Gabe. "How do you match people up?"

"Clients fill out a profile, with a picture, then define their likes and dislikes. An algorithm picks up key words to narrow down potentially compatible people. Then we have that group fill out a more detailed questionnaire."

"What kind of questions?" Dom asked. He looked uncharacteristically interested.

Gabe thought for a moment. "Things like 'If you could share dinner with anyone in the world, who would it be?' Or 'If you could be a character in a movie, which one would you choose?' A very revealing one is 'Tattoo—for or against?'"

"Let's try it," his mother suggested. She looked at Annie and Mason. "You take the quiz."

Annie looked a little startled. "I don't know about Mason, but I'm not looking for a match."

"I know. It's just for fun," Flo said. "You're both single. Gabriel, give them a question."

"Okay." He sat on the couch. "How about which character in a movie. You first, Annie."

"Wow. No pressure." She blew out a breath. "Okay. I'd want to be Wonder Woman."

"You're already a superhero," his mom said.

"How sweet. Thanks, Flo."

"I mean it. Twins? That says it all."

"Actually it's not the superpowers I want," Annie clarified. "But that golden lasso would come in pretty handy. A way to know someone is telling the truth."

"Okay. Good answer," Dom said. "Mason, you're probably going to say Superman."

"No." He'd had time to think. "Sherlock Holmes."

"Because the supersleuth is so in touch with his feelings?" Gabe teased.

"No. He notices little things and figures out who's guilty. I can relate to that. I do a lot of mystery-solving in the ER because people don't always give me all the facts. Their symptoms are very general and vague. So I have to read between the lines to help them. It's my job to figure out what's wrong."

"Good answers, both of you," Gabe said. "But I'm not sure they would intersect for a match."

"Okay, next question," his mother said. "I like the tattoo one. How do you feel about them?"

"Not a fan. Don't have one and no plans to get one," Mason answered.

"Okay. The doctor doesn't like needles," Dominic teased.

"But you were in the army," Annie said.

"A tattoo is not a prerequisite for joining," he answered.

"Annie? What about you?" his mother asked.

She squirmed then sighed. "I have one. And I love it."

Mason looked at her, the skin he could see, and couldn't find her ink. His curiosity cranked up by a lot to know what it was and—more important—where. Discovering the location would involve taking clothes off and his body reacted enthusiastically to that thought.

"Strike two." Gabriel shook his head. "Last one. Who would you want to have dinner with?"

"That's easy," Annie said. "Eunice Golden."

"Who?" they all said at the same time.

"I was an art major. She's a painter and a pioneer in her field, focusing on nude male bodies in her earlier work."

Mason noted that the rest of his family looked as clueless and surprised as he felt. And now it was his turn. "I'd like to have dinner with the Surgeon General of the United States Army."

Gabe gave him a pitying look. "Probably no overlap there."

"Even though that person is a woman, appointed for the next couple years?"

"Too subtle." Gabriel shrugged. "If you were clients of Make Me a Match, you would not be paired off."

"Then it's a good thing neither one of us is looking to do that," Annie said.

"Oh, pooh," his mother said. "A few questions on a quiz isn't everything."

Mason had mixed feelings. On the surface they might not look compatible, but he agreed with his mom that a quiz didn't come with a guarantee of success. Everything in his first marriage had looked ideal, but together he and his wife were a disaster. Still, a quiz was stupid. Right? He agreed with Annie about that. He wasn't looking for a match any more than she was. He'd never failed a test in his life. Surely that's what was bothering him now.

Chapter Seven

Her hormones didn't take that matchmaking quiz but you wouldn't know it by the way they were stirred up.

Annie hadn't been able to stop thinking about those questions, through dinner and the rest of the evening. Now it was quiet in the house. Mason's brothers had gone and everyone else was in bed. The two of them were standing side by side, just putting the twins down. She had the crutches under her arms but didn't put much weight on them. Their arms brushed and she felt the contact all the way to her toes.

According to their answers to those questions, they weren't compatible, but her body wasn't paying any attention. Still, she had another question for Mason. She hadn't wanted to interrogate him in front of his family, but no one else was here now.

"Why didn't you tell me you were married?"

He glanced at the babies, who were drowsy but not sound asleep yet, and put a shushing finger to his lips. He angled his head toward the connecting bathroom and indicated she should follow him. Not wanting to disturb the twins, she limped after him. When he flipped the switch on the wall in his room, a nightstand lamp came on. There was a king-size bed with a brass headboard and an oak dresser with matching armoire.

Mason met her gaze. "I wasn't keeping it a secret. If I was still married, I'd have said something. But I'm not. The fact that I was married just never came up and it didn't cross my mind to mention that I'm divorced."

Logically that was true, but somehow it felt very relevant to Annie that she didn't know he'd been legally committed to a woman at one time. He'd taken that step because he'd been in love. It should simply be a fact from his past, just information, but she was having a reaction to this fact and it wasn't positive. She wasn't proud of it, but this feeling had a good many characteristics of jealousy.

And then she really looked into his eyes and saw the sadness. Facts were one thing; emotions were something else.

"Do you want to talk about it?" she asked.

He laughed but there was no humor in the sound. "You know those were the first words your sister said to me."

"Oh?"

He nodded. "My divorce was just final and I went to the bar. She was already there and came over, sat down on the stool next to me."

"She must have thought you looked sad. Like you do now." She moved closer to where he stood at the foot of the bed. Their bodies didn't touch but she could feel the warmth of his. "Did you tell her what was going on?"

"Only that my divorce became final that day but not why it happened in the first place. She heard the *D* word and suggested that there was a rebound activity guaranteed to take my mind off it."

Annie winced. It was hard to hear about her sister's

behavior. Jess was always there for her and she'd never forget it. "She wasn't a bad person."

"I know. That night we both needed a way to forget the stuff that was eating away at us."

"What were you trying to block out?" she asked.

"Failure. On so many levels." He sighed. "I fell in love with Christy and that was obviously not a success. I was in town to see my family, on leave from the army, when I met her at Patrick's Place, formerly The Pub. That's where I ran into your sister." He smiled. "She was beautiful and funny."

Annie wanted to hear about the woman he'd loved. "So, on the day your divorce was final you went back to the scene of the crime, so to speak."

"Yeah. I guess closure was on my mind. Coming full circle. A place to reflect on what went wrong." He smiled sadly. "The night Christy and I met, we couldn't stop talking. We were kicked out at closing time and sat on a bench outside for hours. Just talking."

"About what?" Annie asked.

"About what we wanted. Mostly that we both very much wanted to have children." He smiled at her. "I love kids. I'm like my mom that way. In fact, I thought about being a pediatrician for a while."

"Why didn't you?"

"I liked the adrenaline rush of emergency medicine."

"So what happened? With Christy, I mean."

"We had a long-distance relationship, but it worked, and then I proposed. We bought a house here in Huntington Hills. After all, I wouldn't be in the army forever and this town is where we wanted to settle and raise kids. We had a church wedding with both families there. She even got pregnant on our honeymoon. Everything was perfect."

"Magic," she said quietly.

That soul-deep sadness turned his eyes as hard as blue diamonds. "Until it wasn't."

"She lost the baby." Annie was just guessing.

He met her gaze and nodded. "We both took it hard, but she was really sucker punched. After all, she'd had a life inside her. And then it was gone. The doctor said we could try again right away, but I wanted to wait. She insisted we go for it and I gave in to make her happy."

Annie knew what he was going to say and just waited for him to put it into words.

"That time she made it almost through the first trimester before the miscarriage."

"Oh, Mason—" She put a hand over her mouth. "I can't even begin to imagine how hard that was for you both."

"And I don't have the words to explain the devastation we felt. The first time we believed—hoped—it was a fluke. Just one of those things. And the doctor assured us that it happens and no one can explain why. No reason we couldn't have more babies without any problems at all. Other couples did all the time."

"But not you." If this had a happy ending, the two of them wouldn't be standing there right now.

"The second miscarriage meant there was a pattern. Made us doubt we could have what we wanted most. Christy wanted to try again, right away, but this time I held firm on waiting." He dragged his fingers through his hair. "When a body goes through trauma like that, conventional wisdom suggests a sufficient amount of time to rest and rejuvenate." He looked lost in memories that were bad and it seemed as if he was going to stay there, but he finally went on. "She was angry. We both knew there was an overseas deployment in my future and she wanted a baby before that. We were drifting apart emotionally and physically. I suggested date nights, brought her flowers, tried to get back the dream we'd both wanted when we first met."

"And?"

"She was closed off. Until one night she came to me and was so much like the woman she'd been. I thought we were finding our way back. We had sex. She didn't mention that she had stopped birth control."

"She got pregnant?"

"Yes." A muscle in his cheek jerked and his eyes flashed with anger. "And she lost that baby, too."

"I'm so sorry, Mason."

He sighed. "That's when she gave up on us. I wanted to go to counseling, try to make things work. There were other ways to have the family we wanted. Surely we could be like my aunt Lillian and uncle Phil. But I couldn't fix what was wrong all by myself. No matter how much I wanted to."

"That's so sad."

"Yeah, sad. A small word for what I felt. I didn't just lose my children, I lost my wife. My family. I couldn't save anything. And I hated that house full of sad reminders."

"That's why you sold it before you were deployed," Annie said.

He nodded. "Most guys who shipped out left behind a wife and their kids. They didn't want to go, but sacrificed that time with loved ones in service to their country. But I couldn't wait to get out of here. I was glad to go."

"To leave the bad stuff behind."

"Yes. And to do some good. I couldn't help Christy, but I saved lives. To the best of my ability I stabilized the wounded, made sure soldiers who experienced traumatic injuries didn't lose an arm or leg. They thanked me for healing them, but it was just the opposite. They healed me." He met her gaze. "Then I got your email."

"About the babies possibly being yours."

He nodded. "I didn't know what to feel. So many times before I'd expected and hoped to have children. I didn't want to go all in again and get kicked in the teeth. Or was it just a cruel hoax? A miracle? A scam?"

"You're not the only one who thought that," she said wryly.

"I could have sent you a DNA sample, but I wanted to meet you—" he glanced past her, toward the room where the two babies slept side by side in a crib "—and the twins before doing it. Just being here made me feel more in control." He shrugged and there was a sheepish expression on his face. "Stupid, really. I know better than anyone control is an illusion. Because if it was up to me, those pregnancies would have resulted in healthy babies not miscarriages."

"And you might still be married," she said.

"I'm not so sure about that. I began to wonder if we just needed to believe we were in love because of wanting children so much. Thanks to science there are more options to have a family and I tried to talk to her about that or adoption, but she couldn't stand that everything wasn't normal, neat and tidy. Perfect. If she couldn't have that, she didn't want anything. Including me. By my definition, that isn't love."

It was such a devastating story of life dumping on him and love lost. And Mason looked so incredibly sad at the memories of the children who would never be. Annie couldn't help herself. She had to touch him, offer comfort. She moved one step closer and rested her crutches against the bed then put her arms around him.

"I'm so sorry you went through that, Mason."

He held completely still when her body pressed against his and didn't react for several moments. Annie was afraid that she'd somehow made things worse and started to step away.

"No."

She looked up and saw the conflict in his eyes just before he pulled her against him and lowered his mouth to hers. That achingly sweet touch set off fireworks inside her. It felt as if she'd been waiting for this since the moment she'd opened her door and seen him standing there in military camouflage, looking as exhausted as she'd felt.

Annie pressed her body closer but it wasn't enough as heat poured through her and exploded between them. He settled his hands at her waist then slid them down to her butt and squeezed softly before cupping her breasts in his palms. The kiss turned more intense as he brushed his tongue over her lower lip. She opened to him and let him explore, let the fire burn.

He backed up toward the bed and circled her waist with his arm, half carrying her with him. The only sound in the room was their combined breathing and it was several moments before they both heard a baby's whimper.

"It's Charlie." She pulled away and started to reach for the crutches but he stopped her.

"Should I apologize, Annie?"

That would mean he was sorry, and she didn't want him to be. She just wanted him so much.

"Annie?"

The whimper became more insistent and she put the crutches under her arms before turning away. "He's going to wake Sarah. You need to grab him, Mason."

He nodded and hurried into the other room.

She was sorry but only because of how very much she wanted him. Giving him that information wasn't smart.

He didn't believe in love any more than she did. So starting anything wasn't the wisest course of action. It had just happened because they were practically living on top of each other.

She could resist him for just a little bit longer. In a short time the cast would be off and she could go back home. And he would close escrow on the house and move into it. Either way, she wouldn't have to go to bed at night with only a bathroom between them.

Just to prove how spineless she was, Annie wasn't sure whether to be sad or glad about that.

It had been several days since Mason had kissed Annie and his son interrupted them. The kid's timing was bad. And she'd never answered the question about whether or not he should apologize for kissing her, touching her. *Wanting* her.

Now he was in bed, alone and frustrated. It was early and quiet, so the twins were not awake yet. He was, mostly because sleep had been hard to come by ever since that kiss. Might as well get up, he thought. There was a lot of house-buying stuff to do today.

He went in the bathroom and listened for sounds and movement on the other side of the door to the room where Annie slept with the babies. It was still quiet. That was good; she needed her sleep. After a shower and shave, he dressed in jeans and a T-shirt, then went to the kitchen.

His mother was there. More important, she'd made coffee. Moving a little farther into the room, he saw that Annie was there, too, already having a cup.

"Good morning," she said.

His mother was standing by the counter in front of a waffle iron. "Morning, Mason. Did you sleep well?"

"Like a rock," he lied. "Charlie and Sarah were quiet all night. I didn't hear a peep from them."

"I know." Annie sipped her coffee. "If only we could count on that every night."

Flo laughed. "By the time that happens, they'll be teenagers staying out all night."

"It was one time, Mom," he protested. "And I lost the car for a month. Are you ever going to let me forget that?"

"No." She gave him a look before turning back to watch what she was cooking. "And someone got up on the wrong side of the bed this morning. You're crabby."

"For being irritated that you still bring up teenage transgressions?"

"I was joking," she said.

He poured himself a cup of coffee. "Soon I will have my own place and you won't have to put up with me being crabby in the morning."

"Don't remind me."

"It's not like I'm going to the Middle East. The house isn't that far away."

She slid a waffle onto a plate and brought it to the table. "But you'll be gone. Everything's changing around here too fast for my liking."

Annie put butter and syrup on her breakfast and cut off a bite before looking at him. "Your mom and I were just talking about this. My cast is coming off in a couple of days and I'll be going back to my apartment with the babies."

"I'm going to miss all of you terribly," his mother said.

Mason had known this moment would eventually come but hadn't expected the announcement to knock the air out of him. He wasn't ready. "Annie, you need to be careful when the cast comes off and you put weight on the leg. Maybe you should think about staying here a little longer."

"I've already imposed long enough." She looked at his mom, gratitude in her eyes. "As much as I appreciate everything you've done, I don't want to take advantage of your hospitality."

"Please. Use us," Flo pleaded. "Stay as long as you want. We love having you here. It will be too quiet without you. I love those babies so much."

"I know." Annie smiled fondly at the other woman. "And they love you. I appreciate the offer and everything you've done for us more than I can tell you."

Mason was moving out soon and had deliberately put off thinking about being in the new house alone. After being with her and his kids, that was a lonely prospect. Because she'd helped him pick out the house, he couldn't help picturing Annie there. And the reminder that she wouldn't be didn't improve his mood. For that reason, he kept his mouth shut. No point in opening it and proving what his mother had pointed out. That he was crabby. If he did, there would be questions and he wouldn't want to answer them.

Annie was almost finished with her breakfast and sighed with satisfaction. "That was so good."

"If you stay, I'll make them every morning. I'm not above using food as a bribe," his mother said.

"Tempting." Annie grinned.

"At the risk of being pushy, since the twins are still asleep, it might be a good idea to get a shower in before they wake up," Flo said.

"That's not pushy. I was thinking the same thing." She stood and grabbed the crutches resting nearby. "Thanks for breakfast."

"You're very welcome. I'll listen for the babies and bring their bottles to you when they wake up."

"Thanks." She hobbled out of the room and smiled up at him as she passed.

Mason's heart skipped a beat and he resisted the urge to turn and watch her limp away. He'd gotten used to watching her, seeing a smile light up her face. And when he couldn't see it every day, there would be a significant withdrawal period.

His mother poured more coffee into her mug and blew on the top. "You should marry that girl."

It took a couple of moments for the words to sink in. And he still wasn't sure he'd heard her right. "What?"

"You should marry Annie," she said again, as if there was any doubt who "that girl" was.

"I can't believe you just said that. It's outrageous even for you."

"What does that mean? Even for me."

"I mean you can't just say whatever pops into your mind."

"I don't." She cradled her cup between her hands and leaned back against the counter. "That thought came to me when I saw your face. After Annie said she was moving back to her apartment. I didn't say it then. I waited."

"My face? What about it?"

"You looked as if someone just punched you in the gut," his mother said calmly.

"No, I didn't."

"Mason—" It was the dreaded Mom voice. "I know you. And if I'm being honest—"

"When are you not?" he asked wryly.

"It's a gift." She smiled at him. "I've never seen you happier than now—since Annie moved in here with Charlie and Sarah. It gives me such joy to see you this way."

He wanted to tell her she was wrong but he couldn't. It was true. He'd told Annie as much and risked her calling him silly. But from here to marriage was a big leap. "Mom, seriously—"

"I can see how much you like each other." At his look of irritation, she sighed. "I'm old, not dead. And I can see when two people have a connection."

"No one said anything about love. I respect and admire her very much but— And, in case you forgot, we were zero for three on Gabriel's questionnaire."

"I'll deny it if you ever tell him I said this, but that quiz is not helpful. I see the way you and Annie look at each other."

"How is that?"

"Like you want to be alone. There were sparks, Mason, and it's more than respect and admiration."

He didn't want to discuss this. It was crazy. Although there was that really hot kiss. "You're imagining things, Mom."

"I have an imagination, I'll admit. But trust me on this, you and Annie have sparks. Successful marriages have started with less. Including me and your dad."

"You weren't in love when you got married?"

"We were young, wildly attracted to each other. And pregnant with you."

"What?" That was a shock. "I never knew that. You had to get married?"

"We didn't have to. Our parents were supportive. But doing the right thing was important to both of us." She shrugged. "The realization of how much we loved each other came after you were born. We were tired and stressed about making ends meet, but our bond and commitment and love grew stronger every day because of how much we both loved you. Your father was the right man for me and my hormones knew it before my heart did."

The union his parents shared was the bar by which

Mason judged success. He had no idea their deepest commitment to each other had started with him. "Still, Mom—"

"You and Annie have two children together. You're parents and good ones. In spite of Gabriel's dopey quiz, you're compatible. I can see it the way you work together with the babies. If there were any cracks, the strain of caring for them would break them wide open. If anything, you two have grown stronger from the experience."

That statement had the ring of truth to it. "Maybe, but—"

"Please don't go by those completely irrelevant questions. Fortunately your aunt Lillian relies on her instincts about a man and woman when she's matchmaking. Her success rate is pretty high, too." She smiled. "That intuition for pairing up a man and woman runs in the family."

"Even if you're right about Annie and me—"

"I am." She pointed at him. "And you're going to say, why rush things? And I will say, why wait? You care and so does she. Together you can give Charlie and Sarah a stable home, a loving environment. And all of that under one roof."

"This idea is crazy, Mom."

She tapped her lip. "And your paternity petition is still pending with the court. It couldn't hurt to show that you're making a legal commitment to their mother, as well."

"We don't have to be married for me to present a strong case. I have the DNA proof."

"Of course you do. And that was one of those things that just popped into my mind. But this isn't. If you don't get out of your own way and marry her, someone else just might snatch her up, right out from under your nose. That old boyfriend could still be lurking."

"Not after what he called my children." Mason still wanted to clock him for that.

"Maybe not him, but Annie is pretty, smart and funny. Someone is going to sweep her off her feet. It should be you."

When Mason was in medical school, there hadn't been a class on jealousy, but that didn't mean he couldn't diagnose it now. The knot in his gut, elevated blood pressure and the pounding in his temples. All symptoms that confirmed the thought of Annie with another guy was just wrong.

But that didn't answer the question.

What was he going to do about it?

Chapter Eight

Annie sat on the medical exam table at the orthopedic office and watched Dr. Jack Andrews cut through her cast. Mason had driven and was standing by her, but there was something on his mind other than freedom for her leg. She wasn't sure how she knew that but she did.

The doctor shut off the mini-saw and set it aside, then pried apart the cast and cotton-like material beneath that was sticking to her skin. He smiled. "How does the leg feel?"

"Like heaven. But it looks gross. All white and shriveled and different from the other one." She glanced at Mason, not sure she wanted him to see the grossness and not sure why she should care that he did. And it was a waste of energy because he'd already seen.

"Don't worry. That's normal for what you've been through." Dr. Andrews was a colleague of Mason's, young and good-looking, but his opinion on the attractiveness of her leg didn't matter.

"It doesn't look normal." She glanced at Mason again to see if he was grossed out. He didn't look repulsed. He looked like Mason. Strong, steady and incredibly cute Mason.

"Soak the limb in warm water twice a day for the first few days and wash it with mild soap. Use a soft cloth or even gauze. That will help remove the dead skin."

"Does she need to take it easy, Jack?" Just like Mason to ask that.

"As you know, the muscles are atrophied from lack of use. I'm going to prescribe physical therapy for a few weeks so the experts can work on teaching you exercises to strengthen it. In a very short time you'll build the leg up again." He met her gaze, his own serious. "Your balance might be somewhat compromised after weeks of not walking normally. Go slow. Use the crutches at first to see how you do. But it won't be long before you'll forget this ever happened."

"I doubt that." His smile was nice, she thought, but her insides didn't quiver at all from it. Not like when Mason smiled at her.

And the experience hadn't been all bad. She'd gotten to know his family, how wonderful they were. He'd been pretty wonderful, too. The twins were lucky to have him for a father. Was he really determined to stay a bachelor? He was so loving with the babies, it was hard to believe he wouldn't meet a woman who would convince him to try again.

"You've been a perfect patient, Annie."

"And you've been a perfect doctor, Doctor," she said. "No offense but I hope I never have to see you again."

Mason laughed. "She means professionally."

"I got that," the other man said. "The feeling is mutual."

She shook his hand. "Seriously, thank you so much for everything."

"You're welcome."

When they were alone, Mason handed her the sneaker she hadn't used for six weeks.

"Thanks, Mason."

"For?"

"Do I have to pick one thing?" She thought for a moment. "First of all for reminding me to bring my sock and shoe. I'd have forgotten if not for you. It seems like forever since I needed it and I'd have crutched right out of the house without it."

"Happy to help."

"I also want to thank you for going above and beyond the call of duty these last weeks. And for being a good father to the twins."

"I should be thanking you. For making sure I knew about them."

"It was the right thing to do." Her stomach did the quivery thing when he smiled.

"Are you ready to get out of here?"

"So ready." The crutches were braced against the exam table and she grabbed them. "Following doctor's orders. No point in setting myself back. But now I can pick up my babies, not just wait for someone to hand them to me."

"How do you feel about grabbing some lunch before we go home to the kids?"

"Would it be all right with your mom? Does she have to be somewhere?"

"It was her idea." He opened the exam room door.

"In that case, I'm on board."

They walked down the hallway with medical offices on either side, then into the lobby area, where automatic doors opened to the outside. Annie was using the crutches to take part of her weight·but felt pretty good moving on her own two feet. No dizziness or pain, just some minor weakness. She felt free, happy, and was looking forward to lunch with Mason.

It was one of those perfect fall days in Southern California and she was enthusiastically on board when he suggested getting sandwiches to eat in the park. There was one a short distance from his new house where they found a picnic table with a roof overhead not far off the cement walkway.

They were sitting side by side, looking at the white gazebo surrounded by yellow-, coral- and pink-flowered bushes. There were towering trees, shrubs, green grass and just a perfect amount of breeze.

"It's so beautiful here." Annie sighed contentedly then took the paper-wrapped turkey sub sandwich and napkin he handed her and immediately unwrapped it.

"Yeah." He set his own lunch on the table and didn't do anything but stare at it.

"I can't wait until Charlie and Sarah are big enough to run around and play on the kids' equipment." She pointed to a bright yellow, blue and red structure with tubes and stairs surrounded by rubberized material for unexpected landings.

"Uh-huh," he answered absently. Definitely distracted about something.

Annie wanted to know what was up with him. Maybe her comment about him being a good father had somehow freaked him out, put pressure on him. With her luck, the bum leg making her dependent on him had made him change his mind about wanting to take responsibility for the twins. Showed him he wasn't cut out for being a dad and he wanted off the hook. She couldn't stand it anymore and had to know.

She put her sandwich down without taking a bite. "Look, just spit it out. Get it over with."

"Spit what out?"

"Whatever it is you're so jumpy about."

"I'm not jumpy." But he didn't sound too sure of that.

"You've been preoccupied since we left the house. The whole time we've been gone you hardly said two words. Except to the doctor. So, just tell me what's going on. I can handle it. I've been alone before."

"What are you talking about?"

"You're responsible enough to not feel comfortable telling me but decent enough to do it to my face. You don't want to be tied down by the twins." The quivery feeling in her stomach became something else that made her want to cry.

He stared at her for several moments then shook his head. "You couldn't be more wrong."

"So I've made a fool of myself and you don't have anything on your mind?"

"No, you're right about that," he confirmed. "I'm actually surprised you know me well enough to recognize that."

"Of course I do." Although she was a little surprised, too. And also really anxious about what was going on in his head. "So, I say again, just get it over with. Please."

"That's what someone says when they think it's going to be something bad."

Damn aviator sunglasses were sexy as all get-out but she couldn't see his eyes. The window to the soul. A clue to what he was feeling. "Because it is bad, right?"

"I didn't think so, but I guess it could be interpreted that way."

"Darn it, Mason. Will you just tell me what we're talking about here?"

"Okay." He blew out a breath. "I was going to ask you to marry me."

Shut the front door! Annie's jaw dropped and she blinked at him for several moments. Unsure what to say, she finally asked, "Why?"

"That should be a simple enough answer but in our case it's complicated." He angled his body toward her. "I don't know where to start."

"So we're not talking love here." Please don't be talking love, she thought. They both had the scars to prove that was a losing proposition.

"Different *L* word. We *like* each other."

"True." And that was so much safer.

"And respect," he said. "I respect you a lot and I'm pretty sure you feel the same about me."

"Definitely." Even when she thought he was going to leave, she gave him credit for doing it in person. "Okay, but we could just go back to the way things were before I broke my leg. I'll move back to my apartment and you can visit any time you want."

He sighed. "I want more. I'll be moving into the house. It just seems like a natural transition to do that together. If I hadn't spent time with you and the kids in the same house, it would have taken me longer to get to this place, but I would have eventually."

"And that is?"

"I don't want to visit my kids. I want to live with them under the same roof, together with their mother. You've said that the apartment is too small and you were going to look for a bigger place." He shrugged. "I just happen to have one. And since the broken leg and living with my folks, you're half out of there anyway. If we just move your stuff to my place, it would be easier. You love the house."

"I do. And your points are all good ones. But we could just live together," she suggested. "Share expenses. Baby-sitting. It's a little unconventional, but this situation is the very definition of that. We don't have to get married to be a family."

He took off his glasses and his eyes were bluer and more intense than ever before. "I want a *traditional* family. For me and for them. With you."

Traditional family. The words struck a chord in Annie's soul, a tune she didn't fully realize had been playing her whole life. She'd never experienced what Mason was offering her. But he had and she'd seen it in action. He knew how to do the family thing. It was as natural to him as breathing. If he was going to abandon her and the twins, he'd have done it already. He wouldn't be offering her a legal commitment.

"Annie?"

"I'm thinking." She met his gaze. "Maybe we should try dating or something first?"

"So you don't want a traditional relationship."

"I didn't say that. Actually, I've wanted that my whole life," she admitted.

"Okay. We could date, but we'll wind up right back here. I feel as if we've been more than dating since we met. And it's been pretty terrific. You. The kids. It's what I want."

His marriage broke up because his wife couldn't have children. She and Mason were already parents. Annie did like him. A lot. It wasn't love, but that was so much better. Who needed drama and heartbreak? He was steady. Supportive. Sweet. She was happy around him and enjoyed spending time together. She looked forward to seeing him after work.

And there was that kiss.

"Come on, Annie." He took her hand and brushed his

thumb over her left ring finger. "This is the right thing to do."

Her exact words just a little while ago about letting him know he was a father. She waited for some sign, a knot in her stomach, a shred of doubt in her mind, something to make her say no way. But there was nothing. Just a feeling that this could work really well.

"Okay, Mason. I'll marry you."

Escrow on the house had closed less than a week ago so Annie had been busy helping Mason move things in. It had kept her too busy to be nervous about the wedding. But two weeks after his proposal they were going to take vows. Things had come together quickly, partly because it was small, partly because Florence Blackburne was a tireless volunteer on their behalf and wanted this to happen.

On Thursday evening two weeks after becoming engaged, Annie and Mason stood in front of someone who was licensed by the State of California to marry them. Flo had found him on the internet. He was a skinny twentysomething who looked like a college student earning extra money. Carla was her maid of honor; Mason's dad was the best man. His mom and sister held the babies, who looked completely adorable. Charlie had on a little black suit and red bow tie that he kept pulling off. Sarah was wearing a pink-tulle, cap-sleeved dress with a darker pink satin ribbon that tied in a big bow in the back.

If anyone thought Annie's tea-length red dress was an odd choice, they kept it to themselves. The bodice was snug-fitting chiffon and the full, flirty, asymmetrical midcalf hem flattered her figure. Muscle was building up in her leg but she was a little sensitive about it being thinner than the other one.

Patrick's Place had been closed for this private function. Carla was BFFs with the owner, Tess Morrow Wallace, and had facilitated the arrangements. Annie was aware that Mason had met his ex-wife here, but the interior was new so she chose to be superstitious about that, in a positive way.

Tables and chairs were arranged to form an aisle for Annie to walk down. Now the Blackburne family formed a semicircle around Annie and Mason in the center of the room. Together they had written their own vows to each other and she was glad there wouldn't be any surprises because the unexpected always had a way of being bad.

Annie cleared her throat to go first. "I, Annie Campbell, take you, Mason Blackburne, to be my husband, and father to Sarah and Charlie. You're a good, decent man who takes care of them and me. In front of everyone gathered here, I promise to honor and cherish you and put the family we're making today above all else."

In his black suit, Mason was more handsome than she'd ever seen him. The blue stripes in his silk tie brought out the intense color of his eyes in the best possible way. And his smile... Her heart fluttered and she wasn't sure if nerves had chosen this moment to trip her up or if it was something else a lot more complicated. He didn't touch her with any part of his body, but their gazes met and locked and made her feel as if he was holding her in his arms.

"I, Mason Blackburne, take you, Annie Campbell, for my wife. I solemnly promise to respect, honor and care for you and our children to the very best of my ability. It's good and right, and I look forward to making a family with you and Sarah and Charlie."

She and Mason exchanged plain gold bands, after which the internet guy said, "I now pronounce you husband and wife."

Neither of them moved and Gabriel Blackburne said, "Isn't this the part where you kiss the bride?"

Annie felt a quiver in her stomach and instinctively turned her face up to look at Mason. He smiled then slowly lowered his mouth as her eyes drifted closed. His lips were soft and chaste but that didn't stop memories of their first kiss from popping into her mind. This felt like a down payment on a promise for later. And it didn't last nearly long enough.

Mason pulled back and said, "Hello, Mrs. Blackburne. How do you feel?"

Good question. This was a done deal now. Legal. She'd made decisions in the past and instantly had second thoughts if not outright regrets. What-the-heck-have-I-done moments. But this wasn't one of them. Mason was all the good things a man should be and there was no denying that sparks happened every time he touched her. Most important, the babies would have their father and a normal life.

"I feel great," she said, smiling back at him.

"Me, too."

"Me, three." Carla hugged both of them. "Congratulations. You make a beautiful couple."

"I couldn't agree more." With Sarah in her arms, Florence gave her son a one-armed hug before doing the same to Annie. "Welcome to the family, sweetheart."

"Thank you." Unexpectedly, Annie's eyes filled with emotional tears. Her voice only caught a little when she said, "It's really nice to have a family."

The rest of the Blackburnes lined up to congratulate them. All but Gabriel, she noticed. The bar was open and he'd walked over for a drink. Then she was swept up in the celebration and Charlie was leaning toward her, wanting to be held. Sarah did the same to Mason.

He met her gaze and there was a tender look in his. "We're a family and as soon as the court recognizes me as their father, we'll be official."

"That won't be long," she said. "But I'm officially starving right now."

"Let's go eat. Mom—"

"On it, honey."

Adjacent to the main bar area was a restaurant where tables had been arranged in long rows to accommodate the family. Two high chairs had been set up on the end for the babies. Florence herded everyone to their assigned places, with Annie and Mason surrounded by their maid of honor and best man.

When they were all in place Flo said, "If Annie and Mason have no objection, I'd like to make the first toast."

He looked at her and she nodded. "Take it away, Mom."

"It gives me great pleasure to welcome Annie to our family. My son is a lucky man." She held up a flute of champagne. "Peace and long life."

Her husband frowned a little. "Isn't that from *Star Trek*?"

"Maybe, but it fits." Flo shrugged and nodded at him. "Okay, best man, it's your turn."

John stood and looked around the table. "It's a blessing to be surrounded by my children and grandchildren to celebrate this happy occasion. Mason, you're a lucky man. Annie, I'm very happy to have another daughter. Congratulations."

For the second time she felt emotion in her throat and tears gather in her eyes. She blinked them away and smiled at him. Everyone clinked glasses, and soon after food was served. There were many volunteers to help keep the babies occupied so that they could eat their wedding dinner without interruption. The meal was followed by a beautiful red-velvet cake garnished with roses around the base. Everyone was mingling, chatting and having a good time.

Then Annie and Mason somehow found themselves alone in the crowd. He had a glass of champagne in his hand and said to her, "So, I have a toast."

"Oh?"

"I'm not a man of words, so don't expect profound."

She smiled. "You do okay."

"Right." He held up his glass. "Here's to us."

"To us," she said, touching her glass to his. "It was a nice wedding."

"Agreed. But on the one-to-ten nice scale, that dress is a fifteen." There was more than a little male interest in his eyes. "Why red?"

"Symbolism and maybe a bit of superstition." She sipped her champagne. "Red can be a sign of good luck, joy, prosperity, celebration, happiness and long life."

He nodded and slid one hand into the pocket of his suit pants, striking a very masculine pose. "All good reasons. And not traditional."

She couldn't tell whether or not that bothered him. "I know we took this step to have a traditional family for the twins, but—"

"You think I'm upset that you didn't wear white?"

"Are you?" she asked.

"No. This couldn't be more different from my first wedding and that's a very good thing. Only—" It looked as if something had just occurred to him. "You've never done this before. It's a really bad time to ask. And, for the record, I'm an idiot for not thinking about it until just now. Are you okay with a small wedding?"

"If I wasn't, you'd have heard. In case you haven't noticed, I'm not shy about standing up for myself."

"Yeah, I figured that out the first time we met. And I quote, 'Do the swab and leave your contact information. Now please go.'"

"Yeah." She grinned. "Not my finest hour. In my defense, I was tired and the twins were teething."

"No, I get it. You're independent and it's one of the things I like about you. I just wanted to make sure you're fine with the size of this wedding because having something bigger would have meant waiting—"

"Speaking of that—" Gabriel Blackburne joined them and had apparently overheard. He had a tumbler in his hand containing ice and some kind of brown liquor. "Why didn't you?"

"Didn't we what?" Mason asked.

"Wait to get married."

Annie guessed Mason hadn't discussed with his brother why they'd decided to take this step. And she couldn't read the other man's expression. It wasn't animosity exactly, more like concern. There was also something dark and maybe a bit bleak, but she sensed that was personal to Gabriel and had nothing to do with her and Mason.

"Don't get me wrong." Gabriel took a sip from his glass. "I wish you both all the best. But why rush things?"

"It's about being a family," Mason explained. "My escrow closed. Annie and the kids were half moved out of her apartment because of the broken leg. It seemed a good time to merge households."

"A merger. My job is turning around failing businesses, but…" His brother's expression was wry. "Be still my heart."

"Annie and I talked this through and we agreed it was the best thing for the children. We want to give them a conventional home. Like you and I had."

"Yes, we did." Gabriel's expression grew just a little darker. "But a successful family starts with a strong core."

"It does," Annie said. "We are in complete agreement about the twins and raising them in a stable and loving environment."

"So you are in love?" Again he glanced at Annie but his gaze settled squarely on his brother. "Because if I'm not mistaken, you were never going there again."

Mason's eyes narrowed but his voice was even and casual when he responded. "Annie is the most courageous and warm woman I've ever met. And it seems to me that if you're this cynical, you aren't the best person to be working in a business that is supposed to help people find their life partner."

"You are so right. That's why my goal is to make that business profitable again as quickly as possible so I can leave." He finished the last of the liquor in his glass. "I'm not telling you anything you don't already know, but this 'merger' will change everything."

"For the better," Mason said.

Annie knew the man meant well but she shivered at the words. Before she could think that through, she recognized Sarah's tired cry and knew Charlie wouldn't be far behind.

"Mason, I think the grace period on the twins' good mood has just expired."

"Yeah."

"I sincerely wish you all the best," Gabriel said again. "You have a beautiful family. I envy you, brother."

Mason smiled and held out his hand. His brother took it then pulled him in for a bro hug. "See you Sunday at Mom's."

They said good-bye and went to retrieve their children from Mason's mother and father. Annie took Sarah and

Mason grabbed Charlie, who rubbed his face against his father's shoulder. It was a classic sign of being overtired.

"We need to get these guys home," she said to Florence.

"Why don't you two stay?" his mother said. "I can keep them at my house overnight."

And that was the exact moment it really sank in for Annie that being married *did* change everything. When you married a man, he became your husband and you were his wife. A couple. And couples had sex on their wedding night.

Chapter Nine

After his mother offered to keep the kids, Mason could have kissed the woman. A wedding night alone with Annie sounded just about perfect to him. Not that he didn't love his children to the moon and back, but… Taking that sexy red dress off his new bride sent his imagination and other parts of him into overdrive. There hadn't been a specific conversation about sex but after that kiss he figured they were good. If one of the babies hadn't interrupted them, their first time would already have happened.

But it felt right to have waited until after they were married. Right for Annie somehow. That was probably stupid, but that's the way he felt.

"What do you think?" he asked her.

Annie looked a little pale and her smile was forced. "That is so sweet and thoughtful. I can't thank you enough for the offer. But we got married to be a regular family. It doesn't seem right not to have them with us on our first night."

Mason had mixed feelings. He felt like biomedical waste because it crossed his mind that he wanted her all to himself. That made him a selfish jerk for not wanting to share her. The other part of him realized how important it was to get this right.

"We appreciate it, Mom. But I agree with Annie."

This was better, he told himself. No pressure on either of them. The twins came first and that meant bathing, feeding and rocking them to sleep. That might happen by midnight and they would fall into bed exhausted, too tired for... Anything.

Mason tried not to be disappointed and almost succeeded. Almost.

They bundled the kids into jackets because the October evening was chilly. Buckling them into the carriers that fit into the car was more of a challenge. Being overtired and out of sorts, they cried and fought the restraints, but he and Annie out-stubborned them.

She hugged his mom and dad. "Thank you for everything."

"You're so welcome, sweetheart." Flo smiled. "I think you'll make my son a happy man."

Annie glanced at him but her expression was impossible to read. "I'm glad you think so."

Mason looked around the pub's dining area and noticed a busboy busy loading dirty dishes from their dinner into a plastic tote. Still, he had to ask. "You're sure you don't need us for anything here?"

"No. We have it covered. Take your family home."

"I like the sound of that." He looked at Annie and she nodded. "Good night, all. Thanks for coming."

His parents had picked up Annie and the twins, so her car was at the house. They walked outside, each carrying a crying infant. Even after they were secured in the rear seat of his SUV the crying continued. It was impossible to have a conversation over the high-pitched wails. Fortunately it didn't take long to get home.

He pulled into the driveway beside her small, compact car. Annie opened the front passenger door and the overhead light came on.

"I'm glad they didn't fall asleep," she said.

"Why?" Because she didn't want to be alone with him? Was she trying to tell him something?

"Because I'd be tempted to put them to bed without even undressing them. They need baths, jammies and bottles. Never too soon to start a routine."

"Good point."

In the house they set Sarah and Charlie facing each other on the family room rug. The settling-in process was ongoing so boxes were scattered throughout and furniture was still scarce. Shopping for it hadn't been a priority. The babies' nurseries were put together, each with its own crib. But the cartons lined the walls in the rest of the rooms and needed to be unpacked.

Annie looked around ruefully. "Is this all my stuff or yours?"

"Fifty-fifty." He settled his hands on his hips, pushing back his suit coat. "And I have one more load from my storage unit."

She sighed. "It doesn't feel like we'll be settled anytime soon."

Was she trying to get a message across? Or was he reading too much darkness into that conversation with Gabriel tonight? Until then he'd felt just fine about this whole thing. Now… Time would tell.

The twins had been quiet since coming into the house, both of them looking around with wide eyes. Charlie rubbed his face, a sure sign of an imminent meltdown.

Annie saw it, too. "I'm going to get out of this dress."

It had been a long shot at best, but there went any chance of him sliding the sexy material off her. She was probably going to slip into something more comfortable but it would likely be sweatpants not lingerie. He wasn't proud of these thoughts, but he was a guy.

"Okay. I'll entertain them while you change for operation bath time."

"Roger that." She smiled then hurried out of the room.

Charlie's whimpers turned to full-blown wails, so Mason unbuckled him and lifted the little guy into his arms. That was Sarah's cue to commence with her own high-pitched vocal demonstration of unhappiness. She arched her back against the straps holding her in, but he didn't want to undo them and have her sliding out of the seat.

He put his son on the rug. *Don't judge*, he thought, grateful the germ police weren't around. He was getting a bath soon. Then he freed Sarah and cuddled her close for a moment while her brother took off on another crying jag.

Mason went down on one knee and put a hand on the boy's belly. "I honestly don't know how your mother did it all by herself."

"It wasn't easy." Annie had quietly entered the room and moved closer.

He looked up. "And yet somehow you made it look easy."

"I doubt that. But thanks." She held out her arms for Sarah. "Now, unless you want soap and water all over that nice suit, you should change into a slicker and rubber boots."

"Understood."

Mason put on jeans and a T-shirt, then grabbed his son off the floor and followed Annie into the bathroom that connected the twins' nurseries. Their small tub was already out on the counter by the sink and she filled it with warm water before handing her baby off to him. He had one in each arm and watched her set out two sets of PJs, diapers and two fluffy towels.

She took Sarah and stripped off the dress, tights and diaper before lowering her into the water. Little hands and feet started moving. Crying stopped and splashing started.

"They do love the water, but there's no playing tonight." Annie washed, rinsed and lifted Sarah out before quickly wrapping the towel around her.

Mason had removed Charlie's clothes while his sister was being bathed. They handed off babies and he took Sarah into her room and dressed her in the clothes Annie had put out. By the time he finished, Charlie was in a towel and on the way to his room. He stood in the doorway, holding his sweet-smelling daughter.

"Assembly line works like a charm," he said.

She looked up for a moment and smiled. "An extra pair of hands makes this so much easier."

"We make a good team."

"Yes, we do." She finished putting on Charlie's one-piece blue sleeper. After picking him up, Annie held him close and brushed a hand over his back while he rubbed his eyes again. "You're a tired boy. Let's give them a bottle and put them to bed."

"The same crib? Or their own?"

She met his gaze, thinking that one over. "I don't know. Thoughts, Doctor?"

"Not a pediatrician but… Sooner or later they have to be in their own rooms. This is a new environment anyway, so it might be a good time to try. The worst that could happen is they won't go to sleep and we put them in the same crib again."

Annie nodded. "And if it works, they might sleep

through each other's fussiness and we'd only have one awake at a time. That sounds too good to be true. But I vote we give it a try."

"It's unanimous," he said.

After bottles, the twins were asleep. They carefully put them in their respective rooms then met in the hall to wait for the crying to start. Five minutes went by and all was quiet. Annie held up two fingers, indicating they should give it another couple of minutes. They both held their breaths but there wasn't a sound.

She angled her head toward the family room and he followed her there. "I am cautiously optimistic that this just might work."

"A wild prediction."

"You're a pessimist," she scolded. And sure enough, ten minutes passed without a peep. "Cautious optimism rules. It would appear they're in for the night. What are we going to do with ourselves?"

Then her eyes widened and a blush covered her cheeks. Any other time the kids would have been fussy and out of sorts, but not now. It had been smooth and easy getting the twins to sleep, but Mason sensed a whole pile of awkward in the room. He knew her pretty well now and there was no question that Annie looked tense.

He had wanted her practically from the first moment he'd seen her and now she was his wife. But he'd been getting vibes from her and not the ones he was hoping for.

There were so many ways this could go sideways and he didn't want to do the wrong thing. He didn't want to be another jerk in her life. That was no way to start out. On the other hand, they *were* married. But one of them had to address this situation.

He cleared his throat. "Annie, you're probably really tired and—"

When he stopped and let the meaning of his words sink in, a charged silence joined the awkwardness dividing them like the wall that once separated East and West Berlin. Her eyes changed color, as if a light had gone out. But that was probably his imagination.

Finally she nodded. "It has been a long day—"

"Right. Sure."

She half turned toward the hall. "I think I'll turn in now."

"Okay."

When she was gone, Mason poured himself a Scotch and leaned against the island that overlooked a family room empty of furniture. If one was into symbolism, this would be a doozy. He had thought marrying her would solve problems and fill up his life. He'd had no idea it would be just the beginning of complications.

What was it she'd said? It was never too early to get into a routine. What did this say about the routine they were starting?

Annie barely slept on her wedding night but not for the reason she should have not slept. And a week later nothing had changed. They slept in the same bed but his long shifts at the hospital and caring for the twins became an excuse for him to avoid intimacy. The rejection hurt on many levels, but what stung most was her poor judgment. How wrong she'd been about the sparks between them. Well, half-wrong, anyway. She was the only one who'd felt them.

They had made legal promises to each other, not physical ones, but she'd assumed that would all work out based on one hot kiss. She'd made the first move then but desperately wanted him to make the first move now. Annie had her pride and didn't want him to sleep with her just because they'd said "I do." Or worse, pity.

She threw back the covers and went into the master bedroom's adjoining bath. Lingering humidity and the sexy male scent of cologne told her Mason had recently showered. Apparently she'd slept harder than she'd thought because she hadn't heard him. Obviously he'd taken care to be quiet. That was thoughtful and he got points, but her anger and hurt refused to budge.

After taking care of business, she checked on the twins and smiled tenderly at each of them still sleeping in their very own rooms. Little angels, she thought. They were safe, secure—loved. That's all that mattered, right? Right.

Still, quiet time was rare and she went down the hall toward the kitchen to make coffee and enjoy a peaceful moment before all hell broke loose. The hallway opened to the family room, which was adjacent to the kitchen. With his back to her, Mason was standing there in blue scrubs because he was on his way to work. She so didn't want to face him. Eventually she'd have to, just not right this minute.

But before she could scurry back to bed and pull the blanket over her head, he turned and spotted her. She froze, feeling like a deer caught in headlights.

"I'm sorry if I woke you," he said.

Don't be nice to me, she thought. *Just don't.* If he was, she would have to let go of her anger and let down the only shield she had to keep out the hurt scratching to get in. She also couldn't ignore him, no matter how ill at ease she felt.

Annie moved closer, trying to act as if all was fine and normal, but her legs felt stiff and trying to smile made her face hurt. "You didn't wake me."

"Good." He nodded a little too enthusiastically, signaling that he felt awkward, too.

She was in the kitchen, but kept her distance from him. "Charlie and Sarah are still asleep."

His gaze didn't quite meet hers. "They must be growing."

"I guess so."

After a few moments of tense silence he said, "I made coffee. Would you like a cup?"

"Yes. Thanks." This was so stiff, tense, awkward and overly polite, it made her want to scream.

He seemed relieved to have something to do and immediately took a mug from the cupboard above the coffee maker, then poured steaming hot liquid into it. Packets of her artificial sweetener were in a bowl on the counter and he ripped one open before shaking the powder in. Then he grabbed the container of flavored creamer from the refrigerator and poured that in, lightening the dark color to the exact shade she liked. The thoughtfulness was both incredibly sweet and super annoying. He held out the cup.

"Thanks," she said grudgingly. She took a sip and noted that it was perfect. This was probably where she should meet him halfway. "How late are you working tonight?"

"It's twelve hours, so seven to seven. Probably seven thirty-ish."

"Ish?"

"If an emergency comes in around change of shift, I could be delayed getting out. Every day is different. Why?"

"I was wondering about dinner."

"Right." He leaned back against the counter and folded his arms over his chest.

Annie swallowed against a sudden surge of overwhelming attraction for the man she'd married. She'd seen him in scrubs before as he'd often come by the apartment after work to see Charlie and Sarah. When they'd been living with his folks she'd seen him before he'd left for the hospital, too. In her opinion the lightweight top and pants looked comfortable, like pajamas, and weren't the sexiest ensemble in the world.

But the über masculine pose he struck drew her gaze to the contours of his chest and the width of his shoulders. She had the most powerful urge to be in his arms, held tight against his body. Except he'd shut the door on that and every night since then rejection grew wider and more painful.

"If you get hungry, go ahead and eat without me."

"Hmm?" What were they talking about? Her mind had gone completely blank.

"Dinner. Tonight. If I'm not home and you need to eat, don't wait for me."

"Okay. I'll make you a plate."

"Don't go to any trouble," he said. "And I'm sure I'll be home in time to help with baths."

"Right." A devoted dad. He wanted to help with the nighttime ritual. "Unless they're really fussy, I'll hold off until you get here."

"Great." Again with the enthusiastic nodding. He was going to give himself head trauma.

But again the sweet consideration irrationally ticked her off. It was official. She was crazy. "Okay, then."

She sipped her coffee and looked anywhere but at him. "If you have to leave for work, don't let me keep you."

"I have a few minutes."

She waited for him to say more but he didn't. Since you could cut the tension in the room with a scalpel, she would think he'd have jumped on her suggestion and hit the road. But, oddly, he seemed reluctant to leave. Of course, that was about his children, not her.

"Would you like some breakfast before you go?" It seemed wrong somehow not to offer.

"No. Thanks, though. I'll just grab something in the doctor's dining room. At the hospital," he added.

"Right. Because it's logical that the doctor's dining room would be at the hospital." Was she awful for not resisting the urge to tease him?

"This is what you might call a 'duh' moment." The corners of his mouth curved up, cracking the tension a little. For the first time, he met her gaze. "What's on your agenda for today?"

Look at him. Asking his wife what her plans were for the day. Just like any normal couple. If he could pretend, so could she.

"I'm going to the apartment to clean out the last of my things."

"You should let me help with that," he said.

How ironic was this? She was ending her old life at the same time she was dealing with the unforeseen fall-out from her new one.

"I gave my notice and have to be out." She wrapped her hands more tightly around the mug.

"But the cast hasn't been off your leg very long. Let me see if I can work something out and help—"

"It's all right." She was touched that his concern seemed genuine. But she was used to doing things alone. That was self-pity talking. She did have backup, just not from Mason. "I can handle it. Your mom is going to watch the twins. And Carla is meeting me there to help. She took a hooky day. Called in sick. Don't tell Gabriel."

"You think I'd rat her out when she's helping you?" It wasn't clear from his expression whether or not he was kidding. "I'm hurt that you think so little of me." He was talking about his male pride but her pain went a lot deeper than that. A place she'd thought was scabbed over and protected. A wound from childhood that she'd actively worked to heal and forget. As much as she wanted to blame him, it wasn't fair. They had moved quickly to marry. Between taking care of the babies and moving, they'd been so busy. Discussing the finer points of this arrangement hadn't been a priority.

"On the contrary, I think you're incredibly honest." She sincerely meant that. "And on the off chance you might run into your brother, it was simply a reminder not to say anything about Carla."

"My lips are sealed."

And so, apparently, was his heart. She needed to do the same. "Good."

He glanced at the digital clock on the microwave. "It's time. I really have to go."

"Have a good day." Wasn't she the world's most supportive wife?

"Hold down the fort while I'm gone." A husband's automatic response.

"Will do," she said.

He straightened away from the counter and hesitated for a moment. Annie had the feeling he was going to kiss her goodbye, a classic husband move, before heading off to work. She held her breath. But hope was a cruel thing because he didn't move close to her after all.

"I'll see you tonight." He turned away and headed for the front door.

Annie heard the soft click of it closing behind him and thought it was the saddest sound ever. On the way to his car in the driveway he would walk across the porch that had caught her heart and reeled in her hopes. It symbolized the dream for a traditional family that she'd had her whole life. But regret flooded her now because she knew all the front porches in the world couldn't fix what was wrong with this picture.

When she'd first met Mason, he hadn't trusted her, what with being the sister of the woman who hadn't told him he might be a father. And Annie hadn't believed he would stick around and take care of his children. They'd been wrong and had become friends, working side by side to care for the twins both of them loved more than anything. Taking the marriage step had seemed perfectly logical but she never dreamed it would create this awful divide between them. They were together legally but had never been further apart.

Chapter Ten

Annie climbed the stairs to her soon-to-be vacant apartment and bittersweet memories scrolled through her mind. Jessica announcing that she was pregnant and didn't know who the father was. The nervous and happy excitement when labor had started. The thrill of the twins' birth turning to fear and unimaginable grief because Jess died. Bringing the babies here when they were so tiny and she couldn't carry both of them up the stairs at the same time. The sheer terror of caring for both infants by herself.

Until Mason showed up and stood right here, she thought, looking at the familiar door. The moment she'd seen him, her life had changed in so many ways—some good, some not so much.

She unlocked the door and carried moving boxes and trash bags inside. The place was empty of furniture. Indentations in the carpet were the only clues that her couch and coffee table had once been there. Now they were in storage until decisions were made about what to do with everything. That seemed inconsequential considering everything else that was going on—or not going on.

"Hello."

Annie turned and Carla stood in the doorway with cups of coffee in her hands. "Hey, you. Thanks for coming."

"Doesn't look like you need much help," she said. "Mostly I came because you promised to take me to lunch."

It felt good to laugh and Annie was grateful to her friend for that. And the coffee. She took the to-go cup Carla held out. "The big stuff is gone, obviously. I need another pair of eyes to make sure I don't miss anything."

"I can do that." Carla looked around. "Where do you want to start?"

"The master bedroom." Also known as the room for sleep because in her world no one was being bedded.

Annie led the way and again only the marks on the rug indicated where the bed and nightstands had been. In the bathroom they set their coffee on the countertop between the two sinks. Annie opened the medicine cabinet while her friend got down in front of the cupboard underneath the sink.

"There's a shower cap here," Carla said. "A couple of gigantic hair rollers. A long-handled back scrubber. Nearly empty bottles of shampoo and conditioner."

Annie glanced away from what she was doing. "That was when I changed brands to get more volume. I kept those for an emergency."

"Do you want me to put these in a box?"

If only hair products would take care of her current crisis. Come to think of it, if she had better hair, maybe Mason would be attracted to her.

"Annie?"

"Hmm?" She pulled her thoughts back to what she was doing.

Carla held up the plastic bottles. "Keep or toss?"

"Throw them out."

"Done." She pulled out a trash bag and dropped the discards into it.

Annie took bottles out of the medicine cabinet and checked each label. There was one that said "Jessica Campbell." Prenatal vitamins. Her sister had wanted the cheapest over-the-counter brand but Annie had insisted she listen to her obstetrician, who'd said the prescription had the right amounts of what she needed for the baby. That was before she'd known there were two. A sob caught in her throat.

She'd been so busy with Charlie and Sarah that she hadn't had time to grieve, and an unexpected pain settled in her chest. It was emptiness and loss and missing the only person she'd ever truly been able to count on to love her.

"Are you okay?" Carla was staring at her.

"Why do you ask?"

"Oh, please. Your face is an open book. Never play poker, by the way. You suck at bluffing."

Annie handed over the bottle. "It just hit me all over again that she's gone and isn't coming back."

"Oh, sweetie—" Carla took it from her and closed her hand over the name. "I wish there was something I could say to make it better."

"Me, too. And I feel guilty."

"Why? You were there for her when she needed you most. And you took in her children without missing a beat." Carla sat back on her heels. "What could you possibly have to feel guilty about?"

"I love Charlie and Sarah with all my heart. They are the best thing that ever happened to me. But at what price?" Tears filled her eyes.

"Annie—" Carla stood, moved closer and hugged her.

"It's not like you made it happen. If you could bring her back, you'd do it in a heartbeat. And Jess wanted you to have the babies. She gave them to you."

"She didn't have a choice. I'm all she had and she's all I had. Our mother and her husband made it clear no help was coming from them. Not that it ever did. In a meaningful way anyhow."

"Their loss."

"And I'm sad that the babies will never know their mom. She was loyal and brave. She stood up for me when no one else would."

"You'll tell them about her," Carla said gently. "And all of her wonderful qualities aren't gone forever. They'll live on in her children."

"You're right." Annie's mouth trembled but she managed to smile. "I need to think about that."

"You haven't had much time or energy to think about anything. You've been treading water and getting by these last few months," her friend pointed out. "And life is give and take, yin and yang."

"I'm not sure where you're going with that."

"Losing your sister was horrible and tragic. But circumstances brought Mason into your life."

Just hearing his name made Annie's chest tighten, but not with sadness. It was way more complicated than that. "Yes. Mason is in my life."

Annie turned back to the medicine cabinet and pulled out a thermometer, antibiotic ointment, peroxide and Band-Aids. First aid supplies would fix a scrape but not what was ailing her.

It was quiet in the room and she'd been too lost in her own thoughts to realize Carla hadn't said anything in response to her Mason comment. In fact she could almost feel her friend's gaze locked on her like a laser beam.

She glanced over her shoulder and knew her inability to bluff was going to bite her in the butt. "What?"

"Something's bothering you. Something besides losing your sister."

Annie didn't want to talk about this but she faced the other woman and prepared to fake it. "No. I'm just tired. It's been hectic. First my leg. Moving in with Flo and John. Settling the kids. Moving again and cleaning out the apartment."

"Getting married." Carla leaned back against the sink. "How's that going, by the way?"

"It's an adjustment."

"Of course. But in a good way." Her eyes narrowed as she looked closer. "Right, Annie?"

"Yes. Of course—"

"Like I said. You suck at bluffing. Something is bothering you and for the life of me I can't figure out what could possibly be wrong. You just married a great guy. He's a hunk and a doctor. Is there any chance that your standards are just a little bit too high?"

Annie crossed her arms at her waist. "I'll admit that on paper my life looks perfect—good job, two beautiful, healthy children and a really hot husband..."

"But...?" her friend prompted.

Annie shrugged. "He doesn't want me."

"He married you."

"For his kids. To be a family. All of us under one roof for their sake."

Carla looked confused. "I really wish it was happy hour and this place had some furniture."

"What does that mean?"

"We could have wine and sit on a comfortable sofa for this chat." She picked up their coffee cups and slowly settled on the side of the tub, patting the space beside her. "This will have to do. Now sit."

Annie sat. "This isn't something girl talk can actually fix."

"Oh, ye of little faith. Besides, you won't know unless you try. I had no words of comfort for you losing your sister, but I've got plenty to say about you and Mason." Her friend was bossy, in a good way. "Now tell me what's going on. The truth. Don't hold back. What makes you think he doesn't want you?"

"He doesn't want to have sex with me."

Carla nearly spit out the sip of coffee she'd just taken. "Tell me I didn't just hear you say that your marriage hasn't been consummated yet."

"Yeah, that's exactly what you heard." Annie told her what happened on their wedding night.

"Okay. But think about this. Everything went down so fast. Maybe he was giving you time. It's possible he really is what he seems—caring and compassionate. That he was simply being a nice guy."

"It's been a week and he hasn't made a move. No guy is that nice." Annie had been miserable when she got here, but not like this. And, so far, talking things over was making her feel worse. "When he proposed, he said we liked each other, which is true. That we were friends, also true. But clearly he didn't mean anything more than that."

"How do you feel? Do you want to have sex?"

Annie thought about kissing him and he sure hadn't pushed her away. "Yes."

"Okay, then. Do something about it," Carla advised.

"Excuse me?"

"Come on to him. It's not the olden days. Things have evolved. Women can make the first move and not be a hussy."

"I can't. I've had enough rejection in my life. Enough humiliation. From Mason it would be—" Annie didn't have the words to describe what a no from him could do to her.

"Wouldn't it be better to know?" Carla asked gently.

Annie was dyslexic and school had been a challenge for her in more ways than one. She'd learned to compensate and be successful. Now her company was one of two finalists for the biggest contract they'd ever had and it was largely due to her vision and artistic execution of the campaign.

Intellectually she knew all of this but her inner child still heard the other kids ridicule her, tell her she was stupid, ugly, an idiot. School had been isolating and lonely, still she'd made it through. But Mason was honest. If she faced him outright and forced him, he would tell her the truth. That they were married friends without benefits. But could she handle hearing it?

"It probably would be better to know," Annie said. "I'll think about it."

Mason had to do something. The situation with Annie was tense and getting worse every day. And it was all his fault. After the problems in his marriage, then the divorce, followed by a year's deployment, he was apparently pretty rusty, socially speaking. He missed the easy conversation with Annie, the teasing and laughter. And the promise of that wedding kiss. But he'd blown it big-time.

So here he was at Make Me a Match. The office was in a building in the Huntington Hills business complex. He parked and exited the SUV, then walked through the double glass doors into the lobby with its elegant marble floor. The elevator opened when he pushed the up button, and he rode it to the top floor, where his aunt Lillian's business was located.

The elevator doors opened into a reception area with comfortable furniture arranged to facilitate conversation. Carla Kellerman sat behind the desk, and he knew she doubled as greeter and his aunt's assistant.

She looked up when he stopped in front of her. "Hey, Mason. How are you?"

"Fine."

"Really? You look terrible."

"Thank you." He felt that way, too, but tried to make a joke.

"Long hours at the hospital? Twins keeping you up at night?" There was an expression on her face: accusation mixed with pity.

"All of the above," he answered.

"How's Annie?"

"Great," he lied. He got the feeling she didn't buy the deception.

"To what do we owe this visit?" She toyed with a pen on her desk. "Since you got married—what was it, ten days ago?—I wouldn't think you'd be in the market to meet someone."

"I'm here to see Aunt Lil."

"I didn't see your name on her schedule. Do you have an appointment?"

"No." He was just desperate. "She was out of town and couldn't make the wedding. I haven't seen her for a while and just dropped by to surprise her. Maybe take her to lunch."

"Too bad. You just missed her," Carla said. "She had a lunch meeting."

Well, shoot, he thought. "My bad. I should have called first."

"Since you're here, do you want to say hello to Gabriel?"

Mason could truthfully say his brother was the last person he wanted to discuss this problem with. "That's okay. Don't bother him."

"Do you want to leave a message for your aunt?"

"Just tell her I was here and I'll talk to her soon." He lifted a hand. "Thanks, Carla. See you."

"Mason, is there anything I can help you with?"

She was Annie's good friend and the second-to-last person he wanted to talk to about this.

"No. It's all good. I'll just be going now—"

"Mason. What are you doing here?" His brother walked into the reception area from a side hall.

"Just stopped by to say hi to Aunt Lil, but she's not here. So I'm going to take off—"

"What's your hurry? Have you had lunch? I was just going to order takeout. Wouldn't mind some company. Come on back to my office."

"Okay." There was no way to make a graceful exit now. "Nice to see you," he said to Carla.

"You, too. Say hi to Annie for me." The woman looked as if she was going to say something more but instead she just smiled.

"Will do."

Mason followed Gabe to an office at the end of the hall. When both of them had walked inside, his brother closed the door.

"What's wrong?" he asked.

"That's direct."

His brother was wearing a T-shirt, jeans and sneakers. Mason had a hunch that, at least for today, his consulting work was strictly behind the scenes and not with clients.

"That's the way I roll. Now answer the question."

He stood in front of the abnormally tidy desk because there were no visitor's chairs in front of it. "Nothing is wrong. Why would you think that?"

Gabe rested a hip on the corner of his desk. "Because you've never dropped in to see Aunt Lil."

"I was deployed. It was a little difficult to commute for a drop-in," Mason said. "And how do you know that? You haven't been here that long."

"I've been here long enough to know that this visit is out of character for you."

"What do you know about character?"

"Okay." His brother looked down for a moment then gave him a wry look. "You're going to mock me because math and spreadsheets and data are my thing."

"Well, yes, that was my plan," Mason admitted.

"It's true that I'm not involved very much with the other part of this business. But since you've been back from deployment, you never just dropped by to see Aunt Lil at work. That's not criticism, simply a fact. From that data I can extrapolate that you have a problem and think our aunt is qualified to advise you. Since you so recently got married, I deduce your issue is in some way connected to your wife. I'm right, aren't I?"

Mason sighed. "You're not wrong."

"I'm listening," Gabe said.

Mason figured it was a symptom of his acute desperation that he was actually considering telling Gabe what was going on. The brother who'd warned him that he might be moving too fast and marriage would change everything.

"I want your promise that you won't discuss this with anyone else. Especially anyone in the family," he added.

"Are you serious? I can't promise that. I'm not a priest or lawyer ethically bound to keep our conversation in the

strictest confidence. No medical privacy issues, either."
Gabe's grin was a clear indication of just how much he
was enjoying this.

"Then I'm not going to tell you." Mason half turned
toward the door.

"Okay. You win. My lips are sealed. But at least can I
have an 'I told you so'?"

"I think you just did." Mason hoped he didn't regret
this. "Now I want you to swear that you won't reveal to
anyone what I'm going to talk about."

"Like swear on a Bible?"

"On the bond of brotherhood," Mason said.

"That's really deep." His brother made a cross over his
heart. "You have my solemn promise."

"Okay." Mason blew out a breath. "I messed up with
Annie. On our wedding night."

"Dear God, Mason. I'm probably not the best person
to help with that. And, for crying out loud, performance
in bed is not in Aunt Lil's wheelhouse, either. Maybe you
should see a doctor—"

"It's not *that*." Once again Mason was reminded that
he was a healer and not so good with words.

"What a relief. So it's not sex—"

"It kind of is."

Gabe shook his head. "Just tell me what happened."

"Everything was fine when we left after the wedding.
We got the twins settled pretty fast. They were both sound
asleep at the same time, which almost never happens. It
was just Annie and me—" When his brother gave him a
get-to-the-point scowl, Mason said, "I was trying to be
sensitive. All the men she's known are jerks and I didn't
want to be another one. I didn't want her to feel pressure
to…you know—"

"Sleep with you?"

For now Mason ignored the irony of a doctor being reluctant to use the words. "It was supposed to be an out if she wanted one."

"What did you say?"

"That she was probably tired."

Gabe gave him a pitying look. "I'll admit I'm better with financial facts than women, but even I know not to tell a woman how she feels."

"I found that out." Mason would never forget the look in her eyes. Emotions had swirled but he'd had no idea what they were. He'd only known that at that moment everything between them changed. In a bad way. "The thing is, it's awkward and tense now. I don't know how to fix it. Doing the wrong thing could be worse than doing nothing at all."

"I had no idea." Gabe shook his head.

"What?"

"That you suck this bad at romance."

"Now you know," Mason snapped.

"I guess I'm not the only Blackburne who focuses on data and logic instead of emotions."

"If this was an emergency room and you were having a heart attack, I'd know exactly what to do. I'm stethoscope and chest tubes, not a matters-of-the-heart guy."

"I get it."

Mason met his gaze. "Since you just admitted you know very little about women, it's quite possible that I just bared my soul and humiliated myself for no reason. You can't help." Mason started pacing. "You're useless."

"I wouldn't go that far. At least, not completely useless." Gabe looked thoughtful. "I try to avoid the interpersonal part of the business but it's impossible to work here and not absorb some things."

"Such as?"

"How to set a romantic scene." His brother shrugged. "We arrange a lot of first dates. I hear things."

"In my case, it seems a lot like shutting the barn door after the horse got loose."

"Ah, yes. You've already met someone and married her." Gabe nodded. "You moved so fast, I have to ask. Have you ever actually taken Annie out? On a date, I mean?"

"It's been hectic," Mason defended. "We have two babies. Then she broke her leg. It's not easy to align everything for alone time."

"Making the most of what you've got is another conversation and not my point anyway. But there are things you can do to maximize the moments you do have."

"Such as?"

"Bring her flowers. Put rose petals on the bed. A bottle of champagne chilling in the bedroom." Gabe threw up his hands. "Google 'romantic gestures.' Because that's all I've got. Or you can ask Mom."

"I'm going to pretend you didn't just say that." Mason barely held back a wince.

"Too far?" Gabe grinned. "But you must see where I'm going with this."

"You're talking about courting her."

"Finally the clouds part and the light shines through." Then his smile faded, replaced by a lost and angry look. "I'm not sure of the rules anymore, but it used to be a kiss good-night on the first date."

"I've already kissed her," Mason said.

"Before the wedding?"

When he nodded, Gabe asked, "And?"

"Hot. Very, very hot."

"Good, you've got some game. On the second date, more kissing and touching. If that works, seal the deal on the third date." Gabe's expression was ironic. "I can't help pointing out that this is something you should have taken care of before the vows."

Mason glared at his brother. "I've lost count. You've said 'I told you so' how many times now?"

"Sorry."

"No, you're not." But Mason laughed.

"No. I'm not." Then Gabe turned serious. "I like Annie a lot. And those kids are terrific."

"You'll get no argument from me."

"I really wish you luck, Mason."

"Thanks." They shook hands and Mason pulled him into a bro hug. "I have to go. Things to do."

And a first date to plan.

Chapter Eleven

Annie left work later than usual, partly because a deadline was approaching and she'd felt the need to put in more time on her graphics for the new contract presentation. Partly to avoid Mason. He was off today and had taken over childcare while she'd gone to the office. Now she had to go home. It took so much energy to be chipper and "normal" when she felt anything but and she didn't have the sparkle to spare.

In spite of that, her heart always skipped a beat when she saw him. Tired after a long hospital shift. First thing in the morning, all rumpled and scruffy. Playing with the babies. When they worked together taking care of Sarah and Charlie, the tension went away and everything was like it used to be before they were married. But when they were alone…

Was Carla right? Should she come on to him? She was too oomph-depleted to think about it right now.

She guided her car onto the street where she'd lived only a short time and a knot tightened in her stomach. After pulling her compact car into the driveway and parking, she got out then opened the rear passenger door to retrieve her laptop case from the seat.

She walked to the front door and sighed with satisfaction over her porch. She did love it. Bracing herself, she went inside and made her way to the back of the house. It was eerily quiet. No baby coos, chatter or even crying. That was weird.

She moved into the kitchen, where Mason was at the counter, his back to her. It was a broad back, wide shoulders. And if things were different between them, she would march over and let herself feel those muscles for herself.

He turned and smiled. "I thought I heard you come in."

That grin was like a direct hit to her midsection and the shockwaves went through her whole body. "H... Hi."

"You had a long day." He glanced at the case in her hand and moved close. "Let me take that for you."

"What?" His hand closed over hers and held on maybe a little longer than necessary before he took it and her purse. "Oh... I can—"

"I'll just put these over here on the floor in the family room."

The manly scent of his skin had her senses reeling with awareness and she missed it when he moved away. Although distance allowed her brain to start functioning again.

"Where are the twins?"

"Asleep." He walked back into the kitchen and went to the bottle of wine sitting on the granite countertop. It was already open and breathing. He poured some of the deep burgundy liquid into two stemless glasses then handed one to her.

"They're actually asleep?" she asked.

"Yeah. No nap today, which I kind of planned." He

moved close and looked down at her. "We did errands. Then I took them for a long stroller ride in the park and they got lots of fresh air. They were tired and fussy for baths, but it worked out."

"You bathed them, too?"

"Yeah. You've been working hard. I knew you'd be tired."

She had been but right now not so much. This new and different Mason had her attention. After a sip of wine she said, "I better get dinner started."

"I already did. It's not fancy," he said. "Salad, twice-baked potatoes and steaks. I'll grill them."

"Wow." This couldn't be real. She must have stumbled into an alternate reality. "That sounds great. I'll set the table."

"Already done."

She glanced over at her small dinette set in the nook. There was a bouquet of flowers in the center and her heart simply melted. She could feel liquid warmth trickling through her as she stared at the white daisies, baby's breath and strategically positioned yellow roses. She walked over and leaned in to smell the sweet, floral fragrance.

"Mason, they're beautiful."

"Did you know that there are meanings attributed to different colored roses?"

"I think I heard that somewhere, but I'm a little surprised that you know."

"I got quite the education at the florist."

Her eyes widened. These weren't just an impulse buy at the grocery store? "You made a special trip?"

"Yeah. The twins won over everyone in the place and I think that got me extra attention."

The babies might have helped a little, but a man as incredibly good-looking as Mason would get attention from women if he was alone. "I'm pretty clear on the significance of red and white roses. But not yellow."

"According to Cathy, of Flowers by Cathy, it means joy, friendship and the promise of a new beginning."

Be still my heart, she thought. Then her practical self shut down any deeper implication. He probably just liked the color.

"They're really beautiful. So cheerful. Thank you."

"You're welcome." He moved to where she stood by the table and held up his wineglass. "What should we drink to?"

The sounds of silence surrounded her and she smiled. "Our healthy babies."

"To Charlie and Sarah." He touched his glass to hers and they sipped. "You must be starved. I'll cook the steaks."

"I'll toss the salad and warm the potatoes."

He shook his head. "You worked today. And this is our first— This is a…" He hesitated then finally said, "This is my chance to pamper you."

"And I appreciate it." More than she could say. "But I think you worked harder today than me. Like a wife."

His eyebrows rose. "That's high praise."

"I mean it." And she was grateful, from the bottom of her heart.

"I'm happy to do it." Intensity glittered in his eyes. Even though no part of their bodies touched, she felt as if he was touching her everywhere.

"And I'm happy to help. But before I do, I'm going to peek in on the twins."

She saw the baby monitor on the counter and they would hear if there was a problem, but she needed to see them. They grounded her and she needed grounding after Mason's sweet thoughtfulness. That made her feel like an ungrateful witch and she didn't mean to be. But she had a hard time trusting the good stuff.

She looked in on Charlie first and smiled at the soundly sleeping boy. He was on his back, arms and legs outstretched as if he appreciated having space all to himself. She couldn't resist brushing a silky blond strand off his forehead and, fortunately, it didn't disturb him.

Then she tiptoed into Sarah's room. The little girl was a tummy sleeper, no matter how they tried to keep her on her back. Annie put a kiss on her finger and touched it gently to the little girl's round cheek. When Sarah moved, Annie froze. After all Mason's efforts, the last thing she wanted was to wake up this baby. She waited a few moments and all was peaceful, so she quietly backed away.

Annie headed to the kitchen, where the French door was ajar. Through the glass she could see Mason watching over the gently smoking grill. The hunter/gatherer, she thought. Today he'd hunted and gathered the heck out of their survival and she didn't know what to make of it.

By the time the steaks were ready she had the salad bowl and potatoes on the table along with the flowers and wine. It suddenly felt very romantic, in spite of the bright, canned light shining down. They sat across from each other and smiled.

"No candles?" she teased.

"Damn, I knew I forgot something." He actually looked upset with himself.

"Oh, my gosh. I was kidding, Mason. This is amazing. I love it."

"Really?"

"Are you serious? I didn't have to cook it. That makes everything fantastic, like going out to dinner."

"Medical school was no culinary institute, so I didn't

learn how to serve elegantly. My service in the army neglected that, too."

"Now you're just fishing for compliments," she said.

"Did it show? And I thought I was being subtle." He grinned then said, "Try your steak. I wasn't sure how you like it. I did both medium-rare and figured I can cook yours more if you want."

"No. Medium is good." She made a cut and looked at the warm, pink center. "This is perfect."

The meat practically melted in her mouth, it was so tender. Suddenly she really was starving and practically inhaled the food and the rest of the wine in her glass.

Feeling the need to explain, she said, "I didn't have time for lunch."

"As a doctor I have to tell you that's not good."

"I was on a creative roll. Doing the last tweaks before we present our concept to the client." She shrugged. "I don't like all my eggs in one basket, which doesn't help."

He refilled her wineglass and she was reaching out when he set it down. Their fingers brushed. The touch was electric and she was sure something sparked in his eyes, too.

He cleared his throat. "What does that mean? All the eggs in one basket?"

"I don't put my creative energy into one concept. It's important to have a choice. So the team brainstorms two or three and we work them up. If we get the contract, the client will choose a direction and we'll put all the detail into that. But there will be enough that they can visualize each one."

"That's two or three times the work for you."

"It's an investment in our reputation. 'The company that works twice as hard for you.'" She rested her arms on the table and smiled.

"Something tells me you're a girl who puts maximum effort into everything, not just the job."

"I always try my best. Even when I was a little girl."

"And your parents didn't see the effort."

"You remembered," she said. A man who listened. It might be his most attractive feature.

"It's their loss. In case I haven't said it before."

She sighed. "Someday maybe I'll believe that. In the meantime, I don't want to lose out on moments with Charlie and Sarah. But I have to find balance. Being able to work remotely helps. And what you did tonight."

"Just pulling my weight," he said modestly.

Of which he had a lot, all muscle and temptingly male. And this change in him just might be leading somewhere exciting. Was she a fool to hope?

"Speaking of cooperation, I'll do the dishes since you cooked."

"Not in my restaurant," he said.

"At least let me help. It's the least I can do."

He thought that over. "Okay."

Together they cleared the table. Since there were no leftovers, it was only plates, utensils and a salad bowl. They finished wine while working and Annie was super relaxed and hyperaware. When their hands brushed exchanging plates, her breath caught. Their shoulders touched and her heart started to pound. She saw his eyes darken with something sexy and wild and she was almost positive it wasn't just her feeling this.

Should she jump his bones?

Fear froze her. If he didn't want her, she could lose even this, and she couldn't bear that. It was selfish, but also for the babies. Together they could provide a stable environment. More selfish, she didn't know what she would do without him or the family she finally had because of him. No, if a move was going to be made, he was the one who would have to do it.

When they were finished, he looked down at her. "I had a really nice time tonight."

"Me, too."

He looked away for a moment then met her gaze. "Would it be okay if I kissed you good-night?"

That was sweet and gentlemanly, almost as if they'd just met and... Was this a date? She smiled and nodded.

The corners of his mouth curved up as he cupped her face in his big hands then touched his lips to hers. The contact was soft and sweet and perfect. Tender and gentle, a gesture of promise.

He pulled back and there was a dash of regret in his eyes when he let her go. "I've got paperwork to do, so I'll say good-night. Sleep well, Annie."

All she could do was nod. She was breathless and wanting and more than a little disappointed. But she knew rejection and this wasn't it. Mason was up to something.

After working three days in a row at the hospital, Mason finally had two days off and planned to put Operation Courting Annie into high gear. He had taken the twins to his parents' house and, after carrying them inside, had gone back to the SUV for diaper bags, favorite blankets and stuffed animals they couldn't get along without.

He put the provisions in the room where the cribs were set up, the same one where Annie had slept. The thought of her sent heat rolling through him. Dinner and flowers had gone well and he had every reason to hope that tonight would, too.

Back in the family room, the babies were on a blanket and Lulu sat patiently between them while they awkwardly patted her furry back. His mom and dad sat on the floor with the kids and the dog; it was a modern Norman Rockwell moment.

Flo stood and walked over to stand beside him. "It feels like forever since I've seen these babies."

"You see them almost every day."

"But it's not the same as having them here," she said wistfully.

Mason watched his daughter crawl over to her grandfather and into his lap. Watching the man who'd raised him cuddle and interact with his own little girl tugged at his heart. He'd been too young to really remember this amazingly gentle and patient side of his dad, so it was cool to see now.

"Mason?"

"What?" He reluctantly looked away and focused on what his mother was saying.

"I said, where is Annie?"

When he'd called to make sure it was okay to bring the kids over, his mom had been on the phone with someone else. She'd confirmed they weren't busy and would love to babysit the twins. Then she'd cut him off. Now she wanted details.

"Annie is at the office, working."

"So why am I watching your children? Not that I mind."

"No, you're just nosy." He appreciated the fact that she didn't interfere but was deeply committed to knowing whatever was shared willingly. "The thing is, I'm going to surprise her at work and take her out to dinner." When you were raised by Florence Blackburne, a guy knew when he messed up and when he did good. This time he'd definitely done good.

"Oh, Mason, that's a wonderful idea. Very sweet and thoughtful of you."

And selfish. But he hoped it would be positive for both him and Annie. He also chose not to share that he'd actually taken his brother's advice and searched the internet for romantic gestures. Since he couldn't sweep her away to Fiji, surprising her at work followed by a dinner out, with candles this time, would have to do.

"I'm glad you approve, Mom." He looked at his father, who had been listening in. "Any objections, Dad?"

"Nope." He let Sarah pull the cell phone from his shirt pocket and grinned at her. "Say hi to Annie for us."

"You know it's Friday. Your father and I aren't working tomorrow. We can keep Charlie and Sarah overnight. If you'd like."

He had been hoping she would offer. Another piece of the plan clicked into place. "I'd appreciate it, Mom. And I know Annie will, too. Thanks."

"Anytime."

Lulu barked once and drew Mason's attention to Charlie pulling himself to a standing position right in front of the DVD stack.

"Red alert," he said.

"We're going to have to move those." His mother hurried over to grab up her grandson. "Come to think of it, babyproofing this house is now a major priority."

He kissed her cheek. "I have to go or my plan to intercept her before she heads home will be a dismal failure."

"Don't you worry. We'll take good care of these little angels." She gave Charlie loud kisses on his neck and he giggled.

"I'm sure the three of you will do fine with them."

"Who's the third?" she asked.

He pointed to the dog. "Lulu. In fact, Annie and I would like to borrow her."

"That dog does love these little ones," his mother agreed. "Now go. We've got this."

"Roger that."

He shook his father's hand and kissed the kids. And, this was a first, he got them to imitate his farewell wave. One of them said what sounded like "Bye-bye" and he'd swear on a stack of Bibles that it was first words.

Part two of his plan was officially in motion, he thought as he drove to Annie's office. It didn't take long and he parked in the lot that had more cars at this hour on a Friday night than he'd figured. Probably not all of them worked at C&J Graphic Design, but that didn't matter. The very definition of surprise meant you had to be flexible in the execution of the plan.

He walked into the lobby, pushed the up elevator button and the doors instantly opened. After getting inside and selecting the floor where her office was located, the nerves hit. What if she thought this was a stupid idea? What if he embarrassed her? And the worst: What if she had no desire to be anything more than what they already were?

The doors opened and across from him there was nothing but glass, the center etched with the words "C&J Graphic Design." He exited the elevator to get a better look at her office. He could see wood floors and cubicles divided by more glass. A doctor could do delicate surgery in this room what with the excellent track lighting overhead. All the workspaces were empty, except two.

Mason saw Annie standing just outside her cubicle, talking to a man who was outside the one next door. He looked to be in his early thirties, black hair and dark brown eyes that kind of smoldered. Surprise. Mason could have gone forever not knowing she worked with a guy good-looking enough to be on the cover of *GQ* magazine.

"No guts, no glory," he mumbled as he pushed open one of the heavy doors and walked inside, moving toward the twosome.

"Who are you?" Smoldering Eyes asked.

Annie turned and her eyes widened. "Mason!"

"Hi." He lifted a hand in a wave and stopped beside her.

"What are you doing here?"

"I wanted to surprise you and take you out to dinner." He met the other man's dark, curious gaze, then looked back at her. "Surprise."

"Mission accomplished. I'm definitely surprised." There was a pleased expression on her face before it slipped a little. "Where are the kids?"

"At the house. They'll be fine by themselves." He grinned to let her know he was kidding. "I had you for a second."

"No." But she playfully slugged his arm. "Seriously, where are they really?"

"Three guesses."

"Your parents'."

"Right in one," he said.

"So there really is a husband?" *GQ* asked.

"Yes." Annie looked apologetic. "Sorry. I should have introduced you. Mason Blackburne, this is Cruz Wright, one of my coworkers."

Mason shook the other man's hand. "Nice to meet you."

"Likewise. So you're the twins' father, the dad who got Annie to say yes."

Was there a hidden message in those words? Had this guy been planning to move in on her when Dwayne the Douche was out of the picture? Unclear.

"I am that man, yes." Mason moved close enough that

his arm brushed Annie's. Meeting her coworker gave him one more reason to be glad that she could do a lot of work remotely.

Just then an attractive young woman joined them and looked him up and down. "So, who's this?"

"Mason Blackburne, my husband." Annie looked up at him. "This is Ella Lancaster, my boss's assistant, and the woman who keeps things running smoothly around here. And she does it with extraordinary grace and good humor."

He shook her hand. "A pleasure, Miss—"

"Ella." She smiled. "Annie's been through a lot in the last year. We were happy for her when she told us she was getting married. It's about time someone lived up to Annie Campbell's rigorous standards."

"She doesn't suffer fools," Cruz explained.

"I suffered Dwayne." Annie glanced up at him and made an "eek" face. "Calling him a fool is an insult to fools."

"Right on." Cruz studied Mason. "Points to you for sticking around."

"He came to surprise me," she explained to Ella.

The other woman sighed and said to him, "Are there any more at home like you?"

"As a matter of fact, there are," Annie said. "He has two brothers. And a sister."

At the end of the row of offices, a door opened and a man emerged. He was in his fifties. Blond hair with gray at the temples, the lean body of a runner. He joined the group.

Before he could say anything Annie said, "Bob, this is my husband. Mason, this is Bob Clemens, our boss."

The man held out his hand. "Glad to meet you, Mason."

"Same here, sir."

"Annie says you were in the army. Deployed overseas recently."

"Yes, sir. I was assigned to a medical unit in Afghanistan."

"Thank you for your service." Bob looked around the group then settled his gaze on Mason. "To what do we owe the pleasure of this visit?"

"I'm here to surprise Annie and take her to dinner."

The man nodded his approval. "She's been working a lot of hours and deserves some quality downtime. The campaign for the client is ready and she needs to relax and have some fun."

"R and R, that's my plan," Mason said.

"Then what are you waiting for?" Bob asked. "Get her the heck out of here."

"Yes, sir." Mason looked down at her and held out his arm. "Let's go."

There was no hesitation or awkwardness when she put her hand in the crook of his elbow. She looked luminous and happy, and that gave him hope that he wasn't messing this up beyond repair.

Now for the next part of his plan.

Chapter Twelve

Annie was literally quivering with excitement as she walked out of the office on Mason's arm. Whatever was going on with him, she was giving this new attitude two thumbs-up and a double arm pump. Inside, of course. It took a lot of concentration to not giggle like a schoolgirl and walk normally. And he looked so sexy and handsome in his jeans, white dress shirt and sports coat. He was out of her league, but she would deal with that insecurity at another time.

Waiting for the elevator, she could feel her coworkers staring through the glass. Mason hadn't picked her up and carried her out in front of every employee, but it still felt like *An Officer and a Gentleman* moment.

She started to slide her fingers from his arm, but he put his hand over hers to keep it there. She smiled up at him.

"This is a very nice surprise."

"I'm glad."

"To what do I owe—?"

Before she could finish her question, the elevator doors opened and they walked inside. Mason pushed the button for the first floor and the ride down was fast. When they stepped out into the lobby, it was as if happiness made her see everything brighter and more clearly. Nothing was there that hadn't been there this morning, but that was before Mason had made the effort to surprise her at work.

In the corner by the tall glass windows there was a grouping of pumpkins, pots of rust-colored mums and a scarecrow announcing that fall was in full swing.

"This will be the twins' first Halloween," she said. "Should we take them trick-or-treating?"

"Affirmative." He glanced at the decorations and let his gaze wander over the whole lobby. "The little kids in costume are the best."

"I know. And it will be really different for me this year."

"Really?" He gave her a wry look. "You think? With two babies?"

"And a house. There aren't a lot of kids in my apartment building, but now I live in an actual neighborhood." She grinned. "It's going to be fun giving out candy and seeing all the costumes on the little ones."

"Logistics," he said thoughtfully.

"What?"

"Tactical operations center."

"You're going to have to translate that into nonmilitary terms for us civilians."

"One of us will have to stay home—tactical operations center or TOC—and give out that candy, while the other takes the twins around."

"Divide and conquer," she said, nodding.

"Right."

She sighed happily. "From my perspective that is a quality problem to have."

"I completely agree." He looked down at her, more carefree than the solemn, serious guy who'd knocked on her door to take a DNA test. "But the night is young and I'm starving. We can talk about this at dinner."

After walking outside into the cool, crisp evening air, she said, "My car is over there. I'll meet you at the restaurant. Where are we going?"

"Nope. It's top secret. I'll drive. We can get your car later." He pointed. "Mine is right there in the first row."

"Okay." At that moment she was ready, willing and able to go with him wherever he wanted to take her.

They strolled over to his SUV and he opened the door for her, handing her inside. For a split second, their faces were millimeters apart. She could feel his breath on her cheek and thought he was going to kiss her. And she wanted him to so very much. The streetlight illuminated his features and there was a hungry intensity there that had nothing to do with food. So when he didn't touch his mouth to hers, it wasn't a soul-wrenching blow. As he'd said, the night was young and they were going to dinner. As surprises went, this one was moving its way into her top five.

He got into the driver's seat and turned on the SUV, then guided it out of the lot to merge with street traffic. It was a little congested right now as a majority of people left work and headed home. She actually had no idea of their final destination.

"So, where are you taking me?"

"Like I said, it's a surprise."

"I thought you showing up unexpectedly at my place of employment was the surprise."

"Part of it," he confirmed.

"But I can't change your mind about keeping the dinner location a top secret?"

"Nope. Although, you'll figure it out soon enough. Short of blindfolding you, I can't keep it clandestine all the way there."

But how sweet was it that he was doing it at all? Annie

pinched herself, just to make sure she wasn't dreaming. The tweak on her wrist told her she wasn't.

As he drove, making left and right turns, the area became more open, less dense with single-family homes and zones where there were businesses and strip mall shopping. Finally, when he turned onto Summit Highway, she knew.

"Le Chêne," she whispered reverently.

"Affirmative."

It was one of Huntington Hills' most highly rated and exclusive restaurants. Upscale, cozy, romantic, historic. She'd only been there once. It was a spontaneous decision Dwayne the Douche had made without a reservation for the busiest place in town. They'd been turned away. So she knew the restaurant was located on a country estate and vineyards. When they slowly drove closer, she recognized the ivy-covered stone exterior that was reminiscent of a French château.

"This place is hard to get into," she said.

"I made a reservation."

Planning ahead, she thought. It was a very sexy quality.

He parked in the lot, then got out and came around to open her door. When she slid to the ground, he put his hand to the small of her back as they walked inside. The interior was dimly lit and had elegant oak wood beams and recessed lighting. The hostess confirmed a reservation for Dr. Mason Blackburne and showed them to a table for two in a secluded corner. There were candles on the table and that made Annie smile.

Tables were covered with pristine white tablecloths and the chairs were oak. It was country elegance with a wall full of wine bottles and lots of wood-framed mirrors.

The server came right over. "My name is Shelly. Can I get you something to drink?"

Mason asked for a wine list and picked out a bottle.

Shelly left menus and promised to be back in a few minutes. It didn't take long and she opened the red blend then poured a small amount in a long-stemmed glass for him to approve. He did and she filled both of their glasses before promising to return to take their orders.

"Let's drink to good surprises always," he said.

Annie touched her elegant crystal glass to his and heard a bell-like tinkling sound. "I can get behind that in a big way."

She took a sip of the dark red liquid and savored the perfect blend of flavors. "This is nice. Thank you for all of this, Mason."

"I have to apologize."

"For bringing me here to this beautiful place?"

"No. For not bringing you sooner," he said.

"You have nothing to be sorry for," she insisted.

"I disagree." He met her gaze across the small, intimate table and the flame in his eyes burned as brightly as the candles between them. "Everything was rushed and clumsy. The house. The wedding. Our first night. It was fast—"

"Is this your way of saying you're having second thoughts?" A familiar knot of apprehension tightened in her stomach. "Do you regret everything?"

"No," he said quickly. "Good God, no."

"Then what?"

"I'm trying to make it up to you."

"And I'll try to communicate my feelings," she said. "You can't read my mind."

"No, but I can read your face. There's been tension between us and it's my fault. I hope this is a new beginning."

Their server, Shelly, returned and took their orders. White sea bass for her and red snapper *meunière* for him. "Are you celebrating anything special?"

"No," Annie said.

"Yes," he said at the same time. "We just got married. No time for a honeymoon and we have twins. But this is a special occasion for us."

"Congratulations," Shelly said. "The twins. Boys or girls?"

"One of each," he said proudly. "This dinner is to celebrate the beginning of our life as a family."

"That's so sweet," the server said. "I'm a sucker for romantic gestures."

Me, too, Annie thought.

When they were alone she cleared the emotion from her throat and said, "So, Halloween logistics."

"Right, it occurs to me that my folks could help. Give out candy at the house while we take the twins out. They won't last long anyway, and it's not like they can eat candy."

She nodded. "Just a symbolic gesture, for pictures and the promise of future family traditions."

"I like the sound of that."

They chatted, laughed and teased until the food came. Everything was delicious and she knew that because he shared his with her and she did the same with him. The service was impeccable and Shelly brought them a piece of cheesecake topped with strawberries, on the house, to memorialize this dinner for them. He paid the bill and they walked outside, complaining about how full they were.

At the SUV Annie hesitated before getting in. She looked up at him and had no idea what he saw in her eyes, but on the inside she was brimming with joy. She couldn't ever remember being this happy.

"Thank you, Mason. I had a wonderful time. I feel like Cinderella and my coach will turn into a pumpkin if I don't leave the ball before midnight."

"This night doesn't have to end," he said softly.

"It does. We have to pick up the twins."

"My folks offered to keep them tonight. I made an executive decision and took them up on it."

Annie knew what he was saying and smiled. "For the record, I'm not tired at all."

"Yeah." He looked sheepish and so darn cute. "That was definitely not my smoothest moment."

"Past history." Annie threw herself into his arms and hugged him then turned her face up to his. He kissed her until she was breathless and finally she said, "I like your executive decisions. Now take me home."

"Can't this thing go any faster?" Annie was in the passenger seat of Mason's SUV. She was only half kidding but the lights from the dashboard illuminated Mason's grin.

"It *can* go faster actually, but I'd be breaking speed-limit laws. I don't know about you, but getting stopped by a cop right now isn't high on my to-do list."

"Mine, either, darn it." She looked at his profile, outlined by passing lights, and admired the straight nose, strong jaw. He was a handsome man, but beauty was only skin-deep. A pretty face didn't reveal character, but what he'd done tonight definitely did. "Mason?"

"Hmm?" He glanced over then returned his attention to the road.

"In case I forget to tell you later, tonight was the nicest surprise I've ever had. No one has ever done something so special for me."

"I'm full of the unexpected," he declared proudly.

Something in his tone caught her attention. It was mischievous, playful. "What?"

"Just stating a fact." Same roguish tone.

"You have something else up your sleeve," she said. "Give it up."

"You are so impatient."

"If I agree, will you tell me?"

"No."

"That's just mean," she said.

He smiled, completely unmoved by her words. "You'll thank me later."

"I guess I'll just have to trust you on that."

"And that's okay," he said softly. "You can."

Trust was the very hardest thing for her to do. Everyone in her world had let her down. Everyone but Jess. Except, in the end, she'd left, too. Not by choice, by fate. Mason was a good man and Annie wanted to have sex with him. She was going to give him her body by choice, but that didn't mean her heart went along. She wouldn't give that up.

"I'm feeling a serious vibe from your side of the car," he said. "You okay?"

"Better than okay." She was in control.

"We're almost home." His voice was edgy and deep with the subtext of what home would be for them tonight.

A wave of anticipation rolled through her and every nerve ending in her body started to throb. She'd been waiting for this possibly since the first time she'd seen him. Maybe not exactly then because she'd been very tired and pretty crabby. But soon after when he'd kept showing up. That was okay. Falling in love was not.

"Here we are." He drove into the driveway. "Home sweet home."

There was a light on in the living room and the babies weren't there. "Do you think maybe we should call your mom and check on Sarah and Charlie?"

"Yeah." He pulled his cell out of his jeans' pocket and looked at the screen. "There's a text from her."

"What is it?"

"She says, 'Babies fine. Don't call me. I'll call you.'"

"Okay, then. Wow." Annie looked at him. "It's a little scary that she can read minds."

"It's a mom thing. She's one, you're one." He shrugged. "Let's go inside."

"Yeah." She opened her door. "I want to see what the surprise is."

Mason got out and came around to her side. He held out his hand and she put hers into his palm, their fingers intertwining as they walked to the front door and unlocked it.

He pushed it wide and said, "Surprise."

Annie's heart melted when she saw pink rose petals on the entryway floor. The trail continued through the family room and down the hall to the master bedroom. On the dresser was an ice bucket with a bottle of champagne and two flutes.

He lifted the bottle and water rolled off. "The ice is almost melted, but it's still cold."

"Oh, Mason—" She moved closer to him and thought surely he could actually hear her heart hammering. "This is incredibly thoughtful. I didn't think you could top picking me up from work and that beautiful dinner, but I was wrong. You were right. I do thank you."

"Yeah?" He was studying her closely and the words seemed to reassure him. "I'm glad. This could so easily have gone seriously sideways."

"It so didn't, believe me." She put her palms on his chest and met his gaze. "I wasn't tired before, but I'm *really* not tired now."

He grinned sheepishly as his hands settled on her waist and pulled her close. "You're not going to forget that, are you?"

"I think the rose petals and champagne bought you a memory lapse."

"In that case…"

Mason lowered his mouth to hers, a soft kiss, but tension had been building all night. And probably even before that. The touch was like accelerant to a glowing spark, igniting it, turning it into a flame that burned out of control. She opened her mouth and his tongue moved inside, caressing everywhere before dueling with hers.

Annie pushed his sports jacket off his shoulders and he dragged it the rest of the way, turning the sleeves inside out in his rush. She started to undo the buttons on his shirt but her fingers were shaking, her hands uncoordinated. He brushed them aside and dragged it over his head.

Light trickled in from the hallway, enough for her to see the impressive width of his chest and the contour of muscle. It was begging to be touched and Annie couldn't resist. The ever-so-male dusting of hair scraped her palms as she moved them over his skin and down his rib cage. She heard him suck in air and flinch as if it tickled—or turned him on.

"You're very forward," he said.

"I've been told I should take the initiative."

"Do I want to know who told you that?" He picked up her hand and softly caressed the palm with his thumb.

"Probably not."

"Even if I wanted to thank them?" he said in a hoarse voice. "And, just so we're clear, I'm definitely not complaining."

He brought her hand to his mouth and sucked on her index finger. Now it was her turn to gasp as the power of that small contact crackled over the nerve endings in every part of her body. She was breathless and feeling like taking more initiative.

"You have too many clothes on," he said.

"What are you going to do about that?" She gave him a sassy look then unbuckled the belt at his waist.

"I'm going to assist you in disrobing." He turned her around so that her back was to him.

She quickly shrugged off her sweater, making it easier for him to keep his promise. He didn't hesitate, instantly lowering the zipper on the black dress. He did it slowly, and only to her waist, then he pushed the material open wider and kissed the exposed skin.

This exquisite torture was making Annie squirm with need in the best possible way. He must have read her body language because with one quick move he had the zipper all the way down. She let the silky black material slide down her body and pool at her feet before stepping out of it.

She faced him in black panties, matching bra and high heels. He wasn't the only one who could read body language. If the intensity in his eyes was anything to go by, he very much liked what he saw.

"You are so beautiful." His voice was hardly more than a strangled whisper.

He put his hands on her waist, grazing his thumbs over the sensitive bare skin before sliding them higher to brush the undersides of her breasts.

The need to feel his hands on her without any material in the way was so strong she couldn't fight it even if she wanted to. She reached behind and unhooked her bra, letting it fall to the floor with the rest of her clothes. Then she took his hands and placed them on her breasts, holding them there. The touch felt so good, her eyes drifted closed, letting her just take in the sensations.

Moments later she felt his mouth on her and the sensations multiplied exponentially. He kissed first one sensitive peak then the other and her legs went so weak she wasn't sure they would hold her up.

"I want you now," she murmured.

"Twist my arm."

He yanked the bedcovers down then removed the rest of his clothes. Annie stepped out of her heels and let him lead her to their bed. She sat then slid over and made room for him. He followed her, gathered her in his arms and slid his hand over her side to the waistband of her panties. He hooked a thumb then dragged them over her thighs and calves, where she kicked them off.

He ran his hand down her hip and over her belly, resting his palm there as he slid one finger inside her. He brushed his thumb over the sensitive feminine bundle of nerves between her thighs and the intense feeling nearly made her jump off the bed.

All the while he was kissing her—eyelids, nose, cheeks, mouth, neck. He kissed the underside of her jaw then blew softly on the moistness, making her shiver before taking her earlobe between his teeth, biting gently, tenderly. The assault on her senses pushed her to the edge.

"I need you. Now—"

Without a word, he nudged her legs apart with his knee and settled himself over her. His chest was going up and down very fast and the sound of their mingled harsh breaths filled the room. Taking his weight on his forearms, he started to push inside her then stopped.

"What?" she asked.

"A condom—"

"Oh, God! I wasn't thinking—"

"I was." He rolled sideways, reached into the nightstand to retrieve one then put it on. Moments later he was back and kissed her softly. "All squared away. Now, where were we? Oh, yes—"

He entered and her body closed around him, welcoming him. She wrapped her legs around his waist, taking him deeper inside, moving her hips. He got the message and slowly stroked in and out, building the tension with each thrust.

Before she was ready, Annie felt herself let go, break apart, setting free waves of pleasure inside her. Aftershocks made her tremble in the most wonderful way and he held her until they stopped.

Then he began to move in and out again. One thrust then two. Moments later he groaned and breathed her name. She kissed his neck and chest and when he buried his face against her hair, she held him until he sighed into her shoulder.

Annie wasn't sure how long they stayed like that and didn't much care. She hadn't felt this good in a very long time, and that kind of scared her. Sex with Mason was different. Oh, the mechanics were the same, but it was unlike anything she'd ever experienced. And there was only one reason for that.

Her feelings were engaged. She wasn't putting any label on them, but something was stirred up inside her. It was ironic that she'd been bothered when he wouldn't sleep with her. And there was that old saying—be careful what you wish for.

Well, she got it. And she wasn't complaining. It was everything she'd hoped for and more. Mason played her body like a violin and her body was happy. But her heart was a different story.

Chapter Thirteen

Annie didn't trust perfect.

She'd grown up in an environment that was the exact opposite of perfect. The absence of crisis was the bar she used to judge the quality of her life. A rainbows-and-unicorns existence made her uneasy but that's how it had been for the last week. Ever since that magical night when Mason had surprised her at work and taken her to dinner, followed by the best sex she'd ever had.

And it wasn't an aberration because it had happened every night after. Even with babies and work, they managed to be together. It was wonderful but Annie was so afraid to go all in and believe this was how things were going to be from now on. She was a little less confident about her control where Mason was concerned.

He would laugh if she confessed her fears, but he couldn't understand. Except for that one bad marriage blip, his life had been smooth sailing because he'd won the lottery in terms of fabulous families. She couldn't relate to that, so it was understandable that he had no frame of reference for her insecurity, either.

Today her insecurities were on parade inside her. They were meeting his lawyer and the family court judge to finalize his legal petition of paternal rights. He was with Charlie in the family room waiting for her to get Sarah ready.

She smiled at the little girl on the changing table, playing with a small stuffed bear as Annie secured the tabs on her diaper. "Daddy is your daddy, right? So what could go wrong, baby girl?"

Sarah babbled an incoherent response. "I know. I'm being ridiculous. Daddy would say the same thing. It's just that I'm nervous. And you need to look your best. So Mommy has to put your clothes on. No flashing the judge, baby girl."

She slid white tights over Sarah's feet and legs, then covered the diaper. After sitting the infant up, she slipped a dress over her head, a simple floral print with a smocked bodice, and black ballerina flats. Last, she put on a headband with attached bow that highlighted her cornflower blue eyes and blond curls. For once, the little girl didn't pull it off. And again the perception of perfection reared its ugly head.

"I have a bad feeling about this."

She sighed then picked up the baby and walked into the family room. Mason had Charlie in his arms, holding the little boy closer and more tightly than usual. He was wearing navy slacks and a long-sleeved white dress shirt with a red-and-blue-striped silk tie. There was a serious expression on his face and her stomach knots pulled tighter.

"You're worried," Annie said.

"About?"

"Court."

"Nervous," he clarified. "There's a difference. Unless you work there, no one wants to go in front of a judge."

"But your lawyer said it's just a formality. All the paperwork is in order."

"He did," Mason confirmed. "So smile, Annie."

"You first," she challenged.

At that moment Charlie babbled something that sounded like "Da-da" and patted Mason's shoulder with his chubby little hand. And that got a genuine smile from his father.

"See? Charlie isn't worried," Annie said.

"Only about getting his next bottle." Mason tested the weight of the boy resting on his forearm. "Have you noticed how heavy he's getting?"

"I have." She nuzzled her daughter's soft cheek. "This little princess is petite and delicate."

"She looks beautiful. And so do you." For a moment his eyes glittered with something other than anxiety. "Is that a new dress?"

She looked down at the belted black shirtdress with its long sleeves and white detailing. Her coordinating heels were low and sensible. Practical but not flashy. For the moment, anyway, she was living a rainbows-and-unicorns life, so why not dress the part?

"Yes, and new shoes." She caught her bottom lip between her teeth. "Do we look like we're trying too hard?"

"Maybe. But justice is supposed to be blind. I doubt the judge will turn down my petition because of our fashion choices."

"So, you're saying I'm being ridiculous?"

He smiled. "Those words did not come out of my mouth."

"Uh-huh." She looked at Sarah. "See? I told you Daddy would call me silly."

He moved close enough for her to feel the warmth of his body and hers responded to it. Smiling tenderly, he said, "You are the least silly person I know. If anything, I'd like to see you develop a silly streak and work on cultivating a little carefree-ness."

"So now I'm too serious?" she teased.

"You're perfect."

"Not even close." And of all the things he could have said, that was the least likely to anesthetize her nerves. Because she didn't trust perfect.

"That's my prognosis and I'm sticking to it." He shrugged. "But we're procrastinating and need to get going. No one will care how photo ready we are if we miss the hearing."

"Right."

They shifted into high gear, working together like a meticulously choreographed ballet. Each put a baby into a carrier then took it to the car and secured it in the rear passenger seat. Annie had packed the diaper bag with bottles, changes of clothes and supplies for any emergency imaginable and set it on the floor in front of Charlie. Mason lifted the double stroller into the SUV cargo area. He'd put on his matching suit jacket and looked like a successful doctor and devoted dad.

Annie smiled at him. "You look very handsome. And pretty soon this will all be over."

"Piece of cake." He kissed her, a brief brush of his mouth on hers. "We got this."

They drove to the courthouse located in an older section of Huntington Hills. It was a complex of buildings and Mason's lawyer met them in the lobby of the family court. The high ceilings made their footsteps echo on the marble floor and the twins noticed. Both of them found their outdoor voices and used them in different pitches that made Annie and Mason wince.

She had just met the attorney and wanted their babies

to make a good impression. Like that really mattered, but… "Sorry about that."

Cole Brinkman didn't seem perturbed by the noise. "This is normal for family court. They're kids and no one expects them not to make a sound."

"So this won't count against us?" Mason asked.

"Of course not," the lawyer said. "Nothing will. Through no fault of yours, you didn't know about them. Now you do and have the science to back up your claim. It's a slam dunk."

"Okay." Mason nodded.

"Just so you're aware, there are other cases in front of this judge, too. There will be other parents."

"And kids?" Annie asked.

"Yeah." Cole grinned. "It's going to be noisy."

"Okay, then."

"We should go in. Judge Downey is hearing the case and his courtroom is at the end of the hall."

They walked in the direction he pointed and stopped at the tall, wooden double doors. Mason pulled one open so Annie could push the twins' stroller through. Cole wasn't lying. By Annie's count, there were about eight or ten couples already seated with numerous children of varying ages.

Minutes after they settled in the first row, an older man came in from a side door near the high bench. Since he had on a black robe, one assumed he was the judge. A woman in a sheriff's uniform announced Judge Downey, a man with white hair who looked to be somewhere in his sixties.

"Good morning," he said. "I've reviewed the documents for all of you here today and we'll try to move things along quickly. Children have a short attention span and I want them to go be kids. So, first case."

It wasn't them. From what Annie could pick up, the couple were aunt and uncle to a boy whose parents had been arrested during a drug sting and sent to prison for illegal distribution. The child was born while the mom was in jail and family had petitioned for temporary guardianship of the infant. They were the only parents he'd ever known. Now they were seeking legal custody. Their home environment was stable and loving, but the court bent over backward to keep children with their biological parents unless that became impossible. It was complicated.

Thank goodness Mason's case was simple, Annie thought. Several more couples and kids were called up, but Charlie was getting restless in the stroller so she unbuckled him and set him on her lap. Sarah wouldn't stand for being strapped in if her brother got to be free. So Annie handed off the boy to Mason and released the little girl, holding her close for a moment.

As proceedings dragged on she pulled out bottles from the diaper bag, then toys to entertain them. That worked for a while but then they started rubbing their eyes. After that there were tired cries and she wasn't sure if it was permissible to get up and move around with them. Mercifully their case was called and they could at least walk as far as the judge's bench.

He smiled. "You have a beautiful family, Dr. Blackburne."

"Thank you. I think so, too." He patted Charlie's back.

"A lot of scenarios present in my court, most of them heartbreaking. And I have to make decisions that are in the best interest of a child, decisions that will affect people's lives forever. And not always in a good way."

Annie's stomach lurched. Was he trying to prepare them for the worst? Something no one could have predicted?

Judge Downey smiled then. "Fortunately your situation is not one of those and the facts speak for themselves. Black-and-white. The DNA results are proof that you are the biological father of Charles and Sarah Campbell. They are a conclusive determination of your paternal rights, which I'm pleased to legally affirm."

"Thank you, sir," Mason said.

"Your attorney also filed a concurrent petition to change their last names and that is granted, too."

"So, that's it?" For a second Annie wasn't sure she'd said that out loud.

The judge smiled. "That's it. I wish every case was this easy. Congratulations."

"Thank you, Your Honor." Mason grinned at her, obviously relieved.

They left the courtroom and shook hands with their attorney. Cole took cell phone pictures of them, their first as a legal family.

They left the building and found the SUV. Mason grinned. "We're all Blackburnes now."

"I know." She had been ridiculous to worry.

This was surreal and so wonderful that there were no words to express her feelings. The last piece had fallen into place and she could hardly take it in. She finally had everything she'd ever dreamed of. A traditional family. She had never really believed that happiness like this could happen to someone who'd come from where she had. But she'd beaten the odds.

On paper and in reality her life really was perfect.

Mason drove his family home from the Huntington Hills' government center but he couldn't be sure he wasn't flying. Since getting the DNA results, he'd been there for the babies. He'd fed them, changed diapers, walked the floor at night with either—or both—when necessary. He'd been doing all the right things because he loved them. But there was something profoundly powerful in knowing the t's were crossed and the i's dotted. His status was legal. His name was on their birth certificate. No one could take them away from him.

"I'm pretty happy right now," he said.

"Really?" Annie was in the front passenger seat beside him. "I'd never have guessed. What with you frowning since we left the courtroom."

"I haven't stopped smiling." He was stating the obvious, which she already knew. "It's the weirdest thing. The proof was in the DNA test but I feel as if a weight has been lifted."

"That's good, because you're stuck with me and the twins now, Dr. Blackburne."

"And I can't think of anyone I'd rather share this with."

There was a smile in her voice when she said, "What a sweet thing to say. I feel the same way."

He glanced over and thought again what a pretty picture she made in her new dress. He also thought how very much he was looking forward to getting her out of it. But that was for later. Right now they had to get the kids home for naps. How ordinary that sounded and how wonderful. He vowed never to take it for granted. This was something he'd wanted for a very long time.

Annie seemed happy, too. They'd worked out the sex misunderstanding and were as compatible in bed as they were out of it. She wasn't demanding declarations of love or a definition of his feelings, and he was grateful for that. He cared about her more than he wanted to put into words. A couple of times leaving the house or on the phone when he'd said goodbye and nearly added "I love you," it startled him. But he caught himself. What they had was pretty damn good.

He wasn't going to rock the boat with a four-letter word. He'd said it all the time to his ex, even at the end when he wasn't feeling it anymore. He didn't want anything to mess up what he had with Annie and the kids, especially that one little word.

"We're almost home," he said. Another four-letter word that felt different from when he'd left this morning. Now it was his turn to be silly and Annie would probably make fun of him, but right now he didn't care. "The meaning of home feels more profound to me."

"Like you got a blessing from the angels?"

"At the risk of you laughing at me," he said, "yes."

"I understand." And she wasn't laughing.

He pulled the SUV into the driveway and turned off the engine. "Would it be too corny to say this is the first day of the rest of our lives?"

"Probably. But I get where you're coming from and share the sentiment. Who'd have guessed the big, bad, army doctor, emergency specialist was such a super softy?"

"That's our secret," he said teasingly. "I have a badass reputation to maintain." Belying his words, he took her hand, bringing it to his lips to kiss the back of it. "Let's go be a family."

She glanced into the back seat and smiled tenderly at the sleeping babies. "Car ride works every time."

"Any chance of getting them in their cribs without waking them up?"

"There's always a chance." But the skeptical note in her voice put the brakes on hope. "The odds aren't good."

"That's what I figured. I'll take Sarah and the diaper bag. You get Charlie." He felt as if he was the commander of a military operation, and life with twins was like that sometimes. Double the work. But he wouldn't change it for anything.

"Sounds like a plan."

Coordinating their efforts, they swiftly and efficiently and—dare he say it?—expertly got their children inside and changed out of their perfect family court clothes. One-piece terry-cloth sleepers were just what the doctor ordered. Each of the babies got a bottle and went down for a nap with a minimum of protest. The magic was still holding.

He and Annie tiptoed from the nurseries into the family room and he smiled at her. "That was too easy. Do you think it's because I'm now legally their father as well as biologically?"

"They're just tired out from a big day," she said. "Or maybe we've banked some good karma."

"Since all is quiet on the home front, would you mind if I went out to do an errand?"

"What do you need to do?"

He grinned. "It's a surprise."

"Oh?" Female appreciation turned her eyes a darker shade of hazel, highlighting the gold flecks. "Maybe champagne and rose petals?"

"You're half-right. We need a really good bottle of champagne to celebrate a really good day."

"But no flowers?" She didn't look the least bit disappointed. "It was a sweet and beautiful gesture that I'll never forget. But those petals were really messy. Until they dried, it was kind of hard to vacuum them up. I watched you struggle with that."

"So the whole thing was wasted on you." He knew better than that.

"Absolutely not." She met his gaze and there was a wicked gleam in hers. "But it's not necessary today."

"Good. Because that's not my plan. I wanted to stop by my mom's and share our good news."

"You definitely should. Flo needs to know," she said emphatically. "I have a little work to do anyway. While the kids are sleeping."

"Okay, then. I shouldn't be too long."

"Take your time."

He nodded and started to turn away, then impulse took over. Moving close, he curved his fingers around her upper arms and pulled her to him, then lowered his mouth to hers. Her body went soft and yielding, and her small sigh of satisfaction made him hot all over. He ran his fingers through her silky blond hair then cupped her cheek in his palm. Her breath caught and she slid her arms around his neck. When he reluctantly lifted his mouth from hers, both of them were breathing hard.

"Are you sure you need to work?" His voice was hoarse.

"Yes. Sorry." And she did look let down. "Bob is doing the presentation to the client tomorrow and I need to go over the sketches and theme one more time, just to make sure it's as perfect as possible."

"Okay. And I really should share our good news."

"Yes."

"'Bye, Annie. I—" He'd almost said it again but stopped just in time. And he wasn't sure how he felt about that.

"What?"

"I'll be back soon. But if you need anything, call the cell."

Mason hurried off and drove to his folks' house not far away. His dad wouldn't be home from work yet but his mom's job was part-time and her car was in the driveway when he got there. He exited the SUV then walked up to the front door and knocked.

Flo answered and smiled instantly when she recognized him. "Mason! This is an unexpected surprise."

"Good or bad?"

She playfully swatted his arm. "Always good to see you. And you know that. Come in."

"Thanks."

"Can I get you something? Iced tea? Coffee? Food?"

"Come to think of it, I'm starving. Didn't have lunch today."

"I'll make you something."

In the kitchen she got out what she needed for a sandwich, even putting on one of the dill pickle slices that he liked. He sat in one of the bar chairs at the island and grabbed the plate she slid over to him.

"Thanks, Mom."

"You're welcome." She walked around the counter and sat in the chair beside his, watching wide-eyed as he wolfed down the food. "Why no lunch? Were you at the hospital? I didn't think you were working today."

"I'm not. But it was a big day. Annie and I went to court with the twins."

"That was today?" Her mouth dropped open and then she gave him the "mom" look. "Why didn't you tell me? I'd have been there."

"That's why we didn't tell you. If something had gone wrong—"

"But your lawyer said there were no problems."

"I just didn't want to take a chance." Now he felt like a little boy caught in a lie. "I know how hard you can take things."

"I admit that, but I'm still pretty good with moral support," she defended. "And you might have needed it. You take things hard, too. Sorry. You got that from me."

"Do you want to keep busting my chops for protecting you? Or do you want to know what happened?"

"Tell me," she said.

He grinned. "It's official. The twins are Charlie and Sarah Blackburne now."

"Oh, Mason." She hugged him. "Congratulations. That's wonderful news."

"It is pretty great."

"And I could have been there to hear it if you'd given me the chance."

"Mom, let it go. I was trying to protect you."

"I'll get over it." She grinned. "I can't wait to tell your dad. Or do you want to talk to him? Since you were obviously trying to protect him, too."

He sighed. "You can tell him. Maybe that will get me off the hook."

"It's a start," she teased.

"Good." He slid off the chair and took his paper plate to the trash. "I have to get back to Annie and the kids. I just wanted to come by and let you know. My next stop before home is for a bottle of champagne."

"You have a lot to celebrate." She hugged him again. "I'm so happy for you, Mason. After all you went through, finally things are going your way."

"Thanks, Mom."

She walked him to the door. "Give my best to Annie and kiss my grandbabies for me. Tell them Grandma will see them soon."

"Will do."

He jogged down the walkway to the SUV parked at the curb and got inside. The next stop was the liquor store and a really expensive bottle of bubbly. He had big plans for it later.

After paying, he got back in the SUV, more than ready to be home with his family.

His cell phone rang and he answered right away, certain it was Annie wanting him to pick up diapers or formula or something. But it wasn't.

"Dr. Blackburne?"

"Yes. Who's this?"

"I'm calling from the lab about the DNA sample you recently had tested."

This was weird. "What about it?"

There was a brief silence before the woman said, "I'm sorry to inform you that the results were incorrect. Recent court action on your motion to claim your parental rights triggered a quality control test here at our company. It turned out there was a mix-up with your sample and the one we received at the same time."

Mason listened to everything the woman said and asked a few questions. He was assured that the tests had been checked and rechecked and the new results were correct. After clicking off the phone, he had no idea how long he sat there. And just like that his world blew up.

"I'm not a father."

Chapter Fourteen

Annie looked at the cell phone in her hand as if it was an alien being. The message from the lab came completely out of the blue and the worst part was that Mason had received the same one. The lab had mixed up the two samples she'd sent. The man who'd signed away his rights to the twins was a DNA match to them. Not Mason.

She couldn't imagine what he was thinking right now. Being a father was so important to him. In fact his first marriage had imploded because his wife had given up on them. Annie didn't quit. She wasn't like that. He would be home soon and they'd talk this through. She would assure him that everything was fine.

But time passed and he didn't come home. She called and he didn't pick up. She left voice messages and he didn't answer. He'd gone radio silent. Once she'd come very close to contacting his parents but decided against it. They would have to know soon, but he should be the one to break that news.

The twins woke up hungry so she fed them then did baths and playtime before getting them down for the night without much fuss. They were obviously still tired from their court outing. It had been several hours and still no Mason.

Another sixty minutes went by. She knew because she counted every one of them. If she didn't hear from him soon, she would find out if his parents had. Worry wasn't something she handled especially stoically.

She was pacing and just about to call Flo when the front door opened. Relief washed over her when he came into the kitchen.

"Mason—"

She moved toward him then saw despair on his face and stopped. He was still wearing his suit but the slacks and jacket were wrinkled, the tie loosened. The crisply pressed-and-perfect exterior was gone and seemed to reflect his inner turmoil.

"Where have you been?" she asked.

"Driving."

"You heard from the lab." She wasn't asking a question.

"I did." He set a bottle of champagne on the granite countertop beside him. A bottle that would probably never be opened. "Turns out we didn't have to get married after all."

The words were like an arrow to her heart and she nearly gasped. She didn't know what she'd expected, but that wasn't it.

"The reasons we got married are still the same."

"What were they again?" His voice was flat, emotionless and just this side of bitter.

"You wanted a family and so did I. Now we have one," she said.

"You do." He dragged his fingers through his hair. "You're their aunt. A blood relative, at least. I, on the other hand, am nothing to them."

"That's not true, Mason. You are Sarah and Charlie's dad. A test done in a lab doesn't change that."

"You're wrong. It changes everything."

"All it means is you probably can't donate bone marrow or a kidney. In every other way you are what you've always been. The man who holds them when they cry. Feeds them when they're hungry. Makes sure their diapers are changed. You keep them safe. Everything a father is supposed to do."

"Annie, it's not that simple."

"It's exactly that simple. You feel the same way about them that you did this morning when you were nervous about what was going to happen in court."

"Yeah." He laughed but the sound was cynical, resentful, frustrated. "The timing of this news is inconvenient. Makes you wonder if fate is having a laugh at our expense."

"What does that mean?"

"I have to notify my attorney about this. It's not as straightforward as it was this morning. The judge should have this information."

"Probably. But I don't think it alters anything. The biological father already signed away his rights. He doesn't want them."

"He did that before test results were in. Knowing for sure gives you a different perspective. Trust me on that."

Annie looked into his eyes, dark with anger and pain. She prayed for the right words to get through to him. "Tell me you don't love them. In spite of this glitch. I want to hear you say that you don't want to be their father."

"I—" He looked down and shook his head. "That's not the issue."

"Are you serious? It's exactly the issue, the only thing that matters."

"I'm nothing to them." He slashed his hand through the air as if severing ties. "I was something for a while. For a few months I had a son and a daughter. For a few weeks I had it all. Test results matter or we wouldn't do them."

"In a medical situation they do, obviously. But it isn't relative to the heart and soul."

"Relative?" His smile was sarcastic. "Are you making a pun?"

"Stop feeling sorry for yourself, Mason." She took a step closer and realized how badly she wanted him to hold her and to hold him back. "They are your children in every way that counts. And they need you."

"I've lost my children. Again." Rage and hurt blazed in his eyes before they went dark. "And there's nothing I can do about it."

"Let's take a time-out." Annie met his gaze. "This has been a shock for both of us. We need to let the dust settle and let it wear off. Deep breath. Decisions should wait until we've processed this completely."

"It's not complicated, Annie. Time and cooler heads won't change the fact that the twins are not mine."

It wasn't the words so much as the look in his eyes that convinced Annie his mind was made up. Nothing she could say would sway him. "Wow, you're not the man I thought."

"What does that mean?"

"I believed you were someone who didn't put restrictions on love. It never occurred to me that you are a man who can't care about a child unless that child has his genetic material."

"That's not fair," he said.

"I think it is," she snapped. "And what about you and me? What happened to sharing this adventure together? You said that to me just today, but I'm getting a totally different vibe now. The fact is that we're married and we have two children."

"You do," he corrected.

"Back to that." She blew out a breath. He was hurt and betrayed and too big for her to shake some sense into him. "So where does that leave us?"

He opened his mouth then closed it again. But emotions were swirling in his eyes: pain, bitterness, betrayal because of a stupid mistake, regret. And that was the one tearing her apart. He was sorry he married her.

Annie hated being right. Mason Blackburne was one more man abandoning her. She should have been prepared for the fact that sooner or later he would back away. Unfortunately she wasn't. She had let down her guard and got a right hook square in the heart.

"Message received," she said. "This is your house. I'll move out, but I'd appreciate a little time to find something for the babies and me."

"Annie, we—"

She put up a hand to stop him. "You made it clear there is no we, so it's a little late to play that card. Until I can move out, I'm taking the master bedroom. I'd appreciate it if you'd sleep in the guest room."

"If that's what you want."

No, it's not what she wanted, but it was the only choice he was giving her. This wasn't a misunderstanding about whether or not they would assume traditional husband and wife roles and have sex. He'd all but told her that since his DNA didn't match the twins', he didn't want her.

"Good night, Mason."

Without a backward look, Annie walked away and down the hall. She went into the room she'd so happily shared with Mason and closed the door to shut him out.

She'd been clueless and overconfident believing she was in control of her feelings. Now she knew that what she felt for Mason was too big to contain. She was head over heels in love with him and knew it for a fact. Because letting him go was so much harder than any rejection she'd ever experienced in her life.

He'd only married her to do the right thing for the children he'd believed were his. It was clear to her now that she would never have married him if she hadn't been in love with him. The worst part was she couldn't even blame him. She'd agreed to everything he'd proposed.

She tried to hold back the sobs, but one escaped before she put her hands over her mouth. Mason had broken her heart but she would never let him know how much he'd hurt her.

Mason was a mess.

That was his diagnosis and there wasn't any medication or therapy that would make him better. It had been a few days since finding out he wasn't a father and he still felt as if someone had cut out his heart and left a gaping hole where it used to be. He and Annie had been unfailingly polite when forced to interact, but every night he heard her crying and it ripped him apart. So he'd decided to do something proactive.

He'd gotten in touch with the twins' biological father. Annie had his contact information in a file, along with paperwork relinquishing all rights to them. Mason wasn't their blood relative but Tyler Sherman was. And kids needed a dad. The guy reluctantly agreed to meet him during his lunch break and suggested neutral territory. Patrick's Place.

Mason had pushed back on the location because it had memories, but the man insisted. It wasn't far from his current landscape job. Apparently he wasn't inclined to go out of his way for his children.

So Mason was waiting in a booth. He glanced around the place where he and Annie had taken vows not so long ago. The bar with brass foot rail dominated the room and there were personal family photos of the owners on the wall behind it. A room adjacent to this one had pool tables, flat-screen TVs mounted on the wall and comfortable seating to watch televised sporting events. Next to that was the restaurant where they'd had dinner with his family after the wedding. The tables were nearly full during the lunch hour. Coming here was a really bad idea.

So he turned away and focused on the front door, where he could see everyone who came in. There were couples, groups of women and men, even lone individuals who'd stopped by for something to eat. But no one who seemed to be looking for someone. The meet time came and went and he was beginning to think he'd been stood up until he saw a guy enter by himself then hesitate and look around.

"Tyler?" Mason said quietly.

"Yeah." He was tall, blond and really young. Dressed in jeans and a navy T-shirt with Sherman Landscape silkscreened on the front.

"Mason Blackburne." He stood and held out his hand.

The other man shook it then sat across from him. He looked acutely uncomfortable. "What's this about? You insisted it was important. You said it was about the DNA test."

"Yeah, you are the twins' father." Mason was surprised those words didn't stick in his throat. A lab test didn't change his love for those babies and that meant he wanted them to have everything they deserved.

"Is this some kind of scam? Annie said the DNA would be done in five business days. That was months ago. Why are you telling me this now?"

Mason swallowed hard. "The lab made a mistake and

we just found out about it. They mixed up the samples—yours and mine."

Tyler looked down at his hands for a moment then blew out a long breath. "I signed a legal document giving Annie sole custody."

"That was before you knew for sure that you're their father. You might change your mind." Mason pulled out his cell phone and found the pictures he'd taken right after court, the day he'd claimed parental rights he wasn't entitled to. "Here they are."

Tyler scrolled through the series of photographs but his expression didn't change. "They look healthy. Cute kids. Look like Annie."

"Yeah."

He handed back the phone. "But why would you think I'd change my mind?"

"I just found out that the babies I thought were mine are actually not. I won't lie. This information hit me pretty hard because I've wanted to be a dad very badly and for a long time. It seemed to me that the man who is their biological father would jump at the chance to claim Charlie and Sarah."

"Does Annie know you contacted me?"

"I didn't want to say anything until after I talked to you. But these kids deserve to know their real father." Since he felt like their real father, it tore him up to even say that.

"Look, I'm not father material and maybe I never will be. My childhood was crap and my old man was a son of a bitch, probably still is. I wouldn't know because I refuse to see him. The fact is I doubt I'd be a very good father because my role model sucked."

Mason had always taken his close family life for granted, until he'd met Annie. She'd told him more than once how lucky he was to have his parents and siblings, and this guy was confirming that.

Mason met the other man's gaze. "So you're sure about this? The decision is right for you?"

"Some choices are hard, but this isn't one of them. Especially because they have Annie and you." He shoved his fingers through his blond hair. "Look, I'm not a complete bastard. If there's a health issue, or someday they're curious about me, I'll do what's right. But as far as raising them? Those kids are better off without me."

"Okay."

Tyler looked at his linked fingers for a moment then back up. "I know what you're thinking."

"I doubt that." Mason almost laughed. There's no way he could possibly know.

"It's nothing I haven't thought about. I should have been more responsible about birth control if I feel so strongly about not having kids."

"Now that you mention it…"

"Believe it or not, I'm very conscientious about that. I wore a condom. It broke, but I didn't think too much about it because Jessica told me she was on the Pill. Those twins were meant to be, I guess."

"Apparently."

"Look, Dr. Blackburne, I made the right call—for me and for them. You obviously care and they're lucky to have you. If it matters, you have my blessing."

Oddly enough, it did matter. "Thanks for not blowing off this meeting, Tyler."

"You're welcome." He slid out of the booth and held out his hand. "Nice to meet you."

"Same here." Mason stood and shook his hand then watched the man exit the way he'd come.

"You look like someone who needs a drink." The voice came from behind him, but it was familiar.

Mason had been so lost in his own thoughts, he hadn't heard anyone approach. He turned and saw Leo "The Wall" Wallace, a former NHL star who co-owned this place with his wife.

"Hi, Leo."

"How are Annie and the kids?"

"Healthy." Physically, anyway. She would barely look at him and cried every night, so there was that.

The big man was studying him intently. "Well, my friend, you look like hell."

"Since when did insulting a customer become a good marketing strategy?" No matter how true it might be.

"It's just an observation and I wasn't kidding about that drink. Have a seat. I'll be right back."

"It's too early," Mason protested.

"You're the doctor but you don't always know what's best."

Mason did as instructed and watched the other man walk over to the bar and say something to the bartender. Instantly the woman got two glasses then took a bottle of some kind of brown liquor from the display behind the bar. She poured, then slid the tumblers across the bar to her boss. Leo carried them to the table, setting one in front of Mason.

"Drink up, Doc. It's medicinal."

Mason looked at it for a moment then, figuring he couldn't feel any worse, he tossed back the contents of his glass. It was smooth going down then burned in his chest and all the way to his gut. At least for a few moments the searing sensation took his mind off the pain eating up his insides.

Leo toyed with his glass. "So, who was that guy you were talking to? The conversation looked pretty intense."

Mason saw no reason not to tell him. His family knew and had tried to help. But what could they say? Words didn't change the results of the test. Talking this through might help. Although he wasn't sure how. It wouldn't change the fact that the rug had been ripped out from under him and the truth he thought he knew was a lie.

"That guy I talked to is the twins' biological father." He explained about the lab error.

"I'm speechless." Leo looked like he'd just been smacked with a hockey stick. Finally he said, "How is Annie taking this?"

"Better than me. She says it doesn't make any difference. Love is all that matters."

The other man's expression turned dark and serious. "She's right."

"Wait a minute. You're a guy. I thought you'd understand."

"You mean take your side. And I do understand. More than you think." Leo tossed back the liquor in front of him then toyed with the glass. "I was married once before. We had a baby boy and I love him more than I can say."

"Okay. Didn't know that, but I'm not sure what this has to do with my situation."

"He's not mine biologically. She lied to me, said she was pregnant with my child, and I married her. After a couple of years when she was having an affair with the guy, she said her son should be raised by his *real* father."

Pain darkened the man's eyes and he sucked in a breath. "The thing is, I felt like his real father. I changed diapers, fed him, played with him, got up at night when he cried. Loved him more than anything. It doesn't get more real than that, but suddenly I had no say in any decisions con-

cerning my son, simply because he didn't have my DNA."
Leo met his gaze. "Everything changed except the way
I felt about him."

"Oh, man—" Mason shook his head. "Now I don't
know what to say."

"Tess and I got off to a rocky start emotionally, but
there was this irresistible physical attraction from the moment we met. One night we gave in to it and she got pregnant. She swore the baby was mine, but I'd been burned
once and didn't want to be made a fool of again. It nearly
ruined the best thing that ever happened to me."

"That's rough."

"Yeah. But now the most wonderful woman in the
world is mine and we have a beautiful little girl." His expression brightened. "My point in telling you this is that I
have a pretty good idea what you're going through. And I
have to say that meeting with the twins' biological father
seems straight up to me."

"I appreciate that." Mason remembered his conversation with Annie the night he'd found out about the error. It
was bitter and full of self-pity. "But Annie... I said some
things."

"People say stupid stuff when they're dealing with really emotional situations. It's understandable."

"Not this."

Leo frowned. "What did you say to her?"

"That we didn't need to get married."

"I'm sorry... What?"

Mason sighed. "I told her—"

"I heard what you said." His friend stared at him as if
he had two heads. "You implied that you only married
her because you believed you were the twins' father?"

Mason winced. "When you say it like that—"

"I'm guessing that she wasn't happy."

"She's moving out with the kids as soon as she can find a place to live," he confirmed.

"You are an outstanding doctor, but communication is not really your thing." Leo gave him a pitying look. "So, genius, why *did* you marry Annie?"

Mason was running on pure adrenaline now and just snapped out the answer without overthinking it. "I'm in love with her and the babies. I love her so much that I'll let her go if that's what's best for them. Even if it kills me."

And just saying those words, he died a little more. But he meant it.

"You're a damn fool, Mason."

"What?"

"This isn't some romantic tragedy. This is real life. You have a beautiful woman who loves you." Leo pointed a finger at him. "Don't give me that look. I know what I'm talking about. You may not believe this, but I'm a lot more than just an ex-jock businessman. I saw the way she was looking at you the night you got married. Right here at Patrick's Place. Trust me. Those were not the looks of a woman getting married just for the sake of the kids."

They had deliberately avoided defining anything besides friendship and respect—even in their wedding vows. And what Mason felt was so much more than that or he never would have proposed in the first place.

"Oh, man… I really blew it," Mason said.

"You think?" Leo pointed at him again. "You gotta fix this, pal. And trust me. It won't be easy."

He was right, Mason thought. He had to fix things with Annie. But how?

Chapter Fifteen

"Bob wants to see you in his office."

Annie was working in her cubicle and looked over her shoulder at Ella, who was standing right outside. "What does he want?"

"Don't know. He just told me to tell you. Consider yourself told."

"Did he look happy? Sad? Mad?"

Ella thought about the question. "Not sure. If people's faces were emojis, I could tell you."

"Point taken. And it has to be said, no one can tell what Bob is feeling. He's remarkably even-tempered."

"He is." Ella studied her. "You, on the other hand, wear your heart on your sleeve."

Annie really hoped that wasn't true. Because then everyone would know how crushed she was about why Mason married her. "Really?"

"Are you kidding? Everyone in the office has been wondering what's been bugging you for the last couple of days."

"No way," Annie said. "I'm the same as always."

"That's not what Cruz says, and he's right next door to you."

"What is he saying?"

"That since the night Mason picked you up here and took you to dinner you've been so bright and shiny it makes his head hurt. But the last few days, you look like someone popped your wedded-bliss balloon."

Hmm, she hadn't realized her cubicle buddy was so observant. Or that she was so transparent. Or that she could miss Mason's touch so much it was impossible to hide her feelings about him. Being humiliated in school because of her learning disability had been the training ground for her poker face. Only Jessica had been able to tell when she was concealing her pain and anguish. But apparently now her coworkers could, too.

"I'm fine. Just tired. With two babies in the house, who can sleep?" Duck, cover and conceal.

Old habits died hard and she didn't want to talk about this. The babies had been sleeping better than those first few months after she'd brought them home from the hospital. It was Mason keeping her up. All the what-ifs and if-onlys haunted her. How could she have been stupid enough to fall for him? That was actually the easiest question to answer.

Chemistry. She'd felt it from the beginning and it wasn't something easily ignored. Plus he was so darn nice, a truly good man. Practically perfect, which was ironic because she didn't trust perfect. Yet she'd started to trust him and her heart hadn't stood a chance.

"I'm fine, Ella."

"Okay." The woman's tone said she wasn't buying that. "But if you need someone to talk to, I'm here."

"Thanks." She pushed the chair away from her desk and stood. "I'll go see what Bob wants."

"Right."

Annie could tell by her coworker's expression that she was hurt and just wanted to help. It was much appreciated, but she was on the emotional edge and desperately clinging to her professionalism at work. And just before a meeting with her boss was not a good time to air out her personal problems.

She walked to his office. The door was open and he was at his desk. "You wanted to see me?"

"Annie. Yes." He took off his glasses and tossed them on the desk. "Come in. Would you close the door, please?"

She did as requested then sat in the chair on the other side of his desk. "Are you firing me? Should I be worried?"

"No." He smiled. "Just the opposite."

"The opposite would be not firing me."

"I'm making the announcement in the morning to the staff, but I wanted to tell you first."

"About?"

"I'm putting you in charge of the campaign for our newest client." Bob's face grew rounder when he smiled broadly.

"We got the account."

"Yes. In no small part because of your talent and hard work."

"It was a team effort," she said.

"A team that you organized and led." He nodded at her. "Congratulations."

"Thank you."

This was a real "how do you like me now" moment to everyone who ever bullied, teased and belittled her. To anyone who'd called her stupid. This was what she'd worked her butt off for. Against the odds and while raising two infants, she'd managed to come up with creative concepts and execute them, enough to impress a major company and get them to trust C&J Graphic Design with their business.

Now she would be in charge of that account. How she wished Jessica could see her now. She should be doing the dance of joy, except none of it meant anything to her because she'd lost Mason and the family they had made together.

To her horror and humiliation, Annie burst into tears. She buried her face in her hands for several moments then pulled herself together with an effort to look at her boss. "Sorry. That wasn't weird at all."

"Not quite the reaction I expected," he admitted.

"Tears of joy. Honestly." She tried to smile but knew it was wobbly at best.

"You should be proud, Annie. It was a lot of pressure and you've handled it with grace, intelligence and enthusiasm."

"Thank you." She brushed away tears that just kept leaking out of her eyes for no reason.

"I think you should take the rest of the day off. You deserve it. Go home. Let off some steam. Be with your beautiful family."

That nearly sent her into another meltdown because that family was gone. But she managed to maintain her composure long enough to thank him again and walk out of his office.

Family. The idea of it got to her every time. It was the opposite of her superpower. It was her vulnerability. For a pathetically short period of time she'd had everything. The babies, a husband and father, in-laws she loved. It was idyllic. Then a lab error had torn her perfect world apart.

She grabbed her purse from her cubicle and managed to sneak out without seeing anyone. She found her car in the parking lot and put the key in the ignition. But where was she going? Mason wasn't working today and had the twins. He'd insisted, but that was probably all about guilt.

He was clear on the fact that he had a legal responsibility to the babies but insisted he wasn't allowed to have an emotional one. With her promotion, she would probably have to spend more time in the office and that meant hiring someone to watch her children. She couldn't count on him. Not anymore.

As badly as she wanted to see Sarah and Charlie, to hold them, she couldn't face Mason in this raw state. So she backed the car out of the space and drove out of the lot. Instead of taking the turn to go to his house, she went in the opposite direction.

For a long time she just kept driving as thoughts tumbled through her mind. She was operating on autopilot, but her subconscious took over. That was the only explanation for how she eventually ended up at Florence Blackburne's house and saw the woman's car parked in the driveway.

Annie made a spontaneous decision to stop. She parked in front, walked up to the door then rang the bell. Flo answered almost right away. She was holding Sarah. In the background Charlie was crying.

"Boy am I glad to see you." The other woman acted as if nothing had changed. "These two are both hungry. I know they can hold their own bottles now, but I prefer to hold them."

"Me, too. But sometimes you can't."

"The downside of being a twin is having to share because there aren't enough adults around to help."

"This isn't one of those times. I'll go get him," Annie said.

Working together, they warmed bottles and settled on the sofa in the family room. Each of them had a baby to feed.

Annie couldn't get the bottle into Charlie's mouth fast enough. But when she did, there was silence as he sucked the formula down. "Where did Mason go? Did the hospital call him in?"

"No. He said he had to see someone and was going to Patrick's Place."

Annie felt a knot in her stomach. "Another woman?"

"If so, I don't think he'd have mentioned that to me," Flo said. Then her expression changed from teasing to concern. "What's going on with you two? He told us about the lab error, Annie. But I'm not sure why your first thought would be about him meeting another woman."

Annie sighed. Her subconscious had brought her there for a reason. Talking to Mason's mother certainly couldn't make things worse than they already were. "He all but told me he only married me because he thought he was the babies' father."

The other woman took the bottle away from Sarah then lifted her up for a burp, and she produced a very unladylike one. Flo rubbed her back and met Annie's gaze. "The truth of finding out he's not their father threw him. Mason is solid and steady, unflappable. But he was rocked by this. And he's a doctor. He relies on lab tests being correct so that he can treat his patients accordingly."

"I get that. He wasn't the only one shocked by it."

"I know, honey. Although it may sound like it, I'm not taking sides. The thing is, when he was married before, having a family was his focus. So many times he got his hopes up, only to be devastated by losing a child. And it was even harder for Christy, his ex." Flo shook her head. "But with Sarah and Charlie, they were here and they were his. And that was a dream come true for him. I don't know what he said to you, but I doubt he was thinking clearly when he said it."

"He said there was no reason to be married."

"Unless you're in love."

When the baby stopped sucking on the bottle, Annie took it away to burp him. "It was a mistake. Gabriel was right. We moved too fast."

"Gabe's experience doesn't make him the best person to be giving out advice. I wouldn't take his words to heart." She smiled at the baby dozing contentedly on her shoulder. "I'm the one who told Mason not to let you get away and implied that your old boyfriend was hovering."

"Why would you do that?"

"Because you're perfect together."

"I don't believe in perfect," Annie said. "And when he proposed, we agreed that love had nothing to do with it."

Flo smiled. "But neither one of you stuck to that, did you?"

"It doesn't matter. I'm moving out of the house with the babies as soon as I can find a place to go."

Mason's mother shook her head. "I can't believe you're really going to split up. Annie, you're part of the family. So are the twins."

"They're not. Now we know you're not related to them by blood. They're not your grandchildren."

"You're wrong about that." Flo's voice was kind and gentle when she said the words. It was also firm. "Sarah and Charlie are my grandchildren and I love them with every fiber of my being. DNA is only science. It cannot tell us who we're supposed to love. That's the heart's job."

"Flo, I can't believe—"

"Believe it," she said. "And I believe with all my heart that Mason loves you with all of his. Don't throw that away because he said something in haste after getting the biggest shock of his life. Fight for your family."

The woman's words were the verbal equivalent of a snap-out-of-it slap. It worked. Annie got the message. Perfect didn't just happen. You had to fight for it.

* * *

Mason left Patrick's Place feeling both empowered and idiotic. The things he'd said to Annie... He needed to see her as soon as possible and headed to his mother's house to pick up Sarah and Charlie. After parking at the curb, he jogged to the front door and knocked softly. Because of Annie, he was aware that when there were babies in the house, ringing the bell put a guy at the top of the most endangered species list.

The door opened and his mom put a finger to her lips and then indicated he should follow her into the family room. "They're asleep."

"I figured. The thing is, I have to get home and—"

"Cool your jets."

"Mom, you don't understand—"

"Baloney. I understand plenty." She gave him a look. "What in the world is wrong with you?"

"That's a broad question. You might want to narrow the scope a bit because there's a lot wrong with me."

"You're so smart in so many ways that it shocks me how you can be so dense about certain things."

"What are you talking about?" he asked.

"I talked to Annie. How could you tell her you didn't have to be married after all?" His mom pointed a warning finger at him. "And don't even accuse her of talking behind your back."

"I wasn't going to—"

"Because I pried the information out of her. She's an amazing young woman and you have handled everything so clumsily."

"Tell me something I don't know."

"This is not a news flash. You really screwed up. I explained how emotionally drained you were after the divorce, but you need to talk to her and work this out."

"I get it—"

"Because Charlie and Sarah *are* my grandbabies and I love them. Annie, too. She's become like a daughter to your father and me—"

When her mouth quivered and tears filled her eyes, Mason felt like toxic waste. What kind of a son was he, making his mother cry? "It's okay—"

"No, it's not. But you're going to sort everything out." She blinked away the tears. "Because ultimately your welfare is on the line. Only you know what's in your heart, but I can say in all honesty that I've never seen you as happy as you've been with Annie and your family."

"I know and—"

"So you have to convince her not to move out. At least encourage her to give it some time, let emotions settle down before making a decision you'll both regret."

"That's my plan. I will—"

"I mean it, Mason. You've always been an over-achiever, so if there's ever been a time to go with your strength, this is it—"

"Mom, stop talking. I just came to get the kids. I'm going to talk to Annie when she gets home from work."

"She got off work early and stopped by to talk to me."

"She didn't take the kids home?"

"I suggested she leave them with me so you two can talk quietly and without interruption. And I'm suggesting the same thing to you. Besides, they're sleeping. Every-one knows you never wake a sleeping baby."

"Okay, thanks."

She smiled. "And, Mason?"

"Yeah?"

"You better explain to Annie who your meeting was with at Patrick's Place."

"How does she know about that?"

His mother shrugged. "She asked where you were so I repeated what you told me, which was next to nothing. She went straight to wondering if it was a woman."

"Great. Like I needed another challenge. And no. I didn't see a woman."

"Make sure she knows that."

He planned to. And it was going to be an uphill battle. She'd told Dwayne the Douche that he'd abandoned her once and she wouldn't give him a chance to do it again. For the first time in his life, Mason wished he was a lawyer instead of a doctor. He needed the right words to heal the harm he'd done to her heart.

The drive from his parents' house wasn't long but it felt like forever. People facing death often said their life flashed before their eyes. Mason had the reverse sensation—life without Annie stretched in front of him. The images were sad and grim, without brilliance or color.

He pulled into the driveway beside her compact car and got out. After gathering his thoughts, he exited the SUV and walked to the front door. He opened it and walked inside. It was unnaturally quiet; a preview of his future if he'd irreparably damaged their relationship.

He couldn't stand the silence and called out, "Annie?"

"In the kitchen."

There was too much square footage between them to accurately diagnose her tone. So he took a deep breath and put one foot in front of the other until he was beside the granite-topped island, face-to-face with her.

"Hi."

"Hi." Her expression was neutral and he didn't know how to take that. If things were normal between them, he would ask about her day. But everything was wrong and what he said to her now would determine whether or not he could make them right again.

He jumped straight into the deep end of the pool.

"I didn't meet a woman at Patrick's Place."

"I believe you. But whatever it was must be pretty important if you had to leave the kids with your mom."

"It had everything to do with their future. And ours," he said. "I talked to Tyler Sherman."

"Their biological father." Her eyes went wide with shock. "Why? He made it clear that he didn't want anything to do with them."

"That was before he knew the test results. I thought he had a right to know."

She mulled that over before asking, "And?"

"The new information didn't change his mind." Mason told her everything the guy had said. "If needed, he'll step up, but feels that day to day the kids are better off without him."

Her expression wasn't neutral now. It was full of doubt. "Were you hoping he did want them now, because you're not their biological father?"

"No. God, no, Annie." He was blowing this. Damn it. "I was trying to do what's right. I would die for Charlie and Sarah. I am and will always be their father. I love them more than I can even put into words. And if he sincerely wanted to be a positive part of their lives, it's my responsibility to look at the big picture and do my damnedest to figure out what's best for them."

"So he doesn't want a role in their lives?"

Mason shook his head. "Not now. But he's not hiding, either. If they have questions eventually, he'll be around to answer them."

"Okay. He sounds like a good guy."

"He seems to be. Self-aware and practical. He cares about the twins, enough to put their welfare first. I respect that."

She took one step back. "Okay, if that's all—"

"That's not even close to all." He wanted so much to have her in his arms, but he was afraid to touch her yet. Afraid she would shrug off his touch and not really *hear* him. "I didn't mean what I said, Annie. About being married. It was a knee-jerk reaction to that call from the lab. Nothing changed for me."

"Oh?" Her eyebrow lifted. "So we're still friends who only like and respect each other?"

"No."

"So we don't like each other?"

"That's not what I meant." This was not going at all the way he'd hoped. "More than anything I want to be married to you. I want a family with you, to raise Charlie and Sarah together with you. They're my kids and it's not in the DNA, it's in the heart. I want to be the best husband and father I can possibly be. Because I love you, Annie."

"Really?"

"With everything I've got. If you give me another chance, I'll prove to you that I will never let you down again."

"Right." She turned away then and walked down the hall toward the master bedroom.

Mason stood there for several moments before reaction kicked in. It was not going to end like this. He wasn't going to let it end at all. Whatever he had to do, however long it took, he was going to prove to her that he loved her and wasn't going away. His military training kicked in and surrender wasn't an option. Army strong.

He marched after her into the room they'd shared awkwardly at first and then with all the passion and intimacy of a married couple. He was so focused on what to say that might persuade her to take a risk on him that it was several moments before he really saw the room.

Rose petals had been tossed on the carpet and the bed.

A bottle of champagne was icing in a bucket and two flutes were beside it on the dresser. Best of all—Annie was there smiling at him. She'd set a scene, just like he had, to work out the bumps in their marriage.

"What's this?" he asked.

"My way of fighting for our family."

"It's a good way." He moved close and put his arms around her waist, nestling her against his body. "So, this— the flowers and champagne—is going to be our thing?"

"Could be," she said. "What do you think?"

"Maybe we should invest in a rosebush." He met her gaze and with all the intensity of the feelings inside him said, "I'm in love with you, Annie. More than I can tell you."

"I know." She settled her hands on his chest. "Deep down I knew that when you proposed or I would never have said yes, no matter how much we pushed the friend-ship angle."

"How could you know when I didn't?"

"It was there in everything you did. Going to work. Feedings in the middle of the night. Walking the floor with a fussy baby." She glanced at the petal-strewn bed. "Making the effort to show me how you felt even when you wouldn't say the words. At night, reaching for me even in your sleep."

"I knew it, too." He pulled her close and whispered against her hair. "Love is also being afraid I'd lost you when you fell down the stairs and broke your leg. I finally know what it means to be in love."

"I love you more." She glanced at the bed again then up at him.

"In case you were wondering," he said, "I'm not the least bit tired."

She grinned. "Me, either."

Epilogue

Christmas Day

Mason parked the SUV in front of his parents' house and smiled at Annie in the passenger seat. The outside looked like a Christmas store had thrown up on it. "So it's the twins' first Christmas."

Annie was staring at the house. Flo had invited the whole family to help decorate, but the scope of it all still amazed her. "Something tells me this has nothing to do with our children."

"You would be right about that. My mom goes all out for Christmas. She's missed having little ones to fuss over and has probably set retail records this year."

A feeling of melancholy slipped into her heart. "Jess would have loved this."

Mason reached over and took her hand, wrapping it protectively in his. "And you still miss her."

"I always will." She had Mason now and the twins. They were happy, healthy and beautiful. Marriage to him was the best thing that had ever happened to her. "I wish she was here."

"She is," he said gently. "She will always be here because a part of her lives on in the twins. And she loved them more than anything."

"How do you know?"

"Because she gave them to you. She trusted you with what she cared about most. And you are honoring her memory by raising them to be the best they can be."

She loved the love shining in his eyes for her. "*We* are loving and caring for them."

"And each other."

"Ma—" That earsplitting screech came from the back seat.

Annie winced. "The pitch of our son's voice could shatter glass."

"Doesn't that make you proud?" he asked. "He's not a year old yet and is pulling himself up to a standing position. Before you know it, he'll be walking. Have you seen how fast he can crawl?"

"Seen it?" she scoffed. "I've had to chase him down. And Sarah is no slouch, either. This 'getting around' thing adds a whole new dimension to parenting."

"I know. Are you as tired as I am?"

"You don't look nearly as tired as I feel. How do men do that?" She studied him. "You complain about being old and tired but you, sir, are better-looking and hotter than ever."

There was a wicked gleam in his eyes. "So, I have a plan. My whole family is here for Christmas. We let them chase after Charlie and Sarah and save our energy. When we get home, I'll have my way with you."

She grinned. "Not if I have my way with you first."

When there was a double outcry of frustration at being

immobilized in the back seat, Annie sighed. "I suppose there's no putting it off any longer. We have to set them free."

"Yeah. Here we go."

They exited the SUV and each opened a rear door. While Mason liberated their daughter, Annie released the restraints, lifted Charlie from the car seat and kissed his cheek. "Is that better, Charlie bear?"

The little boy immediately wriggled and squirmed to be let down but she held on. His grandparents had seen him last night in his white shirt, red-and-green-plaid bow tie and little jeans. Sarah had been wearing her red-velvet dress, white tights and black Mary Janes. Pictures had been taken for posterity. Today for the Christmas gathering they were wearing comfortable T-shirts underneath their sweaters.

Annie looked up at Mason and grinned, preparing to hit him with her most recent Daddy observation. "Our daughter has you wrapped around her little finger."

"Does not," he said.

"Does, too."

They grinned at this now familiar debate then walked up to the front door. Of course Charlie wanted to ring the doorbell because one time he'd been allowed to and had never forgotten.

Flo opened the door and instantly smiled at each baby. "Merry Christmas, my little sweethearts!"

Her husband joined her and beamed at his grandchildren. "Who's having their first Christmas at Grandma and Grandpa's house?"

The twins held out their arms to the older couple and, of course, they were swept into loving hugs and kisses. After the affectionate greeting, they all went into the family room, where everyone was gathered.

The *family* room. A place where relatives were together. To celebrate peace on earth and goodwill toward men.

Or just to hang out on a Sunday. Most people took it for granted, but not Annie. She would never get tired of this.

"Did you see that?" Mason asked her.

"What?"

"They didn't say a word to us. Just commandeered our children without acknowledging our presence." He sighed. "It's official."

"What's that?"

"We're chopped liver."

Annie laughed then slid her hand into his as they mingled with his brothers, sister and parents. There was a gorgeous tree in the corner and wrapped presents were piled underneath it. Lighted garland draped the fireplace mantel, where stockings for every family member were filled to overflowing. It was perfect.

The twins were in the center of the family room, where their grandparents were removing their sweaters. This was it. Annie looked at Mason and grinned. Everyone was watching as if the process were fascinating. When the outerwear was off, the room got so quiet you could hear a pin drop. The message on the front of their little T-shirts sank in.

"'I'm the big brother. I'm the big sister.'" His mother's expression was priceless as she looked at Mason then Annie. "Another baby?"

"Surprise!" they said together.

The tiny guests of honor were momentarily forgotten as congratulations and hugs were offered all around. It didn't last long because Charlie fast-crawled over to the tree and started investigating the wrapped boxes and gift bags. His sister willingly joined in and they had Uncle Gabe's present nearly opened before intervention arrived.

Annie and Mason watched the happy chaos, their arms around each other's waists.

"Are you happy about the baby?" she asked. "It wasn't planned."

"I'm ecstatic. Thrilled. Proud. So lucky. It's the best gift I could have received." He kissed the top of her head.

"Me, too. I feel so blessed. A traditional family is everything I've ever wanted. And you made it possible. I love you so much."

"I love you more," he said. "It occurs to me that we were meant to find each other. In a perfect world we would have met, dated, fallen in love, had an engagement, married and then had children."

"Our story isn't that," she agreed. "But it's perfect for us."

* * * * *

COMING SOON!

We really hope you enjoyed reading this book. If you're looking for more romance, be sure to head to the shops when new books are available on

Thursday 31st October

To see which titles are coming soon, please visit

millsandboon.co.uk/nextmonth

MILLS & BOON

Coming next month

THEIR FESTIVE ISLAND ESCAPE
Nina Singh

An appealing, successful, handsome man was asking to spend time with her on various island adventures but his only objective was her business acumen.

That shouldn't have bothered her as much as it did. But that was a silly notion, it wasn't like she and Reid were friends or anything. In fact, a few short days ago, she would have listed him as one of the few people on earth who actually may not even like her.

"Why me?" Celeste asked. There had to be other individuals he could ask. A man like Reid was unlikely to be lacking in female companionship.

She imagined what it would be like to date a man like him. What it would mean if he was sitting here asking her to do these things with her simply because he wanted to spend time with her.

What his lips would feel against hers if he ever were to kiss her.

Dear saints! What in the world was wrong with her? Was it simply because she'd been without a man for so long? Perhaps it was the romantic, exotic location. Something had to be causing such uncharacteristic behavior on her part.

Why hadn't she just said no already? Was she really even entertaining the idea?

She wasn't exactly the outdoors type. Or much of an

athlete for that matter. Sure, she'd scaled countless fences during her youth trying to outrun the latest neighborhood bully after defending her younger sister. And she'd developed some really quick reflexes averting touchy men in city shelters. But that was about the extent of it.

Reid answered her, breaking into the dangerous thoughts. "Think about it. Between your professional credentials and the fact that you take frequent tropical vacations, you're actually the perfect person to accompany me."

Again, nothing but logic behind his reasoning. On the surface, she'd be a fool to turn down such an exciting opportunity; the chance to experience so much more of what the island had to offer and, in the process, acquire a host of memories she'd hold for a lifetime. It was as if he really was Santa and he had just handed her a gift most women would jump at.

Continue reading
THEIR FESTIVE ISLAND ESCAPE
Nina Singh

Available next month
www.millsandboon.co.uk

LET'S TALK
Romance

For exclusive extracts, competitions and special offers, find us online:

MILLS & BOON

THE HEART OF ROMANCE

A ROMANCE FOR EVERY KIND OF READER

MODERN

Prepare to be swept off your feet by sophisticated, sexy and seductive heroes, in some of the world's most glamourous ar romantic locations, where power and passion collide.
8 stories per month.

HISTORICAL

Escape with historical heroes from time gone by. Whether yo passion is for wicked Regency Rakes, muscled Vikings or rug Highlanders, awaken the romance of the past.
6 stories per month.

MEDICAL

Set your pulse racing with dedicated, delectable doctors in th high-pressure world of medicine, where emotions run high passion, comfort and love are the best medicine.
6 stories per month.

True Love

Celebrate true love with tender stories of heartfelt romance, the rush of falling in love to the joy a new baby can bring, ar focus on the emotional heart of a relationship.
8 stories per month.

Desire

Indulge in secrets and scandal, intense drama and plenty of hot action with powerful and passionate heroes who have it a wealth, status, good looks…everything but the right woman.
6 stories per month.

HEROES

Experience all the excitement of a gripping thriller, with an romance at its heart. Resourceful, true-to-life women and str fearless men face danger and desire - a killer combination!
8 stories per month.

DARE

Sensual love stories featuring smart, sassy heroines you'd wa best friend, and compelling intense heroes who are worthy o
4 stories per month.

To see which titles are coming soon, please visit

millsandboon.co.uk/nextmonth

JOIN US ON SOCIAL MEDIA!

Stay up to date with our latest releases, author news and gossip, special offers and discounts, and all the behind-the-scenes action from Mills & Boon...

 millsandboon

 millsandboonuk

 millsandboon

It might just be true love...

GET YOUR ROMANCE FIX!

MILLS & BOON
— *blog* —

Get the latest romance news, exclusive author interviews, story extracts and much more!

blog.millsandboon.co.uk